The Judas Seat

by

Katherine Pritchett

The Judas Seat

Cover Art by *Kristian Norris*

The Wild Rose Press, Inc.
PO Box 708
Adams Basin, NY 14410-0708
Visit us at www.thewildrosepress.com

Publishing History
First Edition, 2023
Trade Paperback ISBN 978-1-5092-4687-8
Digital ISBN 978-1-5092-4686-1

Published in the United States of America

The lead FBI agent approached her from the doorway of Richard's study.

"Yes?" Terra put down the magazine she had leafed through at least a dozen times without seeing any of the pictures. She rose from her chair, hoping it was news that the crisis Richard was in had been resolved, afraid the news might not be good. Carrie and Paul moved to stand beside her.

"Mrs. Matthews, we've received a tip that there might be another attack." He touched the speaker in his ear. "We have additional agents coming in to surround the house, but I'd like to suggest that you folks all move into an interior room without windows for the time being."

"What room would that be, Barry?" She glanced around the family room. She had fallen in love with this house precisely because every room offered a spectacular view through generous windows. Even the basement was a walkout.

"Well, uh—" He looked around the room, studying each doorway. "What about the utility room?"

"I guess that would work." A room tucked between the garage and kitchen, it contained only a long, narrow horizontal window above the washer and dryer. "But it won't be very comfortable for the three of us to spend the night in."

"No, ma'am, but the word we get is that this will be soon—" The family room picture windows burst inward from a hail of bullets.

Praise for Katherine Pritchett

Dedication

This book is dedicated to the soulmate I found at long last, answer to a prayer I didn't know I was praying.

Prologue

Beijing, China, four years ago…

From the Starlight Restaurant revolving atop the Beijing International Hotel, Chung Hee Yu gazed out over the twinkling lights of Beijing. He sipped at his freshly brewed cup of white tea, delighting in the delicate flavor of the tea, as the city appeared to swirl around him. He smiled as the waiter picked up his plate. Even in his indulgences, he exercised restraint. For the last dinner he would enjoy as a free man, he had chosen a finely-marbled Wagyu steak, but only a five-ounce, medium, with steamed vegetables. Not a huge steak, no calamari, not even American fried chicken, although it was on the menu. Instead of champagne or priceless wine, he had this tea, with a single sprig of fresh mint, slightly bruised to release its flavor and aroma.

"Dessert, sir?" The waiter appeared quietly at his elbow.

"No, thank you." He shook his head. "Perhaps another cup of this excellent tea in a few minutes, if you please."

"Of course, sir." Bowing, the waiter backed away.

Chung Hee watched a commotion two tables away as waiters seated a large group. He recognized the tall man, as noticeable as a giraffe among gazelles, even in this international venue, among the Chinese men being seated. Unfortunately, the man also recognized him and strode toward his table.

"Minister Yu." The man thrust out his hand.

Chung Hee rose and accepted the hand. "Mr. Lowe. How pleasant to see you." Lowe had spent the last month in Seoul negotiating partnerships with Korean auto manufacturers.

"Would you care to join my group, Mr. Yu?" He waved toward the table where his party was settling in. He grinned. "I'm wining and dining the Chinese auto gurus. Might get Kia some competition in the States."

"I wish you luck, Mr. Lowe. But I'll decline your invitation." He glanced out the window again. "I've finished my dinner and am just sitting here relaxing and enjoying the view."

Lowe grinned and winked. "If you change your mind, come on over. Might make the Chinese more anxious to make concessions if they see a South Korean cabinet minister at the table."

Chung Hee smiled. "I wouldn't want to offend my most excellent colleagues, Mr. Lowe." He sat back down. "Besides, I'm simply on a personal retreat, not on official state business."

"Well, it's a pleasure to see you again, Minister Yu." Lowe sauntered back to his table, and Chung Hee returned to his tea. It had cooled more than he would like, but he drank anyway. Hot tea, lukewarm tea, cold tea. Soon it wouldn't matter. He tried to see above the city lights and the smog they had tried hard to control before the Olympics to find the stars, and failed. He satisfied himself instead with the panoramic view of Beijing for what might be the last time.

The waiter reappeared with a second cup of tea.

"Thank you." Chung Hee nodded his thanks. He lingered over the tea, thinking back over his life to this point. During his lifetime, South Korea had become a full participant in the global economy, manufacturing and consuming at alarming rates, and he had allowed himself to be seduced by shiny baubles. The excesses available to those in government service had distracted him from his core goal of leaving the world, and particularly his country, a better place than when he entered it. What he was about to do should further that goal in a single bold move. He finished his tea, left payment for his bill and a generous tip, and then headed for his room.

There he filled a small backpack with the things he would need for his trip. At last, he surveyed the deluxe hotel room one more time. It was a fine hotel, five-stars, utilized primarily for visiting dignitaries and the ever-growing numbers of wealthy tourists. He had visited it many times in the past fifteen years, first as a junior aide to South Korean cabinet ministers, then as Cabinet Minister for Unification himself. But this was a personal trip. He breathed deeply the fragrance of the white roses management had sent to his room, as he realized he would probably soon miss the many luxuries to which he had grown accustomed. Although he sometimes slept on the floor in such rooms, just to keep himself from growing soft, last night he had luxuriated in the king-sized bed.

As he reached for the door of the room, a thrill of fear ran through him; his motives might be misunderstood; he might never get the chance to explain himself; his efforts might end abruptly in failure and death. He accepted the fear as an attack from the enemy—proof his course of action was the right one. With a sigh, he closed the door behind him and walked quietly toward the elevator. Once at the expansive lobby, his rubber-soled shoes made no sound on the marble floor as he walked toward the door to the street without looking at anyone. No one would notice this behavior as anything unusual; in fact, to behave otherwise would arouse suspicion.

Thus unnoticed, he slipped into the evening streets and made his way toward the train station. The crowds he encountered, he realized, were not there when he first accompanied the Cabinet to Beijing fifteen years ago, but China had made many adaptations to bolster its economy, and therefore change the lives of its people, in recent years. At the station, he bought a round trip ticket to Sunchon, North Korea, showing a Chinese passport he had obtained months ago along with the proper travel papers indicating he was on his way to purchase rice for an importer.

He boarded the train, making his way toward the "hard" or cheap seats. Though padded and upholstered, the seat would feel very hard indeed on his long journey. He settled in and opened the newspaper he had purchased on his trip across the city. He kept his small pack, holding only three shirts, a second pair of trousers, and three sets of underwear and socks, on his lap. The light jacket he wore, he knew, would not be adequate for long when he arrived at his destination.

The train jerked several times as each car submitted to the pull of the engines. Slowly the momentum smoothed and picked up speed. The car rocked him to sleep somewhere along the dark journey north and east into the countryside. Thin morning sunlight nudged him awake as the train began to slow. Ahead, around a slight bend in the track, he could see the bridge across the Yalu, with Antung, China, on this side and Sinuiju, North Korea, on the other. Although his stomach tightened, he forced his demeanor to remain calm.

The train stopped to allow the North Korean border guards to enter. Thin, young, and stern-faced, they scrutinized the passengers as if they expected each to be a notorious international criminal. He supposed they would receive a medal and parade for shooting one. He blinked and placed his Chinese passport and papers in hand. The guards passed him by with just a cursory glance at the documents. Thanking God for his part-Chinese North Korean grandmother, he stared out the window at the brown early winter landscape while they completed their review of the car. Finally, the train began to move again. Another thirty minutes and the train stopped at Sunchon, North Korea.

Standing up, unobtrusively stretching stiff muscles, he put the Chinese papers in the backpack, and drew his real passport from his jacket. He stepped off the train under the watchful eye of still more soldiers. Without looking at them, he entered the station and found the office of the station master.

"May I help you?" A thin young woman looked up from her desk.

"Yes, please," he answered quietly. "I have a matter I would like to discuss with the station master."

"What is the nature of your business?" she barked.

"Please, just give him this." He handed her his passport. "I think then he will see me."

She opened the passport, poised to dismiss him and

hand it back, but instead spun around for her boss's office. Seconds later, she returned. "He will see you now."

"Thank you." He had barely entered the office, the door still closing, when he heard her pick up the phone and request soldiers. He stepped toward the desk, where the station master glanced from his passport to his face and back to the passport.

"You are Chung Hee Yu, South Korean cabinet minister?"

"I am."

"Why are you here?"

Chung Hee met the man's gaze. "I wish to defect."

Chapter 1

Nassau, the Bahamas, present day…

The plane rose as if fighting to stay in the air when the pilot lowered the flaps on the approach to International Airport, New Providence Island, Bahamas. Terra McIntyre Matthews sympathized with the plane. Taking off was bad enough, but landings forced her to maintain taut control of her fear. Despite her resolve, her fingers clenched the arm of the seat, and she let out the breath she had been holding. She tried to appreciate the azure water spreading big around the tiny island, but instead let out another breath.

A voice rumbled low in her ear. "You could have had the aisle seat, you know."

She thrust out her chin. "I'd rather see what's coming at me." She turned away from the window, and love for her husband smothered the fear. She tried to soak up every angle of his countenance, the way the light in his brown eyes warmed her to her toes, his broad shoulder brushing against hers. She felt the unfamiliar pressure of the wedding ring as he squeezed her little hand in his long one. "But you already know it." She leaned into his shoulder. "I love you, Richard."

He nuzzled her hair. It still felt strange to wear it short, after having it long for most of her life, but the surgeons had to cut off so much, it seemed the only logical choice. "Not nervous about meeting my parents, are you?"

"I'd be crazy not to be nervous, wouldn't I?" Her stomach hurt from tension as the wheels touched down. "After all, their son was working in Washington, DC, grieving his beloved wife, then out of the blue he calls them to say he's remarried." Her knees shook. "I'm a nobody, and you're the son of a U.S. ambassador."

"Retired ambassador." He tugged her hand, forcing her to meet his gaze. "And you are definitely NOT a nobody." He kissed her forehead. "You are somebody very special."

She felt tension drain from her, replaced by confidence flowing from him to her. "Still, they have to wonder about me. I mean, I'm younger." She sighed. "I doubt I'm what your mother had in mind for your wife."

"My mother didn't choose you to be my wife." He cupped her chin in his hand. "I did." He kissed her. "Besides, Mum will come to love you once she gets to know you." He gathered their bags from under their seats. "Dad will be a lot easier. Just listen to some of his golfing stories and ask his advice on your swing."

She swallowed hard, forcing her fears down to the pit of her stomach. Richard's first wife, Elaine, had been the Boston-born daughter of his mother's best friend. That Elaine had been tall, blonde, classically beautiful, Terra knew from the photos she had seen in Richard's apartment. That she had been a gifted teacher and devoted wife, she learned from Richard's stories. That she had died in the same terrorist attack that nearly killed her husband brought Richard's and Terra's lives together. The plane bumped once before settling to the ground, and Terra gasped.

Terra held his hand tight against the fear, greater than her fear of flying, sweeping over her again as the doors to the plane opened. "I hope you're right." She knew she would regard herself with suspicion if she were Richard's mother.

Then the bustle of disembarking carried them like flotsam toward the shore of the terminal. The heat rising from the tarmac engulfed them the instant they stepped onto the ramp out of the plane. She glanced at the sapphire sky, where gulls called as they circled. Colors intensified, as if she had suddenly stepped from a black and white movie into full Technicolor. Then she looked toward the terminal. Palms surrounding it bent in the steady breeze dissipating the heat. A sweet floral scent wafted to her, mixed with a smell she guessed was surf. A brightly colored crowd surged out of the terminal toward the plane. She scanned the group, wondering which couple would step forward to judge her fitness to be his mate. Richard stopped and opened his arms wide.

Terra tried to hang back as a couple she recognized from the photos in Richard's apartment rushed toward him, but he drew her to his side, making his parents embrace her to embrace him. Up close, their faces blurred, but as they stepped back, they assumed the careful expressions of career diplomats. The seconds they studied her seemed like hours to Terra.

Paul Matthews spoke first. "So, this is our new daughter." As his brown eyes sparkled and his lean face creased in a broad smile, Terra glimpsed the source of the charm that had drawn her to Richard. Richard not only looked like his father, tall and distinguished, although on Paul the dark hair had faded to silver, but acted much like him. Paul took her hands. "Richard didn't do you justice when he described you to us, my dear." He pulled her into a hug. "Welcome to our family, Terra."

He was so gracious she nearly cried. "Thank you, Mr. Matthews." Before she could say more, she felt Caroline Matthews' hand rest briefly on her arm.

"Yes, dear," Caroline said, her voice as cool as her hand had been. "Welcome." Sunglasses shielded her eyes, and her lips appeared set in a resolutely neutral line, as the breeze teased her curly salt and pepper hair.

Terra's stomach tightened again, as she realized Caroline's assessment was not finished.

"Did you read the news today, son?" Paul spoke as he walked toward the baggage pickup. Richard fell into step beside him, perhaps an inch taller than his father.

"You mean about Kim Jong Un?" Richard glanced back toward Caroline and Terra following in silence. Terra nodded as she recognized the name of the North Korean president who had died yesterday. "We saw it on CNN at Dulles while we waited for the plane."

"Then," Paul hesitated. "You don't know about Chung Hee Yu?"

Richard stopped. "What about him?" His voice had taken an edge. Terra moved closer to him.

Paul halted as well. "He's been named acting President of the Presidium as well as Secretary General of the Korean Worker's Party in Kim's place."

"Damn." Richard shook his head. "Should complicate things."

"There's more." Paul watched Richard. "It seems South Korea and China are very alarmed the nuclear threat might escalate."

Terra read a mix of emotions in Richard's eyes—anger, fear, sorrow—she wasn't sure what his actions told her. "Who is Chung Hee Yu?" Although she knew Richard had served as an American diplomat for over a decade, Terra hadn't learned many details beyond the fact he was transferred from Korea to the post in Zimbabwe, where tragedy had changed the course of his life.

"When I knew him, he was South Korean. We were both part of a graduate fellowship study at Oxford. Our group was to study economic interdependence among Far Eastern nations and the European Commonwealth." He shook his head again. "We became good friends and developed some solid theories."

"Why did he switch to the North?"

Richard started walking. "I don't know." She realized the story was deep, and she would have to pry for it. He smiled as if he read her thoughts. "It's a long story, but I promise I'll tell you the whole tale—after we pick up our luggage and get settled in."

"You're staying with us, aren't you?" Terra could hear the strain in Caroline's voice.

"Of course, Mum." Richard threw his arm around his mother. "Then you can monitor if I'm eating right and taking my vitamins."

"Oh, Richard," she protested, but smiled. "I'm supposed to worry. It's in a mother's contract."

He laughed. "And I appreciate the wonderful job you do of it." He offered one arm to his mother and the other to his wife.

"Fine son you are," Paul grumbled. "Take the lovely ladies and leave me to gather the luggage."

Chapter 2

Richard chuckled as Terra bustled about trying to hang up her clothing only to have Janie, his mother's maid, take it from her. He knew the routine and had simply tossed the things he preferred untouched in a drawer and left the rest to Janie, but Terra wanted to do things herself. "It's okay, Terra." His bag sat unzipped on the floor. "Janie takes great pride in making guests feel they have nothing to do but enjoy themselves." He walked toward his wife, patting Janie on the shoulder as he passed her. "It's good to see you again, Janie."

"The same here, Master Richard." Smiling, Janie hung up Terra's silk blouse. "You look good; marriage agrees with you."

"Thank you, Janie." He took Terra's hand. "I certainly agree with marriage." He led her toward the French doors opening to a balcony. "Let's go for a walk along the beach." The balcony ran the length of the house and from it a stairway led down to the garden.

"Richard, I just can't get used to people doing things for me because they're paid to do it," Terra protested as she followed him into the garden.

Richard slipped his arm around her shoulders, savoring how good she felt to him, the solid presence of her in his life, when once he had feared having only memories to hold. "You've been doing it all your life, Terra, only you just didn't think of it that way."

"Explain yourself, dear." Her voice had already relaxed. He could hear the smile in it.

"When you paid someone to change the oil in your car—"

"I did it myself."

"When you paid someone to do your taxes—"

"Did it myself."

He sighed. "All right. When you paid the airline to fly you to DC—" He stopped to look at her.

"No, I didn't fly myself."

"When you bought your ticket, you were paying someone to do things for you because they were paid to do those jobs, and they had the training or the gift for it. Janie likes her work, and because we respect the work she does, we get along fine."

"So, then, tell me about Chung Hee Yu."

He laughed. "I knew you wouldn't let it go for long."

"You're stalling."

"You win, as usual." He took a deep breath, gathering his memories and trying to separate assumptions from facts. "It was a long time ago, just after Elaine and I were married. I was about to be posted to South Korea, but this fellowship came up and the State Department thought, since there were a few bright, young South Korean politicos involved, it might be beneficial for me to participate. Chung Hee and I became friends fairly quickly. He had a lot of questions about western life, religion in particular. Although South Korea has the largest Christian church in the world, Chung Hee had been raised Buddhist."

The memory of a bright October afternoon came back to him. Chung Hee had been deep into religious philosophy that afternoon as they walked, practicing each other's languages. By accident, it seemed, they wandered toward the chapel. As they approached it, Chung Hee moved as if drawn by a magnet. Richard followed him inside, as much from his own curiosity as by the question of why such a shining intellect should be attracted to such a place, ancient and musty by Richard's standards, but new and untried to one of Chung Hee's faith. Inside, Chung Hee stood as if absorbing the whole aura of the chapel, from the stained light in which danced the dust motes of centuries, to the austere altar, with its simple wood cross. Richard's own cynicism quailed before the faith that held up the stone and polished the pews. When Chung Hee knelt before the altar, Richard knelt beside him without question.

"What does it all mean?" Chung Hee asked, raising his gaze to the cross.

"It means—" Richard faltered, unsure of his answer.

"It means what you believe it means." A voice echoed off the stone walls. A priest walked toward them. "How can I help you today, lads?"

Chung Hee scrambled to his feet, bowing as he approached the priest. "Teach me, father," he asked humbly. "I want to know more." Chung Hee had disappeared with the priest into his study, while Richard returned to the dorm, realizing he had witnessed something quite profound, but unsure of its meaning.

He came out of the depths of his memory. "Three weeks later, Chung Hee asked me to be present at his baptism. His conversion to Christianity made me question, and I began to understand more about my own faith through him."

Richard fell silent and Terra simply held his hand as they walked. Through the garden gate and a few more steps, the foliage gave way to the fine white sand beach Richard treasured. He glanced toward the end of it, where it curved out of sight. Heat waves shimmered off the sand near the curve, and for an instant, he saw Elaine in the distance, running toward him, her golden hair billowing behind her. He blinked back the sudden tears, and she was gone.

Terra's soft hand touched his shoulder. "You used to come here with Elaine?"

He nodded and pulled her close to him, her heart beating reassuringly next to his. Instead of a dead wife in the distance, he now had a living wife beside him. Yet Terra had almost paid the same price as Elaine. He spun her so they could view the ocean together, his arms still wrapped around her waist. "I came here, too, after she died, to sit on the beach and watch the tides. I thought about just walking out into the waves and never stopping."

She leaned back against him. "But something kept you anchored to dry land?"

He nodded, and her hands closed over his. They stood in silence while the waves rolled over the sand. Just as he began to feel relaxed by the rhythm of the surf, Terra spoke. "Why did he switch sides?"

"Why," Richard sighed. "I have never figured out."

Chapter 3

After the blinding heat of the sun reflecting off the bright sand and verdant turf, the limestone-floored veranda with the fans swirling lazily in the high ceiling above them felt soothingly cool. At least a dozen different colors of orchids nodded around the edges of the veranda like friendly butterflies. The muted noises filtering through the lacy walls of night-blooming jasmine took Terra back to childhood summer afternoons in Oklahoma—lawn mowers, hedge trimmers, women's low voices, children's laughter. Except in Box Elder, Terra had never heard seagulls and surf in the mix. "So, dear," Caroline Matthews passed a plate to Terra. "How did you and Richard meet?"

"Well, I was working for him," Terra began. She busied herself selecting fruit. How much did Richard want her to tell them? Did they know about the feud with Adler that brought them together? Tea on the veranda might not prove very relaxing.

"You remember, Mum. I told you when Terra first started working for me." Richard reached for the teapot. "More tea?"

"Yes, dear." Caroline held her cup for him to fill. "I remember you telling us you had a new assistant. Then you called to say you had gotten married." She smiled at Richard. "I'm just trying to fill in the gaps."

17

Richard sighed. "Okay, I forget you weren't there for the whole thing." He picked up his own cup to take a sip of tea. Terra guessed he was stalling, trying to decide how much of the story to share. His gaze strayed to the newspaper, where he had been reading about the latest developments on Chung Hee's presidency, as he and his father discussed the ramifications of a Christian at the helm of a county still persecuting them, of a South Korean leading North Korea. Suddenly he slammed his cup down so hard it shattered, sending a flood of hot tea over the table. "Son of a bitch!" He shoved back his chair and spun away from the table. Caroline jumped up to follow him.

Terra noted the thin, straight set of his lips. Folding her napkin as a dam against the tea, she picked up the damp paper to read what incensed him. She scanned the article about Chung Hee, but saw nothing they hadn't already heard on the news or surmised in discussion. She found what triggered his outburst in a short article halfway down the third column. She raised her head. "Adler's been released?" she choked out.

He looked back at her, his voice taut. "National security reasons, isn't it what it says?" Paul reached for the paper.

Terra went to Richard. She felt a tremor in the arm he slipped around her. "I'm sorry, Terra." He kissed her hair. "I thought it was over."

Caroline stepped back toward her husband. Finished with the meager article, Paul looked up toward his son. "The Robert Adler of the CIA who was involved with the attack in Zimbabwe?" Terra still wrapped in his arms, Richard nodded. Paul dropped the paper and folded his arms across his chest. "Do you want to tell us the whole story now?"

Taking Terra's hand, Richard came back to the table. His mother sat, and Janie placed a fresh cup of tea in front of him. He took a long drink and sighed deeply before beginning. He reached out once more for Terra's hand. "Adler sent Terra to work for me, without telling her the story, but of course, I saw through his ruse." He sighed, running his free hand over his eyes, as if going back into the memories was painful. Caroline sat silent, her blue-gray eyes studying first Richard and then Terra. "Still, I decided maybe through Terra I could find out what he was up to, and then she proved to be so gifted at editing, I wanted to keep her on for her sake." He looked deep into Terra's eyes. "Sounds pretty selfish now, telling it like this, doesn't it?"

She put her hand over his. "Not if you were there, Richard."

He glanced at his father. "I was getting close to three witnesses who would incriminate him, swear he used Elaine and me as bait to draw in the terrorists. He had one witness killed, and intimidated another one out of talking to me, and it was coming down to just one last chance." He paused, and Terra squeezed his hand. "I think Adler hoped I would come to care for Terra, and though I tried not to, I did." He stopped to raise her hand to his lips. He stared into her eyes for a long time.

Caroline cleared her throat, and Paul shot a look at his wife. "Then Adler put Terra in jeopardy, hoping I'd give up the chase to protect her. I tried to make him believe I would, but I couldn't." He dropped his head. "I lived for revenge too long; I couldn't let it go." He sighed. "I didn't realize until it was almost too late that living people, going forward into the future, was more important than revenge." He reached up to caress Terra's face, still not looking at her. "My drive for revenge almost cost Terra her life." At last, he raised his head to her and stroked her curls. "And is why you're seeing her with short hair and not the long, glorious hair she had when I nearly got her killed."

He sighed. "And then I found out other people were on to Adler for more than just Elaine's death; he would have been put away anyway. FBI and Interpol were watching him, and letting me be a distraction to him while they made their case." He took a deep breath. "And if I hadn't stampeded him into taking rash action, he might still be in jail."

Terra reached up to touch his cheek. "You had no way of knowing it at the time." She squeezed his hand. "You did more than anyone else to put him away."

He squeezed her hand back. "Than anyone else but you. He nearly killed you."

Paul spoke up. "Adler himself attempted to kill Terra?"

"Yes, he tried to blow her head off." Richard focused on his father. "If she hadn't moved to get away from him, she'd be dead. As it is, the bullet grazed her skull and burst her eardrum." He tried to smile. "So, if she doesn't hear all your stories, be gentle."

Paul ignored the humor. "If he committed an assault with intent to kill, they could hold him on it, never mind the national security charges." He leaned back in his chair. "I smell a rat."

"Any time Adler's involved you can smell a rat." Terra's eyes flashed. "He has always made my skin crawl."

Richard did smile then. "Terra gave him quite a bit

of grief herself." He kissed her hand again. "And saved my life once." He stared deep into her eyes. "Or maybe more than once."

"How are you feeling now, my dear?" Caroline's voice had softened from the tone she had used toward Terra until then.

Terra glanced at her mother-in-law. Unshed tears glistened in her eyes. "I'm feeling pretty good now. A headache once in a while, still have some tones I can't hear, some things are muffled, but all in all, I feel very lucky." She glanced back at Richard. "I really owe Adler a thank you, because without his interference, I wouldn't have met Richard."

He smiled. "And without him, I wouldn't have met you, dear." He looked back at his father. "But I hadn't thought about the assault charges being enough." The two diplomats locked gazes, and Terra could see the wheels turning in both their minds. "There must be more to it." He sipped at his cool tea. "I'll call someone in the FBI and see what I can find out."

Chapter 4

Richard watched his father from the patio door. On the tiny putting green he maintained himself in the yard close to the house, Paul took careful aim on the ball. Richard had learned years ago golf in general and putting practice in particular helped his father to focus, to clear his mind for serious thinking. Richard respected the process and waited until the ball swirled into the cup before stepping onto the flagstone walk.

"What did you find out, son?" Paul asked as he picked up the ball.

Richard walked across the manicured lawn toward Paul. "Absolutely nothing. Agent Prescott was not available. They said he'd call me back."

Paul set the ball on the green, studied the angle, and sank another putt. "And you don't expect a call?"

Richard sighed. "No, I really don't. Just a hunch."

Paul picked up the ball again. "Your hunches are usually pretty good."

Richard nodded. "What do you think?"

Paul set the ball on the green. "I think you need to call another source." He swung. "You have one, of course?"

"Ginny, and a nephew of Rena."

Paul smiled. "A nephew of Rena?" He evidently remembered Richard's youthful escapade in Italy. "The family is speaking to you again?"

"Dad, you know Rena still has positive feelings toward me. It's just her father who hates me."

"I have news for you, son, he doesn't really hate you, he just has to say so. After all, you took his daughter out on a date he didn't sanction and got yourselves kidnapped by the Red Brigade." Paul made another putt. "That he's angry about, but he's very happy you were able to get the both of you free, alive." He pulled another ball from his bucket. "I'm pleased with it myself."

Richard sighed. "We were young and foolish, but it did make her nephew a little more dedicated on the case. He's with Interpol now."

"Do you think you can get any information from him?"

Richard shook his head. "No, but I think Ginny can." Now a globe-trotting journalist, Ginny had introduced Richard to Elaine in college.

"Why haven't you called her?

"I have, got her voice mail. She'll be calling soon."

Paul nodded toward his golf bag. "Good, then pick out a club and show me you remember how to play golf."

Richard touched the clubs without selecting one. "I thought I was through with Adler. He would be brought to justice, even if it wasn't for Elaine's death."

"It could still happen, son." Paul waited.

Richard finally pulled a club from the bag.

Paul cleared his throat. "A wood, son." He handed his putter to Richard. "Not much good for putting."

Richard sighed and accepted his father's club. "I'm sorry, Dad." He concentrated on the ball, on his stance, on the feel and balance of the club in his hands.

Surprisingly, the act of bringing the surface of the putter into contact with the ball at precisely the right angle quieted his agitation, gave focus to his anger. He sank the putt, and the slight elation of it made him feel in control again.

"Helps, doesn't it?" Paul grinned.

Richard nodded. "Yes, it does." He picked up his ball and waited for his father to swing. "It makes me realize I should have played it different."

"No, you did just fine, you sank the putt."

"I mean Adler." Richard stared at the cup, not seeing it. "I could have killed him, then Terra would never have to fear from him again."

"Mark my words, son. You will never regret letting him live."

"But Terra doesn't realize she's still in danger."

"Are you sure she is? What makes you certain he'll come after her?"

Richard looked down at the ground. "I guess I'm not sure. But Bahamian banks are the new Swiss banks. Discreet and safe. Logic says he has some money stashed here."

"You've been around government long enough to know what makes the papers isn't always what's really going on." Paul took aim on another ball. "Maybe he's not as 'free' as the article implied."

Richard stared at his father. "I hope you're right." He looked down. "Terra's been through enough."

"So have you, son." Paul put his hand on Richard's shoulder. "So have you."

Chapter 5

"What would you like to see while you're here, Terra?" Caroline's voice was gentle, though still reserved. She doesn't trust me yet, Terra thought. While Richard and Paul engaged in putting practice, they were sitting on the veranda, having a second cup of tea. A gentle breeze ruffled the gardenias flanking the veranda's entrance to the garden, adding the scent of sand and salt to the heavy perfume of the flowers.

"I don't know," she responded. "Seeing the ocean and the beach was pretty good already."

"You've never seen the ocean?"

Terra shook her head. "DC is the closest to a beach I have ever been."

"Where are you from, Terra?"

"Oklahoma." She laughed. "Just about as far from both oceans as you can get."

Caroline smiled. "Certainly." She picked up her cup. "What brought you to DC?"

"A decent job and a chance to make some changes in my life." She caught the question in Caroline's smile. "My parents died a car wreck while I was in college." She fell quiet, remembering the day her world fell apart. Then she sensed Carrie expected the story to continue. "I had to sell their house and business to settle the estate. I had no relatives nearby, so when I graduated, I accepted a civil service position with GSA in DC."

"And then you met Richard?" Caroline couldn't keep the motherly concern from her voice.

"Not right away." Terra shook her head. "I'd been there about three months, had applied for an open position in CIA, when Adler showed up in my boss's office and asked me to work for Richard to provide him information." She took a deep breath. "It sounded flaky, but he hinted I'd be without any job if I didn't help him. I figured Richard would see through me, not hire me, and I'd be off the hook." She looked at Caroline. "I don't lie very convincingly, and he figured it out right away, but I guess he wanted to know what Adler was up to." She remembered how Richard piqued her interest. Adler told her he was retired and she expected an elderly man, not the handsome writer in his prime. "By the time Richard confronted me about Adler, he was interested in my opinion of his writing—he was my favorite author even before I met him—and I was curious about the situation, because nothing was what it seemed to be." She remembered her confrontations with Adler and the way they were balanced by the excitement of learning about the man behind the political suspense novels she loved. "Adler always made my skin crawl, and after Richard told me about Elaine, I wanted to help him put Adler away."

"I understand how you feel about Adler," Caroline admitted. "After burying Elaine, standing by Richard's bedside, watching him go through the agony of learning to walk again, when we learned what Adler had done, I would have gladly throttled him myself." Terra grinned with a surge of warmth toward her mother-in-law. Caroline caught the look and smiled herself. "Paul's the diplomat, not me."

"You were a mother protecting her cub," Terra said, and Caroline laughed then, a deep infectious laugh. Terra heard a note common to Richard's laugh and recognized the mother in the son. "And you still are, aren't you?" Caroline stopped laughing, and Terra went on. "You wonder about me, since you didn't get a chance to know me before we got married, don't you?"

Caroline looked down at her hands, then back up at Terra. Richard might look like his father, but he had inherited a lot from his mother. "Yes, I wonder, and I worry. He's been hurt enough, and I don't want him hurt again."

Terra reached out to grip Caroline's hand. "Neither do I," she said. "He deserves to be happy, and I will do everything in my power to make sure he is."

Caroline placed her hand over Terra's and said nothing.

Chapter 6

"Oh, please, let us have a reception for you," Caroline implored over a dinner of lobster Cayman style, served in the formal dining room, with more forks than Terra knew what to do with. "We weren't there for the wedding, and I'm sure you haven't had a reception yet."

"Mum—" Richard began.

"Carrie, give the kids a break," Paul growled. "They're still on their honeymoon."

Caroline shot a look at her husband. "Oh, all right, I just wanted to do something nice for them."

"It's very sweet of you," Terra jumped in, still eyeing the firm white meat of the lobster. "How about we talk about it some more, and maybe we can do it before we leave." Now that she had cleared up a few things between her and Caroline, Terra was genuinely enjoying her in-laws.

"How long will you be staying?" Caroline evidently hadn't thought about them leaving.

"Our house won't be ready for a month yet," Richard said. "I thought we'd stay here a couple of weeks, then maybe go see another part of the world." He gave his attention to the dinner.

"You can stay as long as you want, you know." Caroline sounded sincere. "We haven't seen much of you in the past couple of years, and we'd love to get to know Terra."

Richard looked at Terra, and she smiled. "Why don't we leave it open as well, dear."

He shrugged. "Your wish is my command, love."

"But I'll keep working on those manuscripts and still get them to Warner on time." She smiled. "By then the galley proofs of your book will be ready to go over."

He raised his left brow at her. "I gather this will be a working honeymoon?"

"I don't just sit still very well."

He leaned across the table to kiss her. "I know."

"Mr. Matthews." Janie appeared in the dining room doorway. "Telephone for you. It's the State Department."

Paul rose from the table. "I'll take it in the den." Richard had explained to Terra his father had not only been an ambassador but advisor to several Presidents.

"It's not for you, Mr. Paul." Janie shook her head. "It's for Mr. Richard."

Father and son exchanged a look as Paul resumed his chair. Richard stood. "What could they want?"

"Why don't you talk to them and see?" Paul suggested. Richard left the room.

"Do you suppose it has to do with Adler?" Terra asked. This was something new to her. She had no idea what his life as a diplomat had been like.

"It could," Paul said. He leaned toward the doorway, listening. Caroline fiddled with her silverware. Terra watched the hallway.

Richard returned minutes later. Three faces questioned him. Finally, Terra asked, "Well?"

"It was the State Department." He sat back in his

chair and picked up his fork.

"About Adler?" Maybe they still had Adler in custody somewhere.

He stopped with a bite halfway to his mouth. "No." He set the fork back down. "North Korea has agreed to talks about controls on nuclear weapons. They asked me to head the negotiations." He waited, as if expecting more questions.

Terra glanced at Paul. Surely a former ambassador would understand what was going on. "And," his father asked. "What did you tell them?"

Richard shot a look at Paul before facing Terra. "I told them no."

"No?" Paul and Terra spoke at the same time. Paul went on. "Why?"

Richard took Terra's hand. "Because I'm still honeymooning with my wife, and I don't want to leave her halfway across the world for who knows how long." He turned back to Paul. "You know it won't be a fast process over there, could drag on for years." He kissed Terra's hand. "I got married to live with my wife, not leave her."

"But, Richard, if they need you—" Terra gripped his hand. She didn't want him to go, but if the world demanded him, she could live without him for a while.

"They don't," he assured her. "They have other negotiators who are up to speed on the situation, who have been working on it for years. I'd probably be just a figurehead to talk to the media if I went."

"Well, I'm glad you said no," Caroline voiced her opinion. "You've retired, you don't have to go anymore."

Paul glanced at his wife. "So, then, what's on the

agenda for the rest of the week?"

Richard let go of Terra's hand after a quick squeeze. "I thought we'd just go sightseeing, whatever Terra wants to do." He glanced at his mother. "I haven't been here much myself since you settled in."

"Will you have some time for golf?" Paul gave his son the same pleading expression Terra had seen on Richard.

"I'll make time, Dad."

****

Coffee and dessert found them again on the veranda. The evening brought a new symphony from a night life shaking itself awake while the daytime birds came home to roost. Richard moved his chair toward the setting sun. "Look, Terra."

She shifted her chair to face the west as well and caught her breath at a sky saffron, peach, and indigo. "It's beautiful." The brilliant colors of the sunset dimmed the vibrant island colors, found in everything from parrots to flowers to houses to island dress, settling into subtle hues as the intense sunlight waned.

"These islands are famous for their sunsets," Caroline said. "It's from the same clouds that bring the afternoon showers."

"You know, I haven't been to see you often enough to get to know the island." Richard touched his mother's hand. "I'm sorry I've been obsessed these past few years, Mum."

She patted his shoulder. "I understand, son. You were working through your grief." She sighed. "And taking on a mission that evidently needed doing."

"Son, I'm afraid even I underestimated what Adler was capable of," Paul apologized.

Richard noticed the tightening in Terra's jaw at the mention of the man who had terrorized her. "I'm ready to forget about it and move on," he said. His parents evidently understood he wanted to change the subject, as they began talking about the local sights. Terra listened intently, but Richard slipped off into his memories. He had come here with Elaine, while his parents were vacationing in Nassau, and still considering whether to retire there. He and Elaine had enjoyed snippets of the nightlife, but had spent most of their time strolling the gardens and frolicking on the private beach. Their second child was probably conceived on this island, but then they had returned to Richard's job at the Embassy in Korea. Shortly after came his disagreement with the official policy, backing Chung Hee's plan for further cooperation between the Koreas, leading to his posting to Zimbabwe, a second miscarriage, and then Elaine's death.

"You should go down to Cable Beach for a little while, have a drink, dance a bit," Paul urged.

"Dancing on a beach?" Terra asked.

"Cable Beach is not like the beach right out there," Richard explained. "It's on the edge of downtown, has every entertainment you could find on the strip in Vegas."

"Not quite as big," Caroline corrected.

"Big enough." Richard preferred solitude, but he thought Terra might be interested. "Would you like to go for a stroll, love?"

She looked at him, curiosity in her gaze. "If you're not too tired. Maybe for a little while."

He set down his coffee cup. "Let's go, then." He helped her to her feet, noticing a bit of strain around her eyes. "I'll grab you a jacket. It might get a little cool in the dark with the breeze off the sea."

"There's a wrap just inside the door, son," Caroline offered with a smile. "I keep it handy because you're right, it does get cool."

He bundled the shawl under his arm and led Terra down the garden path through the gate to the private beach. He brought her close to his side, and she nestled against him. "Terra, I'm sorry."

"About what?"

"I didn't realize until I was explaining things to my parents how selfish I was."

She stroked his cheek. "I thought you were remarkably self-*less*."

"I guess I was just obsessed and didn't realize how it looked to other people." He caught the flowery scent of her shampoo and rested his cheek against her hair. "You feel good."

She pressed closer to him. "You do, too." She slipped her arms around his waist. "Did we just get here this afternoon?"

He held her close. "Seems like a long time ago, doesn't it?" He felt the deep breath she took. "Are you tired?" Two months ago, he thought he had watched her die. He feared she was pushing herself to act like she had recovered, but in truth, the severe concussion and other wounds she had would take time to heal.

She snuggled her head into his shoulder. "A little." She looked up at him. "But the beach sounds interesting. The lake beaches I'm used to are for swimming and playing in the sand."

His fingers traced her cheekbones. "The beach will be there tomorrow. We can see it in the morning, even go to the Straw Market." He kissed her forehead. "We can dance on Cable Beach all night tomorrow if you feel up to it."

She scanned his face. "It seems like weeks since we've been alone together."

"We're alone now," he whispered, tasting her lips with his, teasing. She kissed him back, demanding a response from him. He tossed the wrap to the sand, lifting her up against him, only to lower her to the blanket. He ran his hands over her body, but when he started to undo the buttons on the blouse, she stopped him.

"Richard!" She sat up, looking around. "Who knows who might be out here." She glanced back at the house. "And your parents are just across the lawn."

He leaned back, his head propped on his hand, smiling. "Whatever happened to 'I'll make love to you at the base of the Washington Monument at high noon?' "

"You're never going to forget it, are you?" She pushed him over.

He laughed and realized it had been a while since he had laughed. Maybe he was as nervous as she was about meeting his parents. "Would you, if I'd said something as memorable?"

"Just wait," she threatened. "Someday you'll say something that will come back to haunt you." She tickled him, and they rolled on the sand, laughing like kids. When they finally stopped, he pulled her into his arms, and they lay on the beach, watching the moonrise and letting the sound of the waves relax them. Finally, he glanced at his watch.

"Are you sleepy yet?"

She yawned. "Mmmmm."

He stood up, and helped her to her feet, brushing off the sand gathered on her skirt. The curve of her hip beneath his hand thrilled him, and the silver shimmer of moonlight on her skin took his breath away. He held her close. "I love you, Terra." He wished with all his heart he could keep danger away from her.

She rose on her tiptoes to kiss him, running her fingers lightly across his chest. "I love you, too." She bent to pick up the blanket. "Let's go to bed." She smiled at him as she straightened. "And I'm not sleepy anymore."

He grinned. "Race you to the house."

She slipped off her sandals and tossed the blanket at him. She would have beat him if he hadn't vaulted the fence to the beach. They were still laughing when they entered the darkened house and climbed the stairs to their room.

Chapter 7

Terra awoke to the weight of Richard's arm across her, his body warm against her back. His cheek, rough with stubble, rubbed against her neck as he breathed. She wrapped her arms around his, reveling in the comfort of the closeness. Outside birds chattered, their conversations as raucous and varied as a crowd at a DC Metro-link station. She raised her head slightly to survey the room. A ceiling fan spun slowly in the high ceiling. Sheer curtains swayed in the salty breeze sweeping in through two pairs of French doors leading to the balcony. Richard shifted in his sleep, moving his leg over hers. She studied him, trying to memorize the lines of his face, care lines as well as laugh lines. Voices drifted up to her from the garden. Caroline and Paul, it sounded like, but she could no more make out the words than she could understand the birds. She glanced toward the French doors. Morning sunlight, growing bolder by the minute, groped its way into the room. She looked toward the nightstand, to see if there was a clock, but found none.

She felt Richard's chin against her shoulder. "You awake?" he mumbled.

"Um-hum." She tangled her fingers in his hair. "Any idea what time it is?"

He nestled his face between her breasts. "Morning."

"Thanks." She giggled. "I already figured that out." She moved closer to him. "Doesn't feel like you're ready to get up yet."

"Oh, I'm ready, all right." She giggled again, for a while.

****

Caroline met them at the foot of the stairs. "Terra, a Mr. Warner's office called for you." She smiled at them, arm in arm coming down the stairs. Terra felt a kinship with this mother whose son's happiness was important to both of them. "They said they received the parcel you sent, the work was exactly what they wanted, and they needed an address to send you more." She paused. "I hope you don't mind, but I gave them this address."

"Thanks, Mrs. Matthews."

Richard let go of Terra's hand and hopped down the last three steps. "Are you sure it was from Terra's office, Mum?" Terra caught a note in his voice she hadn't heard since Adler was put in custody.

Caroline looked from Richard to Terra. "I don't know, I suppose it could have been someone else, but it certainly sounded legitimate." She took Terra's hand. "And you can call me Caroline or Carrie or whatever you're comfortable with, dear."

"Did you send a parcel to Warner?" Richard's gaze bored into Terra.

"Yes, you remember, I sent it the day we left DC."

"Well, then, I guess it would just be arriving at their office, wouldn't it?"

"Yes, and they had said they wanted to send me a couple more manuscripts."

His shoulders relaxed. "Okay, I guess I just haven't

quite trained myself to let down my guard."

She rubbed his shoulders. "Old dogs have a hard time learning new tricks."

He swung her down the last step. "Hey, I learned to use the computer, didn't I?"

She laughed. "Very slowly." She caught Caroline smiling. The worry lines between her eyes Terra noticed when they met had relaxed.

"What would you kids like for breakfast?" Caroline was ever the good hostess.

Richard walked toward the kitchen. "What do you have?"

His mother followed him. "Fruit, cereal, about anything you want, son."

"One day, maybe Terra can make pancakes for us." He smiled for Terra. "Hers are wonderful."

Caroline addressed Terra. "Would you mind one day, dear?"

"Not at all," Terra assured her. "I can't get used to not doing things myself."

"She's very independent," Richard said from the refrigerator. "How about berries and muffins?"

"Sounds good, love."

Richard stood up, bowls in his hands. "Where's Dad?"

"Tuesday is his golf day," Caroline said, amusement in her voice.

"I thought every day was golf day for him." Richard started setting food on the kitchen island. Terra tried to guess where plates and silverware were to help him and not trouble Caroline.

"Oh, it is, but on Tuesdays, Albert Hamilton picks him up, and they join Roger and Fred, play eighteen holes, and have lunch at the Club, then spend the afternoon lying about golf. Would you like tea?"

"Sure." Richard and Terra put together the breakfast, as Caroline busied herself heating water.

"Tuesdays and Sundays are Janie's days off, and Margaret Hamilton and I usually meet for lunch while the men are golfing."

"Why don't you go ahead with your lunch plans then, Mum, and Terra and I will spend the day sightseeing."

"I thought you might want to, son. I asked Margaret to pick me up so you would have the use of the car." She pulled the kettle from the burner just before it boiled. "Just remember to drive on the left side of the road and watch for all the other drivers."

"I will, Mum." Terra nodded at him, and he went on. "Mum, if you want to have a dinner party or reception or something for us to meet your friends, it's okay."

She beamed. "I'll see who is available." Terra surmised many of her conversations with her friends revolved around their children. "Today is Tuesday. What about Saturday evening?"

"Would it work for us, Terra?" Richard had agreed readily to the dinner when Terra pointed out to him it really meant a great deal to his mother.

"Absolutely," Terra said. "And thank you, Caroline, for wanting to host one for us."

Caroline poured water for Terra's tea. "No trouble at all, dear." She slipped her arm around her briefly. "I'm just happy to get to spend some time with you both, and to get to know you."

"And I'm glad to get to know you." She gave Caroline a full hug. "I knew Richard's parents had to be pretty special to raise such a wonderful son."

Chapter 8

Richard tossed a backpack into the rear seat of his father's older model Jaguar. "Do you think there's anything else we need? Like a kitchen sink or two?"

Terra laughed. "We only packed sunscreen, hats, and an umbrella."

"And bottled water, your purse, a jacket, and a partridge in a pear tree."

She settled herself in the Jag. "If it's too much for you, love, I'll carry it."

Richard adjusted the seat. "No, I can handle it. I'm sure I was a pack animal in a former life." He wasn't angry, and he knew Terra knew he wasn't. It was just one more example of how in tune they were, even though they had only known each other six months. He leaned across the gearshift to kiss her before he started the car. "I love you."

She squeezed his hand. "And I love you." She looked out the windshield as they pulled from the driveway. "What's our plan?"

"We don't have one, yet." He started to drive on the right for just an instant before he swerved to the proper side. "Do you want to shop or see the sights?"

She settled back in her seat. He watched the way she stretched. She seemed totally relaxed, not a care in the world. As he would have been had he not learned of Adler's release. Ginny hadn't returned his call yet, and neither had Agent Prescott. Now it was back to the constant state of alertness he maintained for four years. He had grown weary of it. "I don't care, dear." She scanned the scenery around them.

"Well, then, why don't we drive around looking at sights until we see something we want to explore more. We can hit downtown and do lunch on Cable Beach, shop at the Straw Market. We'll stay until you're tired and want to go back to the house." The road went up a slight incline, bringing them to the high point of the island. Richard pulled into a parking spot. "Shall we go see Fort Fincastle right now?" Truthfully, he wasn't keen on the idea of them getting into a crowd of people, where he would have to be constantly watchful in all directions. If Adler were on the loose, he just might decide to wreak vengeance on the man who had ruined his career. Or take a second wife from him.

Terra peered up at the old lookout post. "What is this place?"

"It was a watch tower of sorts, for the good folks to keep an eye on the pirates sailing into the harbor." He consulted the tourist guide his mother had pressed on them before they left the house. "We can climb the water tower and see the whole island." He read the fine print. "Top of the tower is 200 feet above sea level."

"Gosh, Oklahoma is higher." Terra was already scrambling from the car. He had a hunch watching out for her today, without letting her know he was, would test his endurance.

"The Queen's Staircase was carved from solid stone by slaves using hand tools." Richard glanced up from the guide to find Terra already a third of the way up. "Sixty-five steps in honor of Queen Victoria's sixty-five-year reign." He hustled to catch up to her.

"Boy, it's damp and mossy here." She put out her hand to touch the limestone wall.

Though the steps were wide, they felt close. Richard stepped ahead of her to move her out of the tunnel formed by the vegetation across the staircase. Once again, he had to start watching his surroundings for potential threats. Maybe his father was right, and Adler had no intention of coming after Richard. Still, he couldn't shake the gut instinct he needed to maintain a state of high alert until he learned what was going on. He would call Agent Prescott again when he got back to the house. It bothered him, too, that Ginny had not yet called.

"This is awesome!" Terra stood in the sunlight at the top of the stairs.

He was a step behind her, scanning the surroundings for other people. A few widely scattered groups of two to four people wandered lazily around the grounds. He focused for a moment on a lone man at the top of the battlement but relaxed a little as a toddler and a boy of about ten joined him, followed by a woman carrying a baby.

"It looks like the *Titanic*!" Terra started toward the battlement.

He scanned what he could see of the top, a few people up there as well. Nothing appeared to be an immediate threat. Since they were planning their day move by move, anyone shadowing them would have to be behind instead of ahead of them. "It was built to resemble a ship."

As soon as they reached the battlements, Terra went straight to the rail. "Which way is your parents' house?"

He stood close behind her, getting his bearings. He spotted the Atlantis entertainment monolith on Paradise Island, found the downtown buildings, and then pointed. "Right about there." He put his arms around her. "You can't see it for the trees."

She snuggled back against him. "It's beautiful here. Like Eden."

"Um." He nuzzled her hair, forgetting watchfulness for the moment. "It's why so many people come here for vacation and retirement." He looked out over the verdant island to the azure ocean. "They don't think about hurricane season and the fact practically everything they need to support their lifestyle has to be imported."

"Paradise is only an illusion."

"Pretty much." He sighed, content with Terra safe in his arms. "You can enjoy the beauty, but you have to realize there is a balance to come."

"It would probably get boring with no seasons."

"Oh, they have seasons." He chuckled. "Rainy and not-so-rainy."

She giggled. "Back in Oklahoma, we could get three seasons in one day."

He glanced down at her. "How?"

"It might be below freezing in the morning, up to 65 by noon, over 80 by four o'clock." She laughed again. "And always the wind. Thirty miles an hour on a calm day."

"Sounds exciting."

"Not so much." She shook her head. "When contractors put a new highway through town, people brought lawn chairs to watch the cement machines.

With their kids and dogs and big gulp drinks from the local quick stop."

He hugged her. "At least it was genuine." He kissed her neck. "Just like you." He kissed her shoulder. "No pretensions, earthy, just like your name."

She turned to him. "Maybe we should go back to the house." She kissed him long and slow. "Your parents won't be home for a while, right?"

He wanted to give in to her suggestion. "But what about seeing the sights."

She waved a hand over the railing. "They'll still be there tomorrow. I know some sights I wouldn't mind seeing again."

"Seeing?"

She moved hard against him. "Or feeling."

"As you wish, dear one." They scampered down to the car, but he took a different route back to the house, and she nearly lost her idea in her fascination with the colorful splendor around her. He had to agree, the islands were beautiful, with their people dependent on keeping tourists happy and carefree. Yet he knew how hard most of those people had to work to make a meager living. Every place on earth, he decided, had its own kind of beauty. And its own way of testing its people. Terra's Oklahoma had its extremes of weather, a severe test to a people still tied to land and crops. DC had its humidity and its throngs of people, the pressure of discerning reality in a city living on pretension. Colorado had blizzards and the threat of too many people on a fragile land. They finally ended up on Cable Beach, sipping fruit smoothies from a beachside stand, while they strolled toward the shopping at the Straw Market.

Terra explored the market stalls, while Richard trailed behind, keeping watch. He hoped she was engrossed enough in the crafts she didn't notice him constantly scanning the crowd around them. She made it almost the entire way through the market before she found anything to impress her. "What do you think of this bag?" She held up a large straw tote.

He was tempted to shrug but resisted. "I guess it's okay, but the real question is what you think of it."

She looked it over carefully, studying the workmanship, estimating capacity. "I think it will work as a beach tote."

"Okay." He reached for his wallet.

"No." She stopped him. "I want to get it myself." She pulled her clutch from the backpack he carried. "You've bought enough for me. This I can handle."

"You don't have to be so independent." He smiled, despite his words. Her stubborn streak was part of what endeared her to him.

"Yes, I do." She paid for the tote and put her clutch back in the backpack. "I wouldn't be me if I wasn't." She kissed his cheek quickly. "Do you want me to carry the pack?"

He slipped his arm around her. "No, I'm fine for another four or five hours."

"And you don't have to be so chivalrous all the time, either."

He kissed her again. "Yes, I do, and you know it."

She giggled. "We're even?"

He nodded. "Yup, we're even." She headed back the way they had come. "Aren't you going to check out the rest of the shops?" He hurried to catch up to her, once more scanning the crowd he had ignored the last few seconds.

"Nope." She walked backwards, facing him. "I remembered where we were headed when we left Fort Fincastle."

"Oh, that." He picked up his pace.

****

Later, they sprawled across the bed in their room. Terra ran her hand lazily up Richard's spine. Her touch relaxed him, and he nearly dozed. A fresh breeze swept through the French doors, cooling the sweat from their bodies. In the distance, the surf crashed over breakwaters beyond the beach. If only life could stay this simple, this safe. He heard the sound of a quiet car in the driveway. He tensed, assuming it was one of his parents, but wanting to be ready if it was not. Beside him, he felt Terra pull the sheet around her.

They heard the front door open. Minutes later, they heard steps on the stairs. Richard sat up, the blanket over his lap. Whoever was outside rapped lightly on the door. "Richard? Terra?" Caroline's voice was soft, tentative.

"Yes, Mum." He pulled on his boxers, just in case she opened the door.

"I wasn't sure you were here at the house, dear. I thought you might be at the beach." She hesitated. "Would you like to join us at the Club for dinner tonight?"

He glanced at Terra and she nodded. "Sure, Mum. What time?"

"Eightish."

"Okay, Mum. We'll be ready."

"Dress is casual, son."

"Thanks, Mum." They heard her walk on down the hall to her own room.

He patted Terra's hip. "Shall we hit the shower?"

Chapter 9

Richard was ready, of course, while Terra changed into the third dress of the evening. They had plenty of time, but neither of them saw any point in just sitting in their room. They could enjoy a drink and conversation with his parents in the garden while they waited for time to go to the Club. "The dress looks great." It was true, the green of the linen dress brought out the green in her eyes, but then the red dress and the print dress had looked wonderful on her, too. "I like it better than the other two."

"It's not too casual?" She twirled in the mirror.

"It's fine for the Island Club, dear." He had dressed in khakis and a golf shirt. The two times he and Elaine joined his parents for dinner there, he learned the dress code. She was wavering, he feared, possibly going to try out another dress, when there was a knock at the door.

"Richard?" It was his father.

"Yes, Dad." He headed for the door.

"Phone for you." He opened the door and Paul handed him the cordless phone. "FBI," Paul whispered as he let go of the phone.

"Matthews here."

"Richard Matthews?" It sounded like Agent Prescott.

"Yes."

"I'm returning your call about Mr. Adler."

"I saw an article saying he had been released."

Prescott hesitated. "Well, technically, he's been released from FBI custody."

"But he's still in custody somewhere by somebody?"

"Yes, Homeland Security has him now."

"Homeland Security?"

"CIA and Homeland Security." He cleared his throat. "They had some questions to ask him before we could proceed with our charges. They may be filing charges as well."

Richard breathed a little easier. "Thank you for calling, Agent Prescott. I was concerned he was on the loose again."

"I understand, sir. I'll call you if there are any further developments you need to know about."

"I'd appreciate it, Agent. Good-bye."

Terra and Paul had been listening to his side of the conversation. Terra spoke first. "He's still in custody?"

"Yes." He looked at Paul. "Homeland Security. And CIA." While he was happy Adler wasn't free, he feared he would strike a deal while among his own kind.

"Like putting the foxes in charge of guarding the other fox." Paul didn't sound pleased.

"Is he likely to get out?" Richard heard fear in Terra's voice.

"No, dear." He put his arm around her and led her down the stairs. Paul followed, concern on his face. "If HS doesn't have anything to keep him on, the FBI will get to press kidnapping, assault, and attempted murder charges."

"Good." Her shoulders relaxed under his arm. "But why hasn't Ginny called you back?"

He sighed. Terra seemed to have developed the knack for reading his mind. "I don't know."

Paul offered him the phone. "Why don't you call her again?" Richard took the phone. "Her messages may not be delivered if she's somewhere too remote."

Richard dialed her cell phone number. "I don't even know what story she's working on now." He waited while it rang. "Could be Middle East, Iraq, anywhere." He got no answer, and no "leave a message" recording. "Well, I guess the number will be there when she checks it again."

"Is Tony back in Italy?" Terra headed for the garden.

"I suppose." Richard and Paul followed her. "I didn't ask. Luigi was hoping he could take him touring around the U.S."

"With frequent stops at dance clubs, I presume." Paul and Luigi had been friends more than thirty years.

"I would guess, from the way he acted the last time I had lunch with him."

"He's harmless, but he does enjoy watching women."

"Luigi is the one who introduced us to Tony?" Terra's memory needed refreshing.

"Yes."

"Would anyone like a drink?" Caroline walked onto the patio. Her dress, too, was linen. He was glad now Terra had stopped changing with the green dress.

"Sure, Mum. What kind of wine do you have?"

"We have some excellent local wines, son." Paul went to his wife. "You look lovely, Carrie." He slipped an arm around her, and she almost blushed. "Why don't I pour some of the vintage we got last month?"

Caroline caressed his cheek. "It would be sweet, dear."

"Not much for me, Paul," Terra called.

"Terra prefers Kool-Aid to wine, Dad." Richard laughed.

Paul gave Caroline a squeeze before he disappeared into the kitchen. The rest of them wandered to the iron chairs arrayed under a palm tree.

"So, Terra," Caroline began. "Did you see much of the island today?"

"Fort Fincastle." Terra smoothed down her skirt as she settled into a chair. "And Cable Beach and the Straw Market. It is unbelievably beautiful here."

"Yes, it is." Caroline had warmed to Terra. "Paul and I spent several years in England, when Richard was a toddler, and many years in New York and near DC before he was posted to Italy." She reached out to touch Terra's hand. "After Italy, we decided we liked living where it was sunny and warm." She smiled at her son. "But this is close enough to the States making it no trouble at all to visit people we love."

"Well, you'll have to come visit us in Colorado when our house is ready." Terra seemed eager to be hostess.

"Are you having one built?" Caroline asked.

Richard knew his mother tried very hard not to pry into his business, but he understood her curiosity. "No, Mum, but the owners needed sixty days to get moved and then we wanted to have it re-carpeted before we moved in." Richard leaned back in his chair, suddenly realizing he owned a house in more or less of a suburb for the first time in his life. All he had ever owned before was his apartment building in DC. "I guess there is some stress involved with being a homeowner."

Caroline laughed. "Yes, there is son. No landlord to call when something breaks down."

"I can probably fix a lot of things," Terra volunteered. "My dad was a building contractor."

"She roofed houses in high school, just to prove to him she was as capable as any man on his crew." Richard was proud of her initiative.

"You are quite an amazing young lady, Terra." Richard could tell the admiration in his mother's voice was genuine.

"Your butler has arrived." Paul carried a tray of glasses and a bottle of wine across the grass.

"I was afraid I'd have to let you go for being too slow, dear." Caroline stood to help him serve. Richard motioned to Terra to stay seated as she started to move. Paul served her first, a glass only about half full. Terra waited until Richard sipped at his wine to try hers. He laughed as she wrinkled her nose.

"Don't you like it, dear?" Caroline glanced at Paul.

"Yes, it's fine." Terra sipped again. "As wines go, it's very good, very sweet." She sighed. "I could almost begin to like this one."

"I told you she wasn't much of a drink connoisseur." Richard laughed and gripped her hand. This moment felt so ordinary, so right. His wife and his parents enjoying each other's company in paradise, genuinely glad to be together. After the stress of his years as a diplomat and the agonies of the four years since Elaine's death, and then the duel with Adler that nearly took Terra from him, he found it difficult to take such moments for granted.

"Phone's ringing." Paul hustled to the house to answer it. For years, Paul had been tied by international peace to a phone, now he often seemed to forget they were around. Richard was glad his father had adjusted to retirement. Moments later, he was back in the garden with the phone. He handed it to Richard. "For you, son. State Department."

Caroline looked at her husband, questioning. Terra watched Richard.

"Richard Matthews," he spoke into the receiver.

"Mr. Matthews, could you please hold? The Secretary of State would like to speak with you."

"Yes, of course." This was not standard procedure. Usually the Secretary only spoke to someone during a crisis or to congratulate them after it had been weathered.

"Richard." The Secretary sounded like he was greeting Richard after a vacation. "How have you been?"

"I've been fine, sir."

"I hear we owe a great many thanks to you for discovering Mr. Adler's deceptions." There had to be more to the call than this.

"Well, sir, I was just doing what I thought needed to be done."

"As you always do, Richard. As you always do." The Secretary hesitated. "I'm afraid we need you to do just that once more."

"What is it you want me to do, Mr. Secretary?" At the mention of the title, Paul sat forward in his chair.

"You are aware of the crisis in Korea, aren't you?"

"Sir, I'm aware President Kim has died and Chung

Hee Yu has been named to replace him. I also know the situation there has been tense for years."

"Well, it's rapidly going beyond tense. Despite their claims to the contrary, intelligence indicates the North Koreans have finally perfected their nuclear warhead, and the means to launch it."

He felt a chill slide down his spine. It was the same feeling he had when he was briefed about his new post in Zimbabwe. "Definitely bad news, sir."

"The South Koreans have agreed to several different negotiators, but Chung Hee has said he will come to the table only with you."

"Sir, Chung Hee is a reasonable man, at least he was when I knew him. He will accept someone who is more qualified than I am to handle this."

"I don't think so."

"But, sir, I don't have a clue what has transpired there in the last four years. I haven't negotiated since then, either. I just don't think I'm the right man for the job this time. Please accept my apologies."

The Secretary sighed. "I'm sorry you feel that way. I have the utmost faith in your abilities. Please call me if you change your mind. My staff is instructed to put you through directly to me."

"Thank you for your confidence, sir, but I'm sure about this."

"Good-bye then." The Secretary paused. "By the way, congratulations on your marriage."

"Thank you again, sir. Good-bye." He clicked off the transmission and sat staring at the grass in front of him.

"You just told the Secretary of State of the United States of America no?" Paul's voice held a mixture of incredulity and pride.

Richard looked at his father. "What else could I do, Dad?" He handed his father the phone, afraid it would ring again. "I'm not the best man for this job. I'd have to study the situation for weeks before I'd know which way to go, and by then, it might be beyond critical mass."

"You're probably right. Chung Hee's insistence on you may just be a way to stall to gain some advantage for him or some time to get his government up and running." Paul stood. "Shall we head to dinner now?"

Chapter 10

After an excellent dinner with a few of his parents' friends, they returned to the house singing old torch songs. What Paul lacked in talent, he made up for in enthusiasm. His voice and Richard's were so similar, Terra would have had difficulty telling them apart had she not been tucked against Richard's side. Paul swung the Jag into the driveway and stopped in front of the garage. "All right, everybody out while the chauffeur puts the car away."

Richard took his mother's arm on his right and his wife's on his left. Terra thought he felt more relaxed than he had been since they arrived. "He's really enjoying retirement, isn't he, Mum?"

"Thoroughly, son." She glanced up at him. "As you should be."

"I intend to, Mum." His arm tightened around Terra. "I don't plan to get sucked into the mess in Korea." They walked into the house to the sound of the phone ringing.

Caroline hurried on to answer it. Terra could feel the sudden tension in Richard, wondering if it would be for him. Caroline came toward them. "For you, son." She handed over the phone. "It's Virginia."

"Ginny," Richard skipped formalities. "Why haven't you called back?"

Terra tried to guess what the answers were from

just Richard's side of the conversation, but it consisted mostly of him listening. She would have to wait until he told her what was going on.

Caroline's gaze was on her. "You've met Ginny?"

Terra nodded. "In DC just as things started getting serious with Adler." She sighed, remembering how she assumed Richard was interested in Ginny instead of her. After all, they were both writers, although Ginny was a journalist, and most important, Ginny had introduced Richard to Elaine.

"She's been a good friend to Richard and Elaine over the years." Caroline glanced at Richard, still listening. "But sometimes I wish she would settle down and quit following news stories all over the globe."

"I don't think she can stop." Terra admired Ginny's spunk.

"Thanks, Gin, I'll keep you posted." Richard ended his call. All of them looked at him with expectant faces. "It was Ginny," he said with a grin, as Paul walked in.

"We figured it out already," Terra's spirits lifted. It must have been good news for him to tease so.

"Well, she's been in Pakistan, no towers, and hadn't been able to call for a while." He laughed. "Then when she got her messages, she started trying to call my cell phone."

Terra looked at him, drawing a blank. "Your cell phone?"

He nodded. "The one I'm so unused to having I left it in DC."

Terra laughed then. "I guess the old dog can only learn a limited number of new tricks at once."

He put his arms around her. "I never got one, because conversations are so easily tapped on them, that I'm not used to carrying one. Soon, both of us will be carrying cell phones so we can call each other from the next room."

Paul chuckled. "I've seen it, you know." He looked at Caroline. "We got one, didn't we?"

"We got two, dear, so we could keep in touch with each other." She opened the credenza drawer. "Here they are." She touched his cheek. "But we always know where the other one is, and we haven't had anything critical enough to tell each other that couldn't wait."

Terra glanced up at Richard. "You know, maybe cell phones and constant, instant communication makes relationships weaker."

"How so, dear one?" He was looking down, into her eyes, his lips a hand's width away from her, making her lose her train of thought.

"Because you don't learn to listen to where the other person said they were going and when they'd be back. You don't learn to trust your knowledge of the other person enough to make decisions you think they'd approve of."

His face moved closer to hers. "Very wise, love."

"Profound," Caroline spoke, and Richard pulled his head up to look at his mother.

"What did Ginny have to say?" If Terra couldn't get a kiss, she'd get information now, the kiss later.

"She said Tony called her, because he didn't want her to be alarmed by the news articles." He chuckled. "Seems young Mr. Verde is quite fond of Gin, and she is using it like the great reporter she is. Agent Preston called her, too."

"Sounds like Ginny." Though Terra regarded Ginny as a threat initially, her encouragement of the new relationship between Richard and Terra, and her absolute loyalty to Richard and his cause had cemented their friendship.

"She got a bit more info than I did, seems Mr. Adler is bargaining with information he has about operations in other countries." His gaze met Paul's. "Right now, CIA and Homeland Security are both very interested in what he knows about North Korean operations."

Paul moved closer to them. "Does he know what's happening there?"

Richard wrapped his arms around Terra. "Nothing Tony or Gin have been able to find out. She was asking me if I knew what was going on, said she might end up covering the story of the peace talks there." He rested his chin on her head. "Assuming there are peace talks." He lowered his voice below a whisper. "Assuming there is still either a Korea or a world by then."

His arms around her felt heavy. She knew he was thinking about the calls from the State Department, his refusals to participate weighing on his mind. She placed her small hands over his long fingers. "Do you want to go for a walk?"

He sighed. "No, not unless you really want to." He let go of her and stepped back. "I'm tired." He yawned and stretched. "Mum, Dad, I think I'm ready to turn in."

Paul chuckled. "You must be starting to run on island time, son." He moved closer to Caroline. "Nothing seems as important here, when the days are sunny, and the nights are balmy, and there is always plenty to eat."

Caroline slipped her arm though his. "And there have been eighteen holes of golf during the day."

"Ah, yes, the perfect day." He leaned his head against hers. "Goodnight, son, Terra." He let go of Caroline long enough to give Terra a little hug and kiss on the cheek. "Sweet dreams."

Richard took Terra's hand, searching her gaze for agreement to skip the walk. She had only suggested it to give him a chance to talk and to think. "I'm ready for bed, too, love."

He took her in his arms the moment the door to their room closed. Without words, they pulled off each other's clothing, moving slowly but surely toward the bed. Knowing where to touch, how to move, what to do to please the other, they made love with tenderness. Terra knew his need tonight had less to do with passion than with intimacy. He needed the comfort her love gave him, needed to know he could satisfy her completely. She knew, too, while she dozed in total relaxation, he would stare into the dark and think, as he had the night they heard of Adler's release. As he lay on his back, one arm around her, the other tucked under his head, she nestled close, her leg over his, her fingers resting on his chest, and wondered how long it would be before his conscience took him to Korea.

Chapter 11

Richard rose just before dawn and slipped from bed for a run without waking Terra. He was back and in the shower when she woke up. Then he joined his father to walk to a coffee shop a few blocks from their house. Now Richard watched from the kitchen as Terra sat at the table in the garden editing one of the manuscripts Warner's office sent her. Her left hand cradled a teacup, while she occasionally made notes on the manuscript with the pen in her right. She brought the cup to her lips, and his heart flipped as he remembered the first time he watched her reading a manuscript and drinking tea. That day changed the course of both their lives. His mother bustled about the sink beside him, washing an assortment of fruit. "Isn't she beautiful, Mum?"

Caroline glanced through the window. "Yes, she is, son. Beautiful and sweet." She shut off the water. "How old is she?"

"Twenty-four," he answered. He knew his mother would be quicker than he was computing the thirteen-year gap between them.

"Hmmm." She looked out the window again, as if seeing Terra for the first time. "She's younger than I thought."

"But she's been through a lot, Mum." He at first resisted his attraction to her because of the age difference, but her personality won his heart without consulting his brain.

"I know she has, dear." She looked at him. "Losing her parents at such a young age, working so hard, going through the Adler thing with you." She placed the fruit in a basket and handed it to him. "I think she's wonderful, Richard. You'll have some adjustments to make because of the age and upbringing difference, but you seem to be handling things well." She pushed him toward the door. "Now go spend some time with your wife. She shouldn't work through her entire honeymoon."

Richard set the basket on the table in front of Terra. She looked up at him, and the contented look on her face made him feel warm and safe. "How are the manuscripts?" He settled in the chair beside her and picked up a plum.

"Two of these are just not grabbing me, but this one—" She flipped back a couple of sheets. "This one has something keeps me turning pages. It won't take much editing at all to get it ready to go." She laid down her pen. "At least in my opinion."

He watched her face, enjoying the expressions moving quickly over it. "Well, you may be new to editing, but from what you did with my book, I think your opinion is probably right. And Warner seems happy enough with your opinion to pay you for it."

"And about my salary—" He sensed an old argument coming. "I want to use some of my money for the house."

"I already explained to you some of the tenants want to buy their share of my apartment building in DC. The sale and my savings will pay for the house."

He reached out to take her hand. "I've had a lot more years to work and save than you have, had nothing to spend money on after Elaine died." He kissed her fingers. "Why not use your money to re-decorate and remodel the house the way you want it?"

She pulled her hand away from him. "Richard, it makes me feel like I'm being patted on the head and called 'the little woman.' "

She might be little and she might be a woman, but it would never be safe to pat her on the head and ignore her. "Terra, I only suggested it to make things simpler and because I don't care for decorating. You have a better sense of it than I do. When I go into writing mode, I don't even notice if I ate or slept—"

She laughed. "I know." She wasn't sulking, at least.

"Okay." He was willing to compromise. After all, Elaine had not earned a salary except for their first year of marriage, and he had always considered his earnings hers as well, because of the active role she played as a diplomat's wife. Now, he had a new situation to learn to deal with. "Why don't we put the numbers together and you can figure out what you want to put in on the house?"

"That's better." He felt her soft fingers on his arm.

"But," he grabbed her hand. "I don't want you to use every penny you have on it. I want you to always have enough of your own money that you can feel free to spend it without thinking you have to ask my permission."

"Fair enough." She leaned toward him, her knees bumping his. "The carpet layers will be there next week. Are you still happy with the carpet and tile we picked out?"

He ran his hand down her thigh. "To tell you the truth, they could lay something totally different, and I wouldn't know."

Her eyes flashed. "I would."

He laughed again, thinking of the prospect of her reading the riot act to any contractor who tried to pull a fast one on her. "I know you would." He squeezed her hand. "They would regret the day." He pulled her fingers to his lips once more. "All I ask is you consult me on how you plan to decorate my study." Again, he watched the emotions dance across her face. "And I probably wouldn't be thrilled if you painted our bedroom pink."

"I hate pink."

"I know."

"If you hadn't let me spend my money on the house, though, I would have painted your study pink."

"Then I'll let you spend all the money you want on the house. Besides—" He stopped before he voiced the thought.

"Besides, what?"

"Nothing, I'll just need to get busy putting the next novel together when we get home." He had almost suggested he might be halfway around the world while she decorated their home. The feeling he'd had when the Secretary of State told him about North Korea's nuclear capabilities nagged at him, hovered in the back of his consciousness. But equally strong was his conviction there were many others more qualified than he to handle the situation.

"Plus, we'll have the galley proofs of *Quest for the Black Pearl* to review by then."

"True." He heard voices and looked up to find his parents walking from the kitchen.

"Good morning," Terra called.

"Good morning, Terra." Paul took her hands and dropped a quick kiss on her cheek. Richard smiled. His father was always gracious to women, but he had adored Elaine. Now, it seemed he had taken Terra into his heart as well.

Caroline gave Terra's shoulder a quick squeeze. "Good morning, Terra." She slipped into the chair opposite her. "You are up working bright and early this morning."

"I like being the first one up, although this morning—" She glanced at Richard. "He beat me to it." She gestured around the garden. "I love watching while the world is coming awake around me."

Caroline smiled. "Yes, I love to be up then, too. I go for a stroll along the beach and do tai chi and watch the fishing boats sail out of the harbor."

"What a good idea." Richard leaned toward Terra. "How would you like to go sailing?"

"The Hendersons would probably let you use their boat," Paul offered. "I could call him for you."

"Sailing?" Terra's voice trembled.

"You don't like sailing?"

"I've never been sailing."

"Don't they have sailboats in Oklahoma?"

"Yes, but dad and my uncles always went fishing, in little boats with trolling motors." She sat back. "Once I went water-skiing with a church youth group." She shook her head. "I'm not friendly with boats."

He grinned. "Kind of like you're not friendly with planes?"

She nodded. "I guess if I can't control it, I don't like it."

"Richard, if she doesn't want to go, don't insist." His mother could still address him with that tone.

"No, Caroline, it's all right." Terra lifted her chin. "It's an unreasonable fear I need to get over." She faced Richard. "If you're comfortable sailing, I'll go."

Pride for her courage and wisdom made it hard for Richard to speak. Finally, he leaned forward to kiss her. "That's my girl." He rubbed her arms. "I learned to sail in the Med when I was sixteen, Terra." He remembered those eventful years, when he thought he knew so much. Now he realized how much he had yet to learn. "You are safe in my hands."

"I always am," she said, leaning her head on his shoulder.

Paul rose. "I'll go call John about his boat."

Chapter 12

Richard wandered out of the dining room into the kitchen. Janie and her sister were putting the finishing touches on the seven-course meal they would serve in another half hour or so, when the guests had all arrived. Janie's sister, Richard learned from his mother, usually assisted when any of Janie's clients needed extra help on occasion. He and his father spent most of the day on the golf course, while Terra and his mother shopped for new dresses, and everyone kept out of Janie's way.

Right now, about thirty people Richard didn't know from Adam's off ox wandered through his parents' entire lower level, including the garden and veranda. He had grown accustomed to such stilted parties as a diplomat, but now, he found them harder to tolerate, even with the two amaretto sours he'd imbibed already. In the kitchen, he was safe from his mother's friends, all of whom seemed to ask the same questions about his life and most often, Terra. He explained at least a dozen times they met when she worked for him, been married two months; yes, she was younger than he was; no, he hadn't known her very long. He needed a breather. He would have preferred to rescue Terra at the same time, but she was trapped between the rather large Mrs. Beasley and the intimidating Mrs. Smythe-Thomas. He had faced many fearsome dragons in his life, but right now, he didn't have the courage to face those two. Terra was on her own; she would survive.

He pulled a piece of cheese from the serving tray Janie was arranging. She tapped his hand. "How am I gonna get this thing pretty if you keep messin' with it?"

"Sorry, Janie." He grabbed a carrot from a bowl. "It just looked so good, I couldn't resist."

"Mr. Richard, you are just like your father." She nodded at the kitchen island. "Pick out what you want, and then get out of here and let me do my work." She stood with her hands on her hips. "You should get back into your party. It's for you, you know."

He picked up a celery stick. "I know, Janie." He drifted toward the veranda off the kitchen. It was dark and didn't appear to have attracted any guests. "But they're a tough crowd."

She handed him another slice of cheese. "You can handle 'em, Mr. Richard." She waved a towel at him. "Now, shoo."

Chuckling to himself, munching on the celery, he sauntered into the welcoming dark just outside the kitchen. He was alone there. He breathed in night-blooming jasmine. The breeze stirring the palms above him also brought wisps of sound from the nightlife downtown, and always, the undertone of the surf. If left to his preference, he would have refused the party, but it was important to his mother, and pleasing his mother was important to his wife, thus he would accept it. His father, through years of state dinners, had developed more endurance than he had. He walked across the cushion of grass, wishing he could slip off his shoes, and examined the hedge surrounding most of the house, lending it privacy. Soon, he would be considering how to landscape his own home, and wondered if this particular plant flowered. He circled the house, inspecting the plants and delaying his re-entry into the fray. At the side of the house where the dining room opened onto the veranda, he stopped in the shadow of a large palm tree. He had planned to slip back into the party through those doors, but the way was blocked by two ladies whose names he had to work to recall.

"They make a cute couple," the younger woman was saying, as she leaned against the filigreed column supporting the outer edge of the veranda roof. The light barely reached her there. With her meticulous makeup and hair, it was hard to guess her age for sure. The widowed Mrs. Dorchester, he thought it was. Most of his parents' friends were American and British retirees and wealthy business people, though there were a few Europeans in the mix.

"Yes, they do." The older woman, Mrs. Lowenstein, was married to the owner of a jewelry chain. Though she wore plenty of jewelry, it was understated, tasteful, and obviously expensive. He smelled old money. "But I wonder…"

"Wonder what?" Mrs. Dorchester leaned closer.

"I wonder if she really married him for love, or if she has her eye on his money."

"He doesn't have much, does he?" Mrs. Dorchester pulled out a cigarette.

"Oh, from what Caroline says, I guess he does all right with those books of his." Mrs. Lowenstein shook her head. "But he's also got a trust from Caroline's family he's never touched, and he stands to inherit her family business and all that goes with it."

Mrs. Dorchester's lighter flamed. "What is the family business?"

"Caroline's father is a founding partner in one of the oldest investment firms in Boston. Any time he wanted, Richard could be a full partner. He would inherit millions."

As if he wanted to be a part of a stuffy tradition focused solely on money. A desire to do something for humanity was what had driven his mother to enter Vassar for a social work degree and attracted her to his father. "Millions?" The end of Mrs. Dorchester's cigarette glowed. "And she's just a working-class girl."

"Exactly." Mrs. Lowenstein sniffed. "It was the opportunity of a lifetime. She was working for an attractive, wealthy man vulnerable in his grief. What smart girl looking to get ahead wouldn't jump at a low-risk chance like that?"

Low risk, my ass, Richard thought. She was kidnapped, beat up, shot, and subjected to mind games. He stayed put, waiting to see what assessment they would make next, and burning with the urge to set them straight.

"Well, I heard—" Mrs. Dorchester lowered her voice. "I heard when he didn't seem inclined to marry her, she got pregnant to hurry him up."

"Oh, he would, too. He's such a nice boy, and lost those two babies with his first wife."

That did it. Richard gathered himself to step into the light and tell them off when his mother appeared in the doorway. "Oh, there you are," Caroline exclaimed to her guests. "We'll be serving dinner in just a few minutes."

"Wonderful party, Caroline." Mrs. Lowenstein fluttered to the door. She took Caroline's hand. "The kids look happy."

"They are happy." Richard heard a note in his mother's voice telling him she was about to administer discipline. She must have been listening, too. "I haven't seen Richard this much at peace in years, and Terra is just a delight."

"Yes, a delight," Mrs. Dorchester agreed.

"I couldn't have picked a better daughter-in-law myself." Caroline turned toward the house. "She's very independent, is working even on their honeymoon as an editorial consultant." She glanced back at the women following her. "I'm as proud of her as if she were my own daughter."

Richard relaxed in the shadows. Inside her velvet glove, his mother wielded an iron fist. He picked up another amaretto as he went inside the dining room. Just then, his mother entered from the kitchen. "Thanks, Mum." He raised his glass to her.

"For the party? It's a joy to me to do it." She rested her hand on his arm.

"No, for what you said on the veranda."

"Oh, you heard that, did you? Hiding from the party as usual?"

"Yeah, Mum, and thanks."

She leaned close to his ear. "The nosy old biddies don't have lives of their own," she whispered. She squeezed his arm and gathered her guests.

Seated across from Terra, Richard watched her parrying the questions of the guests with grace and candor. She was such a trooper, but he'd learned that as she faced the Adler crisis with him. Tough and cool under pressure, she was. Still, he wondered how many of the other guests looked down their noses at her. He wanted to correct them. It didn't help that five years ago on this night, he was frantically calling medical help as Elaine miscarried their second baby. Three months later, she was dead herself. He was in the wrong mood for a dinner party today. He tried to shake off the melancholy. He looked at Terra, glowing in periwinkle silk serving as a perfect foil to her dark hair and ivory skin, and gave thanks to his Maker she had come into his life. He sipped at his wine and tried to give the excellent meal the enthusiasm it deserved. Normally, he loved Grouper Parissienne.

"You were in foreign service in Korea, weren't you, lad?" Mr. Flanagan next to him had retired as a member of England's Parliament.

"Yes, sir, for six years." Richard picked up his glass again.

"Well, what do you think about what's going on there now?"

"I was there a long time ago." He set his empty glass down, and Janie's sister refilled it immediately. "I don't really understand what the situation is now."

"Oh, but you must have some thoughts about it." Mr. Ellis, on his right, spent his life as an importer in the Bahamas.

Richard glanced around the table to find Terra, Paul, and Caroline all paying close attention to his words. "No, not at all. I'm done with world politics." He drained his glass. "All I want to do for the rest of my life is just be a good husband."

Everyone raised their glasses in response to his impromptu toast.

Mrs. Lowenstein addressed Terra. "So, dear, are you planning a family right away?"

Richard watched through his glass as Terra

responded. "No, Mrs. Lowenstein, we haven't really discussed it much."

Janie's sister refilled the glass and Richard finished his wine again. "You know, Mrs. Lowenstein, that's kind of a private matter between a man and his wife."

Mrs. Lowenstein dropped her fork, and Terra stood up. "Carrie, I think I may have overdone it in the sun today." She dropped her napkin at her plate. "Would you mind if I excuse myself for some fresh air?"

"Quite all right, dear."

Richard felt his mother's gaze upon him. He pushed back his chair. "I'll go with you, love."

Chapter 13

Terra took Richard's arm as they left the dining room headed toward the veranda. "You're drunk," she whispered as they stepped into the dark yard.

"Yes, I am." He swayed before stopping at the chairs off the kitchen. Terra pushed him to sit, and he dropped hard into a chair.

She stood watching as he leaned forward with his head in his hands. "I've never seen you like this."

"You won't very often." He worked at his tie. "Hopefully, never again." He dropped it on the table when he finished untying it. "I normally know when to quit."

"Then what's wrong tonight?" Since she had known him, he had been the model of restraint and logic.

He stood and held out his hand to her. "Let's go for a walk on the beach, and I'll see if I can explain it to both of us." He stepped back inside the kitchen for the beach blanket they'd left by the door yesterday. Holding hands, they walked down the path to the beach gate. By the time they reached the sand, Terra thought he felt steadier beside her. His fitness level must be fighting off the effects of the alcohol already. She waited for him to start the conversation.

"I guess I've just been thinking too much since we got here," he began.

"Don't you always think too much?"

He nodded. "But the news about Adler stirred me up—"

"Me, too." She remembered when the duel with Adler ruled their lives.

"Then there's been the Korean thing." He paused. "And then on the golf course today, I remembered it was exactly five years ago Elaine lost our second baby."

She squeezed his hand tighter, knowing how little the memory of the pain had faded. "I'm sorry." She hesitated. "If I'd known, we could have postponed the party."

"It's all right." He looked out toward the breakwater. "I wanted to get this party over with anyway." He laughed. "It's over for us now. They'll be going home to gossip as soon as dessert is finished."

"It's not like you to be as rude as you were to Mrs. Lowenstein." Unless it was a life and death struggle, Richard was unfailingly diplomatic.

"You didn't hear what she said about you."

"About me?" She thought Mrs. Lowenstein had seemed very kind.

"Yeah, about you." They had reached the end of this stretch of beach, and he looked toward the ocean. "I overheard her and Mrs. Dorchester discussing you when I escaped from the party."

"I wondered where you'd gone."

"I'd had all I could handle for the moment." He stood facing the water. "Anyway, they were surmising you had married me for my money, trapped me into marrying you by getting pregnant."

"They thought I was pregnant?" She'd forgotten

how vicious gossip could be.

He nodded. "And why her question pissed me off so much." He slipped off his jacket. "I was about ready to tell them off when my mum stepped in and did it herself. Politely, of course."

Terra knew they were building a rapport, but never guessed Caroline felt that way about her. "Your mom defended me?"

"Yup, she loves you, Terra. She told them she was as proud of you as if you were her own daughter."

"I had no idea." Terra felt tears gather. "I love your parents, Richard. They have made me feel accepted."

He faced her. "They should love you. You're wonderful."

"As are you." She slipped her arms around his waist. "But, you know, we haven't talked much about a family." She pressed her cheek against his chest, reassured by the strong, steady beat of his heart, and his hands on her back. "How long do you want to wait?"

He was silent so long she wondered if he would even answer her. "A little while." He pushed her away to see her face. "Let's get settled in at home." He stroked her hair. "And I want to be sure you've fully recovered from the ordeal with Adler. Then we can talk about it." The tide sent the water lapping at their feet. "How about a swim?" He let go of her to pull off a shoe.

"We don't have any suits."

Too unsteady yet to stand on one leg, he fell to the sand, quickly tugging off the other shoe and both socks. He smiled at her with the look that always worked with her and his mother. "It's a private beach." He dropped his jacket behind him and fumbled with the buttons of his shirt.

"But what about the guests?" Public nudity had been frowned upon in her small-town upbringing.

"They won't come out here, and if they do, the shock will do them good." He wrestled out of the shirt and stood to unfasten his trousers. "You never skinny-dipped?"

She shook her head. "That was one dare I never cared to accept."

He dropped his pants and stood before her naked. "Well, I dare you now."

"Richard!" She pushed him away, although the sight of his toned body made her hesitate before she did. "Just because someone makes a dare doesn't mean I have to take it."

He ran into the water, diving when it reached his knees. Seconds later, he surfaced fifty yards out. "Water's warm."

"I'm sure it is." She stepped out of her shoes. The powdery sand cradled her bare feet, making her realize how stressful today had been, and how tired she was. She spread out the blanket and sat down to watch Richard swim parallel to the beach.

"It's very relaxing," he called from waist deep water. "It would feel good."

"I'm fine, love." He dove again. When she next saw his head in the water, he was a hundred yards out and still headed toward the breakwater. She stood so she could see him. "Richard?"

"Yes, dear." He stopped swimming to float.

"Don't go out too far."

He waved and started back toward shore. In minutes, he walked dripping from the surf and stood before her. "You should come in."

"What about sharks?"

"Never heard a report of them in this bay." The way he looked at her made her want to be near him, no matter what. He held out a hand to her. "Please?"

She pulled her dress from her shoulders. "How can I ever refuse you?"

Chapter 14

Totally relaxed, Richard and Terra strolled into the darkened house. A faint light came from the den. They walked in to find Caroline and Paul having tea. Richard approached them. "Mum, Dad, I'm sorry about ruining the party."

Paul chuckled. "Actually, this was the best party we've ever had."

Caroline glanced at him, but smiled herself. "You know, son, part of the beauty of us being retired is we don't have to make sure anymore everyone at a party leaves happy."

"I've been wanting to tell that Lowenstein battleaxe off since I first met her." Paul grinned.

Richard laughed. "Dad, I never suspected."

"How was your walk on the beach?" Richard knew his mother noticed they were carrying their shoes and their hair was still damp.

"It was great," Terra jumped in. "We went for a swim, too."

"Beaches are good for swimming." Caroline smiled. "I'm sorry the party didn't go like any of us expected." She stood to hug Terra. "We'll edit the guest list more carefully next time."

"Oh, it was actually fun for a while." Terra hugged her back. "Thanks for wanting to have it. We—"

The phone interrupted. "Shall I get it, Dad?"

"Go ahead, son, you're closer to it than I am." Paul was comfortably ensconced in his chair with his feet up.

"Matthews residence."

"Yes, this is the White House operator. Is a Mr. Richard Matthews there, please?"

Richard sat on the edge of the desk. The feeling he'd had when the Secretary of State called returned. "This is Richard Matthews."

"Please hold for the President." Seconds later, the voice he knew only from television boomed in his ear. He stood as an automatic reflex. "Mr. Matthews, please let me say that, as a nation, we are in debt to you for the sacrifices you have made for your country."

"I was just doing my job, Mr. President." At his greeting, his father sat forward, and Terra and his mother stopped talking. "And, please, call me Richard, sir."

"Well, it doesn't seem right when you're calling me 'sir,' does it?"

"No, sir, er, Mr. President, sir." Suddenly, he wanted the man on the other end of the phone to hurry. Across the room, the look on Terra's face told him she suspected what the call was about.

"Listen, Richard, I don't want to waste your time, so I'll get right to the point." The President paused and when he spoke again, his voice was quieter, and yet more urgent. "We need you if we are going to keep the lid on things in Korea."

"Sir, I really don't think I'm capable of doing what needs to be done there. I'm not up to speed on the situation."

"Son, that's why we have support staff. If you will agree to be our lead negotiator, it will buy us the time to get you completely briefed, and to have our best and most knowledgeable people at your side."

"But, sir—"

"Please, hear me out. Chung Hee refuses to come to the table with anyone but you. It may be he is being pressured by his new government. Lord knows his succession was not expected or well accepted. It may be your presence is only needed to get things started."

Richard felt Terra's hand on his arm. "It's okay if you have to go," she whispered.

He swallowed hard, because she had no idea of what she was releasing him to, of what she might have to endure if he did what his conscience told him he must. "Sir, if I go, I believe I will have to be in it to the end."

There was a pause on the other end before the President answered. "You are probably right. I wouldn't ask if I thought there was any other way to stabilize the region."

He took a deep breath as the sensation of being sucked into a vortex swept over him. "All right, sir, I'll accept the role."

"A grateful world will be indebted to you once more." The President paused again. "I would like to meet with you personally before you go, but for now I'll give you to the Secretary of State."

Richard absorbed all of the information contained in the rest of the call: tomorrow, several foreign service officers would arrive to begin his briefing. The Secretary would call each of the Korean leaders privately to tell them, then would also inform the envoys of the other three nations involved in the negotiations. It would be several days, hopefully, before the press got the news. He would remember all the details tomorrow. Right now, all he knew was he would be away from Terra for longer than he ever wanted, and he would be facing the biggest challenge of his life. When he finally hung up the phone, his family was waiting.

"Back on the job, eh?" Paul's tone was jovial, but Richard knew his father understood all involved. His mother merely gripped his father's shoulder. She knew, too. But Terra stared at him in silence. He had a lot to explain to her.

"Yeah, how could I refuse again?" He put the phone back in the charger. "The briefings will start tomorrow. Dad, would you sit in and advise me until I have to leave?"

Paul shrugged. "Sure, if they'll accept an old security clearance."

"I'll make sure they will." Richard began to accept the full authority as well as the responsibility of his new role. "But right now, let's get some sleep."

"Okay, son, goodnight." His mother kissed his cheek tenderly, and his dad squeezed his shoulder.

He held out his hand to Terra, and they climbed the stairs to their room in silence. He could feel her questions boiling, as if she didn't know what to ask first. He opened their door. "Terra, I don't think you know what I'm getting into."

"Richard, I know I don't have a clue, but I know you had to do it."

He sighed, the weight of it already bearing down. "Yes, I had to, and I'm glad you support me in this." He sat down on the bed and tugged her to sit beside him. "But this will be weeks, maybe months. I don't think it would be safe for you there." He thought over the alternatives. "Would you be okay staying here for a while?"

She nodded. "Sure, but I could go back to DC or on to Colorado, couldn't I?"

Should he tell her she was in danger again? "Just let me know ahead of time if you are going elsewhere." He tapped her chin with his knuckles. "You wouldn't want me distracted by worrying about you, would you?"

"No." She put her arms around him and rested her head on his shoulder. "But I'll worry about you."

He held her and didn't want to tell her that her woman's intuition was correct. "I'll be fine, secure meeting location and a full contingent of U.S. Marines." When she didn't say anything, but just looked up at him with eyes full of tears, he knew she was thinking there had been a full contingent of Marines there the day Elaine died.

Chapter 15

Terra watched through the kitchen window. Seated around the patio table, Richard and Paul were in deep discussion with three State Department experts on the current Korean crisis. They had arrived on the earliest morning flight, carrying bags resembling traveling salesman's sample cases more than legal briefcases. Besides the reams of paper, they brought slim notebook computers, backup USB drives, and two burly Secret Service types. At least Terra assumed it was the role the two men served. They never sat in on the briefing meetings, never removed their suit jackets or sunglasses, and rarely spoke. Terra felt guilty anytime one of them came close, but it was seldom. Normally, they wandered the perimeter of the property. As the mercury in the thermometer visible through the kitchen window crept past 85 on its way to the usual 90 degrees, the experts shed their suit jackets. The perimeter guards did not. The carefree honeymoon trip had changed tenor overnight. She shivered.

"Don't be scared, Terra." Caroline's voice was as reassuring as the arm she slipped around Terra. "They all look deadly serious because they have a lot of information to share with Richard." She observed in silence a moment. "Most of it, he won't need, but he has to know everything he can about the situation if he's to make good judgments."

"It's just very intimidating," Terra said as she watched Richard pass a folder to Paul. Paul opened it, exchanged a glance with Richard, and then the youngest of the experts began to thumb through the folders at his elbow. "I've never seen Richard this way."

"What way, dear?"

"So—" she paused, struggling to find a word to describe the attitude he projected. "So, *in command*." She had been there when he had been in control of a situation before, from working a crowd to doing hand to hand battle for their lives, but then he had been acting alone. "Like when the suits protested when he wanted Paul to sit in on the briefing. I mean, he called the Secretary of State personally, and got Paul cleared immediately."

"Richard is very much like his father." Caroline chuckled. "They appear to be simply charming, humble men, but when push comes to shove, they know how to get what's best for everyone in the long run." Her arm around Terra tightened. "Let's just be thankful it's men like them who have this power instead of men like Adler."

Terra shivered again, remembering the old adage, "Absolute power corrupts absolutely." She wondered what other aspects of Richard she had never seen would eventually surface.

****

Richard threw the file to the table and leaned back in his chair. "There's all kinds of information here, but nothing outside of the change in leadership explaining why we're at a crisis right now as opposed to at any time in the past ten years." Even when he was stationed in Korea, the watchers had feared a change in leadership would destabilize a country already shaky.

"But, sir," Theodore Edwards, the youngest of the experts, looked toward the one on his right. "This is all the intelligence we have about the situation."

The oldest man, John Harris, spoke up. "The South Koreans have been most forthcoming about their information."

"They have a public web site containing a lot of this information." The third expert, Ray Delmonico, joined in. "They don't appear to be hiding anything. Even the Chinese are remarkably open at this juncture."

"I'm not saying the information is not complete." Richard sat forward. "I'm just saying something doesn't quite make sense. There's nothing here explaining why Chung Hee has been able to rise to power so quickly and yet not be able to avert the nuclear threat crisis."

"Well, sir." Harris leaned toward Richard. "If I may put forth a theory."

Richard nodded. "Go ahead. We need all the insight we can get here."

"I believe the North Koreans were quick to advance Chung Hee because of his intimate knowledge of the South. After all, he was a member of their cabinet when he defected."

"Some people have theorized that," Delmonico added. "But others think there's something else behind his rise, like maybe he was an agent for the North all along."

Richard shook his head. "I don't think so. I know Chung Hee personally—at least I used to—and it doesn't fit with what I know of him." The data churned in his mind. It was nearly six years since he'd spoken with Chung Hee. In fact, backing Chung Hee's ideas for collaboration with the north was what ran him afoul of his own ambassador in Korea and gotten him reassigned to Zimbabwe. He looked toward his father, quietly observing, reading files, but making few comments since the briefing started three hours ago.

"Well, son," Paul spoke finally. "I think it's something you'll just have to ask him when you get there."

He stared at Paul for a long time. "I'm afraid you're right, Dad." He stacked the folders. "That's enough for now." The experts shuffled files into their cases. "I know you guys were probably up until the wee hours, got on a plane in the middle of the night, and you've been working your asses off since you got here. Go back to your hotel and get some rest. See some island life if you can stay awake for it." Beneath the damp shirts, their shoulders sagged. They had probably been toiling non-stop on the crisis for months. They knew more about the situation in Korea than anyone alive who wasn't in the middle of it. "And tomorrow, dress is casual. We're not trying to impress anyone here; we're trying to get to the bottom of what may prove to be an enigma. I need you able to think and express yourselves clearly, not dying of heat stroke."

They glanced at each other, until Harris spoke. "Thank you, sir."

Edwards cleared his throat. "About security—"

"We have a security system for the house, and I have a rather large safe in my den," Paul volunteered. "You can leave the papers there—"

"Yes, I'll probably study them later tonight." Richard stood up, amazed at how stiff the tension had made him.

"And I assume you have encryption built into the electronics?" Paul knew the drill better than they suspected. They must have forgotten how many years he served in foreign service himself. And he'd only been retired five years.

"Yes, of course," Edwards said.

Richard nodded toward the brawny men who were just beyond the hedge. "And I'm guessing Moe and Larry or their twins will be staying around tonight."

"Yes, sir." Delmonico put the last of the folders in his case. "High security for you from now until the crisis is ended."

Richard glanced toward the house. He noticed Terra and his mother watching as he got up to pace from time to time. He waved Delmonico to his side. "Does it include my family?"

"Affirmative, sir." Delmonico followed his gaze. "Until the crisis is over."

Richard took a deep breath. The assurance did nothing to ease the queasy feeling in the pit of his stomach. Once again, a storm was gathering, and he feared it would break right over his loved ones.

Chapter 16

Terra twirled before the apartment mirror one more time, with a critical eye upon herself. It was a good suit, neutral beige, conservative. Deciding what to wear had been difficult, especially since her heart hadn't been in shopping. Caroline had been helpful, giving her a general sense of the level of dress expected, but stopping short of making recommendations. With Richard and Paul deep in security briefings, there had been little Terra and Caroline could do but stay out of the way. Caroline had suggested shopping for this particular occasion. Terra suspected it was Caroline's way of distracting both of them from the duty facing Richard. As much as she had bonded with her mother-in-law, however, it felt good to Terra to be back in their District of Columbia apartment, alone. "Do you think this outfit is appropriate?"

Richard struggled to fasten cuff links. He barely glanced at her before responding. "It looks fine to me."

She stepped toward him to help him, and he accepted her assistance with a grateful silence. As she looked into his face, his gaze was on the carpet, but his mind was on the other side of the world. She scanned his face, seeing the lines etched deeper in just a week, noting the darkness under his eyes that said he thought more than slept during the night. She stroked his hands as she finished with the cuff links. "I love you," she whispered. "It will all be okay."

He looked at her then. "This is not an easy task I've agreed to."

"I know." She touched his cheek. "But you will give it the best you have, and your best is better than anyone else I know."

"Thank you, Terra." He leaned against her hand. "You may have to be my confidence for a while." The haggard look returned to his face as he faced his mirror to adjust his tie.

She studied her mirror image one more time and decided she would have to trust her own judgment about her appearance. Richard had bigger issues to worry about. There was a knock at the apartment door. She started toward it, but his voice stopped her.

"I'll get it."

She smothered any resentment of his commanding tone by reminding herself of the security presence surrounding them since the morning after he agreed to serve in Korea. He had certainly been right about the risks they had faced against Adler. Although it went against her natural inclination to do things herself, experience told her to trust him in this, too. She followed him to the living room, where he spoke briefly in low tones to the guard stationed just outside their door.

"The car is here."

She stepped forward to join him at the door. "Let's go, then." Holding hands, they followed their guard to the elevator, where he handed them off to a Secret Service agent in the lobby. The agent escorted them to a black sedan and seated them inside. Terra pretended to observe the scenery speeding by as they headed for the heart of the city, but in reality, she watched Richard. He held her hand, but again, his attention was not in the car. Her heart pounded as they stopped at the famous iron gates. Seconds later, they glided through.

She watched the gates close behind them. "We are at *The White House!*" she whispered to Richard.

Beside her on the limousine seat, he squeezed her hand. "Excited?" He smiled for her, but his expression was still distant.

"Yeah, a little." She squeezed his hand back, to convey her support. "When you promised me sightseeing in DC months ago, you really delivered."

He laughed then, something she hadn't heard in days. Seconds later, the car stopped at the South Portico, and the secret service agent who had collected them escorted them into the Diplomatic Reception Room.

Terra stared at the mural of American life encircling the room, the portrait of Washington over the fireplace, the silk couches, the marble floor.

"This used to be the furnace room, you know." Richard, too, absorbed the surroundings, despite his preoccupation.

"The furnace room? How—" Opening doors cut short Terra's question. Secret Service agents took up position just inside the room, as the President strode toward them. He took Richard's hand immediately.

"Richard, Mrs. Matthews. Glad you could come."

"I'm honored, sir." Richard nodded toward Terra standing beside him. "My wife, Terra."

"Sir." Terra shook the hand of the President of the United States, knees shaking in awe. He was taller than he looked on TV, his handshake firm and confident.

"Mrs. Matthews, I apologize for asking to borrow your husband during your honeymoon."

"Sir, I know you wouldn't ask if it wasn't critical."

"Yes, I'm afraid it is."

At that moment, the First Lady entered the room, coming to her husband's side. "Ah, Laura." He introduced her. She gripped Terra's hand, and Terra noted the easy way they moved in tandem.

"Why don't you and I have tea in the Green Room," she suggested. Terra knew the President needed to brief Richard alone.

"It sounds wonderful," Terra agreed. She studied the woman who walked beside her—slender, poised, classy, with a grace born of walks through fire. "You know the pictures on the website don't do the House justice."

"No, they don't." The First Lady nodded. "When we first moved in, I spent what little spare time I had wandering and just taking it all in." She stopped before a door to an elegant sitting room, where a woman in a gray business suit had just placed a silver tea service on a table probably a priceless antique. "Then, of course, they told me I had to make decisions about what china to display, which paintings went where, and design the rug for the Oval Office."

"A lot to deal with," Terra said quietly, trying to absorb the whole experience of the House.

The First Lady sat on the sofa and indicated the place beside her for Terra. "Kind of like what you've found yourself in the middle of."

"I guess maybe I don't have a full grasp of it yet, Mrs.—" Terra began.

"Call me Laura," the First Lady instructed. "Tea?"

Terra nodded and Laura poured. She handed Terra a cup, then poured for herself. Terra sipped and tried to think of what to say. Her hands trembled.

"What are you worried about the most?" Laura's voice was gentle.

Terra stared into her cup. "I don't know. I'm not sure I know enough to know what to worry about."

"I understand." Laura said. "I can tell you that you don't have to know the details to worry. You just have to know him well enough to read it."

"Oh, I read plenty to worry about in his face." Terra had heard the tension in his voice, felt it as he lay awake beside her in the long nights since he had said yes to the President. "I know he's concerned he's not up to date on what has happened and who the players are."

Laura nodded. "It's why we've had our most informed staff briefing him for the past several days. And why he will have three days for private meetings with key people before formal negotiations begin."

"And he appreciates it, I know." Terra hesitated. "But I sense his biggest worry is something I don't think he can put words to."

Laura caught Terra's gaze and held it. "He's probably thinking about possibilities so horrific he's afraid to put them in any concrete form." She took Terra's hand. "Shepherds who have heavy responsibilities like Richard and my husband often have to protect their flocks from dangers they can't communicate to the flock without stampeding them. I suspect Richard doesn't want to frighten you out of your wits with events he prays will never happen, but yet he has to keep them in mind to prevent them." She smiled, conveying a tremendous empathy. "It's much like being a parent, when you protect your babies from a world that no longer recognizes innocence. Your babies don't understand what you are protecting them from, and you hope they never do."

Terra took a deep breath as her mind tried to touch the hem of some of the fears it thought too big for her to handle. "I guess I just have to focus on what tasks and dangers lying directly ahead of me, and have faith either the worst won't come to pass or the people who are prepared for it are there to handle it."

"You've got it already, Terra." Laura smiled a warm smile that said they were sisters in a common experience. "How about a tour after we've finished our tea?"

"It sounds wonderful," Terra agreed. "I can't do anything about what Richard and the President are discussing right now, nor about the situation itself." She sipped again at her tea, making mental notes about the design of the cups and the upholstery she sat on. "I guess the best course of action is to gather up some stories for my grandchildren. The ones that start, 'You ain't never gonna believe this.' "

Laura laughed. "By golly, Terra, you learn quickly."

Chapter 17

"But, Richard, why can't I just stay here in DC and work while you're in Korea?"

The tone in Terra's voice told Richard he needed to put down the file he was reading and address her issue. He rubbed his eyes, trying to bring himself mentally back to the apartment. "You could, I suppose, dear, but I would worry two places at once, about you and my parents."

"But why would you worry about us?" She had finished editing two of the manuscripts Warner had sent her in the Bahamas; it made sense for her to deliver them to him and discuss her impressions face to face while they were here.

He hesitated. Just as he had been reluctant to explain all of the potential dangers to her during the Adler crisis, he hated to bring up his fears now. He hoped they would prove irrational anyway. But he couldn't ignore them, couldn't concentrate on the negotiations if he wasn't absolutely certain he had done everything possible to ensure the safety of his family. "Please humor me, Terra." Rather than frighten her about the future, he decided to ride on the past. "Remember all of the things I was afraid about when we were dealing with Adler, how paranoid I was?" She nodded; she knew as well as he did many of his fears proved well-founded. "Well, the habit hasn't faded yet.

I don't want to be wondering every day if you are safe when I can take steps to make sure you are."

She cocked her head to one side. "How can you do it?"

He sighed. "The government has offered security for you and my parents while I'm working there."

"Couldn't they provide security here easier than Nassau?"

"They could." He had forgotten how stubborn she could be. "But I would feel better knowing you had Mum and Dad to rely on while I'm gone."

She stared at him, silent so long he began to think the argument was over. "Don't you trust me?"

"What?" The idea had never crossed his mind. "Of course, I trust you. I wouldn't have married you if I didn't trust you." He rose from his chair and crossed the room to take her hands. "If you really feel you have to stay here, I'll make sure the security is arranged." His thumbs caressed the backs of her hands. It amazed him how soft and smooth her skin was, made him wish he wasn't going away. "But I just hate to think of you being alone." He reached up to touch her cheek. "I hope you miss me enough to be lonely."

"Of course, I'll be lonely." She moved into his arms. "I just thought I could keep busier here."

He held her close, trying to memorize the feel of her, to draw on his memory in the weeks to come. "You may be right. But I was hoping you could get better acquainted with my parents, maybe help them keep busy, too."

She looked up at him. "You have an interesting point there. I guess I never thought of it that way." She snuggled her head against his shoulder. "When do you leave for Korea?"

"Friday." It would come too soon; today was already Tuesday. "The day after your birthday." He kissed the top of her head. "At least I won't miss it."

"How about this?" She ran her finger along his jaw. "I'll meet with Warner tomorrow or the day after, check with the contractors on the house, then I'll fly back to Nassau when you leave."

He kissed her nose. "Better yet, how about we fly to Nassau together, then I'll leave from there."

"Better." She had agreed, without him voicing the fears he didn't want to give a name. He had come close to losing her before, in so many ways, he didn't want to take any risks now. For the first time in four years, he looked forward to a future. She spoke again, her voice muffled against his chest. "Richard, are we really in danger while you're gone?"

He hoped she didn't read the deep breath he took as a sign he was lying. "I don't really think so, Terra." He squeezed her tighter. "I just don't want to take any chances." He moved to take her face in his hands. "At least no more chances than we've already taken to put Adler away." He kissed her gently.

"And neither of us faced any risk to do it." She smiled, although he saw tears were close.

"Right." He squeezed her hand and moved back to his chair to pick up the file he had dropped. Before reading again, he allowed himself to wander in his memories. The terrorist attack at the American embassy in Zimbabwe that killed Elaine nearly killed him, too, with gunshot wounds and severe burns to his legs when the limousine exploded. For weeks, he wavered between life and death, not really caring which way it went, until Ginny set him thinking about why the attack happened. As he analyzed the situation, he realized someone set them up as bait. His determination to discover who and bring the person to justice pulled him off his deathbed and into conflict with Robert Adler, who was promoted from station chief in Zimbabwe to Assistant Deputy Director of the CIA. As he got closer to proving Adler's guilt, Adler stepped up the campaign to discourage him, ultimately assigning Terra to work as his part-time secretary. When she began to believe Richard instead of Adler, her faith in him brought her into danger more than once, nearly culminating in her death. He spent over four years anticipating peril around every corner. The possibility of Adler wrangling a deal to get himself released from prison while he was in Korea added to his fears about the situation there. He looked at Terra.

His heart skipped a beat at the thought of this incredible woman committed to sharing the rest of her life with him. His heart constricted as he realized she might be in danger again, either from Adler or from factions interested in influencing the outcome in Korea, while he was halfway around the world and helpless to protect her himself. He looked at her one more time and found her smiling at him. "Thanks for humoring me, Terra."

Her smile deepened, until he saw the dimple that meant she was contemplating something mischievous. "I could humor you a lot more."

He grinned, despite his best intentions to remain serious and focused on the files. "And how could you do so?"

She replied by putting aside her reading, crossing

the space between their chairs, and taking the file from him. Then she settled on his lap. "And you could give me what I really want for my birthday early."

"It depends on what you want." She whispered her wish in his ear. Pulling her close, he decided there would be plenty of time to read on the plane. He kissed her and stood up with her in his arms. Right now, what he needed to do was give his full attention to showing his wife just how much he would miss her.

Chapter 18

Terra watched the plane until it was only a tiny speck against blended sea and sky. She finally lost it in the humid haze. Richard was enroute to his destiny across the world. The ever-present Bahamian breeze lifted her hair from her neck, cooling her face as it dried the tears she tried to hold back. She didn't realize she had clenched her fists as the plane took off until Caroline took her hand. The cheerful demeanor she had maintained since Richard agreed to serve in Korea cracked. Tears slipped silently from her eyes and ran down her cheeks.

"Oh, Terra." She felt Caroline's arms around her, and then Paul's arms around them both, as she let the sobs go. She felt Caroline's ragged breathing, and knew Richard's mother was crying, too, even as she stroked Terra's hair like she would a frightened child. "It will be okay, it really will."

She sucked in air and tried to stanch the tears. "I know it will, Carrie, but—" She took another deep breath and swallowed hard. The tears slowed. "I just miss him already." She brushed her damp cheeks. Paul offered a handkerchief. She took it, mopping her tears. When she looked down at it, mascara covered one side. "I'm sorry, Paul." She looked up at him, saw his eyes, lively brown like Richard's, and the tears started again. "I'm getting very good at smearing mascara all over handkerchiefs."

Paul laughed, then, a deep, hearty laugh to envelop both sobbing women and soon they were all chuckling. "All women are very good at it, Terra." He caressed Caroline's arm. "Carrie is a grade A expert at it."

"Oh, Paul," Caroline growled. "I hardly ever cry."

His forehead creased in a frown, but his eyes still smiled. "Maybe not for me, but you bawl all the way home every time your son leaves."

Terra looked at Caroline then, and hugged her, which made them both tear up again. Paul took their arms and started walking out of the airport. "I think I know something to cheer you both up."

"What?" Terra sniffled.

"Retail therapy." Paul grinned as he approached the car. "I'll take you both shopping, buy you something full of chocolate calories, and then, maybe, a round of golf."

Caroline pinched his cheek. "Paul, the first two will work for us, but you know the golf is for you."

He opened her door. "You mean, not everyone thinks golf is the perfect solution to any crisis?"

Terra hugged him as he opened the back door for her. "Thank you, Paul." She settled in the seat. She waited until Paul slipped under the steering wheel. "I know where Richard gets his wonderful qualities— from both of his wonderful parents." The tears started again, but she stifled them. "I'm sorry for breaking down." She brushed away a few disobedient tears. "Please don't tell Richard."

Caroline faced Terra. "It's a tradition of centuries for women to cry as soon as their men can't see them, whenever they send their men off to a big task. Mingled tears bind communities." She wiped away the moisture from her own face. "It's also a tradition not to let them know."

"We always know," Paul piped up. "But we never let you know we know, so you have the illusion we think you're strong."

Caroline slapped his arm. "We are strong. We just need to vent our fears in a healthy way." She turned back to Terra. "But I know it's hard for you." She offered her hand to Terra. "Just when you've discovered true love and security, it's taken from you, and you are stuck with strangers."

Terra was struck by her mother-in-law's wisdom. No wonder Richard was gifted at dealing with people, good at reading them, so sensitive to her needs. Within the first few minutes, she had been able to see the love Paul and Carrie shared and to see also how much they loved their son, and yet respected his independence. Suddenly, she not only missed Richard, she felt the huge void left by her parents' deaths. Still, she had survived their loss, and the struggles from it. And Richard was only gone for a little while. They would talk by phone and e-mail, probably on a daily basis. She squeezed Carrie's hand. "Thanks, Carrie. You are so understanding." She sighed. "But you don't really feel like strangers, and I'm tougher than I look right now."

"I know you're strong, Terra." Carrie squeezed back. "But please also feel like you can be honest with us when you're scared or lonely or need some space to yourself."

The cell phone Terra had brought back from DC rang. "Hello," she answered.

"Terra, I love you." Richard's voice enveloped her

from the tiny speaker. "I miss you already."

"I miss you, too," she said, trying to keep her voice from trembling. "And I love you, too."

He was silent a moment. "Tell Mum and Dad I love them, too." She heard voices in the background. "We have a briefing now. I'll call you again when we get to Korea." He paused. "Always remember I love you."

"I will," she whispered as the connection closed. Suddenly she felt more optimistic about their time apart. She would have plenty to do, as Warner had given her four more manuscripts, and the galley proofs of Richard's latest novel were due next week. She could edit, and get to know his parents, and explore a tropical paradise. It was all just killing time until she could be together with Richard again. And it wouldn't be long.

Chapter 19

Richard stepped out on the balcony of his room at the People's Retreat in Songdowan, North Korea. They landed in Seoul and met for two hours with members of the South Korean cabinet. Then they loaded up a wagon train of SUVs carrying the American and South Korean delegations, and drove over the 49th parallel. The hair on the back of his neck raised at his first crossing of the once impervious border. Holding the talks in North Korea instead of China had been a major concession on the part of the United States as well as the other nations involved.

He hadn't relaxed at all during the five-hour drive to Songdowan. He already knew the negotiations would be difficult, given North Korea's history of appearing to soften, only to become hardline just as progress was being made. Still the past couple of years had brought a few carefully orchestrated visits between relatives on opposite sides of the parallel. The rest of the industrialized world had responded with assistance after a horrendous train crash in the North, and aid was grudgingly accepted. There was a crack in the arrogant façade.

He hoped he could find a way through it into the hearts of the leaders. His only possibility lay in Chung Hee, in their old friendship, in Chung Hee's exposure to the rest of the world, and, perhaps, in Chung Hee's

Christianity. Now he inhaled deeply the sharp scent of the pines covering the slopes around the retreat. At this altitude and latitude, the air had a tentative bite he knew would turn savage in a couple more months. North Korea traditionally faced heating oil and food shortages every winter. Yet they had stubbornly clung to the Communist way of life for decades, when all around them capitalism waged a quietly successful revolution. Even the Chinese had begun to play nice, courting and winning the 2008 Olympic games. How much longer could North Korea hold its people to a failed ideology? Was Chung Hee the harbinger of change?

The U.S. Marine assigned as his valet, under orders to wear civilian dress clothes rather than his uniform to prevent offending their hosts, stepped to the sliding glass door and saluted crisply. "I'm sorry to intrude, sir, but you have a visitor and I couldn't make my knock heard, sir."

Richard nodded. "Thank you, Lieutenant Jameson." He slipped back inside the suite. Instantly he recognized the trim man standing humbly just inside the entrance.

"Chung Hee, you haven't aged in six years." He bowed and offered his hand.

"You look much the same, yourself." Chung Hee also bowed, then grasped Richard's hand. The handshake, though brief, was firm.

"Well, Chung Hee, we have come a long way from Cambridge." He stood at arm's length from his old friend and wondered how he might have changed on the inside. "Miles and years and experiences." He had opened a door, if Chung Hee cared to explain his defection and rise to power. As hard as American intelligence had tried, no ironclad answers had appeared, only theories.

"Yes, much water under the bridge since then." Chung Hee's expression took on seriousness and sadness. "I am sorry for the great loss you suffered. I didn't hear of it until many months later. I wish to offer my condolences on the death of your wife."

Richard waited for grief to let go of the squeeze it suddenly placed on his heart. Even as much as he loved Terra, as happy as he was with his life with her, he still grieved Elaine. "Thank you, Chung Hee. It was a very great loss."

Chung Hee nodded. "I remember meeting Mrs. Matthews in Cambridge and Seoul. She was beautiful and gracious."

"Yes, she was." Richard forced himself to ignore the pain and made a move to go beyond the required pleasantries. "It is a very grave situation we find ourselves in, Chung Hee."

An inner shield slipped down over Chung Hee's eyes. Where before, Richard had seen the man he had known years ago in England and in Seoul, now he saw only a politician in power. "Yes, very grave. But we will discuss it tomorrow. I came only to welcome you to our country and let you know if you need anything, you have only to ask, and we will do our best to provide it."

There, Chung Hee was using the time-honored royal "we" that connected the leader to the state and submerged the individual. "I'm sure everything will be fine, Chung Hee." Chung Hee's step back from openness disappointed Richard, made him apprehensive about the negotiations. He, too, assumed a distance.

Chung Hee bowed once more, preparing to leave. "I will have tea sent to you immediately. Gi Chu, a member of my own personal staff, is at your disposal while you are here. If you need or want anything, just inform him, and you shall have it."

"Thank you, Chung Hee, the tea will be most welcome, then I think I will retire for the evening."

"Yes, you have had a long and tiring journey." He moved toward the door. "We begin at nine tomorrow?"

Richard nodded. "I have already reviewed the arrangement of the conference room. It should be quite adequate."

Chung Hee paused before the door. "I understand congratulations are in order to you, also."

"Congratulations?"

"On your recent wedding." Chung Hee smiled, the mask gone for a moment. "You are a fortunate man to have two lovely women marry you."

An unreasonable chill raced through Richard's veins. "My good fortune, not theirs." Had he sealed for Terra the same fate as Elaine? He bowed quickly as Chung Hee went through the door and opened the cell phone before the door even closed.

"Hello?" Terra's voice sounded sleepy.

"I'm sorry, Terra, I forgot to check the time difference."

"It's okay, Richard, I'm just happy to hear your voice any time of the day or night."

Her voice sounded like an angel's to him. "Me, too."

"How are things going?" He heard her yawn.

"Chung Hee just came for a visit." There wasn't any security breach in sharing that piece of information.

He learned nothing from the visit.

"How was he? I mean, is he the same man you used to know?"

"Yes, and no." He sighed. "It's hard to tell in two minutes how he may have changed."

"I'm sure you'll get a handle on it soon." Her voice had warmed, not as nervous as when he first called.

"I hope so." He knew he should show confidence to her, but there had to be someone who could share his real feelings while he wore a mask around the rest.

"I know so." Her faith buoyed him. "I have faith in you and as does the President. And your parents. And you know we're unbiased."

He chuckled. "You have a way of making dark things light, Terra."

She laughed. "Sometimes I think it's because I don't have a really good grasp of the situation."

He laughed, too, taut muscles in his back releasing for the first time in twenty-four hours. "Grasp or not, you make me feel better." He took a deep breath, wishing he could hold her in his arms tonight. "I'll let you get back to sleep." He paused. "I love you, Terra."

"And I love you, too, whoever you are."

Laughing, he closed the phone and the connection. Gi Chu entered with a tray. He bowed, though Chu bowed deeper, and indicated a low table. Chu set the tray on it. "Gi Chu at your service, sir."

Richard studied the young man, evaluating, wondering if Chung Hee or the old Committee selected him. Or if he had volunteered. And what his deepest motivations were. And if he had a secret assignment. He wished he had missed the call from the White House, wished he was swimming nude with Terra again, making love on the beach without a care in the world.

Chapter 20

Terra trotted up the beach path toward the garden. A three-mile run along the beach had done much to wring the tension from her, flooding her body with calming endorphins. She paused just past the roses to watch Paul engaged in putting practice. She stood silent as he adjusted his stance, his grip, his posture. He adjusted all again, and then swung. The ball missed the cup by only a fraction of an inch. She heard a muttered expletive, and then he stepped toward the cup to retrieve the ball. He saw her as he turned back toward his putting area.

"Terra." His face creased in a grin that said seeing her brightened his day. In his prime, Paul must have been as much or more of a charmer than his son.

"Good morning, Paul." Picking up the damp towel she had left on the chair to cool her after her run, she crossed the yard to drop a kiss on his cheek as he took her hands.

"Ah," he shook his head. "It's a morning with problems to be solved." He nodded toward the green. "The elements of putting are not working together today, and the problem is to figure out why."

Terra laughed, running the towel over her sweaty face. "I'm sorry, Paul, I don't understand golf."

He laughed, too. "I don't think I do, either." He bent to put his ball on the green. "But the act of trying to get the better of a damn little white ball can be quite cathartic."

"I heard."

"Oh, you caught the little conversation between the ball and me, eh?"

She giggled. "Yes, and I would have probably said the same thing."

"Well, dear." He reached for his golf bag. "What say I teach you to putt, then you can learn the real reason for cursing."

He selected a putter, had her hold it to judge its fit, and then instructed her by posing himself, how to stand, how to hold the club, to align her body with the hole, how to assess the distance. When at last she swung, the ball rolled gently into the cup. Paul bounded the few steps to retrieve it. "I thought you didn't understand golf."

"I don't." She studied the grass. "But this is just spatial relationships, like carpentry." She grinned up at him. "Don't forget, I used to help my dad build houses."

Paul laughed. "And it is serving you well." He glanced up as the patio door opened. "How about a little putting practice today, maybe tomorrow at the driving range, and then a real game of golf by Thursday?"

She saw Carrie bearing a tray of glasses and a pitcher of ice water. "Sounds like fun."

Carrie set the tray down on the patio table. "I got back from my walk and decided a tall glass of water sounded good."

"It does." Terra moved toward the table, conscious she was not as pleasantly fragrant as the roses near it. "I just finished a run."

Paul joined them. "I've been thinking hard about golf."

Carrie laughed. "It looks like we're all using physical activity to distract our minds."

Terra swallowed her water through a throat suddenly gone tight. "It doesn't work completely."

"I know." Carrie slipped her arm around Terra. "But it helps."

Terra merely nodded, her whole chest aching with missing Richard. Funny, she had been alone most of her adult life, and now this man she'd only known six months had become the world to her. There was no explaining it, but there was no denying it either.

"How about lunch in Atlantis?" Paul suggested.

"Atlantis?" Terra smiled, knowing he referred to the exotic resort on Paradise Island.

"It would be a good distraction," Carrie said, thoughtfully. "Shall I go make reservations?"

Terra nodded, certain keeping her mind off Korea would take a lot of effort. Her knees felt weak, probably an over-reaction to the exercise. "I think I'll grab a shower and then a bite of breakfast. Maybe I can get some work done on those manuscripts before we leave for lunch." Suddenly, she felt starved. She headed toward the kitchen, not sure she could make it through the shower without something to eat.

"She's really taking it hard," she heard Paul say in a low voice as she passed through the door. She didn't hear Carrie's response. She grabbed a nectarine and bit into it. She hoped she didn't react to the stress of Richard's absence by eating her way around it.

"I won't," she vowed. "I'll work my butt off

editing, and running, and learning golf and tai chi." In their room, she started the shower, steamy and full force, hoping the hot needles biting into her skin would help her deny the lonely tears running down her face.

Chapter 21

Richard surveyed the meeting room an hour before the negotiations started. He knew today would be passed in wrangling over formalities and implied antagonisms. He sighed. He never had much patience with the petty stuff, even when he made his living at it. Now he had even less. Watching the woman he loved die in his arms for political maneuvering made him focus on more important issues. Today, more than when he first refused the mission, he had the sense he was the wrong man at the wrong time for the wrong job. Aligning his pen and pad at the west end of the round table, facing the door to the east, he bowed his head. He rarely prayed, his faith a dim sense of something greater than himself at work, while he relied on his own resources to solve the problems in which he found himself. But today, he felt, if there was a God, he would need His help to keep the world from taking irreversible steps toward Armageddon. "God, if you hear me, if you think I am worthy of your assistance, please, guide my words today."

His mother would be pleased, he thought. She read her Bible daily and faithfully attended services at the nearest Presbyterian church she could find. But she never pressured him to believe as she did. "Your life is your greatest witness," she would tell him. "You can't force anyone into heaven, you have to love them there."

He rarely gave it a second thought.

He walked slowly around the room, touching the back of each of the thirteen identical chairs. One for each of the six countries involved, plus one for himself, plus one for each delegate's primary aide. Arranged around the room beyond the huge round table would be their support staff—Delmonico, Harris, and Edwards for himself, plus four U.S. Marines in civilian clothing. North Korean State Security troops patrolled the perimeter of the building and maintained guard at the doors. He needed to get a sense of the room, make it his own turf, so he was welcoming them to his territory, not a visiting dignitary on the opponent's field. It was a mind game that achieved little success. Even with the Marines nearby and the security personnel from South Korea, China, Russia, and Japan, he felt vulnerable this deep into North Korea. Despite the world's best intelligence technology, little good information about North Korea was available. He hoped Chung Hee's presidency would change it, but the current situation did not bode well.

Located in the center of the building, the room had no windows. During negotiations, it was good, eliminating distractions, but right now he wanted to synchronize himself with the environment. Truthfully, he wanted to dig a hole and hide in it. He sighed. It was too late for that. He paced the perimeter of the room, noting the chairs placed for each group of subordinates, the table with water, both iced and hot, for brewing tea, with coffee as a concession to the "European" delegates. Except for the aroma of the coffee, the room smelled dead. Another table offered European pastries and Asian treats to soothe the delegates. A covered tray of *gool deak*, delicate honey and sesame stuffed rice balls he rather enjoyed, triggered the memory of when he and Chung Hee, then representing South Korea, met often to plan how to increase cooperation between their two countries, comparing cultures, and hoping for a brighter future. He wondered if Chung Hee remembered as well and had ordered them specifically to please his old friend.

"Sir?" Lieutenant Jameson opened the door just far enough to stick his head inside.

Richard faced him. "Yes, Jameson?"

"Sir, the delegates are arriving, sir."

Richard sighed and bowed his head once more. "Two minutes, Jameson. Give them two minutes to gather, then I'll escort them in." How many new wars could they start in two minutes? Hopefully, all would be gathered by the end of those minutes, and no one would accuse the others of a breach of social etiquette. Lord, help me now, he thought. He stepped to the double doors and opened them wide.

"Gentlemen and ladies," he announced, bowing. "If you will please come into the chamber, we can begin." Immediately the jostling for position began. Each delegation wanted to be first. "Primary delegates first, please, starting with Senator Michaels." He nodded toward the former Senator the President had appointed as special envoy for the situation.

Michaels stepped up to Richard and shook his hand. Michaels was an old Cold War horse, a Representative under Reagan who had recently retired from the Senate after serving as head of the Intelligence Committee. There were rumors of him going senile, that this mission had been a carrot tossed to get him to step down, but his knowledge of past intelligence actions should prove useful.

"Next, Pan Kaitan from China." A slender woman, who could have been anywhere from 30 to 60, glided forward. She merely inclined her head toward Richard, as her silken suit rustled past him. She had risen to prominence because of her brilliance in foreign analysis. The Chinese communists were more than politically correct and adhering strictly to communist doctrine to promote equality between men and woman at the mid-level ranks. In this case, they had been wise.

"Minoru Shirane, from Japan." A somber, stocky man, Shirane had a reputation of being a hard bargainer and a stickler for details. He could prove useful, in a good cop, bad cop kind of way.

"Alexei Patmanov, from Russia." Patmanov had survived all the political restructuring resulting from the breakup of the Soviet empire. The wily old Yakutian was a survivor who would not let any threat to the shared Russian-North Korean border stand. Though weakened by the dissolving of the Union, the Russian bear could still slap a mighty paw down on tiny Chosŏn if no other course remained. His tired blue eyes met Richard's as he passed by.

"Now the delegates from North and South Korea." Chung Hee and his former fellow Cabinet minister, Kim Hyeong, faced each other and bowed slightly before stepping toward the door. Though it was wide enough for both to enter at once, Chung Hee hung back a half-step, as if to allow the guest to enter first.

When the Korean delegates took their chairs, Richard strode toward his, nodding to Jameson. "Now the aides may enter." Richard settled in his chair as the assistants found their chairs and set out their notes. Although many of the aides acted nervous, the delegates around the table appeared cool. They would have looked at home gathered around a poker table. In fact, they were, he thought. Poker with armies, ships, bombs, and economic aid for chips. What cards they had to play, he would learn as the game unfolded. How many of them had an ace tucked up a sleeve, he could only guess.

He waited for quiet to settle over the room, five, ten, twenty minutes, before his silence rang louder than the whisperings in the room. At last, all faced him expectantly.

"Welcome to the negotiating table, ladies and gentlemen." Several aides started scribbling notes. "We have come to a very grave impasse, one that must be resolved without delay." He saw Michaels make a note on his pad. Pan smiled, and Hyeong glanced at Chung Hee. "We must put selfish interests aside and consider what is best for the global community here. While we are delegates from only six nations, we represent the entire world, even those people who may be oblivious to the dangers we now face." He turned slightly toward Michaels. "Senator Michaels, would you care to make any opening remarks?"

Michaels began a speech emphasizing the adamant resolve of the United States that North Korea must cease its nuclear weapons development program. Richard let the words slip to the back of his consciousness. He would analyze the speeches later, reading instead the faces and body language of the delegates. He observed each of the delegates as they reacted to the points of Michaels' address. A headache grasped the back of his head, tightening its grip as the speeches droned on.

Chapter 22

The drive across the water to the island of fantasy, properly dubbed Paradise Island, had been awe-inspiring, but the Atlantis resort itself dwarfed any building project Terra had ever seen. Now, in the Great Hall of Waters Restaurant, seated across from Paul at a table just inches from a glass wall, she stared at the sea life watching her. Floor to ceiling windows, all below water inhabited by sharks and other denizens of the deep, surrounded the dining room. "Now I know how a goldfish feels."

Paul and Carrie both laughed. "Ironic, isn't it." Paul chuckled again. "We're in the bowl and the fish are watching us." A great white shark, about ten feet long, prowled past them. Above the shark, a ray glided like a hawk in flight.

Terra shook her head. "You were right about suspending reality."

"They even have a tour of an 'Atlantean archeological dig' you can go through." The sarcasm crept into Carrie's voice.

"But I thought Atlantis was just a myth?" A waiter bore a plate of something exotic past Terra. The scent wafted to her, and her stomach did a flip-flop. She reached for her water and sipped to still the queasiness. She glanced at the menu, hoping it offered something bland, like grilled chicken and salad.

"A persistent myth," Paul explained. "They have found ruins here and there off various coasts claiming to be Atlantis." He studied the hieroglyphics on the wall. "Myths sell well. Reality is no longer necessary, at least for a few hours."

Terra looked around the room. Because the Great Hall was very popular with tourists, they had to wait until 1:30 for reservations, and even then, every table was either filled or being prepared for the next diners. Three tables away, a tall blond man dining alone met her gaze as she glanced his way. He smiled and put down his menu. At first, Terra ignored him, then when he continued to stare, she brought her left hand to her chin, wedding ring on full display. Though she faced away from him, she could see in her peripheral vision he still watched her.

"Paul, are we really in danger while Richard's gone?" She glanced toward the table near the door their ever-present security escort had selected.

"The question is, Terra, are we ever really safe?" Paul's gaze swept quickly over the room, reminding her of Richard keeping watch over them as they tried to escape Adler's surveillance crews. "Is something in particular bothering you?"

She nodded. "The man dining alone over there seems to be watching us."

Holding up his menu, Paul swiveled in his chair, studying the man as he appeared to be perusing the menu. "His table just happens to be on the way to the men's room." He laid down the menu and pushed back his chair. "I'll take a saunter there to wash my hands."

Terra glanced again at the security man, who pushed back his chair, alert, ready to act. Even with two men watching out for her safety, she felt absurdly vulnerable. Paul walked with a brisk stride past the lone diner, who lost his smile as Paul approached. He watched Paul pass by him, then picked up his menu again.

"Probably just some Romeo entranced by a beautiful young woman." Carrie reached across the table to stroke Terra's hand. Her voice was as calming as her touch.

"I'm sorry, Carrie." Terra sighed. "I don't mean to overreact."

"From what little you and Richard have told us about your last few months, you are probably reacting in precisely the manner you should."

Paul sat. "I think the problem is solved now, Terra." He looked toward the lone diner again, who faced the other window now. He leaned toward Carrie. "Nice to know I'm still an intimidating bastard, isn't it, dear?"

Carrie blushed. "You've never intimidated me, you old softie."

Grinning, Paul dropped his napkin in his lap. "No, but I did frighten any other guy who came around you in college."

Carrie laughed. "I simply told all of them to go away, once I convinced you that you had to win my heart."

He picked up her hand and kissed it. "You mean I didn't have to try as hard as I did to get your attention?"

She leaned toward him to kiss him. "You never had to try at all."

Tears gathered in Terra's eyes, watching the two of them, still so obviously in love. She knew the odds were against her own marriage surviving as well. Her parents had been more aloof, even though she knew they loved each other. Suddenly, she ached anew for Richard, yearning to solidify the bonds they had begun to build.

"What would you like to try for lunch, Terra?" Carrie's voice brought her back to the restaurant.

Another pungent dish passed her, and the queasy feeling returned. "Nothing exotic for me." She sipped her water again. "My stomach seems delicate today."

"Poor dear," Carrie patted her hand. "The stress is getting to you. Why don't you and I schedule a spa day here soon?"

Terra nodded. A soothing massage would help push away the tension gripping her shoulders for what seemed like an eternity but had really only been a little over two weeks since Richard answered the call from the White House. "Sounds like a good idea, Carrie." She laid down her menu and leaned toward Paul. "Paul, do you have any tools at the house?"

He looked up from his menu. "Tools?"

"Yes, I noticed today there is a little drip from the faucet in our bathroom."

"I can call a plumber this afternoon, Terra."

"There's no need, Paul, it's very simple to fix."

Carrie laughed. "Paul once tried to adjust the toilet in our apartment when we were first married." She paused to wipe tears from her eyes. "It ended up flooding the apartment below us, and we nearly got evicted."

"Damn thing was defective," Paul growled. He looked at Terra, smiling. "But if you think you can fix the faucet, I'll gather the tools, as long as you teach me how."

"Deal." Finding something she could master felt good to Terra. Helpless female had never been a role she could handle.

Chapter 23

"How did you think Hyeong responded to Patmanov's closing statement?" In their daily debriefing in Richard's quarters, Richard, Delmonico, Harris, and Edwards analyzed every word of every speech in the room during the day. Though many words filled the air, no decisions had been made, except for an uneasy truce to set the time for lunch. Now, five days into negotiations, Richard probed for any hint that could lead to real progress.

"At first I thought he was agreeing with the idea," Harris spoke, rubbing his forehead. "But then I noticed his aide signaling him."

Richard leaned forward in his chair, his head in his hands. The ache inside his skull had become a nearly constant companion since he arrived in Songdowan. The stress of watching every move, hearing every word, catching every nuance wore on him. Even with his very capable staff assisting, they could find no way to move the process past rhetoric. He spoke with his head still down. "What do you think about kicking the aides out of the chamber?"

He heard a gasp from one of the men. Finally, Edwards cleared his throat. "I think they'd have kittens, sir."

He looked to see if Edwards was kidding. Delmonico chuckled; Harris smiled. "Kittens?" he asked.

"Well, we could always give them away, I guess," Edwards offered.

Richard sat up, laughing for the first time in days. "The most successful outcome from these negotiations—kittens which can be adopted out all over the world, spreading joy and warm fuzzies." They all joined him, albeit hesitantly, in the laughter. "Gentlemen, I think we need a break." He stood, stretching, his muscles so tight he feared they would snap. "Let's knock off for now, and announce negotiations start at ten instead of nine tomorrow."

"And if it changes the time for lunch?" Harris asked.

"They can bloody well learn to live with it," Delmonico growled.

"I agree." Richard rolled his head, trying to loosen up. "If it causes them some inconvenience, maybe it will rock things off dead center." He gathered up his notes. "Have a good evening, gentlemen, and I hope you have a good night's sleep."

They left his suite for their own smaller rooms on the next level up. He changed into sweats and running shoes. He opened the door into the anteroom of his quarters, where Jameson bunked. The Marine jumped up as he stepped through the door. "Going running, sir?" The third day, Richard had begun a routine of a morning run on the beach. Jameson accompanied him, claiming the need to "do PT" to maintain his physical conditioning, but truthfully, Jameson acted as his bodyguard.

"No, Lieutenant, I'm just walking for a little while." He noted the concern in Jameson's face. "I need to think."

"Do you think it's safe, sir?"

"Jameson, there are a couple hundred armed North Korean Security Agents surrounding this place, as well as several patrol boats a mile offshore."

"But they're not our guys, sir."

"I know, Jameson, but sometimes you just have to trust to fate." He gripped the Marine's shoulder. "You wait here and make sure no one comes into my quarters while I'm gone."

"Okay, sir, but be careful."

"I will, Jameson. Your commander would be pleased with the fine job you've done thus far."

"Thank you, sir." The look on Jameson's face said he thought his commander would have been more pleased had he escorted Richard to the beach, but he would obey orders.

Leaving his quarters, Richard walked down an austere hallway to a deck with a narrow set of stairs to the ground. Glancing up at the building, Richard reflected how this compound passed as luxury for the masses in North Korea, but by Western standards, it was more like a cheaply refurbished Army post. He picked his way around the huge boulders scattered from the beach to the building. He suspected the rocky shore was part of the reason this had been selected as a site for a "people's" retreat. Difficult to approach by land or sea, the place was easy to secure. He caught sight of a uniformed DPRK officer with a rifle over his shoulder pacing at the top of the building. He sighed. As long as they considered him an ally, he would be safe here.

Closer to the water, the beach smoothed into deep sand suitable for running. But right now, he was too mentally and physically exhausted to run. Instead, he meandered the waterline, observing the tracks of shorebirds, the mounds of seaweed, the broken shells. Occasionally, he bent down to examine a shell, but mostly he just walked, and tried to rest his mind.

He stopped to stare at the water, waves lapping at his shoes, higher with every swell. Tide was coming in. He looked north, startled to see another figure on the beach. A quarter mile away it was hard to be sure, but the slender build looked like Chung Hee. He glanced toward the sentry, who appeared to have seen the walker, but did not sound any alarm. He walked toward the person. Within another three minutes of walking, he could see it was indeed Chung Hee.

"Hello, old friend," he called in a low voice.

"Hello, Richard," Chung Hee responded with a smile. "Walking and thinking?"

He nodded. They were close enough now to read faces. "And thinking and walking."

"Beaches are good for such things." Chung Hee stopped in front of Richard. "Shall we do it together?"

"A very good idea."

Chung Hee turned to retrace his steps. "Then let's walk and think."

"And talk?" Richard hoped the meeting signaled good fortune and would lead to insight on the negotiations.

"We could talk." Chung Hee clasped his hands behind his back.

Now the door was open, Richard pondered the best way to go through it. He decided to start at the beginning. "Chung Hee, why did you defect?"

"Ah." Chung Hee walked in silence for at least a

minute, while Richard forced himself to stay quiet. "There were many reasons."

"Can you give me one?" Richard knew he was pushing; the man he knew at Cambridge and in Seoul had been his peer. The Chung Hee he walked with now was the apparent leader of a nation with the fifth largest army in the world and the power to begin the destruction of the world.

"For one thing, I longed for my people to the north of the parallel to enjoy the options I had for my life." Chung Hee strolled closer to the water and paused to study a seashell.

"But couldn't you have brought it about by continuing your work toward normalization of relations and open communication between the countries?"

"Perhaps." He looked toward the rugged hills surrounding the enclave. "But most likely not during my lifetime." He kicked the shell. "The people had suffered too long. You know they have been starving each winter for the past decade."

"But has your defection helped them yet?"

He faced Richard. "Haven't there been some visitation and exchanges during the last three years?"

Richard considered what he had learned in his recent briefings. Though much progress had taken place in the past few years, he had been preoccupied with bringing Adler to justice, and had paid little attention until this crisis forced it upon him. "Are you saying your defection was responsible for it?"

"No, others on both sides had been working toward it for years." Chung Hee shook his head. "But my defection gave them more tools to work with."

"How?"

"The people in the north had my testimony as to how things were in the rest of the world." He looked toward the ocean, scanning the horizon. "Even though the news reports they heard were carefully edited to 'spin' the way the regime wanted, enough bits got through to give them some picture." He faced Richard again.

Richard studied his friend's eyes, trying to read what was unspoken there. "What happened when you defected?" he asked softly.

Chung Hee looked down at the sand. "After my first weeks of questioning, I went to a re-education camp where I learned about North Korea." He brought his hands together in front of him, massaging his right one with his left. Glancing down, Richard noticed they appeared as gnarled as the hands of an octogenarian, the fingers crooked, joints swollen. Chung Hee crossed them behind him again. "But after camp, I was brought to Pyongyang, and began to teach them."

Richard sensed, though there was much more to the story, this was all he would get today on the subject. "I remember your baptism there at Cambridge." He watched Chung Hee's face carefully for his reaction. "Are you still a Christian?"

Chung Hee's face glowed. "Yes, and my faith is what keeps me strong, focused."

"But how can you practice it when religion is unofficially banned in North Korea?"

"Christianity does not require a building or an altar." Chung Hee's voice suddenly reminded Richard of the voice of the priest who had begun his conversion. "Or even a Bible. The Lord will write his laws in our hearts, if we will but let Him."

Richard knew his questions had jumped all over the place, but there was one more he had to ask. He might not get this chance again. "Why me?"

"Do you think I have forgotten the man I knew in Cambridge and Seoul who sacrificed so much to try to better the lives of my people?" Chung Hee laughed softly. "One of the spiritual gifts our Lord has endowed me with is discernment."

"Discernment?"

"Yes, He has granted me the ability to see the truth through the lies. Allowing me, at times, to see to the heart of a matter. Or a man." He reached out his hand to grip Richard's forearm. "And He has shown me your heart is good. It is against your nature to do anything but the right thing."

"Then, has He shown you who is stonewalling, and why we can't make progress in negotiations?"

"Unfortunately, no." Chung Hee shook his head. "Sometimes the lies must be peeled away like an onion. Sometimes peeling an onion brings tears." He headed south and picked up his walking pace. "We should go inside; it's getting dark."

Following Chung Hee, Richard sensed the man was the onion he would have to peel, while Chung Hee would do the same to him. Motive by motive, layer by layer, until they stood eye to eye and heart to heart. Richard shivered as he wondered what either man would find at the core.

Chapter 24

"See, Paul, it's very simple to stop a leaky faucet." Terra threaded the handle back on the faucet and handed him the screwdriver.

"I never suspected it was that easy." He turned it on and off, twice. He patted Terra's shoulder. "I always thought plumbers had to burn incense and invoke the gods to get this done."

Terra laughed. She could see where the sense of humor she loved in Richard had come from. "Now you know their secret."

Caroline appeared in the doorway. "You have it fixed already?" She tested the faucet as Paul had. "I was going to bring up coffee and scones, let you take a break."

"Mmmmm, coffee and scones sound good." She knew they were making an extra effort to help her deal with Richard's absence, but it felt good to have someone care that much.

"Well, then," Carrie offered. "Let's go down to the garden and have some."

Terra grabbed the latest manuscript she had been reviewing. So far, she had recommended pursuing two of the eight she had read.

"Do you always work this hard, dear?" Paul held the bedroom door open for her.

She paused, looking back at him. "I don't really

think I'm working hard." She started down the stairs. "Sitting in the garden reading and drinking coffee doesn't feel like work."

"Oh, but it is, Terra." Carrie was already halfway down the stairs.

"Well, Paul and I are going to the driving range this afternoon."

Carrie paused at the foot of the stairs. "Now that will be work."

The cell phone chimed from her pocket. "Hello?" she answered, although she knew it had to be Richard. The only other people who had the number were Paul and Carrie.

"Hello, love." The sound of his voice flooded her with a sense of relief. Somehow hearing his deep voice in her ear reassured her all would be well again. "Do you miss me?"

"Only more than it's possible to miss a person." Paul passed her on the stairs, she assumed to give them some privacy, and she sat down on the step to absorb every nuance of his voice. "Do you miss me?"

"More than I ever thought I could." The longing in his voice made her heart ache for him.

"What time is it there?" If they talked much longer about how much they missed each other, Terra feared she would go back to her room and stay there until he returned.

"It's eleven o'clock at night." She heard him moving around his room. "I'm almost ready to go to bed."

"It's ten in the morning here." She leaned against the stair banister. "I just fixed the faucet in our room."

"Wow, I'm impressed." His pride sounded

genuine.

"The same reaction your father had."

He laughed. "Dad is even more challenged by mechanical things than I am."

"I got that from your mother's story about him flooding the apartment below them."

"Oh, you should hear the long version of it."

"How are things going there, Richard?" She longed to have him with her again, longed to feel just the sense of his presence, much less his touch.

He sighed and took a while before he answered. "Not great, Terra." He paused again. "We're not making much headway." She didn't respond, and he went on. "It may take a long time."

"As in how long?" Dizziness came over her again. She figured it meant her heart had fallen to her feet.

"I don't know. Weeks, maybe." He cleared his throat. "If it drags on too long, I'll call a recess and come for a visit."

"That would be nice." Carrie appeared at the foot of the stairs with a cup of coffee. Silently, she handed it to Terra. Terra sipped, savoring the taste, creamed and sugared just the way she liked it. She nodded her thanks to Carrie. "Would you like to talk to your mom?"

"Sure." She handed the phone to Carrie. Cradling the coffee cup in her hands, she lost herself in how much she enjoyed her husband, in missing him, and wishing he could come back. Carrie disappeared with the phone, and Paul came back with it.

"Don't let them box you in, son," Paul was saying as he started up the stairs. "Love you," he said as he handed the phone back to Terra.

"Richard," she said in a voice half-choked by her

ache for him. "Be careful."

"I will be, dear. We have plenty of security here. The only danger is from headaches and paper cuts."

She knew better. Recent world events had made it clear no one was totally safe, anywhere. "Just, please, keep watch out for yourself as much as you did for me with Adler."

He was silent a long while. "I'll be careful, Terra. I want to get this over and come home to you, to live our lives together."

"I know you do." She took another sip of coffee to try to loosen her throat. "I love you."

"I love you, too."

"Sleep well, and remember me while you sleep." She closed the phone and finished the coffee before she joined Carrie and Paul in the garden.

Chapter 25

Richard sat back in his chair, hard-pressed not to let his frustration show. Halfway through the second week of negotiations, each delegate had expressed his or her own country's point of view often enough he knew exactly where each stood. He thought enough time had passed to allow each nation to have appeared firm; it was time for laying bargains on the table. But despite his probing and suggestions, no one had budged from their original position. Chung Hee insisted softly but firmly North Korea needed to maintain its defensive capabilities, without expressly mentioning the nuclear weapons. Patmanov stressed Russia had North Korean targets in its nuclear grid. Shirane pushed the point that Japan might be forced to develop or acquire nuclear weapons technology, as a sideline to developing nuclear power plants to reduce its dependence on petroleum. Hyeong pleaded passionately for the cooperation and open sharing between the Koreas. Pan repeatedly pointed out the shared border with North Korea and their long history of cooperation, assuring Chung Hee North Korea could rely on China for protection.

"But, my dear Pan, China has been increasingly reaching toward the West for commerce and partnerships." Chung Hee inclined his head and lowered his eyes, as if apologizing for doubting his ally.

Pan's eyes narrowed. "We are merely becoming

full participants in the global community."

In reality, Richard thought, if China withdrew into itself again, it might cripple the global market, based on the volume of goods manufactured in China. He spoke. "And China is benefiting from the partnership, just as North Korea could."

"Chosŏn does not need assistance from any nation to thrive," snapped Kwan Seong, Chairman of the National Defense Commission, declared the highest office of state in North Korea, who had stayed at Chung Hee's left during the negotiations but rarely spoken. Chung Hee and the North Korean foreign minister, Dak Ho, seated behind Chung Hee, exchanged a glance. Gi Chu stiffened in his chair behind Dak Ho.

Richard waited a second to see if any other delegates wanted to respond, before he spoke again into the tense silence. "It's not a question of needing assistance, Seong, it's a matter of finding ways each nation benefits and no one suffers."

Seong gave him a glare, then looked toward Chung Hee. Chung Hee did not face Seong, but sat with his gaze down, and said nothing. Dak Ho spoke. "What, for instance, is the United States willing to do to benefit us?"

Michaels cleared his throat. "It depends on you dismantling your nuclear weapons, Dak Ho."

"We must maintain the ability to protect ourselves, Senator Michaels, particularly since China seems to be allying itself with the West." Seong sat straight in his chair. Across the table, Pan's chin raised.

Michaels leaned forward on the table, his index finger aimed directly at Seong. "You don't have anyone to have to protect yourself against, Seong."

"And if Chosŏn insists on building its nuclear arsenal, Japan will have to take steps to ensure its own security." Shirane's voice was low, but emphatic.

"And if the United States continues to focus its efforts on the Middle East, South Korea will have to take such steps, as well." Hyeong looked as if the thought pained him, but he feared the measures might become necessary.

Richard decided the situation was escalating a little too fast. "Chung Hee," he addressed the nominal leader of the country, trying to engage him, taking the influence away from Seong. "What would it take to get a full accounting of all your nuclear capacities, from power plants to weapons?"

Chung Hee paused a long time before answering. "We would require assurances of non-aggression from the United States." He turned slightly toward Seong. "And we will also need a lifting of the sanctions in place against us."

Richard heard Michaels draw a sharp breath and shot him a glance to silence him. "Anything else?" He heard murmuring around the room as Chung Hee met his gaze.

"Energy assistance." Chung Hee's gaze shifted toward Seong, even though he couldn't see him while he faced Richard.

"I thought it's what your uranium was for." Richard tried to keep his voice calm, reassuring.

"But we still must build the infrastructure to deliver the power." Gi Chu handed him a folder. "With our technology, it would take up to ten years to get reliable, affordable power to the heart of the country. With technology advice and equipment from countries with years of experience, we could do it in three."

Richard tented his hands before him. "And food assistance?"

"If the crops do not do as well as anticipated, it may become necessary."

Richard already knew the crops had produced far less than quota, would not have been sufficient even if the crops had exceeded expectations. "What about medical care, immunizations in the rural areas?"

"We have adequate capability for providing it, but assistance could be useful."

Richard leaned his chin upon his fingers. "What is the most essential need your country has, Chung Hee?"

Now Chung Hee hesitated. "There are many needs." Again, his focus shifted to Seong. "Chief among them is the certainty that Chosŏn remains Chosŏn, with the freedom to choose its own destiny."

"Well, it's sure as hell not going to be free to choose any damn destiny unless you give up the nukes!" Michaels glared across the table at Chung Hee. Chung Hee's lips thinned, and Seong's face went dark red.

"Gentlemen!" Richard rose from his chair. He caught Michaels' gaze and then looked directly at Seong. "Badgering won't get us anywhere." He glanced again at Michaels, who settled back in his chair. Seong's gaze darted to Dak Ho, and he sat very straight in his chair, but did not speak. Richard sighed. "Let's take a twenty-minute break." He remained standing as the delegates moved from their chairs. Then he looked at his aides. The concern he saw in their eyes did nothing to bolster his confidence.

****

After another three hours of wrangling, Richard entered his quarters totally drained. He picked up his cell phone, and punched the button connecting him with Terra, and through her, a world not as grim as the chamber he just left.

"Hello, Richard," she answered.

He didn't speak right away, simply absorbing the sound of her voice, immersing himself in the vision of her, remembering the smell of her hair, the taste of her lips, the feel of her body pressed close to him. "Hello, love." He sighed. "Your voice sounds good to me."

"Your voice sounds pretty good to me, too." He heard her lie back on their bed and imagined himself stretched out beside her. "How are things going?"

"Let's not talk about it." He took a deep breath. "Today has probably been the worst day yet."

"I wish I could do something to help."

"You do, just by talking to me."

She giggled. "That is something I'm very good at."

"I know." He felt better already, and then she began to chatter about her day and getting to know his parents, and hope grew within him again.

Chapter 26

After a dinner he barely remembered eating, Richard headed to the beach for a solitary walk. Too tired to even walk, he simply stood at the water's edge and watched the water lap toward him, back out to sea and toward him again. He tried to let his mind be massaged by the waves, tried not to think of the potential in the negotiating chamber. He was so numb, he didn't even look up to see if Chung Hee shared the beach until the former South Korean was only fifty feet away.

"Hello, friend." He heard Chung Hee's soft hail, and finally summoned the energy to respond.

"Hello, Chung Hee." Richard greeted him and pulled away from the hypnotic rhythm of the ocean.

"You seem troubled, friend." Chung Hee stopped arm's length away from him.

Richard turned back to the ocean. "I am, Chung Hee." He picked up a pebble and flipped it over and over in his hand. "Things very nearly came apart in there today. In two weeks, we've agreed on a time for lunch, because some parties made concessions, and that's about it."

"Ah." Chung Hee smiled. "Have you not come to understand the Asian culture yet?"

Richard shot him a look. "What do you mean?"

"We may not have reached any deals yet," Chung

Hee began. "But many cards have been laid upon the table, enough that we may guess what cards remain, and who holds them."

"But—"

"Patience, Richard." Chung Hee placed a hand on Richard's forearm. "You have made more progress than you realize."

Richard shook his head. "But I don't see it." He glanced at the stone in his hand. "It seems to me each of the delegates is as unyielding as this rock." He drew back his arm to throw it into the water.

Chung Hee's hand on his arm stopped him. "Look more closely at the stone."

With a glance at Chung Hee, Richard dropped his gaze to the rock. "And?"

Chung Hee leaned over him, studying the stone. "See the pits, the fissures?"

Richard nodded. "You're saying the delegates aren't as tough as they first appear?"

Chung Hee shrugged. "They're tough, but they have points of admittance, just like the stone, where water or wind or sand can get in and wear away at them."

Richard juggled the stone in his right hand. "How many thousands of years do you think it took for this stone to develop these fissures?"

Chung Hee smiled. "As long as no one is pushing any critical buttons, we have time."

Richard sighed and dropped the rock into his pocket. "You're not really in charge, are you, Chung Hee?"

"No ruler, even an absolute dictator, is fully in charge of a country." Chung Hee gazed out over the ocean. "There are too many variables, too many wills involved." He faced Richard. "A ruler can only operate with the information he is able to gather."

Richard sensed Chung Hee trying to tell him the truth, without actually saying it. "Who is really running the show, then?"

Chung Hee looked down at the sand. "It takes many hands, many talents, to put on a show." He looked away from the shore toward the building. "All of them are needed, but must be kept in balance."

"And if they get out of balance?"

Chung Hee clasped his hands behind him. "Falls can happen if balance is not maintained."

Richard glanced sharply at Chung Hee. "You're saying—"

"It's time I go in," Chung Hee announced as he moved toward the building. "It might do you good to stay out here and listen to the ocean."

"But—" Richard stood, frustrated, as Chung Hee walked as if he had not a care in the world toward the retreat center. He stared, as Chung Hee ascended the stairs and disappeared into the building. Finally, he gave his attention to the ocean, trying to find the message Chung Hee hinted it carried. He saw nothing, just an inexorable slide in over the sand and out over the same sand. It gradually smoothed away the footprints he had made and rolled a seashell farther out to sea with every wave. Suddenly, the message clicked in his mind, but still left him uneasy. How much time did he have to wash over each delegate to find the fissures in their positions? Would a nuclear bulldozer ride roughshod over the beach of negotiations and render the dance of the waves pointless?

****

Terra answered the phone almost before it rang. She had come to anticipate Richard's late morning calls, to rely on them to truly start her day. The heaviness she heard in his voice the last few days, though, concerned her. "How are you today, love?" she asked, trying to squeeze all her love through the speaker on the cell phone.

"Tired, hon, very tired." He was silent a moment, as if he couldn't think of anything positive to say.

"I wish I was there to give you a massage."

"I don't think I'd be tired then." She heard some enthusiasm in his voice.

"But a massage is supposed to relax you to let you sleep," she teased.

"Not the way you give them." He chuckled. "But I'm not complaining, you understand."

"You'd better not complain, or I'll never give you another one."

"I'd give anything to have one right now." She heard the weariness creep back into his voice, as if nothing he wished could come true.

"Could I come over there?" She tried to keep her tone light. "Even prisoners are allowed conjugal visits."

"But we're not prisoners here, Terra, except of our own consciences." He sighed. "We are all here of our own free will, and free will is what is causing all the conflict."

"Richard," she allowed her voice to express the seriousness she felt. "I know somehow you will find a way through this to end the conflict."

"I hope so, Terra, I honest to God hope so." She heard him take a deep breath. "If we haven't made any progress in the next two weeks, I'm calling a recess." He hesitated. "I may even ask for new delegates."

"It's that serious?"

"Yes, the stalemate is that serious, Terra. Chung Hee seems to think we've made progress, but I just don't see it."

She wished she could put her arms around him. "If Chung Hee sees it, then you must have gotten somewhere. Did I ever tell you that you are too hard on yourself?"

"I believe you did, at least once." He chuckled again. "I love you, Terra, and I miss you."

"Me, too, love."

"Goodnight, Terra."

She closed the phone and tried desperately to visualize herself with him, hoping he could feel her close as she did so. Somehow, she doubted he could.

Chapter 27

"Sir, the helo is ready." Jameson frowned, as if the idea of Richard flying away made him uncomfortable.

"Thanks, Jameson." Richard paused to slip on his coat and grab his briefcase. Late September in Songdowan was getting cold, colder than one would expect from the latitude, but the sea added a chilling effect to the constant wind. It would be even colder on the aircraft carrier.

"I hope you get some good intel," Jameson held the door open for him.

Richard hustled to the improvised helipad at the west of the building. Chung Hee had not been happy about a U.S. Navy Sea Stallion entering North Korean airspace, but it was agree to the landing on Richard's assurances, or call off negotiations. Richard received a cryptic call from the State Department about some new information that could not be transmitted via phone or coded message. The only alternative was for Richard to come to the Pacific fleet carrier for a briefing. Harris accompanied him.

The chopper had been on the ground only minutes before they boarded, and it took off again. The flight was fast and straight, only about fifteen minutes to where the Pacific fleet carrier awaited them well outside the twelve nautical mile territory claimed by North Korea. The chopper touched down smoothly on the deck of the floating city. The take-off and landing consumed more time than the flight itself.

An officer met them on the flight deck as they exited the chopper. "Lieutenant Commander Jones, sir. The Captain's Executive Officer." The officer motioned them forward. "Your party is waiting." Richard and Harris followed toward the captain's conference room.

"So, who is a part of this briefing?" Richard asked Jones.

"I'm not sure, sir. Military intelligence, civilian intelligence. I'm just here to escort you to the conference room."

Must be pretty high-level, Richard thought, if even the Captain's XO didn't know. Or wouldn't say.

He saw the man seated at the center of the table the instant he stepped through the bulkhead into the conference room. He stopped. "You!"

"Hello, Rick." Robert Adler smiled the same Cheshire smile he had used for years. "It's good to see you, too."

Richard strode to the table, stripping off his coat as he walked. Memories of his conflicts with Adler over the years tumbled through his mind. After some clashes through their years at Yale, Adler had been the station chief in charge of security in Zimbabwe the day Elaine died. He then rose to the position of Deputy Director of the CIA, as such the man in charge of every field operation in the agency, but Richard's quest for justice for Elaine's death toppled him from power and landed him in custody. Richard thought the conflict ended with Adler's arrest. Richard faced the man on Adler's right. "Who's in charge here?"

"I am, Mr. Matthews." The man offered his hand.

"Porter, Homeland Security."

Richard gripped his hand briefly. "Why is he here?" He indicated Adler with a nod.

"He has offered some information that might shed light on the situation you are currently involved in." His gaze took in Harris, as if questioning his clearance to sit in.

"Harris is fully cleared; he has been my assistant throughout the negotiations." If Porter relaxed, Richard didn't see it. "Can you fill me in?" He took a seat at the far end of the table, not in Adler's direct line of sight. Adler still watched him and kept smiling. The smile reminded him of a snake about to strike an unsuspecting mouse.

"Well, Mr. Matthews, we have some information." At this his gaze darted to Adler. "There are parties in North Korea who are making a tidy profit running heroin out of the country."

"Colleagues of yours?" Richard glared at Adler.

Adler smiled, again. "Parties known to me."

"What's in it for you?" Richard knew Adler did nothing if it did not benefit him.

Adler shrugged. "Bargaining chip."

Richard slammed his hands on the table. "You think you can bargain away murder, treason, and profiteering?"

Porter slipped into the chair beside Richard. Harris took a chair on the left side of the table. "He won't get out of it, Mr. Matthews." Richard threw him a glance saying he didn't believe him. "He's going to spend the rest of his life in prison. He's just wrangling now for a nicer cell." He leaned back. "It's why we're meeting here and didn't bring him to you."

Adler chuckled. "Where can I go if I escape here?" He raised his left hand as far as it would go, handcuffed as it was to the chair. "You think I can row a life raft fifteen miles to shore? Or fly a chopper myself without getting shot down?" He lowered his hand. "You're safe from me, buddy boy."

Richard tried to force his body to appear relaxed. Truthfully, he knew information from Adler would be suspect, would have to be confirmed. He remembered how Adler manipulated facts to try to make Terra believe Richard was a traitor to his country. "All right, Bobby." He said the name with as much sarcasm as Adler had used with his. "Start laying your cards on the table."

"Thanks, Rick." Adler sat forward. "My information is second and third hand. All I know is someone in North Korea is moving very high-quality heroin into world markets." He paused, glancing around the table at Harris and a second civilian, taking in the two armed Marines standing at ease beside the bulkhead door. Richard thought of a rat checking out the trap he was in. Despite the relaxed appearance he presented, all of Richard's senses stood at red alert status.

"Who are they moving it to?" He tried to read through Adler's jovial façade. A man who had controlled the intelligence moves of the mightiest country in the world did not take on a subordinate role and like it.

"I don't know." Adler met his gaze.

The hair on the back of Richard's neck bristled. He faced Porter. "Well, do you know who?"

Porter shook his head. "It's slipping into all

markets, probably through Cambodia, showing up on our streets, as well as Europe, Japan, everywhere they'll admit they have a problem." He paused. "And we have suspicions, though they're not confirmed, the Chinese are fighting it as well."

"What about North Korea?" Though he had stayed quiet until now, Harris watched and listened. Richard selected Harris to accompany him for this reason. Harris spoke only when necessary. The rest of the time, he simply observed and analyzed.

Porter glanced at Harris, before addressing Richard. "We can't verify it, of course, but we think it's beginning to show up there, too."

"Who?" Richard asked the sixty-four-dollar question.

"We can't find out, yet." Porter looked down at his hands.

"Are they raising it in North Korea?" Though Richard addressed Porter, he watched Adler in his peripheral vision.

"Possible, but we doubt it." Porter pulled a satellite map of east Asia from a folder. "We have a pretty good view of most of the known arable land in North Korea. Nothing there seems to have changed much in the past ten years, at least not of the magnitude to produce this much." He indicated land away from the coastal plains. "And up here in the mountains, the growing season wouldn't be quite long enough, and the logistics of operation would be formidable."

"But not impossible?" Richard's mind was spinning with the potential ramifications.

Porter shook his head. "Not impossible, but unlikely."

"Then do you think they are processing it there?"

"It is more likely, since there are already enough processing facilities throughout Asia, Korea could simply be a storage and distribution hub."

Richard stared at the colorful map and pondered. This put a new wrinkle in the negotiations. He couldn't imagine Chung Hee being a party to enslaving his people or anyone else to drugs, but he also suspected Chung Hee was not in total control of the country either. There were others in the background, watching, if not controlling, his every move. And if the person running the drugs was controlling someone who was controlling someone who was controlling Chung Hee, it might take years to follow the trail to the lair. An unstable regime, a closed country without intelligence available to the rest of the world, it made a perfect shield for an illicit business. Peace and open communications with the free world would threaten the profits. If this intelligence were true, it made sense they were getting nowhere with negotiations. The question was, who at the table was involved? The headache crept up the back of his skull again.

"What do the other countries have to say about it?"

"Well, we've only approached our counterparts at our level, not addressed the Executive Branch as yet." Porter consulted a printout. "The Japanese are very concerned. They have a number of special task forces trying to both find the drug source and educate the public on the dangers of heroin. The Russians won't talk much about it officially, but from grass roots sources, we know they are fighting much the same battle we are. The Chinese don't admit there is a problem, but we've seen a number of likely suspects disappear from public view. The South Koreans have approached the U.S. for assistance." He paused. "And the DEA is trying its best to infiltrate the organization, but it's one of the most elusive they have ever encountered."

Richard stared at Adler while possibilities churned in his mind. Adler met his gaze with arrogance at first. When he finally licked his lips, Richard addressed him. "Spill it."

A flash of surprise flickered in Adler's gray eyes. "I've told you all I know."

"You haven't." Richard folded his arms over his chest and waited. At the edges of his vision, he caught Porter watching him in surprise and Harris suppress a smile. "Tell me what you think you know."

Adler licked his lips again. He moved his bulk forward, unable because of the handcuffs to comfortably rest his hands on the table. "There are always people in every culture willing to trade commodities for other commodities."

"Duh." Richard leaned forward, resting his arms without fetter on the table, the significance of the move not lost on Adler. "Give me specifics."

Adler leaned back, eyeing Richard with a hint of suspicion in his hooded eyes. "Like what?"

Richard suppressed showing his irritation. He felt like a dentist trying to extract a molar with only a human hair as a tool. "Like who wants to trade for what."

Adler looked away. "My sources indicated people wanting to buy consumer goods."

"With what? Heroin, fish? Details."

Adler glared back at Richard. The look said his

hatred and envy of Richard, which had taken root during the days they were both students at Yale, had only intensified. "Cash."

Porter leaned forward. "What currency?" he asked before Richard had the chance.

Alder's gaze darted from Porter to Richard and back. "South African rands."

Porter sank back in his chair. "New players," he muttered.

Richard did not spare a glance at him. "Who was trying to buy the stuff? And what?"

Adler twisted in his chair. "My sources only said Asian. They spoke Mandarin, but not like natives." He fiddled with the handcuff. "They wanted computers."

"What kind of computers?" This seemed to spur Porter on. Richard let him take over the questioning, and watched.

"Laptops, wireless equipped."

Porter glanced at the other man in the room. "It doesn't sound like someone just wanting to watch DVDs or play video games, does it?"

The other man shook his head. "Dovetails with reports the terrorists are going hi-tech." He looked down at his hands. "With the right codes, you can control a lot with a wireless laptop."

Richard looked at Harris, who had been studying possible al-Qaeda links to northeastern Asia before he was assigned to Richard's team. His face went momentarily pale, and his jaw clenched. Richard felt suddenly tired and cold. The situation was more complex than any of them anticipated. It might well be beyond the skill he possessed, or of anyone else on earth, for that matter, for it to be brought under control.

He addressed Porter. "Do you have any coffee?" This might be a very long day.

Chapter 28

Terra smacked the ball from the driving range line and it sailed off. Paul watched it, shading his eyes to see where it landed. "Sweet Mary, Mother of Christ." He whistled. "You swear you've not played golf before?"

She shrugged. "We did a week on golf in high school gym class. But I played softball for five seasons." She set another ball on the tee. "Was that good?"

"Well, back in my prime," Paul puffed out his chest. "I could hit it that far without even trying." She felt him watching as she hit the next ball. "But now, I play more for finesse."

She grinned as the second ball out shot the first. "Finesse is not my strong suit."

He chuckled. "I noticed." He probably referred to walking in on her reading the riot act to the building contractor this morning. The man called to say the tile order arrived, but wasn't exactly what they ordered, did she want him to lay it anyway. Terra asked him for the specs on the tile delivered, and told him in no uncertain terms the only way he could lay that tile was if he knocked two thousand dollars off the cost, as it was lower quality tile. If he wanted the amount they contracted for, he would provide the tile they paid for. By the end of the conversation, he apologized and said he would get the proper tile on the way pronto. "Richard is obviously the diplomat in your family."

It almost choked her up to hear him referring to Richard and her as a family. Carrie and Paul respected their boundaries without conflict. "I guess." She hit another ball, using the same muscles and techniques she had used to garner the best runs batted in average in their league for three seasons. "Paul, what is going on over there?"

He busied himself selecting balls. "Jockeying for position." He handed her another ball to hit. "Everybody playing one-ups-man-ship, trying to gain advantages without giving up anything." He peered into the distance to find the last ball she hit. "Stalling, posturing, theatrics."

She looked up at him before swinging. "Nothing of substance?"

He shook his head. "Not yet."

She swung, and this ball went the farthest yet. "How long will it last?"

He sighed, avoiding her gaze as she looked at him. "No one knows." He gave her another ball. "It may well peter into nothing, blow over, and Richard will come home."

"Or?" She waited.

"All holy hell could break loose."

She swung again, and this ball veered to the left. She stepped away from the tee. "Then what do we do?"

Paul faced her, studying her face before he replied. "Carrie knows the answer better than I do. I spent too many nights in Richard's place." He reached out to squeeze Terra's shoulder. "But I think she would tell you we stay optimistic, keep busy, and try to encourage

Richard when he calls." He let go her shoulder. "And I think she would add that we pray."

Terra swung again, and then stumbled as she stepped back from the tee. Paul grabbed her elbow. "Terra, are you all right?"

She nodded, then shook her head. "I just feel weak and queasy." She held his hand for support. "Do they have something carbonated here?"

Paul led her to a seat in the shade. "I'll be right back."

Seconds later, he appeared with a soda. "Thank you," she said as she sipped with shaky hands.

"What happened?" Paul knelt on the ground before her.

She sipped again, and the bubbles quieted her stomach, brought back her strength. "I don't know." She looked out over the driving range. The heat made the grass waver in the sunlight. The reflection from the club handles flashed back into her eyes and made her blink. "Maybe the heat and sunlight."

Paul took off his cap. "I warned you to wear a cap or something."

"I know." She laughed. "I just don't do hats any better than I do diplomacy."

He grinned at her. "Well, I think we've established you have no trouble driving the ball a sufficient distance." He stood up. "Why don't we head back to the house and plan something sinfully chocolate for the rest of the day?"

She stood without shaking. "You do know the way to a woman's heart, Paul." She started to gather the clubs when Paul stopped her.

"I'll do that, young lady." He took the club from

her. "You just stand there and look delicate and petulant."

"Paul—" she began.

"No arguments." She heard a tone in his voice she recognized from those rare occasions, usually involving life and death matters, when Richard insisted on things being his way. She shut up and stood still. She sipped the soda and growled at her body for being weak. It must be the after effects of the concussion and the injuries she'd suffered at Adler's hands. And the stress of worrying about Richard. Without protest, she accepted Paul's arm as he escorted her to the car.

Chapter 29

The day on board the Pacific fleet carrier had been informative, but raised more questions than it provided answers. The next day's negotiations again went nowhere. More exhausted and discouraged than ever, Richard headed for the beach after the debriefing with his staff. He never knew when he might encounter Chung Hee on his walk. Twice they enjoyed nearly an hour of conversation, but Chung Hee had not appeared now for three days. He paused at the water's edge, selected a smooth stone, and tried to see how far he could skip it across the waves. He lost it over the third crest. He looked toward the north end of the beach, and spied the slight figure clad in black meaning he would talk with Chung Hee tonight.

"Hello, friend," he called as he trudged closer to Chung Hee.

"Hello, yourself." This time Richard turned to retrace his steps as Chung Hee joined him. "You look tired, my friend."

Richard sighed. "I am, Chung Hee." He looked toward the building. "I'm tired of not getting results."

Chung Hee chuckled. "Such an American attitude." Richard shot him a glance and he explained. "You Americans are so impatient. You get a little crowded on your coastline, and you expand the country across the continent. You see a situation in the world, you send in the cavalry for a lightning strike, you declare the problem fixed, and you go home."

"Well, you're right there." He sighed. "I guess John Wayne is still our hero."

"Mr. Wayne is considered a hero around much of the world, Richard." Chung Hee touched his arm. "You Americans lumber around like, what do you say, an ox in a glass house—"

"Bull in a china shop," Richard offered.

"Like it, but because you want so much to help." He smiled. "Your intentions are good, although often a little naïve."

Richard gazed off toward the forested hills surrounding the beach. "Sometimes I wish I was a little more naïve. I might have more hope for the negotiations."

"Hope is the most resilient of emotions," Chung Hee said. "It will spring back when it appears dead."

"Well, I would say it is in ICU right now." Richard decided to risk the plunge. "Do you have any drug problems in Chosŏn, Chung Hee?"

"Drug problems?"

"Yeah, addictions, dealing, smuggling, that sort of thing."

Chung Hee studied the beach under his feet. "I believe it is a problem in every country, every society, today."

Richard walked on in silence, trying to decide if the answer was a shut down, or a slightly open door. Chung Hee spoke again.

"Have you ever been under the influence of a drug, Richard?"

The question caught him unprepared. His mind

flashed back to a memory he hated. "Yes," he said softly. "When I was in the hospital after—" He stopped.

"After Zimbabwe, when you and your dear wife were attacked?"

He nodded, thankful Chung Hee knew enough of the story he didn't have to explain it. "They gave me morphine and opioids for the pain when I couldn't protest." He shuddered. "It took me places I never want to go again."

Chung Hee touched his shoulder. "I had a similar experience." The look he gave Richard warned him not to ask for details. "I don't know what it was, but it made me feel like my veins were on fire, my brain as well. I have no idea what I said while I was under its influence." He stopped, silent a moment, and Richard suspected the experience was during his "re-education." "I, too, never want to visit there again."

Richard picked up another rock, glad as he prepared to throw it, that he resisted falling into dependence on the opioids, and the other crutches he leaned on during his recovery from the bullet wounds and burns, as well as the grief. He rejoiced now in the strength he carefully tested daily, not to lose it. "I can't understand wanting to be an addict."

"I don't think many choose it willingly," Chung Hee offered. "But fewer people in the world than you might think have the choices we have had, Richard." He, too, picked up a rock. "Many people feel trapped by their background, their culture, their families, or their own choices." He made four crests before the rock sunk. "To them, perhaps, a slight high followed by numbness seems like a good thing. Then I think the monster has hold of them while they yet believe they can escape."

Richard searched for another rock. Perhaps rock throwing was primitive man's form of putting practice. "I guess denial is a big part of life for some people."

Chung Hee nodded, another rock in his hand. "The bare reality is too much for some to endure, particularly when hope has been stifled."

They stood facing the water, as the sun set behind them. Slowly, the colors spread from the west to the east, reflected in the undulating water. "Some say sunsets are particularly vivid under the influence of drugs," Richard commented.

Chung Hee shivered. "I saw more dragons than sunsets in my experience." He began to smile. "But when I got my tongue—"

"Excuse me?" Richard had assumed Chung Hee was born with one.

"I'm sorry, I'm speaking in jargon." Chung Hee paused. "In many Christian sects, when one is born again, he receives a special language for understanding and speaking to God." Richard nodded, and he went on. "I attended a revival meeting at the Yoido Church in Seoul. There must have been ten thousand people there." He scanned the sky. "When I prayed to receive my tongue, people all around me began speaking in what sounded like gibberish. I closed my eyes, and suddenly I was hearing music, like whale song, only deeper and yet higher, and seeing colors ebbing and flowing, like the Aurora borealis, but much more vivid. The colors seemed connected to the music. Some notes sounded discordant, but also harmonious, like I was seeing and hearing the full spectrum humanity could experience and beyond. It was in tones I couldn't understand, but yet somehow I did, like there were translators built into my heart, if I made the choice to be receptive." He paused, studying the vivid colors in the sky, and smiling. "It was as if I was hearing a harp played by the Creator's own hand, hearing the voice of God and seeing the purest elements of being, hearing a chorus of the Creator's plans for us, the notes resonating throughout eternity."

Richard didn't know what to say. He felt he had been allowed to see a facet of Chung Hee few people ever would. Yet he didn't completely understand what he had seen, nor did he know what to do with it.

"Just take the truth the Lord has placed in your heart, my friend. Learn to hear His voice, which is more often still and small than it is majestic and colorful, and let Him guide your choices."

As the sun set, the wind crept in over the sea, bringing a damp chill that soaked through the sweats Richard wore. He shivered, less sure than ever what direction to take the negotiations next.

Chung Hee glanced at Richard. "I think it is time we go in, friend." He bowed slightly toward Richard, who returned the move. "It is getting cold and dark."

"Goodnight, Chung Hee," he called as the dark figure grew faint against the dusk. "Thanks for the insight."

Chapter 30

"Elmer, there are big problems with Richard's galleys." Terra paced the garden, cordless phone to her ear.

"What's wrong, dear?" Richard's publisher was a gallant man, had been quite nice to Terra when he met her, but she doubted he was taking her seriously at the moment.

"The last set of edits on *Quest for the Black Pearl* appears to have been ignored." She paused to watch their security presence make a sweep past the property perimeter. Though they had installed a bank of surveillance monitors and microphones in Paul's den, the men made random patrols of the property as well.

"I'll get on the phone with Editing and find out—"

"Never mind, Elmer, I went back through and re-did them. I'll send the galleys back to you today or tomorrow."

"Okay, Terra. I'm sorry for the mix-up." There was a momentary silence, then Elmer cleared his throat. "How is Richard doing, Terra?" Elmer watched the news, of course, and knew what one of his most profitable authors was involved in.

"He's making progress, Elmer," she said. "But diplomacy is slow business."

"Well, I'm glad they're getting somewhere. The news media isn't very optimistic."

"You know how the media is, Elmer." She forced brightness into her voice. "Good news doesn't sell."

"No, I guess not. I'll look for those galleys in the next few days."

"Thanks, Elmer." She clicked off the phone.

"Maybe you are more of a diplomat than I thought, Terra."

Paul's voice startled her. She set the phone on the glass patio table. "Well, I didn't want anyone to get the impression things aren't under control there."

"Good policy, dear." He glanced back toward the kitchen. "And I didn't mean to intrude. Carrie sent me out to let you know lunch is ready."

"Thanks, Paul." She picked up the phone to take it back into the house. "I'm famished." She entered the cool kitchen, where Carrie was setting the table in the breakfast nook. She leaned over to hug her mother-in-law. "The table looks fabulous, Carrie."

Carrie laughed, surveying her work. "I'm not much of a cook, but I do one hell of a centerpiece."

"It's okay, Carrie. I'm much better at fixing plumbing than I am at cooking." She put the phone back in its cradle. "Can I help?"

"You can get the salad from the fridge. Janie did most of this yesterday."

Terra carried the large bowl of greens to the table. She felt like she could eat the whole bowl. Carrie set a plate of steaming clams beside the salad. The scent reached Terra, and suddenly, her stomach felt rocky. She sat down. "Carrie, would you mind if I just had salad?" When Carrie looked at her questioningly, she explained. "I've never been very good at handling exotic food, and I guess my experimenting with island food is catching up to me."

Carrie gripped her shoulder. "How about a ham sandwich instead?"

Terra nodded. "That sounds good."

She caught the glance Paul and Carrie exchanged before Carrie went to the refrigerator. She wanted to get up and help, but her knees felt weak. She sipped at her water, then Carrie appeared with an ample sandwich. "Thank you, Carrie. I hate to be such a bother."

"No bother, Terra." Carrie seated herself and spread her napkin over her lap. "But are you sure the concussion isn't still affecting you?"

"That's probably it," Terra said, taking a bite of the sandwich. "And the stress of worrying about Richard."

"Yes, it's wearing on all of us, but on you the most." She watched Terra munching away at lunch. "Will you allow me to see if I can get you in to my doctor to make sure you don't have complications from the concussion?"

"Well." Terra hated doctors, hated admitting she couldn't handle whatever life threw at her. But she couldn't deny bright sunlight seemed to be troubling her more since she suffered her concussion at Adler's hands. "I guess if you think it would be best."

"I'll call as soon as lunch is over."

"Yes," Paul agreed, his eyes showing concern. "Richard would fire us as parents if we didn't take excellent care of you."

****

Terra walked from the examining room toward Carrie seated in the waiting room. Carrie stood up at her approach. "Well, dear, what did they say?" She bent to lay the magazine on the table. "Are you healing from the concussion?"

In shock from what she had just heard, Terra dropped to the chair beside Carrie. "My head is fine." Carrie slipped back into her chair, as if sensing there was something amiss. "But there's a good reason for me to be feeling this way."

Carrie leaned closer. "What dear?"

Terra stared at her shoes. She hadn't wanted it to happen this way; she had imagined a totally different scenario. "I'm pregnant."

Carrie's mouth dropped open, and a thousand emotions played across her face before she could speak. She gripped Terra's arm. "That's wonderful, dear."

Terra looked up at Carrie. She wasn't supposed to share the news first with her mother-in-law. Her husband, the father of her child, was supposed to hear it first. "Yes, but, Richard—"

Carrie looked thoughtful. "How are you going to tell him?"

"Well," Terra had thought it over a great deal in the fifteen minutes since she got the word. "For now, I'm not."

"I see." Carrie gathered up her purse and Terra's. "Let's get to the car and talk."

Terra started to explain as she settled in her seat. "He can't be distracted right now." She leaned her head against the back of the seat. "He's got his hands full with the delegates at the moment. If I tell him, he'll either lose concentration or he'll call it off, maybe even quit."

"He won't quit," Carrie said, with a note in her voice saying she wished he would.

"I didn't think so." Terra stared out the window at

the palms going by. The stroboscopic effect of trees alternating with the bright ocean made her queasy again, and she closed her eyes. At least she knew she could still handle stress well. "Plus, there's the fact of Elaine's miscarriages."

"True." Carrie headed down the road to their house.

"It would have to weigh on his mind, make him worry." She sighed. "I can't tell him just yet."

"How soon, then?"

"He said he would call a recess if it went on very long." She longed to have him here beside her right now. "Maybe then." She rested her chin on her hand. "What I don't understand is how it happened."

Carrie made a noise that sounded like she had choked. "Well, dear, if you don't—"

Terra's face went hot. "I mean, I know *how* it happened. It's just I don't know when. I mean, we'd been careful. Except—" A memory came to her. The night of the eventful reception, on the beach. They'd been too caught up in the moment to consider consequences. "Never mind."

"As long as you're clear on how, dear." Carrie chuckled as she parked the car in the driveway. She glanced out the window at Paul hurrying toward them. "What about Paul?"

Terra looked at him, almost to Carrie's door. "Can he keep it secret?"

Carrie grinned. "It will be tougher to keep than the state secrets he's handled all these years, but yes, we can trust him." She hugged her quickly. "And, Terra, congratulations." She let go of her. "But let's get Paul sitting down before we tell him."

"Good idea," Terra said, reaching for her door handle.

Chapter 31

The past four days had been more arduous than the first two weeks. Even armed with the knowledge of what might be fueling the impasse, Richard was unable to move negotiations off what seemed to him dead center. Only his nightly phone calls to Terra, just before he went to bed, kept him from sinking into hopelessness. Her unique spin on life lifted him up, transported him from a grim conference table to the tropics. She had given him a new perspective on golf, and her version of the interchanges with Elmer and the contractor, verified by his father, made him glad she was part of his team and not his adversary. Still, talking to her was not a satisfactory substitute for holding her in his arms and delighting in her expressive face. He sighed and pulled on his running shoes. The early mornings had become cold enough he began wearing both a regular sweatshirt and a hooded pullover one. If the negotiations dragged on another month, he would have to add a layer of thermal gear. He hoped it didn't take that long. He opened the door to the anteroom.

"Good morning, sir." Jameson jumped up from the floor where he was doing pushups.

Richard merely shook his head at the young man's eagerness. "It's morning, anyway."

Jameson opened the door into the hallway.

"Where are you from, son?" Richard made

conversation as they picked their way around the boulders to the beach.

"Macksville, Kansas, sir." Jameson was stretching, as antsy as a racehorse revved for the post.

"Kansas?" Richard laughed. "I'll bet you've heard 'I don't think you're in Kansas anymore, Toto,' a hundred times."

"Make it a thousand times, sir." Jameson smiled. "The Marines have taken me all over the world, but it's what I always get."

"Well, how does the weather here compare with home?" Richard had nearly completed his stretching on the way to the beach.

"Pretty boring here, sir." Jameson glanced around him. "Not much change from day to day. What changes there are, are gradual." He grinned. "Now at home, we can get three seasons in one day."

"That's what I hear." Richard bent into his last stretch. "My wife's from Oklahoma. She says the same thing."

"Oklahoma's got nothing on Kansas, sir." Jameson started down the beach. Richard caught up and they ran the first leg of the beach in a companionable silence. Though at first he didn't see the need for the Marines, more than once he had been glad of Jameson's steadfast presence. He seemed easygoing, but there was no doubt in Richard's mind the young man could be a formidable obstacle when necessary.

They picked up the pace when they turned at the end of the stretch and ran back toward the conference center. Richard glanced at Jameson. The kid wasn't even breathing hard yet. "How many years am I spotting you, Jameson? Ten, fifteen?"

"I'm twenty-seven, sir."

"Ten years, then." He pushed harder to make sure he kept up.

"You're in good shape, sir." Jameson picked up the pace a few seconds.

"Are you married, Jameson?" Richard pulled ahead by a hand's width.

"No, sir, I—" Jameson stumbled, and Richard's momentum carried him three, four strides past the Marine. Richard stopped, and then he heard the muffled report. Instantly he dropped to the ground, crawling back to Jameson. With his gaze on the hills, he scanned for the sniper, even as he reached for Jameson to turn him over. The dark stain on the sand and Jameson's fixed stare told him there was nothing he could do for his running companion. From the south, near the compound, he saw the North Korean Security Policeman who secured that end of the beach when they ran closing on them, rifle at the ready. From the north, the soldier posted there ran toward them. Another shot barked, and the soldier from the south tumbled. The one from the north end of the beach dropped to the prone position, scanning the hills, rifle at the ready, as he worked his way in a crab crawl toward Richard. Richard started rolling toward the wounded soldier, hoping to secure his weapon and return fire. Suddenly, he felt a sharp sting in his shoulder. He had time to note the fluffy end of a dart before he lost the ability to move. A vivid image of Terra's face looking up at him from a moonlit beach swam before his eyes. Then his world went black and silent.

Chapter 32

Harris burst into Delmonico's quarters. "Ray, I hear gunfire!"

Delmonico, slipping on his shoes as he went, followed Harris back into the hall. Above them, he heard running feet, lots of them. Harris pounded on Edwards' door. Edwards opened it at the second rap. "What's going on?"

"I don't know," Harris said. "But it doesn't sound good."

They reached the balcony at the same time. Below them, the beach swarmed with security personnel, rifles at the ready. The other three Marines who assisted with security in the chambers had joined them. The throng parted and Delmonico saw a man down on the beach. He reached for his cell phone. "Gentlemen," he said, punching in the numbers for a secure line to the Pacific fleet carrier. "We are definitely in an 'oh, shit' situation."

"I'll go down and assess." Harris started down the stairs.

"I think I can tell you what you'll find," Delmonico said.

"What?" Harris paused, looking back at the senior staffer.

"Jameson dead and Richard missing."

"What makes you sure?" Edwards asked.

"Marine issue O.D. sweats on the downed man. Richard was wearing black." He scanned the crowd once more, hoping his gut was wrong. "If there had been an assault, and Richard was there, they would have hustled him back up here pronto, fully surrounded by security." He looked beyond the crowd, wondering how anyone could have penetrated security and then vanished so quickly. "The fact they are running around like hounds that have lost the scent tells me we have a missing person." The connection to the Pacific fleet carrier clicked through. "Operation DMZ North has been compromised," he said slowly. "I repeat, Operation DMZ North has been compromised."

Chapter 33

"I want some answers!" Senator Michaels thundered at the rest of the delegates. Not only was Michaels angry someone had kidnapped an American diplomat, he was scared for his own safety. If they were daring enough to take Richard, wouldn't they see a former Senator as a bigger prize? Thank God he was securely asleep in his quarters when it happened. Even now, he wasn't fully dressed, just his shirt, pants, and slippers. Still, it was his duty to step in and take charge.

Chung Hee stood before him with his head slightly bowed. "I am as shocked as you are, Senator." He met the Senator's blazing blue gaze. "Not only was Richard our best hope as facilitator, he was also my friend."

"Some friend you've proved to be!" He didn't like the turncoat Korean, didn't trust him, any more than he trusted any of the Communist bastards. They didn't value life the same way Westerners did.

Chung Hee stood without responding to the remark. "Senator, our soldiers are scouring the grounds at this moment, helicopters are covering every inch, our ships are securing the sea perimeter, and we have more troops on the way." He paused. "And our people are interviewing everyone on the grounds to find out what they may have seen. Your marines and diplomatic people are talking to them as well." He faced the Senator again. "And I understand your military and intelligence networks have been notified."

Delmonico's doing, with his call to the Pacific fleet carrier. Michaels didn't know who Richard met there the day he spent on the ship, but he knew Richard learned something unsettling. "And they may seriously rain on your little parade here, Chung Hee, until our man is found."

"There is no 'parade' until Richard is found, Senator. Only rain," Chung Hee said softly.

Damned little gook was playing simple, Michaels thought. Acting all wise and Confucian-ly. Michaels could see through him, though.

"Senator," Chung Hee continued. "Has anyone notified Richard's wife and parents?"

Chapter 34

Paul had all but given his study over to the security men who set up their equipment there. It was the room of the house he used the least anyway. In fact, he seldom entered the room at all unless he wanted to read without any distractions, or to simply sit back and reflect on the life he had led, surrounded by the mementos he collected, mostly books. Now with Terra in the house, it seemed boring to just sit. He was passing by the room on his way to the garden when one of the security men called to him.

"Mr. Matthews, could we see you a moment?"

"Certainly." Paul went into the room. A table held a bank of monitors covering the grounds. His own security system provided an adequate second line of defense. Microphones had been strategically placed near entry points to the property. It was an impressive display of technology. "Is there a problem?"

The most senior of the security men nodded. "You should probably sit down, sir."

The warning chilled him to the core. Those words usually preceded bad news, such as when they got the word Elaine was dead and Richard not expected to survive just over four years ago. He dropped into the chair behind his desk. "What's wrong?"

"I don't know exactly how to say this, sir—" The security man stood in front of Paul's desk. "Except to just say it. Your son has been kidnapped."

Cold fear flooded his entire body. Richard had been right, not wanting to take the assignment. And what about Terra? And the baby? Yet they hadn't said he was killed. "Give me details."

"About six a.m. Korean time, four p.m. here, he was running on the beach with his Marine bodyguard. Someone shot the Marine, and two of the Korean security people, and he simply vanished before anyone else could get to him."

Paul's shoulders sagged. Such an operation must have had inside help and been extremely well-organized. "What are we doing about it?"

"North Korea is conducting an air, sea, and ground search. Our U-2's are flying thermal imaging sweeps. Pacific fleet carrier is listening and has been given approval to fly over the area with choppers. We're trying to home in on the GPS signal from his cell phone, but it appears to have disappeared. All personnel on site are being interviewed by the North Koreans and our intel people."

He sat and thought. What more could be done? Bloodhounds? He was sure they had covered it. "Keep me posted on any developments, good or bad, no matter how small, no matter when." He stood up. "I'll go break the news to the women." He stopped at the door. "I'm sure whoever took my son has underestimated him." He looked toward the kitchen where Terra and Carrie were making scones. "It's not over till it's over."

He stood in the hallway and reflected. Richard had been kidnapped before, when he was only seventeen, while Paul was Ambassador to Italy. He managed to get himself and his date away from the Red Brigade then.

And he had checked himself out of the hospital against the advice of his doctors after Elaine died. Even though the doctors had doubted he would walk again, he had healed himself and gone on to bring Adler to justice for Elaine's death. No, his son had a way of beating the odds, of never giving up no matter how hopeless the situation. He stood a little longer, and prayed. Then he walked toward the kitchen.

The sight there nearly moved him to tears. His son's wife, with his son's child in her womb, and his own wife companionably, cheerfully baking side by side, bonding over generations, as women were good at doing. Women were also good, he reflected, at living through bad news. He stepped toward them and switched off the TV. Even though it was tuned to the cooking channel, it wouldn't do to have a reporter break in with a news flash. "Hello, girls."

"Hey, Paul." Terra nodded at him, flour halfway to her elbows, hands deep in dough.

He stood nearby until they finished kneading the dough, patting it into circles, and sprinkling it with sugar. When it went into the oven, he knew it was time. "Wash up and sit down, girls." Heavily, he slipped into his chair at the breakfast nook.

Carrie gave him a look of alarm but said nothing while she rinsed the flour from her hands. Terra's washing up took longer, as Carrie gently scrubbed flour from her forehead and nose for her. Then Carrie walked toward the table and sat down. Terra bounced into her chair. Since she knew the reason for her nausea, it didn't seem to bother her. In fact, she glowed, like most pregnant women, as if she knew a secret no man could ever understand. He only hoped she could retain the glow when he broke the news to her.

"Ok, Paul, what's up?" Carrie's gaze on him was steady.

He took a deep breath, looking at Terra, then back to Carrie. "We just got word." He paused, wishing he could pad the words somehow. "Richard has been kidnapped."

Carrie gasped, but Terra simply stared at him, as all the color drained from her face. Her mouth moved, but no words came out. She shook her head and clenched her jaw, and the color came back. "What happened?"

Quickly he explained what the security men had told him, leaving out none of the details. He knew they would hound him until they had it all anyway; he might as well just lay it out for them. Carrie reached out to take Terra's hand and Paul's. He gripped hers hard, saying nothing. They had faced similar news before. He had learned then having only one child made a parent terribly vulnerable. But Terra, he didn't know how she might handle this, what effect it might have on the baby.

Terra got up from her chair and stared out the window. Outside, the early evening sparkled with the satisfaction of a beautiful day and the promise of a glorious night, as if their world had not suddenly stopped turning. Her hand wiped away a few tears. Then she faced him. "They didn't think he was dead, did they?"

Paul shook his head. "Logic says there would be no reason to take him if they simply wanted to kill him."

Carrie got up to put her arm around Terra's shoulder. Terra reached for Carrie's hand and gripped it. "Richard is the most amazing man I have ever met,

Paul." She closed her eyes. "He rescued me when Adler took me, he fought off three muggers to save my life, and he managed to stay one step ahead of Adler all the time." She opened her eyes again. "He's not dead, I know it. And he will find a way to escape, I know that, too."

Paul got up and put his arms around both women, both totally his responsibility for the moment. "I know it, too, Terra." They stood there for a long time.

Chapter 35

His thirst was the first part of him to return. Before Richard could open his eyes, he could feel his tongue, thick and dry in his mouth. Then the splintering pain in his head overrode the thirst, but only for a moment. As the thirst began again, he felt the ache of not being able to move, of his arms in an unnatural position behind his back. And then the cold seeping into his body. He forced his eyes open, despite the pain in his head, and tried to orient himself to the world around him. At first, he could see only light and shadows, but he kept blinking and finally realized he was in a cave or a shack, lying on a dirt floor, with his arms tied above the elbow behind him, his legs pulled back and tied to his arms. About all he could move was his eyes and his fingers. He saw movement and more light, as something that appeared to be a door opened and someone came close to him. He struggled to watch the person as it bent over him. It appeared to be a young Asian man, maybe in his twenties, wearing layers of worn clothing. He couldn't tell from the dress whether he was Korean, Chinese, Russian, or Japanese. He decided he would guess Korean. "Where am I?" he croaked in Korean.

The man simply stared at him. Then he moved behind Richard to check the rope. Richard tried again, this time saying "Good morning," in Japanese. Still no response. He tried greetings in Russian, Mandarin, and the two words he knew of another Chinese dialect he didn't remember the name of. Still nothing. He wondered if the man was deaf or mute.

Another man, this one younger and thinner than the first, entered the room. Again, he tried the litany of languages, even including English this time. The younger man stared at him, then spoke quickly to the other man. "He is awake?"

Korean. Richard recognized the dialect and could adapt. "May I have some water?" he asked.

The first man glared at the second. Then he circled behind Richard and slammed his rifle butt down on Richard's hands. Trussed as he was, Richard could only writhe away, and then the rifle butt came down again. And again.

"Stop," the younger man said. "We have to keep him alive." He left the room. "I'll get water."

The first man kicked Richard in the back, above the kidneys, and spat on him. "American!"

The younger man returned with a basin of water that looked like it had been dipped from a muddy river. He held a cup to Richard's lips. Richard decided dysentery gave him a better chance for survival than dehydration. He sipped as much as the man would let him have. He looked into the man's face. Probably not even twenty. Maybe he could play on the young man's kindness. "Thank you," he said softly in Korean. The young man stood up. And then he kicked Richard in the face. Richard felt something snap in his right cheek before he passed out.

Chapter 36

"Senator Michaels, the scenario we have been able to piece together is that a sniper picked off your Marine and our security people from above, while a small boat of some kind beached and made off with Mr. Matthews." Chung Hee's chief of security spoke without emotion, just the facts.

Michaels mastered his temper since meeting with Chung Hee, but inside he still seethed. "And what have you been able to find in the search?"

The chief thrust out his jaw. "We found a rubber boat in a small cave about three kilometers north of the beach, near a dirt trail that can barely support vehicular travel."

"And have you shut down all the roads out of here?" Damn, these people didn't know how to think for themselves.

"We have shut down the highways, but there are many trails like this one that will take time to find."

The main highway from Pyongyang was a six-lane marvel of engineering, without much traffic, Michaels reflected. Roads to the agricultural collectives, however, were little more than ox-cart tracks. They had to have the highway for show, while their people starved. "What you are saying is these bastards gave you the slip?"

"We are doing everything we can, Senator." Chung

Hee's quiet voice intruded.

"And we are lining up our troops at the border, in case anyone tries to slip across," Patmanov offered, a cup of espresso in his hand. "Our submarines are moving closer and listening." He nodded at Chung Hee. "Fully in cooperation with the DPRK, of course."

Chung Hee nodded. "Of course."

"Our troops are also tightening our common border," said Pan. Michaels glared at her. Damn chinks, sending a woman in pants to do a man's job.

"And we have a carrier with search and rescue helos that should arrive within two hours." Min Shirane had said little during the negotiations as yet. The Japs appeared to be waiting to see what side would win.

Hyeong spoke up. "Seoul has its troops at the ready. We are watching the roads, the sea, the air."

"Well, I can tell you the US of A is damn well taking action." He didn't elaborate, as he really didn't know what more could be done, and studied the players in the room. Good God, we came here to stop a global crisis, and now we seem to have created one.

Chung Hee spoke softly. "It appears the Four Horsemen have gathered at the gates."

Chapter 37

Richard lay staring at the fire in the center of the hut. He had no idea what time it was or even what day. He hadn't worn a watch for his run on the beach, and they had taken his cell phone. The way he felt when he woke up, he must have been out for a very long time, and the effects of whatever they used to drug him hadn't worn off completely. A few hours after he awoke the second time, they untied him, dragged him outside to use the latrine, and allowed him to sit up for maybe half an hour to swallow some broth with a few grains of rice and tiny bits of pasty vegetables in it. Then they gave him a cup of water and tied him up again. They tossed a thin, dirty blanket that didn't cover much over him, and then the older one rolled up in a heavier blanket near the door, while the other one went outside. Periodically, the man outside came inside the hut for a few minutes, looked at Richard while he added a log and warmed his hands over the fire, and then went outside again.

Richard dozed, despite the cold, but he couldn't stay asleep long. His arms and legs tingled from the awkward position, his hands and face throbbed. His fingers were probably broken, or at least dislocated, maybe his cheekbone, too. His wedding ring was gone, too, although now he gave thanks it was, because if he still wore it, his finger would have swollen around it.

His stomach rumbled, from the lack of both quantity and quality of food and water. His hosts, however, hadn't eaten any better. It looked like they took turns with the same filthy blanket. He endeavored to pull his body into a tighter ball, to get more of him under what blanket there was, but it did no good. He tried the techniques he used while recuperating from Zimbabwe to hold the pain at bay, but he couldn't maintain it for long.

He thought of Terra, but thinking of her caused him fear, that he might never see her again, fear of how she was taking the news. If he thought long about her, he might not be able to summon the presence of mind to figure a way to get back to her.

The cold became too much of a factor to deal with. It took on a tangible quality, creeping into the room, laying its icy hands on him. It entered his lungs like the frigid breath of an ogre. The fire flickered like a friendly beacon, licking the logs, teasing warmth from them. The fire and the cold battled for him, tugging him back and forth between them like a rag doll. He knew there was something very important he needed to think about, but for now, all his mind could grasp was the cold. His only desire was to conserve heat, to not move. He prayed for the fire to get closer. Just as his mind went almost as numb as his body, the younger man entered the hut again to feed the fire. He stared at Richard for a long time, and then he nudged the other man with his foot.

"Your time," he said in Korean. "I get the blanket now."

Cursing, the older man crawled from the blanket. Richard closed his eyes until he could barely see and hoped they assumed he was asleep. Still, he made out the older man's hostile glare as he warmed himself over the fire before he went outside.

Chapter 38

A long, tense week passed since Richard's kidnapping. The State Department called every day with updates, but, in reality, there was nothing to update. He had vanished into thin air. No ransom demands, no taking credit for the kidnapping by any terrorist group. Just prolonged, ugly, frustrating silence. Terra went mechanically about the business she had to conduct, like this phone call with Elmer.

"Thanks for making those changes, Elmer." She wished he would hurry with the conversation.

"No problem, Terra. I'm happy to take care of my favorite author." He paused, and she knew the question coming. "Have you heard any news about Richard?"

"Nothing much." She gritted her teeth to keep from telling him to mind his own damned business. "The people in charge are doing everything possible."

"If there's anything I can do, just let me know." His voice sounded sincere, and she knew he was, but there was nothing he could do, nothing any of them could do, without some clue, some lead.

"Thanks, I will."

"You know, it sounds almost like he's living the plot of one of his own novels."

Terra knew it wasn't the first time. "Well, living it is not nearly as much fun as writing it. Or reading about it."

"Oh, Terra, I didn't mean to make light of the danger." He paused again. "It's just he happens into situations most people would never imagine." Another silence filled the line. "I'm sure he'd much rather be dreaming these things up from the safety of his recliner."

"I know he would be. He's been talking about the next book and getting it put together." He had set himself a deadline of sketching out the plot before they moved to Colorado. Now—

"Well, there is one up side to the situation."

"What?" Terra couldn't imagine anything positive coming from Richard's kidnapping.

"His first five books are selling like hotcakes. We've had to order a second printing of *Capricorn Revisited*, and we've doubled the first run of *Quest for the Black Pearl*."

"That's great." She knew the flat tone of her voice would dampen Elmer's enthusiasm.

He took the hint. "Take care, Terra. You, Richard, and his family are in our prayers."

She hung up without a response. Dropping the phone on the table, she felt a need to hide, to master the tide of emotion rolling in. She feared it would take her with it when it rolled back out. She made it to the shelter of the rose arbor and dropped to the ground, her head on the stone bench. She sobbed so hard she had hiccups by the time Paul found her there.

He helped her to her feet and sat her on the bench. "There, there, Terra." He rubbed her shoulders and held her hands. "It's okay to cry. You can't be a rock all the time."

She cried and clung to him, not even able to

express the many fears dancing in her mind. "I'm sorry, Paul." She tried to wipe away the tears to make them stop, but they just kept coming.

She felt his hands steady her shoulders. "Tell me what you're afraid of."

She shuddered and couldn't face him. "I'm afraid they'll never find him." She sniffed and rubbed her eyes. "I know I said I was sure he was alive and he'd make it back to us, but—" The tears welled up again. "What if I was wrong?"

He took a deep breath. "If you were wrong, if we were all wrong, then there's nothing we can do about it. If we're right, there's nothing we can do from here, either."

She looked at him. "Do you think we should go to Korea?"

He shook his head. "Absolutely not. We'd just give whoever did this more targets." He gripped her hands. "What I mean is, there is no action we can take ourselves to change the outcome. It's in the hands of the experts on the scene, and I understand there are a great many of the world's best handling things."

"Then what do we do?" Though she knew he spoke the truth, it did nothing to allay her fears.

He tipped her chin up to study her eyes. "Shall we pray?"

Confused, she stared at him. "But I thought Carrie was the church-goer. Richard told me you spend Sunday services on the golf course."

He smiled, and it did reassure her a little. "Just because I'm not inside a building with a label on it doesn't mean I'm not worshipping my Creator, nor does it mean I don't believe in God." He studied the ground. "I wouldn't have made it through some of the situations I've faced, including ones where Richard was in peril, without relying on my God." He faced her again. "And that is the one thing we can do for Richard right now." He looked deep into her eyes. "We can pray for him."

He waited until she nodded and took his hand. Then he bowed his head. "Father, you know the situation we find ourselves in. You know where Richard is right now, what he is facing. Only You can get him out of it. We ask, Terra and I together—and You promise wherever two or more are gathered, You hear our prayers—You would protect him now, You would bring him back to us safe and sound, and You would let him hear Your voice and know it is to You he owes his rescue." He squeezed Terra's hand. "Amen."

"Amen," she said. Surprisingly, she felt stronger, calmer, more optimistic than she had in days. "Thank you. I guess it was just what I needed."

He smiled. "I needed it myself." He stood. "Now, why don't you go in and splash some water on your face while I see what Janie and Carrie have concocted for lunch?"

Chapter 39

"Gentlemen and Ladies, we have some news to report," Chung Hee announced in the conference room. All attention focused on him. "We have found an abandoned vehicle, about twenty kilometers from here, with traces of Richard's DNA in it."

"DNA?" Delmonico asked. "From what?" He knew exhaustive DNA tests took time, twelve hours at minimum, but there was an experimental method from Cornell University that could complete a preliminary analysis in thirty minutes.

"Hair," Chung Hee responded.

Delmonico let out the breath he was holding. At least the DNA wasn't from blood. He feared the new boss he had grown to respect would be brutally killed and never found. He and Harris each made a trip to the Pacific fleet carrier in the week since the kidnapping to question Adler further. As near as either could tell, the man told them everything he knew.

"Well, now you've found the vehicle, what else are you doing?" Michaels threw his weight around again.

Since Richard's kidnapping, Michaels appeared to assume Richard's role as lead negotiator, even though none of the other delegates supported the assumption. The man's animosity toward all the other countries was painfully evident, and his manner suppressed any real communication. Delmonico vowed in his next coded report to the State Department, he would request Michaels be recalled and a new delegate named to replace him.

"We have concentrated the search to the west and north, toward the direction in which the vehicle was found." How Chung Hee managed to stay calm in the face of Michaels' needling, Delmonico could only guess. "There are tracks of another vehicle near it, and your intelligence people are trying to match the casts of those tracks with various tire tread patterns." He addressed the entire room. "It is only a matter of time before Richard is found and rescued."

Delmonico stared at his shoes. He wished he could share Chung Hee's optimism. Inland North Korea covered a lot of rugged, remote territory, sparsely populated and harsh in climate in late September. If Richard even remained in North Korea. With the week passed, Richard could be anywhere in the world by now. He figured the odds of finding and rescuing Richard, without some sort of demand or communication from the kidnappers, were about as good as his chances of winning the lottery. Which were zero because he never bought a ticket. Maybe he and Harris would return to the Pacific fleet carrier tomorrow and lean a little bit harder on Adler.

Chapter 40

Richard held out his hand eagerly for his cup of broth. Meager though it was, it represented the only sustenance available. If he refused it, he would only grow too weak to find his way out of the situation. The third day, they tethered him by one hand like a dog on a leash to a log support near the back of the hut. It had taken all day for him to regain much use of his arms and legs after being trussed as long as he was. He had a range of about three feet in which to move.

The first few days, he had had to use his hands like paws to hold his cup, but now, nearly ten days after his capture, if his mental accounting of days could be trusted, he could bend his fingers somewhat. He flexed them at every opportunity, trying to maintain circulation and flexibility. His face no longer throbbed, though it felt crooked.

They took him outside for latrine use now twice a day, and he observed carefully on each trip. It was indeed a hut, albeit part dugout, where they kept him, with a battered canvas tarp for a door. He watched for a trail, a road, anything telling how they got in and out of the area. The ground in front of the hut was trampled, and faint tracks led both directions away from it, but neither seemed more used than the other. The trees, mixed pines and something resembling aspens, told him the camp was high above sea level, but he hadn't been able to judge whether he was north or west of Songdowan. And he had no idea how far.

Every day, he tried to connect with his captors or to learn who had him. He got nothing. Any attempt he made at conversation, particularly with the older one, got him slapped or punched. They rarely exchanged more words with each other than they had the day he came to.

Now, he sipped his broth, and studied the two once more. They kept the supplies somewhere outside the hut and seemed to forage daily for firewood. If they communicated with anyone else, they must do it away from the hut, as he neither saw any radio equipment nor heard any conversations. He decided to ask them a question, but waited until he finished his broth. On the second day, he spoke to them, and got the broth knocked from his hand. He got no refill that day. He learned to wait. He drained the last drop from his cup and set it down. "Have you asked a ransom for me yet?"

Both men stopped eating to glare at him. The older one came to him, picked up his cup and smacked his face with it. The blow jarred his teeth together. But at least he got to finish his meal. The guard walked back to his lunch without speaking. Richard settled on his blanket at the back of the hut. He lay down and closed his eyes almost completely. After they finished eating, both men went to the door of the hut, where they spoke in hushed tones. He strained his ears and could pick out some words, none of which made any sense. Shipment. General. Signal.

The younger man re-entered the hut, glanced at him, and stacked the little bit of wood he had brought in. He heard nothing from the older one. He sat up. "Latrine?" he asked submissively.

The guard glared at him. "You've been." He dropped the rest of the wood. "Wait."

"Please?" Richard squirmed. "The water isn't what I'm used to."

The guard grunted. He left the hut and returned minutes later with a couple of cans of the soup and another armful of wood. They seldom brought either much food or wood into the hut during one day. Richard wondered if this one was preparing for the other one to be gone. He watched another trip or two. A bucket of water. And more wood. The young man set his rifle by the door.

"Latrine, please?" Richard pleaded again.

The young man studied him and finally stepped forward to untie him. Richard rose to his feet as if weak. He wavered as he walked ahead of his guard toward the door. The young man jerked him back and stepped past Richard to pick up the rifle. Slinging it over his shoulder, he jerked the rope again, and led Richard down and what appeared to be south away from the hut. Richard stumbled and wobbled until they stopped, and the young man nodded toward the designated area off the trail.

Richard started to shuffle past him, then spun around to catch the guard full in the face with an elbow punch. The guard staggered back, reaching for his rifle, fumbling to swing it from its position slung over his back to bring it to bear on Richard.

Richard grabbed for it as well. He was able to wrestle it partially away from the guard, enough to swing the butt of it into the man's gut. The guard let go of the gun and doubled over. Richard swung the gun against the man's chin. His head snapped back as he slumped to the ground.

Richard stood over him, breathing heavily. The short battle had sorely taxed the nourishment he'd had the past week, and now his hands throbbed again. He had to think fast. He should probably kill the guard, but he couldn't bring himself to take a life unless he had no other choice. There had been enough dying around him in his life already. He rolled the guard to his stomach, removing his belt. He belted his arms behind him, as they had done to Richard. Then he checked his pockets for anything useful.

"Aha!" He seized the pocketknife and cut the rope from his wrist. There was nothing else of use—no coins, no watch, nothing. No wonder these men had been a party to kidnapping him, if their own existence was so meager. It would have taken little promise to enlist their aid. He slipped the knife into the front pocket of his sweatshirt and picked up the rifle.

Half jogging, but endeavoring to be quiet, Richard retraced his path to the hut. There he picked up the matches, the sole spare clip for the rifle, and the cans of soup. He took a deep drink of the dirty water. As a final thought, he grabbed his thin blanket and the other one. He tied them into a bedroll with his former leash and stepped outside the hut once more. He stood for a moment, pondering. Down the path he had just come, he would encounter the man he had tied, who might even now be awake again and heading his way. Take the wrong path of the others, and he risked running into the older guard. He doubted gaining the upper hand over him would be as easy as it had been with the younger one.

He glanced at the sun, shrouded by clouds low in the western sky. He needed to make time. At last, he selected a path that looked like it had not had traffic as recently as the other. "And I took the path less traveled by," he muttered, quoting his favorite Robert Frost poem. "Let's hope it makes a difference." Settling into a steady trot, he headed downhill.

Chapter 41

"This was a great idea, Carrie." Terra lay on her side, submitting to the skilled hands of a masseuse at the Mandara Spa at Atlantis. Soft Asian music surrounded her. Water cascaded down a glass wall, providing a soothing undertone to the experience.

Carrie lay face down on a table a few feet away. "I thought it would help you deal with things, dear."

"Too bad Paul wouldn't come." She giggled, remembering Paul muttering something about a horse-faced German sadist, before he took his golf clubs to the links. One of the security men accompanied him, also armed with clubs, and another now sat outside the room they occupied.

"I think his last massage experience was in Switzerland, with a very stern masseuse who believed 'no pain, no gain.' " Carrie laughed. "And it could be he fears relaxing too much. You have no idea how loud he snores."

Terra giggled again. She closed her eyes as the masseuse worked on her. The special pregnancy massage was designed to optimize her circulation and muscle tone, while encouraging her to relax. She could enjoy nine months of this. Still, her thoughts were on Richard; in fact, she could only stop thinking of him for a few minutes at a time.

"Carrie, do you have any instincts on how Richard

is? Or where he is?"

Carrie didn't speak right away, and Terra feared what her answer might be. Finally, she heard a soft reply. "I believe he is alive. I don't know where he is, but I feel he is working his way back to you."

Terra had been holding her breath, awaiting Carrie's response. "I believe he is, too. Coming back to us."

"Oh, he loves Paul and me, don't ever doubt it." She paused. "But it's you he'll risk everything to come home to, which is as it should be." She looked at Terra. "You have to do everything you can to make sure he comes home to a healthy wife carrying a healthy baby."

"I will." Terra ached to be face to face with Richard right now, to watch his eyes as she told him he would be a father, to encourage him as he settled into the role.

"And if it takes these massages on a regular basis to help you deal with the stress, we'll do it."

Terra sighed, as her muscles relaxed even more. "It would be tough, but I'd make the sacrifice."

Carrie looked at her and grinned. "And if you need me to accompany you, I'm willing to do that, too."

"You are going to be a wonderful grandmother." Her throat tightened as she remembered her own parents would never have the chance.

"Just don't be upset if I spoil the little one."

"You have to." Terra sighed again, about to drift off to sleep. "It's your job."

Two hours later, after rain shower water therapy, they met Paul under a canopy in the Point Restaurant and Bar. They all learned the lesson not to expose Terra to exotic food for the moment, and this outdoor restaurant, located beside the pool and providing a spectacular view of the harbor, served light fare. Terra ordered a salad, grilled chicken, and a tall glass of milk.

Paul chuckled as she dug into her food with gusto. "You certainly are eating for two today, Terra."

"Paul, hush," Carrie chided him. "She's been eating like a bird this week. She has some catching up to do."

Terra took a big gulp of the milk. "I do think the massage helped."

Paul sighed. "Well, the golf was most therapeutic."

"No one around to see you fudge on your score?" Carrie nudged his elbow.

Paul sat up straight. "Schmidt can vouch for me." He glanced at the security man who accompanied him. Schmidt and the man who guarded the door for Terra and Carrie sat at the bar, with sandwiches and tall glasses of iced tea.

Suddenly two men, one bearing a microphone, the other a large video camera, appeared behind Carrie. "Mrs. Matthews, what can you tell us about the status of your husband's kidnapping?"

Terra froze with a forkful of salad halfway to her mouth. "What?"

Carrie tried to turn, but the men had her boxed in on either side. Paul rose as best he could with the camera man looming over him. "That will be enough!" he commanded in a low voice. "Get the hell out of here!"

The man with the microphone leaned closer to Terra. "Did you have the chance to tell your husband you're pregnant before he was kidnapped?"

She threw down her napkin and stood. The man

took a half step back, perhaps because of the security men hustling his way. Or maybe it was something in Terra's face that moved him as she stepped away from her chair and grabbed his wrist. "Listen, you little creep," she said in a clear, quiet voice. "If I ever see you around me or my family again, you'll wish it was only a lawsuit you had to worry about." The security men stepped between him and Terra, and forcibly, none too gently, moved him and his camera man away from them and toward the hotel security staff arriving. Terra stood with her hands on her hips, glaring after the intruders. Finally, she dropped to her seat and picked up her napkin.

"Damn." Paul whistled in admiration. "The mother tiger in action."

Terra looked first at Paul and then at Carrie. The look of concern in Carrie's eyes settled her down, made her think about what she had just done. "I'm sorry, guys." She put her hands in her lap. "I think I let my temper get the better of my judgment."

"Oh, but what a temper. And what a line." Paul reached out to pat Terra's shoulder. "I'm glad you're on our side, dear."

Glancing at him, she couldn't suppress a grin. It had felt good to dump all her frustrations on the intruder, to let him know, in no uncertain terms, exactly how she felt about him. "Still, I should have just kept my mouth shut. It will be all over the tabloids tomorrow." She looked up at Carrie. "And we may be sued. After all, I did touch him and threaten him."

"We'll deal with it if it comes, dear." Carrie looked from Terra to Paul and back. "What concerns me is how they found out about the baby. And how many other people know."

The blood drained from Terra's head as the impact of what Carrie said hit her. Suddenly exhausted, she propped her chin on her hands. "I have a feeling that this will come to no good."

Carrie nodded. "You'd better tell Richard yourself at the very first opportunity."

If I ever get the chance. And the tears came.

Chapter 42

Delmonico glanced up from the corner where he, Harris, and Edwards were discussing how to corral Michaels until the old fool could be sent home. Chung Hee's head security advisor entered the room. He and his group fell silent, trying to guess by Chung Hee's reaction what news the man carried.

Chung Hee faced the crowd gathered around the table. "Ladies and gentlemen, we have news to report!"

Richard found? Could they be that lucky? Delmonico held his breath.

Chung Hee waited for relative quiet. "With the assistance of thermal images from American planes, we have been investigating possible hideouts deep in the mountains." Delmonico knew the images provided by the planes pinpointed areas inhabited by humans. They had begun to systematically search each one. Silence fell on the room. "Our troops have located a hut DNA shows was occupied by Mr. Matthews not long ago."

"Well, where is Matthews now?" Michaels grew more obnoxious with each passing day. State promised to recommend replacement, but it hadn't happened yet. Michaels' hardline rhetoric echoed the speech the President had given announcing Richard's kidnapping. The Commander-in-Chief had issued a promise of American retribution when the culprits were found.

Chung Hee faced him. "We don't know for sure.

He was not at the hut when our troops arrived." He scanned the crowd. "It appears that he was held there as little as thirty-six hours before. The hut was abandoned by the time troops investigated. An American criminal investigative technician accompanying our troops took the DNA samples that have been evaluated."

Delmonico moved from the corner to the front of the crowd. "What kind of DNA this time?"

Chung Hee hesitated. "Blood."

Delmonico swallowed hard. "How much?"

"From the reports I've heard, very little." He bowed his head ever so slightly toward Delmonico, as if sympathizing. "Not enough to indicate a wound of any danger."

"Any indication what happened, why the place was abandoned?" He sensed Harris and Edwards behind him.

Chung Hee shook his head. "The troops looked the area over carefully, following the instructions of your investigative person. There appeared to be signs of a struggle, but the ground was too hard to find tracks to follow." He met Delmonico's gaze again. "The troops are still there, bringing in more scientific equipment to get more information."

Delmonico faced Edwards and Harris. "From what I've heard about our boss, he's not a quitter." In the dossier presented to him along with the assignment to assist Richard was his history of tough negotiating, considering the best interests of all sides, no matter what, and his incredible recovery by force of will from the injuries in Zimbabwe.

Edwards nodded. "If anyone could make it out of this mess, he can."

Delmonico caught Harris' look. Harris knew, as well as he did, the odds were still against Richard.

Chapter 43

Terra heard drums beating. Or was it thunder? Or the hoof beats of running horses? She rolled over, trying hard to stay asleep. Sleep was a rare enough commodity of late, broken either by nightmares or nausea. The sound came again, and Terra lifted her head from the pillow, halfway out of sleep now. "Terra!" It was Carrie's voice, accompanied by a knock on the bedroom door. She hopped from the bed and ran to the door.

The look on her face, she knew, read she was prepared to slip toward joy or anguish. She couldn't tell by Carrie's expression which way to go. "What—"

Grasping Terra's hands, Carrie pushed into the room. "They've found the hut where Richard has been held!"

"They've found him?"

Carrie sat on the edge of the bed, pulling Terra with her. "No." She looked down. "The place was abandoned about two days before they found it."

Terra stared at her, searching for some reason to hope. "So, no sign of Richard?"

Carrie slipped her arm around Terra, holding her hand. "They found some blood."

"Blood?" Terra felt her control slipping. "Richard's blood?"

Carrie nodded. "But not much, nothing to suggest

he was badly injured."

Terra collapsed in sobs on Carrie's shoulder. "What kind of animals would take someone who was just trying to help the world?" Carrie's body shook, she was crying as well. "And not tell us why?"

Carrie held Terra's shoulders. "I know Paul is concerned there have been no demands from the kidnappers." Terra searched Carrie's eyes, a mother's eyes, and found a shred of hope there. "But, Terra, I choose to believe the reason the hut was abandoned is Richard escaped."

Calm settled over her. "I believe you're right, Carrie." She had to believe it. To believe otherwise meant she was alone again. That the baby growing inside her might never know its father. She wouldn't face the possibility unless it came to pass. For now, she needed to be strong, she needed to believe. She took Carrie's hand. "Carrie, would you pray with me?"

"Of course, dear." Carrie hugged her, and then, heads bowed together, they prayed for the man they both loved to be brought home safely.

Chapter 44

Three or four hours after leaving the hut, Richard found a small stream. Studying it, he decided it was at least as safe to drink as the water he had been consuming. Squatting beside it, he rinsed his hands in the chilly rivulet, then scooped up several handsful of water to drink. He rubbed his face with water and dried it on his sweatshirt. After more than a week of wearing the same clothing, he wasn't sure this made him any cleaner, but he felt better.

His right cheek was tender as he rubbed it, but it hadn't yielded to the pressure of his fingers. He could feel the stubble on his face. He was perhaps a week past needing a haircut when he was taken; he probably would frighten anyone he might encounter now. If they didn't smell him coming in time to run away.

No matter, no time for bathing in a creek not deep enough at any rate. Nor was it warm enough to risk the exposure, even if he wasn't afraid of being followed. Periodically, he moved off the trail, little more than an animal track, to watch and listen behind him. As yet, he detected no one following him.

Ruefully, he wondered what Terra would think of his appearance now. Would she recoil from his filthy appearance? Or would she be as overjoyed to see him as he would be to see her that appearances wouldn't matter? He stopped the thought before he explored it.

He knew Terra, and his parents, were under incredible stress because of his absence. He remembered the look in his parents' eyes as they stood over what they feared would be his deathbed after Zimbabwe. He vowed never to put them, or Terra, through that kind of agony again. He shut down the train of thought through force of will. Thinking of them would allow desperation to enter his mind, and desperation clouded his logic.

Changing from thinking to acting, he studied the sun, half hidden by a growing cloud cover. Another hour, perhaps two, of good light. It might give him enough head start to keep him safe from his captors, if they were pursuing him. He had to assume they had contact with others, that a large group might even now be hunting him. He assumed North Korean troops, at least, maybe a coalition force, were also searching for him. The trick, if he encountered people, would be to tell friend from foe. He set off downhill again, still following the stream.

Another hour brought him to the end of that particular trail. The stream disappeared over a precipice through the only visible way down. The jumble of jagged rocks far down at the bottom of the waterfall told him a daring dive was not the way to escape. He rotated slowly, scanning the walls that funneled into the waterfall. No way out but up. He retraced his path into the forest, trying to find a vantage point from which to find the best way out.

Cautiously, he stepped into a small clearing that might afford him a view of the mountains around him. Just in case, he unslung the rifle from his shoulder and held it at the ready, safety off. Scanning the edges of the clearing, he climbed onto a fallen tree trunk, hoping to see over the forest. The added height didn't help much, but he thought he could see a notch between the peaks around him opening to the southeast. Watching the perimeter of the clearing, he worked his way into the forest in the direction of the notch. Once he was twenty yards inside the forest, he clicked the safety back on the rifle.

The track he found to follow, however, soon led uphill. Pausing to get his bearings on the fading sun, he decided to continue on the upward path. It at least led south. Another half hour or so, and he came to a tiny overhang forming a cave of sorts not far off the trail. He knew he would have to eat and rest soon, or he would not be able to continue the next day.

Dropping the blankets at the back of the cave, he dug out one of the cans of soup. Russian military issue, he guessed, studying the can. Probably surplus from a long time back. With the pocketknife, he punched it open enough to be able to drink the contents. He shuddered at the first swallow. Even though it had been tucked into his sweatshirt, it was cold enough the fat content of the broth was congealed lard, the broth itself watery and flavorless. He stared at the can for a moment and forced himself to down more. It was all he had for the moment, and he was too close to the hut to risk a fire to heat it. He considered saving half of it for breakfast but decided it might encourage animals to get into it. He finished it, more than doubling his caloric intake from the previous day. He hoped it would carry him a long way tomorrow.

He spread the thin blanket on the uneven ground of the cave and drew the thicker one over himself. Cradling the rifle in his arms, he made himself as comfortable as he could. To shut down his mind, he counted backwards from a hundred. Somewhere in the forties, he drifted into a light sleep.

Chapter 45

Terra had begun stopping in Paul's study periodically throughout the day, to check on any possible updates. She knew the men there would search out Paul if they had anything to report, but she wanted to see for herself. Now she stepped through the doorway. "Any news?"

The man seated before the bank of monitors put down the newspaper he was reading and jumped from his chair to face her. He stood, his gaze dropping to her belly for just a second as he scrambled to his feet. The tiny gesture told Terra the security men knew of her pregnancy. At least one of them heard the exchange between her and the reporter. Thankfully, it would most likely be weeks before she started to show. "Nothing new, ma'am."

She moved closer to study the screens. "What are they doing to find Richard?" She could see each boundary of the property, as well as the beach running from the house to the sea. The beach where their baby had been conceived.

The man offered her his chair and she slipped into it. "The same as yesterday, Mrs. Matthews." He paused to study a person strolling down the road, but relaxed when he recognized Janie, leaving the house after her workday. "They are following all the leads from the thermal imaging, roughly two hundred troops fanning out from the hut." He met her questioning glance. "But whether he's traveling alone or is with his captors, he has a two- or three-day head start on them." He pulled his paper from the table and folded it to hide the third page story about the situation. "One man alone or a small group can easily outpace an army trying to stay coordinated."

She stayed silent a moment, studying the monitors, the printouts, the listening devices, the box of donuts, and the plethora of coffee cups. "What are his chances?"

The man met her gaze briefly and looked away. "Ma'am," he paused. "I hate to sound like I'm not optimistic, but—" He looked around the room as if to see if anyone else was listening. "Every day that goes by without some communication from the kidnappers revealing a motive or what we can do to get him back reduces the odds."

She forced herself to remain calm, pushing logic into command, though her heart pounded from fear for Richard. "And if he's escaped them?"

He shook his head. "There's a lot of country between the hut and Songdowan." He picked up a document stamped "classified." "It's rugged country, relatively high altitude, not many roads, not many inhabitants." He looked up from the document. "And the long-range weather forecast is snow."

Terra looked at her hands, staring at the wedding ring that now seemed a part of her. "I believe he's escaped them," she said firmly. "And I believe that he will make it out of those mountains, against any odds." She looked back at the security man. "Do you know my husband?"

He shook his head. "No, ma'am. Never had the privilege of meeting him. I rotated in after he left for Korea."

She stood. "Then you have no way of knowing how resourceful he is." She smiled at him as she left the room. "If you knew him, you would give him better odds."

Chapter 46

Richard awoke from his fitful sleep to mind-numbing cold. Forcing his stiff body to move, he sat up, shivering. A wan light filtered into the cave. Night was over. Shaking his head, giving himself an internal pep talk, he folded the blankets and rolled them up. Every muscle, every joint, every fiber of his being ached as he stood up and stepped out of the cave.

He searched for the sun as a point on which to get a bearing, but the cloud cover was so thick, he couldn't see it. Remembering it had set behind the cave, he turned to his right and worked his way down from the cave to the track he had followed this far yesterday. Just before he entered the trail, he paused to look and listen, then relieved himself. Another few seconds of listening, and he again headed what he hoped was south. The trail continued to lead upward. He would have preferred to angle down, but at least it was going the right direction. He had to assume he was inland from Songdowan, and still in Korea.

He walked steadily, for at least three hours, always ultimately uphill, even though the trail might go down for a few hundred yards. He drank from any stream he crossed. He rested for a few minutes every hour or so, sitting with the rifle across his knees and leaning against a tree.

Last night's supper had long since faded from his

muscles, but he refused to eat the second can until he stopped for the night. He considered saving it, trying to go another day without eating, but he decided to trust something else would sustain him. By nightfall, which came earlier because of cloud cover, he had found nothing that would serve as shelter. He debated trying to keep walking, but he knew that, in the dark, he risked falling and injuring himself to the point he might be unable to continue his journey. He finally found a tree with low hanging branches. After consuming the last can of food, he crawled under the branches with the rifle and blankets hugged to his chest. Another fitful night passed.

The next day began the same as the second. Around mid-day, as he rested against a tree, eyes closed and bone weary, something struck his face. Startled, he opened his eyes to ice pellets raining down on him. "Well, that just bites," he muttered. "Sleet." He rose, his mission now to find shelter. The sleet lasted only minutes, before it changed to ghostly silent snow.

Chapter 47

The SUV carrying Senator Michaels pulled out of the courtyard of the Songdowan People's Retreat. Delmonico breathed a sigh of relief.

"Thank God, he's gone." Harris muttered. Delmonico shot him a look. Harris caught his glance. "I was considering assassinating him myself, just to shut him up."

"Not very diplomatic, John." Delmonico grinned. "But I don't think you were the only one leaning that way."

"Any idea who is coming to replace him?" Edwards gazed down the nearly empty highway. They had been told to expect a new delegate to be named by the end of the week.

Delmonico shook his head. "I think there is some conflict over who to name. The Senate is pushing for a Democrat, but the White House is leaning Republican."

Edwards let out a short laugh. "God forbid they should let qualifications enter into the choice."

Delmonico sighed. "For the moment, gentlemen, we are it. We are all the official State Department representatives the U.S. has here. Our military presence here, small as it is, isn't even considered."

He thought about the searches being conducted. The thermal imaging scans had been tightened to pinpoint a single human. "And with our troops mixed in with theirs, and the Chinese and the Russians, sweeping the woods, and the Japanese cutters and the Russian subs closer to the shore than the Pacific fleet carrier—" He shivered. "Let's hope we get someone with some tact."

Chapter 48

The snow continued throughout the day. It slowed Richard's progress, made the going treacherous as he worked his way ever higher along the faint trace. He rested now every half-hour, trying to find somewhere, tree branches or earthen bank, to give him some relief from the snow. It changed from the dry fluffy substance he first encountered to wet, clinging, slippery stuff. He had to keep moving until he found shelter, or it would get the upper hand.

Already, his swollen fingers throbbed with pain at every heartbeat and his cheek ached. His feet, now damp, burned. He recognized the effects of growing hypothermia. Clenching his teeth, he pushed off from the hillock he had leaned against and trudged along the trail again, one slow step after another.

Two hours later, hoarfrost around his nose and mouth, he stopped in a grove of dense pines that shielded him from some of the snow. It was afternoon, he knew, but without the sun, he had no way of guessing how late it was. He took a deep breath, filling his lungs with cold, damp air. He scanned the grove, finding a trunk that appeared nearly dry. Wrapping the blankets around himself, he squatted against it. Against his will, though he fought the urge, his eyelids closed.

****

Richard opened his eyes with sudden panic.

Disoriented, he forced his mind to inventory his situation. He had feeling in all limbs and extremities, and he was warmer than he had been when he had taken shelter. Though the hunger in his stomach gnawed at him, he could ignore it. He still had control of the rifle, though it was cradled in his arms, his hands tucked into the pocket of his sweatshirt. His feet, still cold and damp, felt a little dryer than they had when he stopped.

He looked beyond his personal space. Very little snow had fallen on his blankets, and only a dusting covered the ground around him. The intertwined branches of the pines formed a tent that shielded him from the worst of the snow. Past the lowest hanging limbs, he could see the snow continued, but not as heavy as when he had stopped. He had no idea how long he had slept, whether just minutes, or overnight. He suspected, though, from the relative dryness of his clothing, it had been at least several hours, most likely though the night.

Assessing his chances, he decided to push on. He knew he could only survive a few days without food, and there was no chance of finding any under this particular tree. He had rested and knew that, eventually, rest would not help him without sustenance. He had to move while he still could.

After shaking the snow off the blankets, he wrapped them around him again and pushed though the branches to step back onto the track. Glancing the way he had come, he saw no evidence he had ever been there. The light snow that continued would eventually hide any tracks he made as he traveled. Any pursuit would have to give up now, although he realized it could be the good guys trying to find him just as easily as the bad guys. How he would know the difference, should he encounter someone, he could only leave to chance.

He trudged on. Within an hour, the snowfall grew. Daylight or not, he had trouble finding the path, and he stumbled more than once.

At last, he stopped under a pine at the edge of the track. He stood, too tired to even lean against the tree. He thought the track leveled out as he walked, but he couldn't be certain. The past hundred yards had been an effort, as he ordered his legs to move each step. He reached the end of strength, the end of his will. He wrapped his arms around the tree and rested his forehead against the rough bark.

"Lord," he sighed. "I know I haven't been a very good disciple." A bitter tightness held his throat. "I've tried very hard to be a good person, to do the right thing, the fair thing, every time I had a choice to make." A single hot tear welled up. "But, Lord, I'm at the end of 'do.' There is nothing more I can do to get myself out of this mess, to get back to the job I believe You want me to do."

He sank down to his knees against the tree, scraping his face on the bark. "I surrender, Lord. I know now it was You who got me out of events that should have killed me. I confess, I was angry with You when my babies died, and then Elaine. I thought I could manage this peace process with my own wit and my own skill. But I was wrong—"

He waited, curiously calm. "I surrender, Lord. I give in. My will is useless against the odds I face now." He swallowed hard. "I ask only, Lord, if Your will is I die here in this wilderness, that You help Terra and my parents cope, You give them peace and comfort."

By this time, he could no longer tell if he was speaking the words or thinking them. Or if they simply poured out of his heart. He thought briefly of Chung Hee's description of his connecting with the Creator. He closed his eyes. Total relaxation engulfed him, and he heard soothing sounds without words in his mind. Gradually, he realized he felt lighter, as if a weight had lifted from him. He raised his head from his hands. Blinking, not even certain if he was still alive, he looked around, and suddenly had the urge to stand, to begin to move again. Without hesitation, he entered the path and began to walk. He still felt cold, but the despair had gone.

Now, he was certain the track led downward. Within another hour or so, he had dropped several hundred feet. The snow was lighter and the air slightly warmer. The path jogged to the right, and there, in a clearing, sat a tiny house with a faint light shining through its windows.

He stopped. "Lord," he said, as snowflakes dusted his face. "Thank you, from the bottom of my soul, for whatever You did back there." He looked toward the house, not fifty yards away from him. "And thank you for this."

Cautiously, though trusting the house was a gift of life to him, he approached the front door. He laid the rifle behind a bench beside the door. He had to come to this door in peace, armed with only his faith. He knocked.

Seconds passed, and he raised his hand to knock again, when the door opened a hand's width revealing a wizened, elderly woman. She looked at him with wariness in her eyes. He bowed. "Please," he said softly, in Korean. "May I have shelter for a while?"

After staring into his face for what felt like a lifetime, indeed would probably mean his life if she refused, she nodded and glided aside. He stepped over the threshold into a tiny, but immaculate home. The warmth from the fire in the hearth enfolded him. He could smell something cooking.

He feared his legs would give way beneath him, when she indicated a chair at a small table with a wave of her hand. He sat, utterly spent. He looked at her again. "Thank you." He pulled the blanket back from his face. "You have saved my life."

She stood a yard away from him. "I know who you are."

The muscles in his jaw flexed. Would she turn him back over to his captors? Before he could speak, she picked up a bowl from the cabinet at one side of the room.

"You were kidnapped while you were trying to help us. My neighbor has a television, and we saw the news there." She dished up something from a pot on the small stove. "Are you hungry?"

"Yes, ma'am," he answered. Thank you, again, Lord, he thought. She is friendly and knows what I need. He smiled, as he wondered if she was what an angel looked like. She placed the bowl and a spoon in his hands.

He tried to remember his manners, but hunger overrode diplomacy, and he emptied the bowl in seconds. Then he gulped down the cup of water she handed him while she refilled the bowl. He stopped after the third bowl, afraid to overload his shrunken stomach with too much food. "Thank you, again."

She nodded. "If you can help us through this crisis, soup will be nothing." She sat across the table from him. "If you can't, if no one can, nothing will matter."

"What does the news say?"

She glanced at her hands. He saw they were worn and wrinkled, like her face. "I last heard two days ago. But it said all the countries involved in the peace talks were trying to find you."

"Did they say if anyone claimed responsibility for the kidnapping?"

She shook her head. "No one has."

Curious. Why take him if they had no objective? Unless the objective was confusion. Or chaos.

"My husband will be home in the morning," she said. "He's at the farmer's market selling our excess produce." Restrictions against private enterprise had relaxed as famine invaded the North with regularity every year. Evidently, their industry was paying off.

"How far is this from Songdowan?"

She thought for a moment. "A little more than a hundred kilometers."

He did some mental calculations. A well-conditioned runner with a support crew could cover the distance in eight to ten hours. In his state, it would take days, maybe a week. "Could I borrow enough food from you to sustain me on the trip?"

"I would have to ask my husband." She looked down at the floor. "It could be dangerous for us."

He realized she had taken a tremendous risk to even allow him in the house. He wanted to reassure her she would be rewarded and not punished for her assistance, but he knew any promises he made could prove empty.

"I cannot guarantee your safety, nor can I even be sure I will actually get back to the negotiating chamber." Though he realized the task before him seemed almost impossible, he was buoyed by the instinct that chance alone had not brought him through the snowstorm to her door. "All I can do is my best to get there and bring peace between your country and the rest of the world." He reached across the table to cover her hand with his. "If I can get to Songdowan, I will find some way to repay to you ten-fold what you have done for me, without putting you or your husband at risk."

She stared at him, her lips pursed as she appeared to consider his words. "I'll discuss it with my husband when he arrives." She stood up and leaned forward with her hands on the table. "I have some extra blankets. You can make a pallet on the floor by the fire." She stepped toward a doorway to another room. "You might want to eat some more before you sleep."

Chapter 49

Terra walked into the kitchen, her stomach clamoring for food. "Good morning," she said to Paul and Carrie seated in the breakfast nook, as she opened the refrigerator. She poured herself a glass of milk. Grabbing a bowl, spoon, and box of cereal, she made her way to the table to join them.

"Good morning, Terra," they said in unison as she set the bowl on the table.

"Still eating for two, I see." Paul eyed the bowl she heaped with cereal.

"Stop it, Paul." Carrie pushed a bowl of fruit toward Terra.

Terra simply raised a brow at him, as she munched away. She downed a third of the milk in one gulp. "Anything new this morning?" She didn't have to clarify the subject. There was only one incident on which they wanted to hear news.

Paul and Carrie exchanged a look. "We were just discussing the weather," Carrie offered.

Terra put down her spoon. "I know the forecast there was for snow."

"It hit." Paul nodded. "Grounded the planes and choppers, called the troops back to shelter."

Carrie covered Terra's hand with hers. "Don't worry, Terra. He's had all kinds of emergency training. He knows how to survive off the land."

She glanced down at the cereal, suddenly hungry to finish it. "Its's the craziest thing, Carrie." She held Carrie's hand and reached out for Paul's. "Today, I'm not worried any more, at least not deathly afraid like I have been."

Paul looked from Terra to Carrie. "Woman's intuition?"

Carrie raised her chin. "Maybe." She squeezed Terra's hand. "I've been feeling a sense of peace today, too."

Terra smiled at her, happier than she had been since their ordeal began. "Good." She let go of their hands and dug into the cereal again.

Chapter 50

"Helping you would put us, has already put us, at risk," argued the husband as Richard sat across the table from him the next morning.

Richard sipped at the tea and finished the bowl of rice porridge. It warmed him, rebuilding his spent energy reserves. He understood the man's dilemma. Though Richard was in favor with the current regime, the situation could change with any shift of power. Anyone who aided him might expect cruel retribution. Drawing attention to themselves could sign their death warrants. He bowed his head. "I understand. I am already deeply indebted to you. Your wife saved my life last night giving me food and shelter."

The husband sighed. He had refused to even give Richard his name, and forbade his wife to as well, simply calling her "wife," so great was his fear. "I want to help. I believe you, in your heart, want what is best for our people." He leaned forward, his voice dropping to a whisper. "But Chung Hee will not always be President, nor may he be in charge even when he is. We don't know if we can trust him, or anyone else." He sat back in his chair and crossed his arms over his chest. "We have to look out for ourselves."

Richard was in the same boat as his hosts. Taking a chance on their hospitality was a risk for him. At another house, he might have been shot, or handed over to the people who had taken him, or held for a reward. The hundred kilometers back to the People's Retreat was a race over unknown obstacles. He could trust to assistance from no one.

He took another drink of tea, and then the wife refilled his cup. He stared at the fire and thought. The snow had stopped during the night. With sufficient food, he could probably make good time, particularly as he got closer to better roadways, though he might have to travel parallel to them or at night to escape detection. He faced his host again. "If someone stole food from your larder, and you never saw who it was, you could not be at fault for helping the thief, could you?"

The husband smiled. "No, no one wants to help a thief make off with their hard-earned goods." He looked toward his wife. "But if the thief were to steal food, he might get stuffed peppers just cooked, and a few jars of *kim-chi*."

His wife nodded, already gathering ingredients. "And rice balls wrapped in steamed cabbage."

"And if I make it back to Songdowan, and officials can be convinced to distribute food aid throughout the region, everyone will benefit, not just the victims of thieves."

The husband stood and offered his hand. "Sometimes it's good to be robbed."

"There is one more thing," Richard said. "Just outside the house, behind the bench, is a rifle I already stole from the people who held me."

His host's eyes widened. "It should be brought in and oiled," he insisted.

Richard stepped outside to retrieve the gun, surveying the clearing before he dug the rifle out of the snow. His host was right. Another day or two, and it would be rusted beyond use. When he came in with it, his host had laid the table with gun oil and a cleaning cloth. Now Richard stared in surprise.

"Reserves," the old man said, nodding toward an ancient rifle in the corner by the door.

Richard glanced at it. A 1940's era Chinese-made rifle, probably handed down from World War II. Together they stripped down and oiled the Russian .762 Richard had appropriated. Richard knew how to break it apart and reassemble it, but his fingers would not work properly to allow him to do it, no matter how much he willed them to bend the way they should.

"I wouldn't expect a diplomat to know how to field strip a rifle." The old man took the gun from him.

Richard studied his own stiff fingers as he tried to flex them. "I asked for weapons training just in case." He looked up as the old man fitted the parts back together. "When I started as a diplomat, the world was not a very safe place."

"It still isn't." The old man grinned, handing the reassembled rifle to Richard to wipe down one more time. "But I guess you already know it."

Richard merely nodded as he ran the oiled cloth over the entire gun. Then he set it in the corner beside the old man's weapon. When he returned to the table, the old man had poured him a cup of tea.

"It's good we decided to do that," the man explained. "The rifle was so dirty it might have blown up in your face if you tried to use it."

"I hope I don't have to."

"We hope that as well." They sat in silence by the fire, while the aroma of beef-stuffed peppers and cabbage filled the air.

Thank you, again, Lord. You got me out of the snow, fed me, showed me the hearts of the people, and now I'll trust to you to get me back to the coast.

Chapter 51

"Yes, Sir, Mr. Secretary, I'll do my best."
Delmonico hung up the phone in his quarters, where he,
Harris, and Edwards had met to discuss the day and
make their daily report to the State Department.

"Well," Edwards questioned. "What did he say?"

Delmonico met Harris' gaze and then glanced at
Edwards. "They're not sending anyone to replace
Michaels."

"What?" Edwards stood. "Why not?"

Delmonico stretched and sighed. "They fear
sending anyone new into the situation might further
destabilize it. At the very least, the formalities would
have to start over and they think losing what little
momentum we have will doom the talks to failure. Or
basically, the Democrats and Republicans couldn't
strike a deal." He stared at his shoes. "So, for the
moment, I'm in charge."

"Damn, Ray." Harris looked at him, and there was
no envy in his eyes, only pity.

"What do we do?" Edwards spoke with the
impatience of youth. Delmonico studied him, knowing,
despite his age, Edwards was the most knowledgeable
non-Asian alive regarding the nuclear and military
capability of North Korea.

"We try to keep any spark from getting near this
powder keg we're sitting on, that's what we start with."

He leaned toward Harris. "John, do you think Adler is telling us all he knows?"

Harris took his time responding. "No, I don't think he's told us everything he knows," he said finally. "But in my gut, I believe he has told us everything he knows about who might be responsible for taking Richard. I think he has connections that go that far, but I don't think Adler personally has had any dealings with them he's aware of."

"Do you think whoever has Richard knows how much Adler knows?"

Harris began to smile. "What do you have in mind, Ray?"

Delmonico grinned. "How about putting up a lightning rod?"

Chapter 52

Traveling mostly at night after he left the pastoral shelter of the highlands, Richard made good time. His week-long trek across the land showed him just how desperate the food shortages were within the country—meager gardens, skinny cows, and people without much laughter.

He found Bible verses he hadn't read in years running through his mind as the miles passed behind him. "Blessed are the meek"—certainly this was a meek and humble people. "Blessed are those who are persecuted"—doubtless this was true as well. "Blessed are those who mourn"—plenty of mourning here already, and more to come unless there were changes. The country needed reform. But was Chung Hee the right man to bring it? "Blessed are the merciful"—could he be merciful, if those responsible for his kidnapping and the suffering within the country were brought before him to be judged? Just before dawn of the sixth day out from the tiny house, he spotted a highway sign that indicated "Songdowan, three kilometers."

The long part of the journey might be over, but the hard part remained. He had to get inside the negotiating chamber without giving his enemies a chance to stop him. The fact that he didn't know friend from foe made that task especially difficult. Finding a slight depression within a grove of trees a couple of hundred yards off the road, he laid out his bedroll on a scrap of tarp the husband had found for him. He ate a nourishing meal of wrapped rice balls and the last of the *kim-chi*. From the bottles of water they filled for him, he drank deeply and lay back on the bed to think through his options.

He considered the approaches to the Retreat, the guarded points, the distance from guard post to building. He asked for a tour the day he arrived, to assess the security as well as have a feel for the place. He left the data to simmer in his mind, as he cradled the rifle and settled in for sleep.

Mid-afternoon, he awoke, ate a bit more, and reconsidered his possible alternatives. At last, as the night grew deep and still, he slipped into the ditch beside the road and started walking. A kilometer from Songdowan, he left the roadway, and worked his way through the countryside, avoiding buildings of any kind. Just before dawn, when he could see the outline of the lights from the People's Retreat, he made his camp.

He awoke about noon. He ate the last of his food, ensuring there would be nothing to trace back to his hosts. He buried the water bottles. Looking around his camp, he marveled at how easily the veneer of civilization had slipped from him, leaving only the primal instinct to survive and outwit those who preyed upon him. Taking the rifle, he worked his way silently through the forest.

A hundred yards out from the retreat, he spotted a sentry patrolling what appeared to be the new perimeter. Since he was taken, they moved the safe zone farther away from the building and the beach. He watched as the sentry made regular sweeps back and forth over a two-hundred-yard pattern. Once he had the timing down, he moved closer to the patrol sweep.

When the man was patrolling about sixty yards away with his back toward Richard, peering instead deep into the forest, Richard crept across the man's path. By the time the sentry swept past the point again, the bushes stopped quaking, and Richard was halfway to the building.

A few feet inside the last of the belt of pines surrounding the retreat compound, Richard halted. He knew the quickest route from the door he now watched to the conference room on ground level. He inventoried the sentries. Now four instead of two on the roof. Their pattern was more irregular than the one in the forest. Two guards occupied the gatehouse near the entry road. From this vantage point, he saw no other sentries.

Carefully, watching the open area as well as uphill toward the perimeter guards, he sneaked around the building to where he remembered trees nestling up against it. Just around the corner from those trees opened a doorway into the main reception area. Keeping pine boughs between him and the sentries, he walked toward the building's deep overhang. Under the overhang, he moved on stealthy feet toward the door. He paused beside the door to steady his ragged breathing and slow his pounding heart.

He grabbed the door handle in his left hand and burst through the opening with the rifle in his right. "Nobody move!" he barked in Korean. The receptionist froze with wide eyes. The guard standing beside her raised his hands. "I'm Richard Matthews, and I need to get to the conference chamber without anyone inside knowing I'm here."

The guard nodded, his breathing fast, but his voice calm. "I recognize you, Mr. Matthews." He glanced down at the receptionist. "We could arrange an escort."

Richard shook his head. "That won't be necessary. You two will serve as my escort." He motioned with the rifle. When they had both moved away from the desk, he reached behind him to close the door and lock it. Then, taking the guard's pistol in his left hand, he let them move ahead of him toward the conference chamber. The girl shook as silent tears ran down her face.

The armed guards at the conference room doors reached for their sidearms as Richard and his escorts approached. "Don't touch your weapons," Richard ordered.

"It's Mr. Matthews," said the guard from the front desk. "He only wants to enter the chambers."

"He can't go in with the gun." The man on the left started to lower his hands.

Richard clicked the safety off the rifle. The man stopped moving. "It appears we have a stalemate," Richard commented. He motioned with the rifle. "You two put your guns on the floor and move toward the end of the hall."

Hesitantly, they complied. "Now, go back down the hall past the door." He laid the weapons he carried beside the guards' guns while they walked away, watching him. He followed them about six feet behind. They appeared confused, looking first at each other, then at him.

"Go on past the door," he ordered. They walked on. He stopped before the double doors. Taking a deep breath, he stepped forward and threw open the doors of the chamber.

Chapter 53

The delegate let his attention wander from the arguments around the table. They had gone nowhere since Matthews disappeared, although the Senator had provided amusement. Now the Americans had put the low-ranking underling in charge. He leaned back in his chair to consider his comely assistant.

Seated behind him, she bent her head seriously over a notepad, trying to capture the most important of the statements whirling around her. He noted the ripe swell of her breasts beneath the business suit she wore, the smooth curve of her calf encased in the silken stocking. He bit his lower lip as he decided tonight was the night he would summon her to his room, and she would learn that the real reason she was ordered to accompany him on this trip had nothing to do with her stenographic skills. After all, a man under as much pressure as he was during these negotiations needed a release from the stress.

His ears caught the whispering of aides near the door. Listening closely, he heard voices outside the chamber, but the doors were designed to keep what went on inside the chambers secret, and what went on outside isolated there. He shrugged. Probably just a changing of the guard. He glanced at his watch. Or the arrival of lunch. He reached for the remainder of the azalea-topped *wha jeon* on his plate at the table. He had barely finished half of the sugar-sprinkled sweet rice cake. He looked forward to savoring the excellent meal they would be served. He glanced at his assistant, licking his fingers as he finished the cake. Imagining himself plunging deep into the delights of the pretty young woman only heightened his enjoyment of the *wha jeon.*

Suddenly the doors to the chamber burst open. He jumped with surprise, turning toward the door to see a filthy apparition stride into the chambers. As his heart slowed, he recognized Matthews under the dirt and beard. The room fell silent as Matthews stood glaring around the room. The American, Delmonico, got up from Matthews' former seat to stand behind it. Chung Hee smiled and bowed his head.

"I'm back," Matthews announced, his voice harsh. Once again, his gaze swept the room. "Delegates, the games are over." With every eye on him, he marched around the room to his place at the head of the table. Leaning forward, resting his hands on the table, he surveyed them all one more time. The delegate noticed Matthews's hands—dirty, swollen, distorted, as if they had been broken.

Matthews spoke again. "The rules have changed, ladies and gentlemen." He waited while they absorbed his words. "From now on, only delegates and the staff I choose will be present in the room." A gasp circled the room. The delegate glanced toward his stenographer.

"From now on," Matthews continued. "You arrive at the chambers when I say and you leave when I say." The delegates began to look at each other and at their staffs. "Meals and breaks are at my order." A muttered rumble began.

Matthews stood staring, until the rumble died, and the delegate could hear the other people in the room breathing. All of them. "And from now on, no arguing about who will sit where." No one else spoke. "You will sit where I tell you, when I tell you." He pulled his hands deliberately off the table, every person in the room watching him. "You will rotate chairs when I tell you, until each of you has the chance to sit in the Judas seat." Slowly, moving from delegate to delegate, he stared each of them in the eye. The delegate resisted the urge to look away, to swallow hard, when it was his time.

Finished, Matthews stood straight, and backed a half step away from the table. "And for one of you, it will fit like a glove." Fear began deep in the pit of the delegate's stomach and climbed toward his throat.

Matthews stood silent a moment, as no one moved in the chamber. "The proceedings are on recess for the moment." He turned away from the table. "We will reconvene in five days, precisely at nine a.m. Korean time." He faced them again. "Don't be late." A buzz went around the room. "You are dismissed."

Chapter 54

"Good night, Paul." Terra bent down to kiss Paul's cheek as he sat in his chair on the patio. She leaned the other way to kiss Carrie. "Good night, Carrie."

"Good night, Terra," they spoke in unison. She smiled. They did that often, saying the same thing at the same time. She wondered if she and Richard would ever have the chance to develop that harmony. She sighed. A surreal peace had enveloped her for the past several days, keeping her fears at bay like a fire keeps a wild predator out of the circle of its light. Perhaps it was because she had begun the habit of praying every morning before she arose and every night as she drifted to sleep.

When the snow slowed in Korea, the flights resumed and troops began the ground search again, but no trace of Richard could be found. The security people looked grim, and Terra could tell by the tightness around their eyes that Paul and Carrie suffered from the lack of news. But for some reason, Terra found reason to hope. And beyond hope, she felt an anticipation. Maybe it was no more than her raging hormones, but she didn't want the feeling to evaporate.

The phone rang. "I'll get it," Terra announced. After all, she was standing and closest to the house.

"Let me." Paul leaped to his feet and beat her to the door, belying his age. She hung back, knowing he wanted to be the one to intercept news, to try to cushion the blow if it was bad. Carrie stood and put her arms around Terra. Neither spoke; they simply moved into the kitchen to watch as Paul picked up the receiver.

"Oh, God!" His knees buckled, and Carrie trembled. He thrust the phone toward Terra.

Swallowing hard, staring at Paul as he took Carrie in his arms, she put the receiver to her ear. "Yes?"

"Terra." She collapsed against the wall, as the voice she feared she would never hear again reached through the line to surround her.

"Oh, Richard," she cried, sinking into a chair near the phone. The tears began. "Are you all right?"

"I'm a filthy dirty sight, but I'm safe back at the retreat." She shook as relief flooded her. "I love you, Terra." She heard him take a deep breath. "I was afraid I'd never get to say that to you again."

She forced words from her throat. "I was afraid I'd never hear you say it again. And I love you much more than anyone could ever love someone."

"No, I love you more." He laughed. "But we can wrestle to see who wins tomorrow, because I'll be landing in Nassau about ten tomorrow morning."

Her stomach flipped. "The negotiations are over?"

"No, but I called a five-day recess." She heard the joviality leave his voice. "I have to come back and finish this, Terra, but I also had to see you again, to try to make up to you what I've put you through."

"Richard, you didn't do a thing. It was those monsters who took you."

"Nevertheless, it was me who agreed to do this, who put myself in harm's way." He sounded like he was chastising himself. "I never wanted you to have to

246

worry like this." Silence fell. "I love you, Terra, and I'm coming home to you. It will only be for a little while this time, but when this crisis is over, I swear I'll never leave you like this again."

She cradled the receiver as if she could touch his face through it. "It's okay, Richard. Now that you're safe, everything will be fine."

He didn't respond right away. "Well, there is one thing you can do for me."

"What, love?" She would do anything for him.

"They took my wedding ring. No one's found a trace of it yet."

This was a simple task she could handle. "I'll call the jeweler and order another one tomorrow."

"Thank you, Terra. I didn't want to be without it." He fell silent. "I'm going to take a shower now, Terra. I can't stand the smell anymore." His voice grew gentle. "And you need to get some sleep."

She laughed. "As if I could sleep now that the world is revolving again." She ran her fingers over the mouthpiece. "I love you, Richard."

She looked up from the phone to see Paul sitting at the table with his head in his hands. Carrie leaned over him, encircling him with her arms. She went to them, hugging them both. "He's alive!"

Carrie wrapped her arm around Terra's. Tears ran down Carrie's face, and Paul's shoulders shook as he sobbed. He looked up at Terra. "Terra, I was afraid we would lose him." His voice broke, and he dropped his head again. They all cried tears of joy and relief. Finally, the flood stopped.

Carrie looked first at Paul, then at Terra. She sighed, her breathing still ragged. "And now," she said, grasping both their hands. "We give thanks." They bowed their heads.

Chapter 55

"What can I do for you, sir?" Richard's new valet, Lieutenant Ryman, stood at attention beside the desk where Richard hung up the phone. Although he had to have heard the exchange between Richard and Terra, his face showed no trace of emotion.

Richard glanced wearily at the young man. "Could you start the shower for me while I brush my teeth?"

"Yes, sir." Ryman bounded into the bathroom. Richard struggled to his feet, finally aware of how much his ordeal had taken from him. He looked forward now to clean teeth and a clean body, to rest in a soft bed on freshly-laundered sheets in a warm, dry room, things he had grown to take for granted. Never again, he vowed. He would never forget how primal existence could be. He filled his toothbrush with paste and brushed for several minutes, while steam filled the room. Ryman laid out several thick towels. "I'll be right outside if you need anything, sir." Saluting, he backed out of the room and closed the door.

Richard wiped the steam from the mirror with his hand. He stared at the ghastly reflection he saw facing him, before the steam reclaimed the mirror. No matter, he would forever remember that sight. Bloodshot, tired eyes; haggard face; shaggy, matted hair; scruffy, filthy beard. He looked at his body as he stripped off the clothes he had worn for so long. He had lost weight, much of it muscle mass, and his skin sagged. He stepped into the shower, and simply stood under the pulsing hot water for several minutes.

He emerged from the bathroom a half hour later, clean and wrapped in a soft, warm robe. Ryman jumped up from the chair he'd been sitting in. "Sir, would you like me to shave you, sir?" He stopped. "I mean, I know you hurt your hands and all, sir."

Richard sank into the chair by the desk. "No, Ryman." He ran his hand over the beard, now clean. "I almost shaved it off, and then I decided to keep it, as a constant reminder to the delegates of what I went through for them, of what someone among them perpetrated."

"Good thinking, sir." The hint of a smile tugged at Ryman's mouth.

"Ryman?"

"Yes, sir?"

Richard hated to ask the question; he was certain he knew the answer. "Jameson?"

Ryman hesitated. "Military funeral with full honors at Arlington already, sir."

Richard's shoulders sagged. "I was afraid of that." He looked Ryman in the eye. "And yet you followed orders to put yourself in the same position."

Ryman did not flinch. "I consider it an honor, sir." He went on. "We know what you are here to do. It's not an easy task, nor one most men would take on, but you have sacrificed to do it, and we are willing to do the same to help you any way we can. Sir."

Humbled, Richard took the conversation a different direction. "Can you get the address for Jameson's family?"

The question appeared to take Ryman by surprise. "I will find it, sir."

"Good." Richard looked in the desk drawer. "Then can you get me some stationery, preferably identifiable as American, and a pen?"

"Certainly, sir." He spun to leave the room. "Will official U.S. Marine Corps stationery do, sir?"

"That it will, Ryman. It will be perfect."

Ryman brought a notepad from his own gear with his own pen. He stood alongside as Richard gripped the pen and tried to write. The fingers wouldn't cooperate at first, and he crumpled the first sheet of paper. He massaged his fingers before he tried again.

"Would you like to dictate while I write it for you, sir?" Ryman offered.

Richard shook his head. "This has to be from my own hand, Ryman." He picked up the pen and began again, aware that Ryman was reading over his shoulder.

Dear Mr. and Mrs. Jameson,

It is with deep sorrow that I write this letter. Your son was a fine young man, and I was proud that he was serving with me on this mission in which we are engaged. He gave his life trying to protect me and the mission. With humility I promise you that I will never forget his sacrifice as we endeavor to complete this mission for the good of all humanity. You can rest assured his death was not in vain.

With deepest sympathy, Richard Matthews.

He looked at Ryman as he finished. "Do you think it will do, son?"

The young man blinked. "It's—it's just fine, sir."

"Now, what about the North Korean security officers?"

Ryman looked confused. "Sir?"

"I saw one of them go down for sure, the other one was under fire, and I'm sure there were more responding." He paused. "What was the outcome?"

"One DPRK officer dead, two wounded. One of the wounded is already back on duty, the other one is in the military hospital at Wonson. Doubtful he will walk again."

Richard bowed his head. He had been at that same hospital this afternoon, when Korean doctors x-rayed his face and hands and told him that he had healed enough that any improvements in form or function would require extensive surgery. He declined; there was no time, or need, for that now. "Then ask if I can speak with the officer back on duty at the first opportunity, if not before I leave for Nassau, then when I get back."

He pulled the pad toward him again. "Get clearance for us to make a stop at the hospital before the plane leaves tomorrow." He picked up the pen again. "And get me the name and address for the family of the officer killed."

"Yes, sir." Ryman saluted and left the room.

He began the same letter again, this time in Korean.

Chapter 56

Terra paced the terminal as the U.S. Air Force jet circled Nassau International Airport. She slept little last night, in fact spent an hour just sitting with Paul and Carrie, in silence, content to share good news for a change. Paul's collapse on learning of Richard's safety surprised her, as Paul was a rock for her in the weeks since Richard's kidnapping. To know that he was as fearful as she had been all along made her appreciate even more all he had done to help her cope. All night she grappled with the same questions roiling in her mind now: how to tell Richard of their baby, how he had changed from his ordeal, how much longer the negotiations would drag on. Behind her, Paul and Carrie held hands and waited. The U.S. security staff held the media at bay outside the waiting area.

She shielded her eyes with her hand to watch the jet as it touched down at the far end of the landing strip. She stood on tiptoe as it rolled closer to the terminal, as if she could somehow reach the door faster that way. The instant the uniformed airport staffer moved aside and unlocked the velvet rope between her and the door to the tarmac, she was running toward the plane, the U.S. security man assigned to her in hot pursuit.

The disembarking stairway hadn't quite touched the plane when the door opened. The first person out the door, an airman in dress blues, secured the door.

Terra reached the bottom of the stairs as Richard stepped through the doorway. He bounded down the steps two and three at a time, while she flew up them toward him. Richard caught her mid-stride. He lifted her against him, his arms around her so tight she feared he would crush her. Her hands caressed his face as she kissed him like he was the oxygen she had been deprived of for too long.

"Other people might like to get off the plane, son." Standing at the foot of the stairway, Paul had to shout to be heard over the idling aircraft.

Richard lifted his face from Terra's lips. He smiled at his father. "I guess I could move on down the stairs, Dad." He kissed Terra one more time, before he slipped his arm around her waist and they reached the tarmac. The only other people down the stairs were the security officers assigned to Richard.

Richard let go of Terra long enough to fold his parents in a hug. "I'm sorry for what I put you through," he said softly, in a voice that choked.

Carrie placed her hand on his shoulder. "You're safe now, that's all that matters."

Paul started to shake Richard's hand, and then, tears in his eyes, he hugged him again.

Richard put one arm around his mother and pulled Terra forward to encircle her as well. "It's amazingly good to be here with you." He looked down at Terra and kissed her again. She leaned against him, enthralled by the solid feel of him beside her where it felt like he belonged.

He kissed her again after they settled in the back seat of the Jag. She ran her fingers over his left cheek. "The beard is an interesting look."

He sighed, nuzzling her chin with it. "I hope you don't mind." He leaned back, as if studying her reaction.

She giggled. "It's a new experience."

He smiled with his mouth, but she saw something different in his eyes. "I thought it might be a good reminder to the delegates."

She squeezed his hand and saw a grimace pass over his face. Looking down, she saw how bent and swollen it was. She made her touch on his hand feather light and looked up at him, wide-eyed. "Richard, what happened to your hands?" She felt, rather than saw, Carrie turn in her seat and Paul look at Richard in the mirror.

He took his battered hand and caressed her cheek. "Just part of what happened while I was gone." He glanced toward his parents. "Nothing serious; I'll heal. Medics already checked me out."

She studied him closely. Under the beard his face looked different, aside from the fact that he was much thinner. "What else happened to you?"

He shrugged, as if it was of no consequence, but his eyes still held the serious expression. "My right cheekbone is broken, some fingers dislocated. This late after the injuries, there's nothing much can be done, unless I want extensive surgery. Otherwise, I just lost weight."

She stared at him, wondering how much to push, and how much to wait for him to tell her. It had taken a long time and a lot of trust for him to tell her the story of Elaine, but that was before they were married, before they were even lovers. She swallowed hard; as much as she loved him, there was much yet she didn't know about him, about how he thought. She glanced toward

Paul and Carrie. Even though they acted like they had relaxed, she could tell that they, too, burned with questions. Paul wheeled into the driveway, the security car behind them. Though a TV news van approached the driveway, security moved them along.

Terra waited for Richard to get out of the car before she scrambled after him. He moved stiffly, wearily. She longed to take him somewhere she could hold him, nurture him, make him forget about what had happened on the other side of the world. He took her hand and pulled her close to him. "How about helping me put away my luggage?" he whispered as he kissed his way from her mouth to her ear.

She grinned. "That might take a while." When she looked into his eyes, she saw the old Richard. Suddenly, she wanted to get reacquainted with that man.

The four of them walked in silence to the house, followed by the two security men. Inside the house, Richard started up the stairs, holding Terra's hand. "We're just going to put my things in our room."

Paul paused on his way to the kitchen. "We won't wait lunch on you," he chuckled.

"Paul!" Carrie slapped his arm, then looked at Terra and smiled. Terra felt her cheeks redden. "Lunch will be in the fridge when you're ready for it."

"Son." Paul hung back another second. "It's good to have you back, safe."

Terra watched father and son exchange a look. "It's good to be back, Dad." He glanced at Terra. "We'll be down in a bit."

Terra heard Paul's laugh as he walked into the kitchen.

Richard gathered her against him. "Now why do you suppose they think it will take us so long to put away a few shirts?"

She pulled his tee shirt loose from his jeans and ran her fingers over his ribs. "I'm sure I don't know." He dropped the bag on the steps. With the clumsiness of his injured hands, he had to leave the buttons and zippers to her, and she obliged, backing a step toward their room for each fastener.

****

"Wow!" Terra gasped, as they settled, exhausted, among the pillows.

"I'll add that to my resume," Richard mumbled, his face buried against her shoulder.

She felt him shift, getting comfortable. His body alongside her was heavy, totally relaxed. She studied it, looking for new scars, some indication besides the cheek and hands of what he had suffered at the hands of his captors. She decided to wait for the story. Her need to know could be subordinated to her need to help him heal. She took a deep breath, sensing that now would be a good time to tell him about the baby. She stroked his soft beard. "Richard," she whispered.

His only response was deep, slow breathing.

"Well, that's a first," she muttered. She stretched herself out next to him. "Just don't let it become a habit." In a few seconds, she drifted off to sleep.

****

Three hours later, Terra awoke alone. For a moment, before she was fully conscious, she feared she had dreamed Richard's homecoming, that he was still lost without a trace. Then she heard the shower running. She slipped from the bed and into the bathroom. He must have heard the door close, because his hand reached out to her from behind the shower curtain. Without a word, she stepped into the hot spray with him. He pulled her close, his hands and his mouth hungry, tasting every inch of her, as she responded in kind. They melted together under the waterfall. He might have lost weight, she thought, but he was even stronger than ever. Finally, as the water started to turn cool, they soaped each other's bodies. Neither of them had yet spoken.

"Richard," she began as his lathered hands ran over her stomach. His response silenced her.

When at last they stepped from the shower, she clenched her teeth. She had to tell him, she thought as he dried her shoulders. "Richard," she started.

"I'm starving," he announced. He pulled the towel from her and ran into the bedroom. "Race you to the kitchen."

Laughing despite her frustration, she grabbed another towel to finish drying. By the time she entered the bedroom a few seconds later, he was backing out the door zipping his jeans, with a tee shirt in his hand. "Last one to lunch does the dishes."

She threw her towel at him and sat down to dress. Maybe tonight, she thought.

****

Standing at the island, Carrie shot Terra a look as she walked into the kitchen. Richard was already seated at the breakfast nook with Paul, wolfing down a huge sandwich and salad. Carrie handed her a glass of milk, her eyebrows asking a question. Terra shrugged and shook her head. Pursing her lips, Carrie made a sandwich for Terra.

Terra carried her plate to the table. Richard shot her the conspiratorial grin that always melted her. She stared at him, lost in the reality of sharing the same room with him again. Carrie joined them, bringing a pot of tea to the table.

"Well, son," Paul picked up his teacup. "What can you tell us about what happened to you?"

Richard set down his sandwich, chewing slowly, and wiping his mouth with his napkin before he spoke. "There's really not a lot to tell, Dad."

Terra paid close attention to what he said by his actions. Something had happened, something that changed him somehow.

"For starters," Paul began. "How did they get you?"

Richard looked down at the table. "Snipers shot my bodyguard while we were running on the beach." He pushed his plate away, the remains of his sandwich apparently forgotten. "Then they hit me with a dart of some sort. Next thing I knew, I woke up in a hut in the mountains." He looked down at his hands, massaging them. "After I got back, our people told me they got me away with an inflatable boat, then switched me to a vehicle."

He looked out the window, and Terra thought how different the balmy Bahamian fall was from the snowy mountains he had escaped. "I don't remember anything until I woke up in that hut. They kept me there about a week or so, then when the second guard was gone, I knocked the other one out and got away." He picked up his teacup and sipped slowly. "Then I hiked through the mountains, till I came to a cabin, where they sheltered and fed me, gave me food for the rest of the trip." He looked at his father. "Now, that is classified. Officially, I stole the food from them." He set down the cup, his fingers tracing the rim of it.

"When I get back, I need to get Chung Hee to agree to food aid for the interior region, but I'll have to tie it to something else, to keep from bringing suspicion on them." He sipped again. "Anyway, I got to the conference, let them know I was back and in charge and called a recess." His gaze met Terra's. "I have three and a half more days with you."

The table was silent for several minutes. Finally, Carrie placed both hands on the table. "Well, then." She rose. "Let's try to put the meat back on you while you're here." She picked up a pad and pencil from the side of the refrigerator and began taking inventory.

"Is there anything I can do, son?" The look on Paul's face said that he read much between the lines of the story. Terra vowed she would ask Paul about it after Richard left.

Richard glanced at Terra before he spoke to his father. "Just take care of Terra and Mum, and yourself, for me." He picked up his cup again. "I do have some briefing documents to look over while I'm here. Evidently a lot went on behind the scenes while I was gone. I might bounce some ideas off you, if I could."

"Certainly, son." Paul smiled, though his eyes, too, looked serious. "I'm at your service."

Sensing that Richard was in a mood to work, Terra stood. "I'll give Carrie a hand and then work on some manuscripts."

Richard grasped her arm. He ran his hand down to meet hers and brought it to his lips. "I won't be long, love."

She leaned forward to kiss his cheek gently. "I'll be close by." She watched Paul and Richard walk toward the formal living room, Richard explaining some of the maneuverings of the delegates as they went.

She joined Carrie at the refrigerator. "Doesn't he trust us with the story?" she asked Carrie. Richard could be secretive, she knew, when lives were at stake. "Or does he think we wouldn't understand a complicated situation?"

Carrie glanced after them. "He trusts us. And he knows we are intelligent enough to understand any complex issue." She gripped Terra's shoulder. "But there are security issues, clearance, our own personal safety, that come into play."

"How?"

Carrie perched on the barstool. "If, for instance, we knew all of the details, we could be very valuable to anyone who wanted to control Richard. We could be kidnapped and pumped for information." She met and held Terra's gaze. "And, believe me, Terra, some of the factions in this world can make people talk, no matter what." She looked down a minute, and Terra wondered what Carrie had seen during the forty plus years she had served at Paul's side. "We deduce a lot from what isn't said, and what we read in the news, but the less specific information we have, the better it is for us and for them." She indicated Richard and Paul with a nod.

Terra sighed. "Well, that's a relief, I guess." She stared toward the study. "I was afraid he didn't trust me."

"I'm sure he trusts you, dear, but he also loves you so very much, he doesn't want to put you in jeopardy if there is any way he can help it." Carrie set down her grocery list. "You didn't tell him?"

Terra shook her head. "First, he fell asleep as I was starting to tell him, and then, every time I tried, he changed the subject." She looked down. "It's almost like he senses there is something big we need to discuss, but he's afraid of what it is."

Carrie gripped her hands. "Give him a little time to adjust, Terra. From what Paul said about the terrain and the length of time he was gone, he must have been through hell. I mean, look at his face and hands. Those are just the injuries we can see." She smiled. "Experiences like that change a person, make them question things they had assumed."

Terra's heart fell to her toes. "Do you think he's wondering if he should have married me?"

"Oh, no, of course not, dear." Carrie hugged her. "But he's probably worried that you may feel he misrepresented himself, that this type of ordeal wasn't on the table when you married."

Terra raised her chin. She was not a quitter, a fair-weather lover. Richard should know that after she stood by him through the Adler nightmare. "I promised to love for better or worse, no matter what."

Carrie touched her cheek. "He'll come to see that soon enough. Just love him and give him time." She looked off in the distance. "Maybe it would be better to wait a day or two for the news. He's still readjusting to normal life, just like a released prisoner of war would be. It shouldn't take as long as some of the POWs, because he wasn't captive for as long, but it is a process, just like grieving."

"You could be right." Terra looked at what Carrie

had written on the list. "Well, what are we going to feed him?"

Chapter 57

"What you're saying is that someone at the table was responsible for kidnapping you?" Paul stood, rubbing the back of his neck. "Do you have any idea who?"

Richard hoped his father's instincts, honed through years of negotiations, could help him figure it out. "No." He looked down again at the materials Delmonico prepared before they left Korea. The resourcefulness of his staff of three amazed him. Delmonico and Harris, both separately and together, had pumped Adler six ways to Sunday. Though they got no hard information, they had a hunch. And they suggested a plan. Not a plan he liked. He hoped his father could help him find another alternative.

Paul came back to the chair. He sat, elbows on his knees, chin propped on his hands. "Let's analyze this." He straightened. "Who loses if North Korea gives up its nuclear weapons capabilities?"

"Everybody wins, except North Korea. They lose the only real bargaining chip they have. No one would be afraid of them anymore, no one would care, they would have no power." He took a deep breath. "They would have no choice but to play nice, to open up, join the world."

"So, who loses if they open up?"

"That's what angle we've been looking at. There's

the heroin connection. They would lose a safe haven for supply. We've narrowed it down to North Korea being a distribution and storage hub. There's a lot of money up for grabs there, and you know as well as I do that money buys power."

"Do they control anyone at the table?"

Now Richard stood and stretched. "That's what we can't seem to find out."

"Do you think Chung Hee is really in charge of the country?"

"I doubt it." Richard had tumbled this question over in his mind many times since the first call from the State Department. "I think he's sincere in wanting to help, but I can't imagine the men who have been the power behind the throne all these years actually letting go, especially to a non-native, non-Communist, who's turned his back on one country already. I don't see how they can trust him, but they are certainly willing to use him."

"Who else would lose?"

Richard shrugged. "Nothing but speculation." He wandered over to look out the window. From there, he could view the garden, where Terra sat at the table, head bent over a manuscript. Leaving her was the hardest part of this assignment, even harder than the physical suffering he underwent to get back to the table. The only thing worse than leaving her was the knowledge of what Jameson and the North Korean soldiers had sacrificed, and those were sacrifices the men would have made no matter who was leading the negotiations.

But Terra had not been aware of what might be asked of her when she signed on to be his wife. When they married, he had no intention of rejoining the diplomatic corps. Even though he planned to make it clear to the President and Secretary he was through when the negotiations were over, he knew that, should a similar situation arise again, he could not refuse.

There was something she wanted to talk to him about, something she found difficult to broach. He suspected she had reservations about what she had gotten into, about the vast differences in age and background that they thought love and shared experiences would overcome. Right now, he had enough to face without dealing with that subject. When the negotiations were over, they would have to confront realities. Maybe they had rushed to marry too soon.

But he remembered how utterly lost he felt when he thought he watched her die. Not even when he faced his own death in the snow in Korea had he felt his life so close to over. She was truly the one who made his life worth living, the one worth dying for. There was work to do on their relationship, and it could not proceed while the crisis in Korea loomed over the entire world. He had to find a resolution and soon.

"If North Korea even opens up, never mind it becoming a democracy, South Korea would be faced with the very real possibility of reunification. That threatens their autonomy. Especially since the North Korean military machine is one of the mightiest in the world." Richard sighed. "Japan, China, and South Korea face the likelihood of thousands of political refugees flooding in and overloading their social systems." He paced. "Russia really wouldn't be affected much." He stopped to stare out the window again. "And if North Korea actually gives up its nuclear weapons, we would have to make good on our promises to help them."

Paul joined him at the window. They both stood in silence for a few seconds. "Let's take a different approach, son."

Richard tore his gaze away from Terra. "What do you mean?"

"Who wins if the North opens, if the nuclear program stops, if a lasting peace develops?"

"Everybody wins." Richard stared at his father.

"But some win more than others." Victory never went equally to all winners.

"And if the stalemate continues?" Paul continued.

"Japan might be forced to develop nuclear weapons in self defense, whereas right now, they are trying to build a reputation for being one of the peacekeepers. Russia might have to position their nukes closer to the peninsula. China would have to choose between backing North Korea and joining the rest of the free world." He rolled his shoulders, trying to release the tension that would not go away. "We would have a build up to Armageddon."

"What can you offer Chung Hee to get him to dunk the nukes?"

"That's just it, I don't have much to offer. They want to bargain with the U.S. alone, but we won't agree to that. We not only want them to get rid of the weapons, we want them to improve their human rights record before we will help. That's a lot to ask of a country still emerging from the 1950s. We need to give them a way out. In the words of Sun Tzu, 'To a surrounded enemy you must leave a way to escape.' " A plan began to form. His father's wisdom helped him discover the way, just as it had when he was young and learning to navigate the world. Paul never told him what to do, but asked the questions that helped him find his own answers. "And if the only way to escape is the one we choose, everyone just might win." He slung his arm over his father's shoulder. "Thanks, Dad."

Paul gripped his arm. "Son, I'm just glad all those years I spent making mistakes are helping you now." They stood together in silence for several minutes. Finally, Paul spoke quietly. "Do you want to tell me what happened to your hands and face?"

Richard shot a glance at his father and decided the old man could probably handle the story. His mum and Terra probably could, too, he just wasn't ready to watch their faces as they heard it. "The guys who were holding me didn't like Americans."

"Americans in general or you in particular?" Paul wasn't watching Richard's face, just staring out the window and letting the story unfold.

"I think it was Americans in general." He sighed. "But me in particular whenever I tried to talk to them." Richard took his arm from his father's shoulders and began to massage his fingers. He caught Paul's glance at his hands. "Rifle butt for talking." He saw the tightening around Paul's mouth.

"And the face?"

"Kicked for saying thank you for a drink of water." He sighed. "All on the first time I woke up in the hut."

"Damn, son." Paul took a deep breath. "You'd better do everything you can to get it wrapped up over there."

Richard looked out the window toward Terra. "No one wants that more than I do, Dad."

Chapter 58

Terra looked up from the manuscript to Richard halfway across the lawn walking toward her. Barefoot, wearing worn jeans and a tee shirt, he looked relaxed, like he'd just played chess with his father instead of asking advice to keep the world from exploding. Her heart pounded in her chest at the thought that this remarkable man who held the fate of the world in his hands wanted her in his life, that because of that, they had created a new life to nurture together. She closed the manuscript as he plopped into the chair beside her. "Did you solve the problems of the world, dear?" she asked.

He took her cheek in his hand and drew her close to kiss her tenderly. "Almost, love." His fingers caressed her neck.

She covered his hand with hers. Then she kissed his palm. She stroked the swollen knuckles and kissed his hand again. "Why don't I get some lotion and massage your hands?" She looked up to see him staring at her with a look of such tenderness that she swallowed hard.

He leaned closer, resting his head on her shoulder. "I was thinking about a stroll on the beach."

"The security monitors can see the beach." Her face warmed. "The whole beach." She saw that sparkle in his eyes that she feared lost forever.

"Is that a problem, love?" he asked, grinning.

"Not for me. Or probably for you." She leaned her forehead against his. "But I'd hate to embarrass the security people." She stroked his chin. "I mean, you'll be gone from here again in a few days, but I have to face them in the hall."

He sighed. "Oh, well, if you'd be embarrassed to be seen walking on the beach—"

"We wouldn't just walk, and you know it," she laughed. "But a massage would help your hands." She stood up. "Wait right here. I'll be back in a flash." She jogged into the kitchen where Carrie kept a tube of lotion for after dishes and gardening. Carrie and Janie were gone to the market. She picked up a towel and popped the lotion into the microwave for one minute. *Maybe I can tell him while he's relaxed from the massage.*

She started toward him. He was leaning back in the chair, his legs stretched far out in front of him, his fingers laced behind his head, eyes closed. In the sunlight, she could see the new lines of care etched on his face, the shadows that spoke of his weariness. She leaned over to kiss his forehead.

He held out his hands for her. "Minister to me, my angel."

She laid the towel across her lap and took his right hand in hers. It was the most deformed, joints swollen so the fingers moved just out of alignment. She smoothed on the warm lotion and felt him relax beneath her fingers. Gently she worked the lotion in, stretching the fingers, massaging the joints. Then, resting the right hand in her lap, she started working on the left.

"Where did you learn to do this?" His eyes were

still closed.

"I served as trainer on my softball team as well as playing," she told him. "Our whole team played hard."

"Pedal to the metal, just like you do?"

"Yup." She worked her way up his arms to his elbows. "Plus, your mom and I have been getting massages to deal with the stress."

"Not Dad?" He grinned, although he kept his eyes shut.

"Nope, not your dad." She giggled. "I heard the story." Now might be a good time, she thought, let him relax just a little more, and then I'll tell him he's going to be a father himself in less than eight months.

"Mr. Matthews!" One of the security men intruded on their little spa. "I hate to interrupt, but—" He stopped about six feet from them. "There's been a mining accident in Russia, over a hundred men trapped." Richard sat up straight. "And Patmanov's grandson is one of them."

"Is Patmanov pulling out of negotiations?"

"We think so, sir. He went home for the recess, is at the mine now." The man hesitated. "And the Secretary thinks it might look good for the solidarity of the nations if you visited the site, lending him your support."

Richard dropped his head to his hands. He sighed. "And I suppose they want me to get going right away?"

Terra could see the tension grip his shoulders again. Not this soon. He hadn't even had twenty-four hours! He'd only walked out of three weeks of limbo a little more than a day ago. He needed rest and recharge before he took on the future of the world again. "But he just got here!" she addressed the security man directly.

He looked at her, as if he understood that she was right, but knew that his chain of command was direct from the President. He might later regret fearing the President more than an enraged wife.

Richard reached for her hand without looking at her. "It's okay, Terra." He stood facing the security man. "I'll talk to the Secretary, get briefed on the situation." He glanced back at Terra. "Then I'll decide what I have to do." He held her for a moment. "I won't go unless there's no choice," he whispered as he kissed her cheek.

She stood, silent and rebellious, as he walked into the house without looking back at her. They couldn't expect him to just throw himself back into the fight like that. Right now, she'd like to talk to the President herself; she'd tell him a thing or two! With a deep breath, she pushed down her anger. This decision was Richard's to make, his responsibility, based on his judgment of what was best for the world at large, not on his own health or Terra's wishes. She walked into the kitchen to replace the lotion and towel.

She stood over the sink, gripping the edge of the counter so tight she wasn't sure if her fingers or the tile would give way first. Taking another deep breath, she began to pray. "Lord, I don't want him to go yet. In fact, I don't want him to go at all." She took a deeper breath and her grip on the tile relaxed. "But You know what he has to do, as does he." She swallowed hard. "If he has to go, I'll trust that You'll get him home safe this time like You did the last time." And, Lord, she thought, if it's best not to tell him about the baby right now, give me some sign. If I need to tell him, give me an opening that I can't miss.

She left the kitchen looking for Richard just as he walked out of the study toward her. She knew her expression questioned him. He took her arm and led her toward the kitchen. "Well," she gulped. "Are you going?"

He pulled her gently against him. He stared into her eyes before he answered. "I have to go." He cradled her face against his chest as her tears started. His arms wrapped around her felt good; it was where he belonged. "There have been some other developments that just came to light." He rested his chin on her head. "Delmonico and Harris are already boarding a plane headed this way, due in—" He glanced at his watch. "About an hour and a half." With his hand under her chin, he tipped her face up to look at him. "They only had about three hours with their families," he said softly.

She stared at him through her tears. "It almost makes me regret the three hours we wasted sleeping."

He hugged her again. "It wasn't a waste, Terra." His hands caressed her back. "Falling asleep next to you and waking up the same place is what I've been missing the most."

She pulled her head back to stare at his face. "Really?"

He smiled. "Well, almost the most."

She tried to laugh, and that started the tears again. "So, what do you miss the most of all?"

He whispered his answer in her ear, and she laughed and cried at the same time. She clung to him and he to her in silence for several minutes, just sharing the same space, breathing the same air. Finally, she pulled away. "We need to call your mom back from the market," she said, brushing away her tears and sniffling. "And find your dad." She unfolded her cell phone.

"Dad was in the study when we made the decision." He took the phone from her. "He's already called her."

She tried to master her fear, show him how strong she could be. "I'm going to miss you," she said very softly, standing straight before him. "But we'll be fine. We'll take care of each other."

The way he looked at her said that he wanted to fold her in his arms again, but that he respected her strength. "I know you will." He smiled. "You are the toughest, most strong-willed woman I have ever met." He reached out to caress her cheek. "But you also have a soft side that I like very much."

She went into his arms again, strength gone for the moment. Should she tell him now, when they felt so very close? She looked up at him. "Richard—"

"Oh, Richard!" Carrie flew through the kitchen door. Richard let go of Terra to hold his mother. Lord, if that's not a sign, Terra thought through clenched teeth, then You sure have a funny way of testing me.

Chapter 59

Twelve hours later, after a transfer from the U.S. Air Force to a commercial jet for a Berlin to Moscow flight, then a shuttle from the Russian Air Force, Richard, Delmonico, and Harris stood in a tangled knot of people grouped around a command post tent on the rim of what looked like a giant meteor impact crater in Mirny, Sakha Republic, former Soviet Union. The four-thousand-foot-wide, two-thousand-foot-deep hole was "Mir," the world's largest diamond mine, operated by private-federal-state conglomerate Almazy-Rossii-Sakha—ALROSA. The wind swept across the flat terrain and circled around them like a hungry wolf hoping to pick off a straggler. They huddled together as much for warmth as for information. Despite the thick coat, hat, gloves, and scarf, Richard shivered, his hands aching.

"Damn, it's cold." Harris's teeth chattered.

"Ordinarily one of the coldest spots on earth," Delmonico offered through blue lips.

"Let's talk," he said, walking away from the group.

Looking back as if they missed the communal warmth already, they followed him. "What's up, boss?" Delmonico asked.

"Have you seen Patmanov?"

Delmonico shook his head. "I think he's down near the mouth of the mine, trying to get the latest updates on the rescue efforts."

"Canadian and South African teams are on their way, but these Russians have as many mining experts as anybody." Harris was shivering in earnest now.

"We'll get back to shelter quickly," Richard promised. On the U.S. plane, they had received a briefing on the situation. Evidently, a helicopter had crashed within the crater, trapping the miners inside the underground mine at the bottom of the pit. "Can you get me clearance to get down to the mine entrance?"

Harris shook his head. "Tried already. Safety reasons, they said, but the guns they carried said security had something to do with it, too."

"Patmanov is a partial shareholder in ALROSA. He worked for them for years, before he went political. That's why his grandson is with them, too, I suppose," Delmonico added.

Richard glanced at the official now addressing the media. "Then see if you can get a message to him that I'm here. The Secretary indicated that Patmanov wanted to talk to me specifically." He shivered again. "Now let's get back to where somebody else can break this infernal wind." His staff grunted assent as they bent into the wind to rejoin the group.

A reporter huddled near the edge of the bank of cameras and microphones tapped his cameraman on the back as Richard and his men approached. "Mr. Matthews," the reporter addressed him. "Would you care to give us a statement as to why you are here?" Though he spoke as if considering every word, his English was flawless.

Richard stepped toward the man. With a deep breath, he stifled his shivering. "I'm here simply to express my concern and the concern of the American people for your countrymen trapped in the mine." The reporter nodded and left the microphone in Richard's face. The camera kept rolling, and a couple of other cameras and microphones pointed his way. "And I'm here to offer my support to Alexei Patmanov, my colleague in the negotiations in North Korea."

"How are negotiations proceeding since your return to the table?"

"We expect to make substantial progress when we resume after this short recess." If they didn't make progress, he would send them all home and convene a new delegation.

"And is there any lead on who it was that kidnapped you?"

"That is still under investigation." An investigation that could not seem to find any information, he declined to add. He had said enough; he needed to wrap up the interview. Only seconds of it would make it on air, anyway. "Right now, I just want my friend Alexei to know that I am praying for his grandson and all the others in the mine." He nodded toward the reporter.

"Thank you for the interview, Mr. Matthews." The reporter faced his cameraman and began giving his wrap up. Other reporters surged forward, clamoring for air time.

"I've given my statement," Richard said. "If anything changes, we can do another interview."

The ALROSA official began to speak again, updates on the progress, but Richard knew so little Russian, he could only guess at the contents of the speech. He stepped close to Harris and Delmonico. "Well, maybe that interview will get my message to

Patmanov." He looked back toward the crowd of media. "It would be interesting to see what spin that gets on the Russian news tonight."

"Sounds like they almost have the fire out," Delmonico said. He had been trained as a Russian linguist during his Army days.

"That's good." Richard closed his eyes for a second. He had slept on the long commercial flight from Berlin to Moscow, and briefly on the Air Force flight from Nassau to Berlin, but overall, sleep had been scarce in the past forty-eight hours. He almost longed for the bed in Songdowan.

His farewell to his family, too, replayed in his mind whenever he let it wander. Terra and his mother crying, tears in his father's eyes, even the security people looking glum.

"Take care of them for me," he whispered in his father's ear as he hugged him.

"I will," Paul promised. "I'll take care of them all." And then he kissed Terra one last time and trudged up the ramp onto the plane. And now he was freezing his ass, and it seemed many other body parts as well, for what seemed to be no reason. Yet somehow, in his gut, he knew that his presence here was necessary.

"Richard." Alexei Patmanov spoke quietly from behind him.

He shook the delegate's hand. "Alexei, I'm sorry for the tragedy here. What happened?"

"A terrible accident," he said, loud enough that the media could hear him. He moved closer to Richard, leaning forward to hug him. "We need to talk," he murmured. He let go of Richard. "Would you like to accompany me to the Church of the Holy Trinity in town?"

"I would be happy to accompany you there." Richard covered his surprise. The old Russian had been distant, cordial but not particularly cooperative, during the negotiations.

"Do you think that's wise, boss?" Delmonico stepped toward Patmanov.

Patmanov nodded. "I understand your security concerns, Mr. Delmonico." He indicated a roomy SUV, with two large men standing beside it. Behind it sat an identical vehicle with identical men. "Richard may ride with me in my vehicle, with my security staff, and you can follow in the second vehicle, or he may ride with you in the second and meet us at the church." He stood waiting.

Richard glanced at Delmonico. He knew Ray was fearful of another kidnapping, yet he felt that Patmanov would not have offered him the choice of vehicles if it was a setup. "I'll ride with you, Alexei."

Richard and Patmanov settled themselves in the back seat of the SUV. "I never thought of you as a religious man, Alexei." Richard began the conversation.

Patmanov shot him a look as he unwrapped the scarf from his neck and removed his gloves. "As I've heard it said, it's better to live as if there is a God and find out there isn't, than live as if God doesn't exist and find out he does." Patmanov smiled as warmly as the wind that swirled around the mine. "A practical man always hedges his bets."

Richard removed his scarf, but not the gloves. His hands still ached. "A time comes when you have to choose one side or the other."

Patmanov smiled again. "And I pray that God will

grant me the wisdom to know when that time comes."

Richard sighed. Patmanov might want to talk, but it would be on his terms. "Any word on your grandson?"

Patmanov glanced at the driver and security man seated in the front seat. "The fire at the entrance is almost out." He looked toward Richard, and Richard saw something that could be fear in his eyes. "When the fire is out, we can send rescue crews in to see if anyone has survived."

"Have you had any communication from inside the mine?"

Patmanov looked back at the men in front. "Not much." He folded his scarf. "Some radio contact at first. Nothing since I got to the site."

"What happened?" Richard watched Patmanov as they drove along tree-lined streets. Mirny had been carved out of the Yakutian wilderness after the discovery of diamonds in the 1940s and 1950s. All of the town development had been based on that discovery. The mine was operational before any houses were built. "I heard a helicopter crashed."

Patmanov nodded, as the vehicle rolled down a broad avenue. "The wind currents from the mine make low level flights over the mine dangerous. It's a restricted, no-fly zone." He met Richard's gaze, and Richard felt a chill. Patmanov knew more than he was saying right now. Richard glanced at the two men in the front. He hoped Delmonico and Harris were careful what they said in the vehicle behind him. "Apparently the pilot lost control, or got disoriented, and strayed in." He twisted his gloves. "The crash evidently disabled the mine's mechanism for getting people and ore in and out." Patmanov looked out the window. "I was among the first people to settle here, you know."

"All I read in your bio was that this was where you lived." The dossier had not given great detail.

"I was twenty at the time and answered the call to build the great diamond city for the State." He smiled. "We lived in tents and worked in unbelievable cold to get that mine up and running, to get the processing facilities built. Then we finally built houses and hospitals." He looked at Richard, a bit of pride in his outthrust chin. "Many said it couldn't be done, a city couldn't be built on permafrost, but we did it."

"It must have taken incredible determination and discipline to endure that."

Patmanov smiled, this time with some warmth. "It did. Those of us who have been here from the early days say that it made us stronger."

The vehicle pulled to a stop before a church of clean white lines topped with three golden domes. Patmanov wrapped his scarf around his neck again and pulled on his gloves. He looked up at the domes. "Ah, the church that ALROSA built." He glanced at Richard. "Since ALROSA is controlled by Moscow, that makes it the church built by Communists and diamonds."

Richard exited the vehicle immediately behind Patmanov, as one security man stayed with the SUV and the other followed them inside the church. The vehicle bearing Harris and Delmonico parked just behind theirs. Richard hesitated on the steps until he saw his staff following them. He glanced at the large gold cross above the doors to the church. Lord, help me now, he prayed.

Patmanov removed his scarf and gloves and hung up his coat before entering the sanctuary. Richard followed, watching carefully. Patmanov touched his fingers to the holy water, crossed himself and genuflected. Then he turned to his security man. "Wait here," he ordered. A hint of a scowl crossed the man's face.

Richard met Harris's gaze, as Delmonico was still hanging up his coat. He inclined his head in the direction of the security man. Harris nodded and took a seat in the back pew. Seconds later, after crossing himself, Delmonico joined him. Richard followed Patmanov to the altar. Patmanov kneeled, and Richard kneeled beside him close enough that their shoulders almost touched. Patmanov was silent for nearly a minute, and Richard suspected that, despite his light words in the car, he really was praying for his grandson's safety. Patmanov raised his face to the crucifix centered at the back of the two-story sanctuary. "This was no accident," he murmured.

Richard had to listen hard to hear him. "Our coming here?"

"No, the helicopter." He clasped his hands before him. A casual observer would assume he was praying fervently. "The pilot was warned three times he was in danger, in a restricted airspace. It wasn't just the wind that pulled him in. He dove."

Richard tried hard not to look startled. "Sabotage?" He took a deep breath. "Who?"

Patmanov bowed his head. "Hard to say." He shifted his position, as if to relieve his knees. "It's top secret, but the mining operations underground were not supposed to start for eight more years. Instead, they started about ten months ago, ahead of schedule, to keep the diamonds flowing so the South Africans wouldn't get a bigger share of the market."

"Industrial sabotage?"

"I don't think so." Patmanov looked up at the crucifix again. "Even though ALROSA is primarily state-controlled, some in the government are in the pocket of the Russian mafia. And it is said the diamonds are linked with heroin." He glanced at Richard.

Richard met his glance. "It was a warning?"

"Someone in the world does not want Russia involved or our peace talks to succeed."

"A warning to me as well, then?"

A smile touched the corners of Patmanov's lips. "It appears that their first warning to you went unheeded."

"Well," Richard smiled grimly. "Shall we say I'm a stubborn man?"

"I would choose the term 'determined.' " He looked at the cross again. "Much like we were when we built this city." He rose stiffly, crossed himself, and genuflected once more.

Richard stood, glanced at the crucifix, and breathed another prayer for assistance. "I shall continue to pray for your grandson's safety," he said as they walked up the center aisle toward the security men. Obedient, the man who rode with Patmanov waited until the diplomat was within a yard of him before he began speaking in rapid Russian. Richard saw Delmonico listening intently, Harris watching.

Patmanov smiled. "It seems our prayers were heard." He enfolded Richard in a bear hug. "My grandson is safe," he said, stepping back. "They are working now on a mechanism to get the workers out." He looked at the floor. "But there were ten men killed, another twenty with various degrees of injury." He met Richard's gaze. "We should continue to pray for those men and their families."

"And for all those around the world who work in harm's way," Richard said.

Patmanov nodded. "Are any of us really safe anymore?" He walked toward the narthex where his coat hung. "But my grandson was instrumental in keeping the men calm and organizing triage for the injured."

Richard placed his hand on Patmanov's shoulder. "I think he inherited some qualities from his grandfather." He slipped into his coat. "See you back at Songdowan."

Patmanov nodded, but Richard read doubt in his eyes. Somehow, he had a feeling he would never see the Russian again.

Chapter 60

Harris rocked back in the seat of the Russian Air Force plane. Though it was "heated" inside, he still wore his coat, hat, and gloves. "Why don't we ever get called to a crisis on a beach in the south of France." He shivered. "Or Maui."

Richard glanced at him. "Be careful what you ask for, John. You may get it." Knowing that whatever they said was probably listened to, perhaps even taped, they kept the conversation light, although Richard was practically bursting to share what he had learned, to get their analysis of it, to see what they might have learned from the Russian staff who might not have realized that Delmonico spoke Russian. Yet, he knew that security meant the conversation would have to wait until they got to Songdowan, and then only after an electronics sweep of the room.

Harris and Delmonico were nearly as exhausted as he was. Even though Edwards had been disappointed at staying behind, he volunteered to maintain the presence at Songdowan, because Harris and Delmonico had wives and children who missed them. He said his cat would get over it if he didn't visit.

Richard leaned the seat back and closed his eyes. Sleep would be the best use of the hours from Mirny to Songdowan. The Russian jet had been cleared to land at Wonson, although the crew was not to disembark. They would be refueled, and then expected to take off immediately. Now that Russia was no longer exclusively Communist, relations with North Korea were strained, more like distrustful neighbors than allies. Yet he was so accustomed to forcing himself to stay awake that sleep didn't come easily.

To relax his mind, he tried to avoid thinking about Patmanov's conversation, about having to question Adler again, and instead to think about his future with Terra. Their short time together just before he left had reassured him of the steadfastness of her love for him. Now, he just missed her.

To keep that feeling from overwhelming him, he tried to think of the house that awaited them in Colorado when this crisis was over. Four bedrooms and three baths on ten acres. It was far more house and land than they needed, but Terra loved the layout and the view, and convinced him that they would be happy to have the room someday. Maybe they would get a couple of horses, or a goat. He supposed they would have a dog and a cat.

He pictured himself working in the study, Labrador retriever curled up on a rug at his feet before a roaring fire in the fireplace. Then as his mind slipped toward sleep, a cat entered the study, the dog chased the cat into the fire and the whole room went pink before it disappeared into the fireplace. His body jerked, and he awoke with a start. He looked around him.

Harris, his hat pulled down over his face, breathed easily, his hands relaxed in his lap. Delmonico snored, head back, legs stretched out before him. Richard wondered at the weight they had carried while he was gone, how they would have handled the negotiations if he never returned.

He settled back in his seat again, and this time imagined himself chopping wood for the fireplace, Terra tending the flowers around the woodpile. He counted each swing of the axe. Somewhere around thirty, he dozed off again. This time, the bump of the plane landing woke him.

****

"Okay, that's what I learned from Patmanov," Richard wrapped up his summary of the conversation in the church. "What did you hear?"

"There was a little more than what he told you about his grandson," Delmonico reported. "Seems his bodyguard also told him he was needed back at the mine, something about the helicopter."

Harris shot a look at Delmonico. "We've suspected for some time that the Russian mob was trying to get a piece of ALROSA, just to give them another commodity to control." He shook his head. "But a suicide pilot doesn't sound like them."

"No, but it does sound like someone recruiting extremists to do their dirty work," Edwards spoke up. "Convince a fringe group that you want to bring down the capitalist dogs, and they'll jump at the chance. Just don't tell them you're planning to replace the dogs in charge with dogs of your own."

Harris nodded. "Yeah, this little stunt probably financed another six months of insurgency somewhere."

"Do you think it is directly tied to our negotiations here?" That was the main question at the moment, the one that concerned Richard the most.

"That's hard to say, boss." Delmonico squirmed in

his seat, as if he didn't like what he was about to say. "I think we need to pay another visit to the Pacific fleet carrier."

"I hate to admit it." Richard sighed. "But you are probably right."

Delmonico glanced at Harris. "Well, boss, while you were on your jaunt around the countryside, we cooked up a little plan."

Edwards and Harris both sat forward but remained silent. Evidently taking their silence as a go ahead, Delmonico plowed forward. "We've questioned Adler, and we feel he has told us everything that he thinks he knows." He paused.

Richard nodded. "Go ahead, Ray."

"But whoever is behind the logjam here doesn't know that he hasn't given us any useful information." He took a deep breath. "What about bringing him to the conference chamber, and just having him sit there? Use him as bait to draw out the culprit."

Richard smiled. "That would be poetic justice." Adler had used Elaine and Richard as bait in Zimbabwe, and it cost Elaine her life.

"They might try to contact him," Harris contributed.

"Or silence him," Edwards offered.

"But bringing him out of a controlled location makes him less secure." Richard rested his chin on his hands. "He's a slippery snake, and I'm afraid he'd find a way to slither away while he's here."

"We'll make it clear what will happen to him if he tries anything." The set to Delmonico's jaw said that he must remember some of the skills the Army taught him and wouldn't hesitate to use them.

"I don't know, guys." Richard stood up. "Let me think things over." He stretched. "We still have two days before the delegates are due back." His staff stood as well. "Let's take some R&R till after dinner, then we'll meet and look at the options again."

Chapter 61

"I won't go along with it." Robert Adler, handcuffed again to the chair in the Captain's conference room, folded his arms across his chest the best he could with such a handicap.

Richard gave Adler a smile without warmth. "Whether you go along with it or not, just your presence in Songdowan sends a message." He sat back in his chair and stretched his arms far above his head. He saw Adler's jaw clench. "Face it, Bobby, you're in a corner. The only way out is the direction I choose."

Adler's eyes glittered like polished granite. "And what would I get if I did cooperate?"

Richard swung around in his chair, as if Adler's compliance meant nothing. "That would be up to the President." He leaned forward on the table. "Maybe a nicer cell, access to a library to write your memoirs." He shrugged. "Some of the charges against you are too big to drop."

Adler glared. "Some of them can't be prosecuted due to national security."

Richard stifled his anger. Right now, he wanted more than anything to make sure Adler went into a cell so deep he would never again see the light of day. He had spent four years proving Adler's guilt. Many had died at various rungs on Adler's ladder to near-absolute power.

After Richard ran the idea past the Secretary of State, the President had called the Attorney General to discuss options regarding Adler. They agreed that the situation in Korea was grave enough to require sacrifices and bargains. They just hadn't yet told Richard what the final price would be, leaving him with only the possibility of a carrot to dangle before Adler. He doubted that Adler would take such bait. "Well, Bobby," he nearly choked on the name. "Some of them can be pursued without any breach of security." He sat straight in the chair, his elbows on the table. "And some of those carry the death penalty."

Adler stared at him. To Richard he looked like a rat testing the trap he was in, trying to find an unseen hole he could enlarge to escape. Though the expression on Adler's face did not change, Richard felt a chill thinking that he could somehow slip away, to renew the contacts he had built over the years, to resume orchestrating power plays throughout the world. As he studied Adler's eyes, he thought he saw hope instead of hatred. His stomach tightened at the look.

"Okay, Rick," Adler said with an oily smile. "I guess I could do you this favor." He leaned forward, just his hands on the table. "For the sake of our old friendship."

Richard had to swallow hard to keep from saying what he felt. "For the sake of what future you have left, Bobby." Had Adler seen some advantage to the offer, an advantage Richard and his staff had missed?

"But you realize my life might be at risk if I do this for you." Adler smiled like he already had a plan.

Richard stroked the beard he kept as a reminder of his ordeal. "All of us take that risk when we answer the call to serve our country, Bobby."

Adler blinked. "What security do you have to offer me?" He nodded toward Richard. "I mean, it didn't take much for them to breach it before."

Richard looked toward Delmonico, who spoke with a barely suppressed smile. "Mr. Adler, we have adequate security in place to assure your safety to our satisfaction."

Adler sat back in his chair. "To your satisfaction?"

"Yes, and I'll be there in the room at all times. That's enough security for me."

Adler looked harder at Delmonico, as if assessing his abilities. "What if it's not enough for me?"

"Then you go as a prisoner under guard." Delmonico looked like a mountain not to be moved.

Richard covered his smile with his hand. Despite his primary motive of drawing the world back from the brink of a nuclear abyss, Richard enjoyed seeing his former nemesis at his mercy. *Forgive me, Lord,* he thought. *I know vengeance is for You, but could I watch while You administer it?*

Chapter 62

"I could get hooked on this *kim chi*," Harris remarked. "It's spicy, sour, and sweet, all at the same time. Like my grandma's green tomato chow-chow."

"It is pickled vegetables, usually cabbage, and almost as much a staple as rice," Richard explained. "Nearly every meal includes it."

"Like *nopales* in Mexican cooking," Edwards offered.

"*Nopales*?" Delmonico was nearly halfway through his main course.

"Pickled prickly pear cactus." Edwards had grown up in Texas, Richard remembered from his bio. "It's readily available, green and nutritious. My mother was half-Mexican," he added. "The last thing a culture gives up during assimilation is its food heritage."

"That's a good thing." Delmonico finished his course. "I love trying different ethnic foods, but you have to be careful that you don't get the Americanized version of it."

"Taco *gringo*?" Edwards grinned.

"Exactly." Delmonico put down his fork, a concession to the Americans and Russians. "Go to a typical Chinese buffet, and you are getting what they have learned Americans think Chinese food is." He nodded toward Edwards. "Or Taco Bell."

"Did you ever try Southern ethnic?" Harris said,

West Virginia coming out in his drawl.

Delmonico nodded. "Sweet tea and fried chicken. With collard greens."

Richard picked at his *gye ran mal ee*, or omelet roll, and relaxed in the fact that his staff had bonded. State put them together specifically for the negotiations. Though Delmonico and Harris worked in the same building, they were not on the same team until Kim's death, when State called the two of them together to run potential scenarios. Edwards was added to the team two days before their arrival in Nassau. Their bonding rendered them more effective at handling their specialties, secure in the knowledge that the other members of the team were handling theirs, and allowed Richard to focus on the other subtleties of the negotiations.

"Ah, my friend, I see you have arrived early." Chung Hee, alone, entered the dining hall.

Richard stood to shake Chung Hee's hand. Chung Hee's appearance meant he might get the opportunity to discuss some issues with him soon. "Won't you join us?"

Chung Hee looked over the table full of Americans. "I believe I will, if it will not inconvenience any of you." He pulled out a chair. "My staff is busy working on a project that I needed a break from." He ordered a bowl of *sollongtang*, then addressed Richard. "I expected you to spend as much time as possible with your wife."

Richard shrugged, wondering if Chung Hee already knew why he cut short the visit with Terra. "I thought it best to offer support to Patmanov and our Russian friends in their tragedy."

Chung Hee nodded. "I hear that they have the issue under control now." He bowed his head briefly. "We are thankful that the death toll was not much higher."

"It well could have been."

"It's a dangerous world we live in these days."

"Yes," Richard agreed. "More every day."

Chung Hee's soup arrived. His dinner epitomized what Richard respected about Chung Hee. *Sollongtang* was made of whatever chopped bones and cheap meat was available, simmered for hours with a few vegetables and spices, then poured over rice and jazzed up with spicy sauces. For many of his countrymen, it represented a meal much richer in protein than they usually enjoyed, though it would not satisfy a Western appetite for long.

Contrasted with the recently deceased leader, who employed a host of premier chefs to prepare rare delicacies daily, Chung Hee's dietary style as well as leadership more closely paralleled Ho Chi Minh than Kim. It was, Richard suspected, not only his character, but also a technique to ally himself with the common North Korean. Though it was not safe to publicly admit it, most North Koreans realized that the ruling elite lived well.

"Thank you," Chung Hee said softly in Korean to the girl who served his soup.

Richard handed her his plate. "*Jal muk ut sup ni da*," he offered the traditional Korean thank you for his meal. He caught Chung Hee watching the exchange and saw a slight smile lift the corners of his mouth before he bowed his head, probably saying a silent grace before he began his meal.

Richard sat in silence, sipping tea, while Chung

Hee finished his meal. How much did Chung Hee really know about what was driving the crisis, steering it in a different direction than the players at the table wanted it to go?

"I think we're gonna go to our rooms, boss." Delmonico placed his silverware on his plate. Edwards and Harris, already finished, nodded their agreement.

"Okay, guys." Richard glanced at his watch. "Let's meet at ten tomorrow, my room."

"Roger, boss." His staff left the room, and he and Chung Hee were alone.

"You have good people working with you," Chung Hee commented.

"Yes, I do." Richard set down his teacup. "I didn't choose them, but the State Department did an excellent job of it." He met Chung Hee's gaze. "Did you select your staff?"

Chung Hee put a spoonful of soup to his lips. He sipped the broth slowly, then put his spoon back in the bowl. "I chose Gi Chu personally, but Seong and Dak Ho had already been selected for their positions, therefore it seemed logical to keep them there."

Meaning he had no choice in the matter, Richard thought. Yet he doubted that either of them was the true power, they were simply the puppets, while someone else choreographed their moves. The dossier on the situation said that they had been minor aides to Kim; their function for Chung Hee was a promotion of sorts. He decided to take the conversation in a circle that might eventually lead back to this subject from another angle.

"I had an epiphany there in the forest," he remarked casually, holding his cup to his lips.

Chung Hee smiled. "I thought I could see a difference in you." He set down his spoon. "Would you like to tell me about it?"

"Simply that I came to the end of my will and had to surrender to His." Richard set down his cup. "I was ready to let go and die, but then suddenly I felt my burden lift and had the urge to get up and walk again." He picked up the cup again. "That's when I found shelter and food."

Chung Hee nodded. "I understand you broke into a home and took what you needed." He sipped at his soup, nearly hiding the smile that said he suspected the real story but would not give it away.

"Yes, that's what I did." He sighed. "But there wasn't that much to take." He took another drink of tea while Chung Hee sipped his soup. "The food aid really will be needed this winter, Chung Hee."

Chung Hee set down his spoon again. "I know that. I will do my best to see that the aid is accepted and properly distributed where it is needed most."

Richard thought about his response long enough that Chung Hee finished his soup. "Who will you put in charge of the distribution, Chung Hee?"

Chung Hee picked up his teacup. "Probably Gi Chu. At least I will make it his responsibility. Others will likely do the distribution."

"Would it be acceptable for you to accompany some of the shipments into the countryside?"

"I do not—"

"Exalted Leader." Seong had entered the room without either of them hearing him. "Your presence is greatly needed in your chambers."

"Can it not wait until the tea is finished, Seong?"

Chung Hee sipped at his tea, and Richard thought he saw a spark of defiance in the new President's eyes. "You should sit down and have some tea and a bite to eat yourself."

"I apologize, Mr. President, but the need is urgent." Seong remained standing, his glare at Richard saying exactly what he thought of the Americans. Then he glanced at Chung Hee. "Your staff requires your presence very much, sir."

Richard nodded at Chung Hee. "Perhaps we can finish the conversation another time, Mr. President."

Chung Hee rose. "Perhaps." He reached across the table to shake Richard's hand. "For certain, we will meet again at negotiations."

Richard watched Chung Hee leave at Seong's side. He now knew beyond a shadow of a doubt Chung Hee served as a figurehead only. But why? Was his presidency merely to dupe the rest of the world into thinking that North Korea changed in order to gain the assistance they desperately needed? Or give them time to assemble enough nuclear weapons that they could simply take what they wanted? He would have to be on his toes when the negotiations resumed day after tomorrow.

Chapter 63

Before the talks resumed, Richard announced that he would allow the primary delegate and one aide into the room. Edwards, Harris, and Delmonico sat behind him, spread out enough that they had a good view of the entire room. In the corner to Richard's left, Adler occupied a chair. He wore no handcuffs, but the Marines in the room never let him out of their sight, except in his quarters or a single-occupant restroom. He was accompanied on all breaks by at least one Marine.

At the appointed time, the delegates gathered outside the chamber. Patmanov's principal aide, Boris Rostopol, approached with the secondary aide. "Mr. Matthews, I regret to inform you that circumstances prevent Mr. Patmanov's presence at the table." He ducked his head, and his hands trembled. "I have been appointed to fill his position for the moment."

Richard nodded and indicated the chair to the right of his. "Have a seat, then."

Looking for all the world like a kid wearing his father's boots, Rostopol slipped into the chair. He lacked Patmanov's poker face, instead showing frightened eyes to Richard, his every sentence uttered as if he would have to verify it with Moscow before it would stand. Though it would not be safe nor wise to dismiss the Russians, Richard knew deep in his heart that they were no longer players in this negotiation.

Shirane appeared at the door. "*Origato.*" He bowed slightly, as he greeted Richard. "We are pleased that you are back in charge."

"We are pleased to have you back as well," Richard responded. He indicated the chair next to Rostopol for Shirane, who took his seat without comment, and bowed ever so slightly to the Russian.

He seated Pan at his left, with Hyeong beside her delegation and Chung Hee between Hyeong and Shirane, almost directly across the table from Richard.

"Ladies and gentlemen," he said when they and their aides had all settled in with their drink of choice on the table before them. "It's time that we roll up our sleeves and get to some serious work."

All appeared to nod assent. On the edge of his vision, he saw Adler lean forward. It would take a lot of concentration for Richard to focus on the negotiations and not wonder what Adler's next move would be.

Chapter 64

Terra paced the length of the patio, kept under the overhang by a short deluge during Nassau's rainy season. "But Richard, the house is ready, and I'm running out of things to do here." She glanced at Paul and Carrie, sipping tea at the table and trying not to eavesdrop. "I mean, you can only play so much golf." She grinned as Paul gasped and grabbed for his chest at the suggestion.

"I know, Terra." Richard's voice sounded tired, but not as hopeless as he had been now that negotiations, under his rules, had resumed. "I guess it would make security easier for the FBI if you were stateside."

"Exactly." Terra flashed a thumbs up to Paul and Carrie. The house being ready made a perfect excuse for them to go to Colorado, where Terra could begin pre-natal visits with the physician who would deliver the baby. "And if we want to get any outside painting done or landscaping planted, we have less than a month to complete it before winter sets in."

"Well, it has arrived in earnest here." Richard sighed. "We have a good six inches of snow here, and more than a foot farther from the coast."

"How much longer do you think it will take?"

"I don't know." She heard him hesitate. "We were able to offer food aid to the interior of the country in exchange for an agreement to consider allowing the

International Atomic Energy Agency in to inspect."

"But not an agreement to actually let them in." It seemed the trade-offs were not very substantial, which dovetailed with what the media reported.

"No, we're just not getting very far."

"Any idea why?"

He sighed. "Some ideas, no proof. But—" She heard him take a deep breath. "I'm going to throw out a proposal tomorrow that might break new ground." His voice lowered again. "It remains to be seen if it will go any further."

She wished he might pull off an incredible coup. "If anyone can do it, you can, Richard."

"I hope I can accomplish something," he said wearily. "I want to come home to you."

Telling him then about the baby danced on the tip of her tongue, but she waited. If he could do what he hoped, he would be home shortly, and she would have the pleasure of watching his face when he heard the news. "I want you home with me, too." She glanced toward his parents. "I'll let you know when we leave for Colorado."

Chapter 65

"Gentlemen and ladies, I have a proposal to place on the table." Richard waited until all the delegates focused on him. Today, a week after negotiations resumed, he rotated all of them to the left, placing Rostopol on his left and Shirane on his right. "As you all know, North Korea has relatively few modern manufacturing plants, but rich deposits of minerals in the mountains." He paused, as most of the delegates nodded. Chung Hee stared at him, as if he anticipated what Richard would say next. "If the DPRK is agreeable, would any of your countries be interested in building a steel processing facility near the mines as a cooperative venture?"

A collective sharp intake of breath circled the table. Finally, Chung Hee spoke. "I will agree to take the proposal back to the Supreme People's Assembly," he said. The light in his eyes, that only Richard could see from his angle across the table, said that he would do everything he possibly could to make the cooperative venture a reality.

"I will approach the Cabinet with the idea," Hyeong nodded. Hyeong's aide smiled and made furious notes.

Beside Chung Hee, Dak Ho studied Chung Hee, as if deep in thought. Chung Hee did not face him.

"My ministers have indicated that several of our

industrial leaders would be interested in participating in a joint venture." Shirane acted like Richard's suggestion had just opened a candy store for resource-starved Japan.

"Our committee would not object," Pan offered. If their manufacturing capabilities continued to grow, China might benefit from such a venture in the future, but for now, having the North Korean nuclear beast declawed to stabilize the region was their primary objective.

Rostopol refused to meet anyone's gaze. "I'll advise my committee."

Richard felt for Adler in the periphery of his senses. He could hear the man squirm, as if the proposal made him uneasy. He glanced around the table and saw Dak Ho looking toward Adler's corner. His mind leaped to a connection; he vowed to watch for further exchanges between the two. He would also alert his staff. "Very well, then. We have an agreement to look toward the future." He looked to Chung Hee, keeping Dak Ho within his line of sight as well. "Food aid is now being gathered to be ready for the coming winter. Chung Hee, what about letting nuclear inspectors into your facilities?"

"The Committee has agreed to discuss that option." Chung Hee kept his face very controlled. Dak Ho stared at his back.

Richard pressed. "When do you think they might have an answer for us?"

"We will meet later today, to set a time to discuss it."

"Then, ladies and gentlemen, do we have any other issues to bring to discussion?" No one spoke. "All right, we are adjourned until tomorrow morning at nine a.m."

****

The next morning at nine sharp, the negotiators reassembled. Richard left the seating the same. He would rotate them later, when he chose. Because he rotated them each day, sometimes two seats in the opposite direction, not moving them kept them off balance. He hoped to encounter Chung Hee on his evening walk, but he never appeared. Today he forced himself to concentrate, as Terra had told him last night that they would be enroute to Colorado today. He would try to wrap up by early afternoon, so that he could verify that they arrived safely.

"Well, delegates," he opened the talks. "Do we have any new developments or decisions today?"

Chung Hee spoke. "The Committee is still considering both of the motions from yesterday."

Richard suppressed a sigh. Delay was a standard North Korean tactic. "It would be most productive if they could give us an idea by the end of the week."

Chung Hee nodded.

"My ministers are prepared to meet with even a few days' notice to discuss details of us building a steel processing plant in a mutually agreed location," Shirane presented. "We believe that it could be most beneficial to both our countries."

"If you have any more information I could take to my committee," Chung Hee offered. "I would be most happy to present it. More details might bring forth a decision more quickly."

"We have a number of proposals we could advance tomorrow," Hyeong said. He glanced at Richard. "Might we have a private meeting with Mr. Chung Hee and his ministers to discuss these matters?"

Richard looked to Shirane and then Chung Hee. "If the other delegates have no objections, it might be very beneficial."

Shirane frowned. "I would not object if Japan would be offered the same courtesy."

"I will see if two such meetings could be arranged and when." Chung Hee looked toward both delegates.

Richard hoped he hadn't created a new international crisis, with Japan and South Korea competing for who would build the first factory. However, he anticipated that conflict could be resolved by both countries investing in North Korea's future. Such a development would bind the region economically in a way that no military alliance could. The meeting dragged on, discussing possibilities for China and Russia to invest in the Korean peninsula, without much discussion over what Chosŏn was looking for.

Chapter 66

Richard went to his quarters hopeful. Though nothing had yet been agreed to, the fact that they moved beyond repeating rhetoric signaled that the focus had changed. Now all parties appeared to be thinking to the future, a future where everyone could win.

Ryman was waiting beside the door when he entered his quarters.

"Has my wife called?" Richard asked before he even closed the door.

"Yes, sir," Ryman appeared glad to pass on good news. "She said they landed in Denver about sixteen hundred." He checked his watch. "Allowing time to rent a car and drive, she thought they would be there a couple of hours ago, sir."

Richard smiled. "Thank you for staying behind to wait for the call, Ryman." He flipped open his cell phone.

"It was a pleasure, sir." Ryman backed out of the room to give him privacy for his call.

Terra's voice on the other end sounded excited. "Richard, the place looks great!"

He smiled at the enthusiasm in her voice. "I trust then that the proper tile and carpet has been installed?"

"Yes, they did a fantastic job of it." He heard her moving around. "Your mom and I are looking over the house and drawing up a decorating plan right now." She laughed, her voice like a refreshing fountain to him. "Your dad is trying to decide where you need a putting green, even though it's dark. And he's already found the hot tub on the deck."

He hesitated, glad they all bonded thoroughly, suddenly wishing he could be a part of it. "Sounds like I'm better off over here; you'd have me working if I was there."

She laughed again. "There will still be plenty to do when you get here, Mister." He could almost see her pause to survey rooms. "How are you at hanging wallpaper?"

He laughed. "About as good as I am at taping boxes." When he packed up some of his things to move her into his apartment, the taping mechanism nearly defeated him.

"Then your job is to be my assistant," she ordered. "How are things going today?"

"Better." He slipped out of his tie. "They are at least thinking about what I proposed." He shrugged off the jacket. "I think we can finally get things moving, and it may not take much longer."

"That's great! I wish I could be there to give you a hug."

"I wish you could, too." He ached with wanting to hold her. "But if you were, who would ramrod getting the house ready?"

She laughed. "Oh, we could just wait, and you could do all the work while I supervise."

He laughed, too. "That's what I figured." He hated to end the call. "I'll talk to you tomorrow. I love you."

"And I love you, too."

Buoyed by her enthusiasm and the progress the

talks were making, Richard changed into running clothes. Ryman jumped up from the magazine he was reading as Richard appeared in the anteroom. "Ready for a run, sir?"

Richard nodded. "Today seems like a pretty good day, doesn't it, Ryman."

"Yes, sir." Ryman signaled the Marine who would also run with them, trying to shield Richard with their bodies. They all knew that their routine was for effect only, that if the perimeter were breached, bodyguards would provide no safety, but without their weapons, there was little else the Marines could do to protect him. He hated to put them in jeopardy, but their orders would not permit him to dismiss them. Bound together, they formed a team, pushing each other to get the most from each run.

Four North Korean soldiers stayed close to them, rifles at ready, constantly scanning the hills and sea around them. Richard wondered if they, too, understood the futility of their mission, should opposing factions determine that Richard needed to be removed from the mission permanently.

"Afternoon, Darnell." Richard greeted the Marine assigned to them today.

"Afternoon, sir." Tall and lanky as opposed to Ryman's stocky, lineman's build, Darnell hailed from North Dakota. Ryman called St. Louis home.

They jogged around the boulders, warming up before they hit the beach to run in earnest. Richard stretched fully, hoping he could keep up with the younger men. "How are things at home, gentlemen?" Richard asked as they reversed at the north end of the beach for the second leg of the run.

"Fine, sir." Darnell, as usual, spared few words.

"Fine for me, too, sir." Ryman had more to say. "My mom sent me video of news coverage of your kidnapping, and some newspaper and magazine clippings, too."

"That should prove interesting, looking at it from this vantage point, Ryman."

"Yes, sir." Ryman paused. "And, by the way, sir, congratulations."

Richard began to feel the burn, before the endorphins took over and the runner's euphoria hit. "Congratulations for what, Ryman?"

"On your pending fatherhood, sir."

Richard skidded to a stop, the Marines sweeping past him. "What are you talking about, Ryman?"

Ryman jogged back to face him. "It was on a news report, and in a couple of tabloids."

Richard's heart pounded in his ears so hard he could barely hear Ryman. "Are you sure it wasn't just tabloid gossip?"

Ryman looked as if he expected to face a firing squad for divulging national secrets. "I'll let you judge for yourself, sir. You can watch the video and read the articles when we finish the run."

"The run is finished, gentlemen." Richard started down the beach at a faster pace than they normally ran. The Marines kept up with him, and in seconds the three of them were gathered around a tiny DVD player in Ryman's quarters.

Richard leaned closer to the screen as video, apparently taken at a restaurant while Terra dined with his parents, showed the reporter shoving a microphone in Terra's face. He saw her blank look at the first question, but when the reporter asked her if she'd had the chance to tell him she was pregnant before he was kidnapped, the expression that crossed her face verified what Ryman had told him. Then he caught the look she gave the cameraman, just before they stopped the video, and knew that the man had felt her wrath. Stunned, he sat on Ryman's bunk.

"Here are the tabloids, sir." Ryman handed him pages cut from a couple of supermarket rags, all reporting from a patient in a doctor's waiting room or a receptionist for a massage therapist. He didn't need to read them, though he did. All he needed was the look in Terra's eyes when the reporter asked her that question. She couldn't lie to save her life.

She could, however, keep a secret, it seemed. He reviewed his short trip to the Bahamas after his escape. Maybe that was what she had kept trying to tell him, and he had avoided. Suddenly, fear seized him. She couldn't be more than two, maybe three months pregnant, and it was at three months that Elaine lost their babies. He needed to be with Terra, to stand by her if things went wrong, to be there to help if they went right.

"Ryman, get a plane ready as soon as possible to take me to Colorado." He opened the door to his quarters to change and pack. "Ten minutes, if you can."

"Sir, what about the negotiations?"

"Two-day recess, maybe longer. We'll let them know." He slipped out of the sweatshirt. "And have my staff come to my quarters immediately."

Edwards arrived while he was still changing. By the time he slipped into jeans and a sweater, Harris and Delmonico had seated themselves on the couch.

Evidently Ryman filled them in, he realized as he viewed their troubled faces. Delmonico spoke, "Are you sure you should go home right now, boss?" Harris and Edwards nodded their agreement.

His sense of responsibility hammered away at the mountain of his fears. The fear remained, impervious to any logic. "I have to."

Delmonico cleared his throat. "Sir, couldn't you discuss it by phone, or wait another week or so?" He glanced at his partners. "I mean, sir, we just began to make progress today."

Richard stared at them. "I know that, men, but there are reasons I have to go." He didn't elaborate, as his reasons tumbled over and over in his mind.

"Then we'll wait here, sir," Harris promised. "And we'll pray that things will go right both here and at home for you."

Richard glanced at Harris. Should he have a little more faith, wait it out a week, ask Terra on the phone? The fear gripped his heart again, and he shook his head. "I have to go."

Chapter 67

The journey to Colorado involved many changes of transport: a helicopter to the Pacific fleet carrier, a jet fighter to Germany, a transport to Fort Carson, and another helo to Estes Park, with a final transfer to a sedan driven by an FBI agent. On the first helo, it occurred to him to order that his trip be a surprise to Terra and his parents.

He thought a lot during the journey. Until the moment he boarded the chopper, his staff had continued to urge him to delay a few days, cool down, focus on the negotiations, but he knew that, until he saw Terra face to face, he would be useless as a negotiator. He thought that he had learned to read Terra very well, but now, he doubted himself. And he worried if she had healed enough from the injuries Adler had inflicted to carry a child, worried if she was ready to have children, worried how she would cope if she miscarried, without him there beside her.

He wondered how he would cope if she lost the baby. The memories of both miscarriages with Elaine haunted him; for months afterward, he asked himself if he could have done anything to prevent them. As he stared out different aircraft windows at the same world rushing by, he feared a pattern had developed in his life, wherein the things he longed for most—home and family—would exist forever outside his grasp.

By afternoon of the next day, as the car started onto the gravel road leading to his new home on Dry Gulch Road six miles northeast of Estes Park, he was still worrying. For the first time, he realized how isolated the house was, their nearest neighbor a good three miles away, closer to Estes. The driver gained on a hard-used pickup truck ahead of them on the road. Richard wondered where it was going, as the road led only to the few residences in the area. He gritted his teeth when the truck took a left into his driveway. "Stick close to that truck," he ordered the driver.

The sedan wallowed on the sand drive. Richard found it hard to see the pickup around the cloud of dust it raised. He thought he saw two heads in the cab, but then the dust roiled up again. The closer the sedan came to the truck, the faster the truck drove. He tightened his seat belt and still had to brace himself with his hand against the dash to stay in the seat.

Finally, the truck skidded to a halt in front of the garage, the sedan seconds behind. The truck doors flew open while he was unbuckling his seat belt. He was just standing up when Terra bounced out of the driver's door and her security man from the other, gun in his hand at his side.

"Richard!" She waved a hand at the truck. "Look, honey, I bought myself some wheels!" She ran toward him. "Are you home for good?"

They met at the back of the truck. He caught her hands, holding her back to look into her eyes. "Why didn't you tell me?"

She blinked. "Tell you what?"

He felt her hands trembling. "I saw the video from the restaurant."

Her face went pale. "Then you know?"

"Is it true?"

She nodded. "I tried to tell you, but something came up every time."

He folded her in his arms, suddenly relieved to have the barrier of the secret removed, as if he could protect her by the simple act of knowing. "Are you okay?"

"I had my first doctor's visit this morning. We are doing fine, and the baby is due about mid-May."

At that moment, his mother appeared in the entryway, ochre drops of paint spattering her face and clothes. "Richard, what are you doing here?" She set down the paint pan and roller in her hands. "I'd hug you, but I don't want to get paint all over you." She frowned. "Is the crisis over?"

"No, I—"

"Son!" His father's face appeared over the edge of the roof. "Did you finish up?"

He shook his head. "What are you doing on the roof?"

"I'm cleaning the gutters, and I'm not on the roof, I'm on a ladder." Paul's face disappeared as he backed down the ladder. "Would you rather have Terra or your mother up here?"

"No, and I'd rather not have you up there either." He glanced down at Terra. "Why not hire the gutters cleaned?"

She shrugged. "It's a simple procedure. Rain is forecast tonight, and any handyman I tried to hire couldn't get to it for a week or more. The aspens next to the house have dropped so many leaves into the gutters, we risked getting water around the foundation. I wanted to do it myself, and your dad refused to let me."

"As well he should." He took her hand and started for the house. "Can we talk?"

Paul tried to lower the extension ladder, confounded by the mechanism. Terra started toward him to help, but before she could reach him, the security man took the ladder from Paul.

Following her, Richard shot her a look. "Who are these people and what have you done with my real parents?"

"What?" Terra stopped and stared at him wide-eyed.

Released from his fears by the normalcy of the scene around him, he laughed. "Mum and Dad have always hired most everything done. You've heard the plumbing story." His mother reached him then, still wiping paint from her hands. "A couple more months with you, and they'll be building their own house."

"Well—" Terra looked around her at the FBI agent stowing the ladder in the garage, and the agent who had driven Richard from Estes Park standing with a confused expression behind the truck. "I guess I plead guilty to just being myself." Chin up, she looked into Richard's eyes. "I don't know how else to be."

He put his arms around her, and she melted against him. "Terra, you are a catalyst for change in my life." He kissed the top of her head and smiled at his parents as they gathered around. "And evidently in my parents' lives as well."

Paul grinned. "I'm going to learn plumbing." Carrie rolled her eyes and shook her head.

Terra looked up at him. "You've made a few changes in my life as well, dear." Her arms tightened around his waist. "One of which we need to discuss."

"Absolutely." He kissed her gently. "Do my parents know?" he whispered.

She nodded. "They've been wonderful support."

Paul cleared his throat. "Why don't I throw a few steaks on the grill?" He glanced toward Carrie.

"And I'll clean up the paint and start a salad and something to go with steaks." She patted Richard's shoulder with her cleanest hand, leaving an ochre smudge on his jacket.

Terra looked toward the agent who was still standing behind the truck. "You might as well join us for steaks," she suggested. The agent assigned to her already closed the garage door and waited behind Richard and Terra.

Richard chuckled. "Catalyst for change, that's what you are." Arm in arm, he and Terra walked into the nearly empty house, where she began showing him her ideas, including paint chips, wallpaper samples, pictures of furnishings and wall hangings. She wanted to take her time shopping for furniture, she explained. He simply nodded, overwhelmed by her energy, and embarrassed by his panic.

Without many comments, he followed Terra and then his father around the house and grounds, trying to absorb the visions they painted of their ideas for the house. He hadn't given it much thought after they closed the purchase, immersed first in introducing Terra to his parents and then in the Korean crisis. The simple dinner his parents prepared surprised him.

"I had no idea you could cook a steak, Dad." He laid his silverware on the plate and leaned back from the folding table. "And, Mum, that was a fantastic salad." He rested his arm across Terra's shoulder.

"I think we've caught Terra's excitement about the house," Paul said, reaching for another honeyed biscuit.

"And I'm learning how much fun doing things for myself can be, son." Carrie smiled across the table at Terra. "Your beautiful young wife is a marvel and a delight."

Terra ducked her head, but Richard caressed her neck. "Yes, she is, Mum." He leaned over to kiss her gently. "But I need reminded of it from time to time."

Carrie laid her napkin on her plate. "Then why don't the two of you go spend some alone time together. Paul and I can clean up." She stood. "After all, you came halfway around the world to discuss something very important with Terra, and you've hardly said a word about it yet."

He glanced at his mother, saw his father nodding in agreement. "You were in on the secret?"

Carrie nodded. "Terra made the decision first not to tell you right away, and after the three of us discussed it, we agreed it would be best."

"We just never expected it to take this long, son." Paul picked up his plate. "It's not my time to do the dishes, Carrie."

"Yes, it is, Paul." She picked up her plate and Richard's and held out her hand for Terra's. "Besides all you have to do is put them in the dishwasher."

"There may be golf on TV."

"It will wait."

Richard rose from his chair and grasped Terra's to pull it back for her. He took her hand to steady her as she stood.

"I'm not as big as a house yet that I need help

getting up, Richard," Terra growled at him.

"I'm not helping you because you need it, I'm helping you to show you how much you mean to me." He smiled down at her, her little hand still grasped in his.

"Oh." She moved against him, wrapping her arms around his waist. "Then, thank you." She looked up into his face, then called to Paul and Carrie busy at the sink. "Night, Paul. Night, Carrie."

Carrie walked toward them and put her arms around them both. "Good night, kids." She kissed Terra's cheek first, then Richard's. "Go, talk about your baby."

"Night, kids," Paul called, elbow deep in suds. "And, son, congratulations. I hope your child is as great a blessing to you as you have been to us."

Richard felt Terra squeeze his hand. "Thanks, Dad," he choked from a throat suddenly gone tight.

"You must be nesting already," he commented as she led him into their bedroom and closed the door. At the moment, the room contained only a mattress on the floor and a folding chair.

"Just trying to stay busy, and not think about you being away from me." She sat on the mattress and patted a spot beside her. He stared at her, memorizing the vitality of her. "I've missed you."

He sat down beside her and then drew her back to cuddle her in his arms, bodies touching at as many points as possible. "And I've missed you," he whispered as he kissed his way down her neck.

Finally, they stopped to breathe. She ran her fingers lightly over his injured cheek. "Are you upset about the baby?"

As some of his fears came crowding back, he gathered her hand in his and brought it to his lips. "I'm upset I wasn't here for you, that you didn't get to tell me the way you probably wanted to. I was afraid you weren't ready to have a baby, that maybe you were keeping the secret all alone."

"I was shocked when I found out—after all, we'd been careful—"

"Then, when—" He couldn't remember when they'd not used protection.

She grinned. "That night on the beach, after the dinner party."

"Oh." The memory came back vividly.

"Anyway, I had to share the news with someone. It never occurred to me not to tell your parents." Tears gathered in her eyes. "They've been as supportive as my own parents would have been, maybe even more so." She buried her head against his chest. "I only hope I'm half the mother your mom is."

He stroked her shoulders. "You'll be fine." He laughed. "Besides, Mum is good because I made her work hard at it."

"That I can believe." She studied his face. "I hope our baby is more like me, the obedient child."

Laughter took him over completely, as he envisioned a tiny rebellious Terra. He imagined their child, blessed both with her stubbornness and the independent streak he had carried all his life. Terra's laughter joined his, and they lay side by side, until finally he could laugh no more.

"I think we're in for trouble." Terra sighed. She rolled on her side, her head propped on her arm. "But on the bright side, we can always bring your parents in to baby-sit."

"If they're smart, they'll just laugh about paybacks and refuse."

She threw her arm across him and rested her chin on his chest. "Somehow, I don't think they'll do that."

He caressed her shoulders, staring into the green pools of her eyes. He never tired of losing himself in their depths. His fears, shoved away by their laughter, resurfaced. "But we have a lot to go through before we get to that point." His fingers traced her lips, the most expressive lips he had ever seen. "And now I'm more worried than ever."

"That's why I didn't tell you right away; I didn't want you to worry and be distracted so you couldn't handle the negotiations. I never thought it would be this long before I got the chance. And I tried to tell you when you came back to Nassau, but you kept changing the subject." She kissed his fingers, sending tingles throughout his body. "I knew what had happened with Elaine would never be far from your thoughts." She squeezed his hand, gently. "But, Richard, I'm not Elaine, and there is no reason to believe that the same things will happen to me. I discussed it with my doctor, and he reassured me that all indications are that this will be a normal, very healthy pregnancy." She smiled. "You are going to have to take it on faith that everything will be fine." She ran her hand down his ribs and slipped her fingers inside his jeans. "Call it woman's intuition, but I just *know*."

"Well, I can't lay claim to woman's intuition." He tugged loose the bandana that held her hair. It had grown a couple of inches since he first left for Korea. He tried to silence the voices in his mind that nagged at him, that whispered that normal human happiness was not for him. Lord, please, let me have faith, he prayed. He let the thoughts of what Terra's hands were doing to him, and what his hands were doing to her, drown out the negative. He paused for a moment. "I feel like such an idiot that I put people through so much inconvenience to get here to ask you in person what I already knew was true when I saw the video."

She laughed, working at the button of his jeans. "Well, they cut the shot before the best part."

"You giving the reporter a piece of your mind?" He unfastened his own jeans, kicking them to the floor as the negative voices went unheard.

She nodded, slipping quickly out of her shirt. "Your dad applauded."

"Still, it was pretty irresponsible of me to leave the negotiations right now." He reached out to run his fingers over her breast. He was almost past caring about anything outside the room.

She grasped his chin, forcing him to look at her face. "Richard, you have been through hell without much break for the past two months. I would say you are entitled to just a tiny bit of irresponsibility, particularly when you consider what happened with Elaine."

"Still, would you mind if I went back tomorrow morning?" Now that his fears had been diminished by the light of reality, he felt guilty about being gone.

She pressed herself, naked, against him. "You'll just have to make tonight memorable enough to tide me over."

He wrapped his arms around her, holding her as close as he possibly could. "I'll do my best, love." He kissed her deep, feeling her respond, in rhythm with her without even having to think about how to move. "And, if I fail, I'll just have to try again."

She giggled. "At least we don't have to worry about birth control for a while."

****

Richard awoke startled. For a second, he didn't know where he was, thought he was back in the hut, dreaming. Then he felt the warmth of Terra's skin against his, her back to his chest, her head cradled on his arm. He marveled at how close they had been, not just skin to skin, not just physically joined, but emotionally and spiritually one being for a short, but incredible span of time. He couldn't drift back to sleep just yet, though. Guilt flooded him as he remembered how critical a situation he had fled, driven by irrational fears. Gently he rolled away from her to search for his cell phone somewhere on the floor. Lying on the edge of the bed, he punched the code to dial Delmonico. "Ray?" he whispered.

"Yeah, boss." Delmonico's voice sounded tense, and Richard wondered how the delegates had reacted to his absence.

"Ray, I just wanted to let you know that I'll be back tomorrow." He sighed, knowing that the advice from his staff had been sound. "You can let the delegates know."

"Will do, boss. Is everything okay there?"

"It's fine, Ray." He sighed involuntarily as Terra rolled over and wrapped herself around him. "You guys were right to advise me to wait."

Delmonico chuckled. "Just speaking from experience, boss. Once it gets to this point, the women are in charge, and there ain't a thing a man can do about it."

"You're right about that, Ray." He clenched his teeth as Terra began to touch him in ways that made conversation all but impossible.

Delmonico went on. "The recess may work to our advantage. Your being gone really threw the delegates for a spin, though Chung Hee just smiled. And by the way, boss, congratulations."

"Thanks, Ray. See you tomorrow." He gasped. "I'll let you know what time as soon as I know." He had to use all his concentration to make sure he pushed the "end" button on the phone. He certainly didn't want his staff to hear what was happening next.

Chapter 68

Richard felt a surge of adrenalin as the chopper neared touchdown at Wonson. He spotted Delmonico waiting for him beside the SUV. His visit with Terra reassured him, and he was now ready to focus on getting the negotiations wrapped up. He felt like a soldier gearing up to charge the last hill and win the war. Then he could claim his hero's reward and settle into domestic bliss.

As he left Colorado this morning, it had seemed frantically normal—him rushing around to pull on his coat against the cold rain that began in the night, while he was saying his good-byes and gathering the furniture brochures Terra wanted him to take, all the while sipping from a hurried cup of coffee—he could hardly wait to embrace that life as his own. And bring a new life into the world, to nurture and protect as his parents had protected him. He felt a part of an incredible looping ribbon of heredity, reaching far back into the past and stretching, he hoped, far into the future. If he could successfully bring about peace in the coming days.

"Afternoon, boss," Delmonico greeted him with a grin. "That well-rested look you have now will disappear in a few months."

"I'll welcome it," Richard responded truthfully. Some of Terra's optimism had rubbed off on him, and now he actually dared to hope he would hold his child soon.

"You'll be able to rest again in about twenty years," Delmonico promised. "Maybe."

"Only if we can wrap this up the right way." He stepped into the SUV.

"Yeah, boss." A change in Delmonico's tone made him face his chief of staff. He read concern in the burly man's gaze.

"We'll need to have a staff meeting right away," he said, glancing at the driver. North Korean, not cleared, the vehicle probably wired. His sense of well-being retreated to the core of him, as he settled into battle-readiness. Delmonico simply nodded and sat quietly on the drive back to the Retreat at Songdowan.

Richard propped his elbow on the armrest and stared out at the damp gray early winter countryside. Maybe Terra had been right when she argued with the messenger who told him about the situation in Russia; he had needed a bit more rest before returning to the fray. Whatever Delmonico's tone hinted at, he was ready to handle it.

Back in Richard's quarters, his gathered staff greeted him with troubled faces, their congratulations sounding hollow. "Okay, guys, what's up?" he said as he slipped out of his coat.

"Shirane is packing up to leave as soon as possible." Edwards offered.

"Why?" That put a new wrinkle in things. It could leave the South Korean offer the only one on the table.

"Ricin scare in the subway. Message just came about an hour ago. All he told us was that it was a generalized threat, but our sources say that it'll happen unless Japan backs away from the plant in North Korea."

Richard dropped to the couch. "Damn." He thought quickly through options. "See if Shirane will meet with me for a few minutes before he leaves."

Edwards summoned a messenger. "There's something else," Harris spoke quietly.

"What?" Richard gave him his full attention.

"Nothing I can prove, but I have the hunch that Adler is communicating with someone here."

"Who?" He would see if Harris's hunch matched his.

"Hyeong's assistant."

"Oh." That was a different take than he had expected. "Why?"

"They've been making eye contact a lot." Harris paused, running his hand over his face. "And it seems to go beyond that." He hesitated. "Hand gestures, raised eyebrows, kinda like baseball coaches, you know?"

Richard replayed his memories from the negotiations. Hyeong's assistant had seemed focused on the negotiations, professional, just what he would expect. "Are you sure she's not just flirting?"

"Well," Harris admitted. "God knows I have no clue what a woman thinks, but there are many more men in the room that I would consider more attractive than Adler if I was a woman." He looked down. "Not my area of expertise." He sighed. "And you wouldn't think a logical woman would be attracted to a man who would spend the rest of his life in prison."

"Check out the letters to prison inmates all over the country," Delmonico growled. "No logic there."

"We'll watch him even closer, John." Richard

looked down at the floor. "I don't discount your hunch, it's just that I suspected someone else." He rolled his head, his shoulders tight with tension. "Can we get some surveillance equipment into his room without the North Koreans knowing?"

"Well, sir," Edwards responded, grinning. "I've been thinking about that." He pulled a piece of paper from his pocket. "Considering what I know to be available on the Pacific fleet carrier, I think I can set up a micro-transmitter and a tiny video feed that will cover most of the room."

The staff's resourcefulness buoyed his spirits. "How soon can you get it done?"

"First thing in the morning. I can fly to the carrier and install it while you're in negotiations."

"Then do it." He faced Delmonico and Harris. "In the meantime, we have to watch Adler carefully." He caught Harris' glance. "I don't think the South Koreans are the only ones he's in touch with."

"Sir?" Edwards interrupted. "If we can get hold of Adler's shoes, I think we can plant a transmitter in one of them, maybe catch what our observations might miss."

"Do that, too, Ted. Let's leave no stone unturned." A knock sounded at the door, and Edwards answered it.

"Shirane says he'll see you in his quarters if you can be there within the next fifteen minutes," Edwards reported.

Richard stood. "We can discuss this more later." He headed for the door. "I'll call you when I get back from Shirane."

****

Minoru Shirane was packing his own bag when

328

Richard knocked on his door. "What's the situation, Mr. Shirane?" he asked.

Shirane stopped and extended his hand to Richard. "There is a threat at home, and I must return there as quickly as possible."

Richard shook his hand and bowed. "Is this tied to our negotiations here in any way?"

Shirane shot Richard a look. "No, evidently their objective is to stop our whaling operations." He picked up a tiny paper cat from the dresser top.

"Do you do origami, Min?"

Shirane shook his head. "No. At least not much anymore." He rotated the cat to view it from all sides. "My daughter made this for me when she was about ten." He studied the cat some more. "I had been trying to teach her the basics, and she surprised me with this one evening." He held the cat toward Richard. "If you look closely, there are 'Hello, Kitty' faces on both sides." He smiled, as if caught up in his memories. "She was fascinated by 'Hello, Kitty' at that phase and had everything about it, including this stationery." He looked at Richard. "She still carries a 'Hello, Kitty' backpack as she rides the subway every day on her way to university."

"I understand." Richard saw a parallel between the situation with Shirane and Patmanov. "Will your aides stay?"

Shirane shook his head. "We are all leaving now." He placed the paper cat carefully in his toiletries bag. "I don't know when, or if, we will return." He went to the dresser to pick up more personal items. "Perhaps the negotiations will be satisfactorily resolved quickly."

"Are your people still planning to meet with the

North Koreans about the plant?"

Shirane looked at him for a moment, before giving his attention to his packing. "I cannot say right now."

Richard sighed. "Godspeed, then, Min."

Chapter 69

Richard left Shirane's chambers more certain than ever that someone within the peace process was trying to derail it. Deep in thought, he went the wrong way in the corridor heading back to his own quarters. He didn't realize his mistake until he looked up toward what he thought was his room to see a Marine sitting in a chair outside a room, while another Marine leaned against the wall across from the door. He smiled. Even in civilian clothes, their military bearing was unmistakable. He had come to Adler's room without planning to, and now he made an impulsive decision.

"Afternoon, Marines," he greeted them. They snapped to attention, the one in the chair standing, the moment they saw him.

"Afternoon, sir," they responded in unison.

"How is our prisoner today?" He stared at Adler's door, refining what little plan he had.

"Quiet, as usual, sir," the taller, older Marine answered. "No phone, no TV, no computer." He nodded toward the door. "Not much he can do in there but pace."

"He already had lunch in the dining hall, with us, sir," the younger man offered.

"Was there anyone else in the hall when you were there?"

The soldiers exchanged a look. Finally, the older

331

one spoke. "We were sitting in the far corner, sir, but I think there was a group that came in after we got our food."

"Who?" He faced the older Marine.

"I think it was the Japanese delegation, sir." The Marine looked worried. "And the South Korean delegation was coming in as we were leaving." The Marine glanced at him. "Should we begin making him take meals in his room, sir?"

Richard stared at the floor for a few minutes. "No, not yet." He looked at the door that would allow him to face his nemesis. It seemed their jousting would never end. Taking a deep breath, he knocked. The older Marine unlocked it.

Adler took several minutes to answer the door. "Yes?" he said without opening the door.

The Marine reached across Richard to turn the handle, allowing the door to swing inward. "Hello, Robert," Richard greeted Adler with more respect in his voice than he had used on the ship.

Adler blinked, then stepped back from the door to allow Richard to enter. "Hello, Rick." He backed a couple of steps into the austere room. "This is a pleasant surprise."

Richard shrugged. "I took a wrong corridor on my way to my room and decided I would stop to see how you are faring."

Adler stared at him, suspicion in every move he made. "I'm doing okay." He walked to the chair and picked up the shoes he had evidently been polishing. He eyed the expensive oxford with a half smile. "It must have been ten years or more since I shined my own shoes."

"Why don't we let the Marines do them for you?" If he agreed, it was an unbelievable stroke of good luck. Or divine providence.

Adler cast him a sidelong glance. Richard knew he must suspect something. "You know, Rick, I'd have to be a fool to trust you to do something for me just for kindness."

"And I'd have to be a fool to expect you to trust me." He sighed and perched on the edge of the bed. "I'd say trust is something we'll never have between us."

"At least that's honest," Adler grunted. He rubbed on the shoes another moment, then set them down. "And I think I'll take you up on that offer." He wiped his hands on a clean cloth. "I guess I'll get used to doing such things in prison, but I'm not there yet."

The hairs on the back of Richard's neck rose. A cornered cobra was more dangerous than one who had an escape avenue. And he had certainly been instrumental in putting Adler in a tighter corner than anyone else. "No. And if you can help us out in this situation, you may end up in a prison where you won't be breaking rocks."

Adler sighed and leaned back in the chair. "But still a prison." Richard felt a chill, knowing how many rocks Adler had wriggled out from under during his career. "What do you think I can do to help you?"

"What intelligence do you have about North Korea?" he began.

Adler shrugged, holding his hands up to show them empty. "You have all the intel there is."

"I have all that's gone through channels." He drew his knee up to his chest, appearing relaxed. "I want what's not been verified, or what is so secret you can't even share it with the President."

Momentary surprise registered in Adler's eyes. A smile crossed his lips. "What makes you think we hold anything back?"

"C'mon, Bob, I'm naïve, but I'm not stupid." He smiled, too. "I know that only a very little of the intel that comes into your office makes it to the Joint Chiefs. There's simply too much of it for them to digest. Hell, a lot of it doesn't even make it to you. It's buried on some specialist's desk, where he's written up a very concise summary, that you condense to a sentence or less." Adler studied him, wondering, Richard thought, where he had come up with this sudden knowledge of CIA operations. Evidently, Adler did not realize that Harris had come from CIA.

Adler rested his elbows on the arms of the chair, tenting his hands before him. "Then what makes you think I have any more intel on this situation than you do?"

"Because I know you're a smart man, and you always know more than you want anyone to think you know."

Adler smiled. "Thanks for the compliment."

"No compliment, just fact." Richard pressed the flattery. "You had to be more aware than anyone that the situation here was preparing for the eventuality of Kim's death. You had to have some idea of what was playing behind the scenes."

Adler's smile faded. "You know that North Korea has been one of our toughest nuts to crack over the years."

"I do." Richard nodded. "But I also know that if

anyone could crack it, you could."

Adler stayed silent a moment. "If I had any information that you could use, why should I share it?"

Richard studied him. Lord, if you gave me discernment, let it be strong now. "Maybe because it's the right thing to do." He looked down at the floor. "Maybe because the world could die without it." He sighed, knowing the only thing that would move Adler. "Maybe because it could improve your lot in life to have helped out here."

"What kind of help would it give me?" Adler's eyes narrowed, and in that instant, Richard knew that Adler did indeed know more than he had shared.

Richard shrugged. "Life in prison is still life in prison." He met Adler's gaze. "But if I told the President that you had helped me, the man who had a big part in putting you away, if I argued for clemency for you, maybe you'd get the time at a nicer prison, get a few more perks."

Adler smiled. "Like I said, life in prison is still life in prison."

"Your choice." He stretched his leg. "If you could tell me, for instance, who the key players are behind the throne and what their angle is, I would be very grateful and willing to bend the President's ear."

Adler nodded. "But the President won't always be President. There'll be another one someday. And then another one after that."

"I guess it all depends on how much help you prove to be and how much concession is granted in writing."

"I guess." Adler smiled, leaning back in the chair and stretching his arms far above his head. Richard noted that Adler had lost weight since his capture. Always a big man, the Adler Richard had faced four months ago was bulky, almost corpulent. The man before him now was leaner. And probably meaner, Richard surmised. "I'll let you know if I think of anything."

Richard recognized a dismissal. He stood. "And I'll let you know if the President comes up with any offers." He picked up Adler's shoes and walked out of the room, closing the door behind him, knowing that Adler watched him as he left. He raised the shoes as he paused at the door. "We'll have these back to you early in the morning."

He nodded as the older Marine locked the door. He motioned to the man when the door was secure. They stepped a dozen feet away from Adler's door. "Report to me who comes and goes wherever he is." Deep in thought, he walked toward his own room.

****

"I'm pretty sure our intelligence is right on the Japanese situation," he said to his staff, after he recounted his discussion with Shirane. "And I think their offer of cooperation with North Korea will be withdrawn."

"Damn." Harris hissed. "That means that somebody is trying to maneuver the negotiations to exclude everyone except the Koreans."

"It looks that way, John."

"And Adler has to be involved somehow," Delmonico added.

"Yeah, well, I gave him some food for thought," he admitted. Briefly he told them of his encounter with Adler. "Ryman is polishing his shoes right now."

336

Edwards brightened. "Then I can get a bug in them tonight, if I can contact Pacific fleet carrier."

"Relax, Ted." Richard smiled at the young man's eagerness. "He'll suspect something, will probably tear them apart tomorrow." He settled back in his chair. "Let's give him a day or two to decide we're not up to anything before we plant the bug in the shoe."

"You think it's wise to talk to Adler alone, boss?" Delmonico had been quiet since Richard mentioned the visit. "I mean, he could try to get the best of you, hold you hostage or something."

"He could try." Richard felt the calm that came from knowing he had beaten Adler in the past. "I'm careful, boys. Don't forget that we've jousted before." He sighed. "And after tomorrow, we'll have surveillance in his room."

"Still, boss, I don't trust him as far as I can throw an aircraft carrier." When Harris shot him a puzzled look, Delmonico shrugged. "I could toss Adler pretty far, and I don't trust him that far."

Richard laughed. "I don't trust him, either, Ray, and I won't let my guard down." He felt better than he had in weeks. "But it did shake him for me to visit him. Not at all what he expected." He stood up. "Let's knock off for the day."

****

After his staff left, Richard changed into running shoes and slipped on a heavy coat against the chill dusk would bring. Ryman and Darnell joined him as he left his room, followed at about twenty yards by their North Korean armed guard. "No run tonight, guys, I just want to walk and think."

"Yes, sir," both Marines responded. They hushed

the chit chat they had begun on the way to the beach. He walked half the length of the beach in silence, kicking the occasional rock, watching the wave pattern on the sand. He looked up to find Chung Hee just a few yards away.

"Good evening, Chung Hee," he called in Korean.

"Good evening, Richard." Chung Hee joined Richard where he had stopped, his own security staff a few feet away from him. The Marines, eyeing the cadre of North Koreans surrounding them, backed off far enough to let the two diplomats talk in privacy, and stood alert.

"Safety makes it difficult to have a solitary walk, does it not?" Chung Hee commented, his back to the security staff.

"Yes, it does," Richard agreed. The hair on the back of his neck bristled as he felt the North Koreans watching him. He faced the ocean, but his attention was on the people surrounding him. He switched to English, hoping few of the soldiers could speak it. "It is most unfortunate that the Japanese have had to leave."

"Yes, most unfortunate." Chung Hee glanced at Gi Chu, and Richard realized that the young man understood their words. He prayed that Chung Hee had chosen Gi Chu for his loyalty and not to satisfy the Party rulers. "I hope they can avert the potential tragedy."

"It seems terrorists are trying to control every government these days." Richard watched a North Korean patrol boat sweep the bay in front of them.

"So it seems." Chung Hee sighed. "People who believe deeply in a cause sometimes become single-minded and lose compassion for others."

He gritted his teeth. Getting information about the real situation from Chung Hee had been difficult before, but with witnesses hanging on their every word, it was now nearly impossible. He decided to take a different route, see if he and Chung Hee could communicate between the lines. "I think I pulled a very foolish stunt, calling a recess to visit my wife."

Chung Hee shot him a look. "Foolish, perhaps, but understandable if one knows your history."

Richard nodded. "But it was selfish of me, putting my own desires above what is best for the world at large."

"Sometimes one learns much more from a foolish mistake than from a wise choice."

"Have you ever learned from such a mistake, Chung Hee?" He watched the North Korean leader in his periphery.

"Yes, many times." Chung Hee clasped his hands before him. "Usually from trusting the wrong person."

"Ah, yes, my experience as well." He dug a hole in the sand with his toe. "Trusting the wrong person can thwart your plans."

"All too often," Chung Hee agreed, nodding to emphasize his agreement.

He is not achieving his goals with the staff he has at present, Richard thought. How can I find out who he trusts?

"The best way to trust the right person is to choose yourself who to trust." Chung Hee offered.

Does he mean my staff, Richard wondered, or his own? "Very true."

"For instance, my friend," Chung Hee continued. "I trust your judgment as to situations and people." He smiled at Richard. "The Lord has gifted you with discernment, as well, even though you may not know it." He looked out over the sea. "Our choices now will have repercussions long after we are gone." He glanced down at his watch. "We have an important day tomorrow, Richard. We should get our rest." He bowed slightly. "I pray you will have a peaceful sleep."

Richard bowed, too. "You, too, Chung Hee." He stood at the shoreline watching Chung Hee and his entourage trudge toward the retreat center. Gi Chu paused at the top of the stairs to look back toward Richard, then disappeared into the building.

Richard sighed. Chung Hee trusted his judgment about people. That must mean he could trust his own staff, which meant that Chung Hee did not trust his own, except for Gi Chu. Logically, then it followed that Richard could trust Gi Chu. And that no one on earth could trust Adler. He took a stride toward the building and Darnell and Ryman fell into step beside him.

Back in his room, he found sleep elusive, and picked up the cell phone to call Terra. The absolute contentment in her voice, as she bounced from talking about the sofa group she'd found to veiled promises about what they would do with each other when the negotiations were over, reassured him, gave him something besides the mysteries in North Korea to occupy his mind. After he closed the phone, he drifted off quickly to sleep.

Chapter 70

"So, South Korea is still committed to moving forward with the steel manufacturing plant in North Korea." Richard needed confirmation that some progress had remained since negotiations resumed.

Hyeong nodded. "We are also committed to helping our northern brothers improve their electric power delivery infrastructure." He stared across the table at Chung Hee. "If we have assurances of non-aggression, and a full accounting of nuclear weapons."

Chung Hee bowed his head. "You have my personal assurance that I have no desire to attack my neighbors." He met Hyeong's gaze. "I have hope that this cooperative venture will be the first of many, and that such ventures will lead to open travel and communication between our countries."

"But we must be able to protect ourselves." Dak Ho placed his hands squarely on the table before him.

Richard shook his head. "What do you need to protect yourselves against, Dak Ho?" He found the constant reference to threats against North Korea grating.

The North Korean foreign minister glared at him for a moment. Before he could respond, Chung Hee spoke. "We are a small country, Mr. Matthews, surrounded by super powers, or—" He nodded at Hyeong. "Allies of super powers." He sighed. "We merely want to keep the means to protect ourselves in case balances of power shift." He looked down at his hands. "In both the distant and recent past, we have seen unexpected attacks from governments that professed peaceful intentions. Such as Hitler's systematic takeover of Europe and Iraq's invasion of Kuwait." He swept his hand around the room. "Today, we are at peace with our neighbors, but who can say what could evoke a change of heart tomorrow." Dak Ho and Seong nodded agreement, perhaps the first time in the negotiations that the North Koreans had reached such unity.

"How can a full accounting of your weapons, to the proper international authorities, hinder your security?" Richard felt compelled to press harder. Thus far, none of the agreements were finalized, nothing signed, no real change since the crisis had arisen.

Chung Hee smiled. "Do you lay every card on the table when you open a hand of poker, Richard?"

"No, I don't, but this is much more than just a poker game." He glanced around the room. "Every country represented at this table has allowed nuclear inspectors into the country and made a full accounting."

Pan Kaitan blinked, and Hyeong looked down at his hands. Rostopol squirmed. Richard realized he had blundered by assuming too much. In reality, the Russians couldn't say for certain where all of their nuclear weapons were after the breakup of the Soviet Union. China certainly had a few aces up its sleeve, and the United States wasn't about to divulge any secret weapons research at Los Alamos. He backed off. "Then what kind of assurance can you give us?"

"We can sign the Nuclear Non-Proliferation Treaty

that was negotiated a few years ago, but never ratified by our country."

Now Richard blinked. This was something that no one thought would ever happen. "You would do that?"

"As a gesture of trust." Chung Hee's gaze was level, but now Seong and Dak Ho stared at their President in surprise.

Richard suspected that the treaty might yet go unsigned, but the offer was important. "I'll see how quickly I can arrange that."

"If the treaty is signed, South Korea is prepared to begin earnest negotiations on the plant, as well as further visits between family members across the border," Hyeong offered.

"That would be very satisfactory." Chung Hee smiled, but Seong's face grew dark. Dak Ho glanced once at Adler's corner. Richard allowed himself a shift of his eyes to see if he could read Adler's expression. All he saw spelled agitation on Adler's face as he toyed with a pen.

A knock sounded at the door and one of the soldiers inside opened it. A messenger hurried toward Chung Hee, hesitated, then approached Richard. "Excuse me, sir," he said hesitantly, his gaze darting to Chung Hee and Dak Ho. "But there is an urgent phone call for Pan Kaitan that they say won't wait."

Richard nodded at Pan. "Take the call," he said, as she rose from the table. "We'll have a short recess."

He stood and stretched as the delegates milled around. Some headed for a mid-morning snack at the refreshments table. Dak Ho left the room and Richard decided to do the same. He stood in the anteroom, enjoying the sunlight pouring through the windows, watching with his peripheral vision as Dak Ho entered the nearest restroom. Adler came through the doors, *wha jeon* and coffee in his hands, and joined Richard at the window.

"Quite a productive morning you've had in there, Matthews," he commented.

Glancing over at him, Richard shrugged. "We'll see if any of it goes anywhere." He noted that Adler wore the shoes Ryman had polished to a gloss last night.

They stood in silence until Adler finished his pastry. The man twisted around, as if to find a servant to take his coffee cup and finally placed it on a low table. The Marines assigned to him stayed no more than three feet away from him. "Nature calls," Adler offered. He walked toward the restroom, followed by his Marine shadows. Richard watched, as he entered the same room Dak Ho had just exited. A question began to form in the back of his mind.

"Mr. Matthews," Pan Kaitan addressed him quietly near his elbow.

He read concern on her normally smooth face. "Did you get the call?"

"Unfortunately, yes." She looked down, and when she faced him again, there was a crease between her eyes. "It seems that a demonstration is gathering in Tiananmen Square, and all of us are being called back to Beijing to display the solidarity of the government."

"A demonstration?" He suppressed a shudder at the memory of the last one. "May I ask what about?"

"Disparity of wages," she admitted. "We have a gap between the lowest paid and highest earning of our people, and the demonstrators want the government to intervene." She glanced around the anteroom. "All of the people's representatives need to be there to assure them that we are seriously listening to their concerns this time. We hope for a peaceful outcome, but—" She looked toward Chung Hee and Hyeong conversing over tea. "It seems that our presence is not actually needed to come to a peaceful and satisfactory resolution here at this time."

He bowed and extended his hand. "Your presence has been most helpful at getting the negotiations to this point, Pan." She squeezed his hand. "I thank you for your insights and wish you a good outcome on the situation you face at home."

"Thank you," she said. "I'll take my leave of Chung Hee and begin preparations to depart."

****

Because Pan's departure disrupted the flow of the day's negotiations, Richard ended the day's work at noon. He and his staff would meet after lunch, but he headed to his room to call Terra.

"Oh, Richard, it's good to get two calls from you in the same day," she bubbled as she answered.

"Same day to you, different days to me," he growled playfully. "How are you feeling?"

"Great, morning sickness is about over. Although it was never just morning." He heard her shift in the folding chairs she had purchased as temporary furniture. They could use them on the lawn in the summer, she had argued. "You know, living in the city was fun, but I hadn't realized how much I missed rural life."

"Rural life? You're less than ten miles from Estes Park and shopping."

"Yes, but it's nice to know that I can step out into my own yard and no one will complain if I mow too early or play the stereo too loud." She lowered her voice. "Or if we frolic naked in the yard."

He liked that idea. "Wouldn't it be a little cold right now?"

She giggled. "It would be chilly, but then we'd have to snuggle really close to warm up." She giggled again. "We have most of the landscaping done, at least as far as we can go in the fall, and the rooms painted that I know what colors I want. We're going to Fort Collins to shop for furniture on Friday. If it's nice tomorrow, my security guy and I are going to start walking the fence line to see if it needs repairs."

"Fence repairs? To keep in our jackrabbits?" She couldn't sit still, had already edited the manuscripts Warner had sent her and finished proofing his galleys. He wondered if a baby would slow her down at all.

"Good fences make good neighbors. Besides, we'll need a pony for the baby and that will mean we have to get horses for ourselves, and maybe a calf or lamb for him or her to play with."

"Whoa, there, land baron, we have ten acres, not ten thousand."

"Well, I just found out that the 160 acres between us and the McGrath ranch is for sale. We could lease it out to a rancher to run a few cattle, have fresh organic beef for ourselves and more room to roam."

"I suppose you'll want to buy Wyoming next."

She laughed. "Not unless land prices go down more."

"Just be careful out there. Remember, it's rattlesnake country, even in the fall."

"I'll wear boots and, besides, Erik carries a gun."

"You'll make an old man of me, Terra." He sighed, wishing it was him she was walking the fence line with. "And wear out the FBI."

"No, I'm going to keep you young." She giggled again, then her voice grew soft. "I love you so much. Are you getting close to a resolution?"

"Maybe." He sighed, hoping the Chinese pullout didn't take the negotiations back to deadlock. "I'll call you before I go to bed."

"Which is when I get up." Her voice grew soft. "It's much better waking up to your scratchy face on my shoulder than it is to your voice on the phone."

"Yes, it is. And that's how it will be again, as soon as possible." He hung up, suddenly aching with the need to get this over with, to stop considering the world at large, and instead concern himself only about his own life.

Chapter 71

He phoned in his report to the State Department on a secure line. The Secretary did not sound as happy as he had expected, and as he was changing for lunch, he got a call ordering him to report to the Pacific fleet carrier within the hour. His staff arrived for their briefing shortly after that.

"Well, sir, that just gives us a cover to get the electronics for Adler's room without any disruption to the negotiations," Edwards offered.

Richard nodded, although a gnawing sensation in the pit of his stomach argued that something was about to go wrong. He decided to bring the entire staff, in order to immediately assess whatever development awaited them on the carrier. Delmonico made the necessary courtesy arrangements for their Sea Stallion taxi to land.

****

Bundled in extra sweaters and their warmest coats, they hopped off the chopper to the flight deck of the Pacific fleet carrier, to be immediately escorted to the Captain's ready room. The Captain himself awaited them.

"What's up, Captain Verain?" Richard asked as they shook hands. He took in the video screen and electronics setup at the front of the room.

"Not sure, sir, we were just instructed to set up a

teleconference video feed." He glanced at Richard's staff. "Only top secret security clearance in the room, sir."

Richard nodded. "My staff is fully cleared."

"Most of mine is not, sir, so it will just be me, my XO, and our intelligence officer here to run the equipment."

"That's fine." Richard made his way toward the conference table. "I guess we're ready whenever the feed is."

The Captain spoke into the receiver. After a few seconds of static, the face of the President of the United States appeared on the screen, and his booming voice filled the room. The Captain dialed down the volume. "Good afternoon, gentlemen and officers," the President said. "Can you hear me?"

"We hear you, sir," Richard responded, glad the Captain had adjusted the speakers.

"Good. I'll cut right to the chase." The President, speaking from the Oval Office, rested his hands on the oak desk. "The Secretary of State briefed me on the latest developments over there, and I want to know what the hell is going on."

"Sir?" Richard sat up straighter. Beside him, his staff squirmed.

"Everyone is bailing out of the negotiations, and the North Koreans are offering the same empty promises they have always offered in exchange for our help. Why?"

Richard stood, so the President could see him clearly. "Sir, I believe that there are factions at work orchestrating the situations that have taken the Russians, Japanese, and Chinese out of play. In short, sir, they've been blackmailed."

"By whom?" No one had ever accused this President of beating around the bush.

"We don't know, sir. As always, intel on North Korea is spotty, but we suspect it's someone within the country who is trying to protect a heroin smuggling operation."

"Have you asked them? You're supposed to be friends with their President." He heard the implied doubt in the President's words.

"I have asked Chung Hee, but I don't believe he is at liberty to be completely open with me. He has only limited power, and I have not been able to find out who has the rest of it."

"Well, keep digging. All of the intel we have is available to you."

"I know that, sir, and I'm keeping abreast of what new developments come up, but it's very tight."

"Also, Richard, no aid until they sign the nuclear agreement AND let the human rights people into the country."

"Sir, that's a lot of concessions to expect from them. I believe if we can get international groups in to distribute the food, they can observe other issues, and we can keep the door open to further exchanges. Not to mention the lives that might be saved."

"I guess you didn't hear me, son. I said no food until the nukes are secure."

"Sir, that takes us right back to where we started. They'll start threatening to launch a strike."

"Then we can move a Nautilus class sub thirteen miles offshore and see how they like it."

"Thirteen miles off North Korea is also within

striking distance of Japan, Russia, and China, sir. They might view it as a threat."

"Well, then, they'd better help you put the pressure on the North Koreans."

"If they stay in the negotiations, they face chaos and murder at home."

"There are risks involved in keeping the world safe."

Richard looked down at his hands. He hadn't realized until that moment that he had a death-grip on the edge of table. He took a deep breath and faced the screen again. "Sir, in a game of nuclear chicken, if no one swerves, everybody loses." He saw the nods go around the table, wondered if the President could see them as well, or only his face illuminated by the President's image on the screen. "The whole world."

"So, you're telling me that I'm wrong?" The President's face was dark and serious.

Richard took another deep breath. "In this instance, I guess I am, sir. From where I sit, I think we can accomplish much more by giving a little than we can by pushing a lot. Right now, we have a small window of opportunity while Chung Hee wields what little power he has to open up North Korea and get it fully involved in the world. Once that begins, it will be hard for them to shut down again, and economic pressure from their own people will make them change faster and more peacefully than force ever could." He stood silent, fully expecting to be dismissed from the negotiations. At least if he fires me, Richard thought, I can go home to Terra and the baby. Although if the next negotiator does what the President wants, my baby may be born in nuclear winter. He met the pixeled eyes of the man who had the power in his hands to destroy the world. Or hold it back from the brink.

The President sat back in his chair, stroking his chin. He glanced at someone beyond the camera lens, probably the Secretary of State and the Chairman of the Joint Chiefs, perhaps even other advisors. He placed both hands on the desk and stared at them. Finally, he looked into the camera again. "Well, son, I have to hand it to you, you have more grit than most. And you've most certainly proved it over there." He leaned back in the big chair. "All right, go ahead your way for now, but don't set any offers in stone until they're run by us."

Richard nearly dropped into his chair as his knees went weak. "Yes, sir," he responded. "I will do my best to bring a solution that will be equitable for everyone."

"That's what we need, son, that's what we need. Thank you for coming over to the ship for this little chat."

"Yes, sir." The feed ended and the screen went blank, leaving the room dark enough he hoped the staff couldn't see his face. No one spoke, the only sounds coming from the radioman shutting down the equipment.

Into the silence, Delmonico whistled. "Brass balls, boss, that's what you've got." He saw Delmonico's tense grin. "Brass balls."

Chapter 72

The brisk wind whipped Terra's hair into her face, making it hard for her to see if the pliers gripped the right piece of wire. Her security man for the day took the pliers from her and twisted the splice into the wire. Then, as Terra had showed him, he slipped one handle of the pliers through a loop in the splice and spun it until the wire was taut. "Thanks, Erik," she said as she stepped back from the fence.

"No problem, Mrs. Matthews," he said. "You know, Mrs. Matthews, I don't believe I've ever even touched a barbed wire fence until today." He handed the pliers back to her and waited for her to start again down the fence line.

"City boy, eh, Erik?"

"Seattle, ma'am."

"Well, that's certainly a bigger city than I'm from. Box Elder, Oklahoma, population 3,628." She shaded her eyes to peer down the fence line. They had come about three-quarters the length of this leg of the fence, the one along the driveway. "I think we can get about halfway around today, don't you?"

He glanced back toward the fence they had just inspected. "That depends on how many breaks we find, ma'am." He patted the roll of wire in his pocket. "And on how long the wire holds out."

She grinned. "Well, we'll just hope we don't find

more breaks than we have wire." She started toward the corner, assessing the fence as she went. This felt like many jaunts with her maternal grandfather, when she shadowed him, as eager to learn the farm chores as any of his grandsons. The rush of memories warmed her against the early November chill. "At least the cold snap makes it unlikely we'll find any rattlesnakes today."

She saw Erik's face pale as he glanced at the ground around him. "I hope not, ma'am."

She laughed at his fear of the snakes, comforted knowing that she would be able to pass on some of her rural roots to her child. Ten acres wasn't a working, self-sustaining farm, but it was enough to teach a child the cycle of life and death, of planting and harvesting, of seasons, and hard work. She was also glad that Paul and Carrie would be an intimate part of the baby's life. Her grandparents played a large part in grounding her and ensuring she grew up enveloped by love, maybe not spoken but certainly demonstrated. Paul would probably have been with them walking the fence today, had he not had to attend to some legal business by phone and fax. She hoped to be finished with the fence by the time he finished with the call.

A swirl of dust approached from the south. Erik stepped in front of her, standing alert as the vehicle approached. It swept on past the pasture and driveway, leaving a gradually expanding fan of dust to settle as it sped north.

She laughed. "You can relax now, Erik." She went around him to eyeball the next section of fence. "Not much traffic out here."

"Can't be too careful, ma'am." he said, handing her

the roll of wire as she pulled out the pliers to repair another break.

****

"Thank you, Chung Hee. I'll inform our people, and we will get the arrangements made." Richard leaned back in his chair with satisfaction. North Korea had just confirmed agreement to sign the nuclear pact, pending a time to hold the ceremony. The signing might yet fall through, but for now, it ranked as an incredible coup.

"And our delegation is prepared to meet with your people next week to begin discussions about the steel plant." Hyeong's smile could have illuminated a small room. He told Richard quietly yesterday that the cooperative venture was something his government had sought for years.

"All right." Richard glanced at his watch. "Let's take a twenty-minute break, and then come back to discuss the food aid distribution." He nodded at Chung Hee, who nodded back as he rose.

Hyeong's pretty assistant flashed Richard a shy smile as she slipped out of her chair. She bumped into Edwards. He put out his hands to catch her, and she stumbled against him before she could regain her feet. Was she just a flirt, he wondered, or was she trying to distract all the men? He glanced toward Adler's corner to find him watching the girl, too. Looking back at Richard as the girl made her way out of the room, Edwards shrugged and grinned. Richard sighed. The tenor of the negotiations had changed from one of hostile tension to almost that of a friendly office party. That change could prove dangerous.

Dak Ho was deep in conversation with his

stenographer. She had rejoined the group in the room with Richard's permission after the departure of the Chinese delegation, meaning the table remained full and positions rotated at Richard's whim. She nodded at Dak Ho's last comment, a serious expression on her face. She was as pretty as the young South Korean woman, Richard noted, but not as noticeable due to her severe business suit and demure demeanor. Dak Ho placed a hand on her shoulder, and she stiffened briefly, holding her breath until Dak Ho dropped his hand. Dak Ho turned from his chair, face to face with Richard. He bowed almost imperceptibly, but his face showed no submission.

Richard bowed deeply. "Congratulations on the strides we are making today, Dak Ho."

Dak Ho held himself up straight. "I just hope that the progress does not slip." He left the room.

Richard watched his back as he walked away. He glanced at the stenographer, Bo Bae, he thought her name was. She met his gaze for only a fraction of a second before she lowered hers. Hugging her notepad to her chest, she waited for him to pass before she stepped away from her chair.

Tension gripped Richard's shoulders. The tone of the negotiations might have changed on the surface, but the hostility remained simmering beneath. He searched for Adler, finally finding him in the anteroom with a cup of coffee and an apple Danish, staring out the window, Marines two paces behind him. He noted the positions of the other delegates as he approached Adler. Hyeong and Chung Hee stood together near the refreshment table, apparently sipping tea. Wearing his characteristic somber expression, Seong stood at Chung

Hee's elbow. The women chatted together a few feet from them. Rostopol and his entourage gathered around a couch in the anteroom, coffee cups steaming in their hands. Richard approached Adler. "Morning, Robert."

"Morning, Richard." Adler nodded. "Which Marine should I thank for the great shoeshine?"

Richard shrugged. "It depends on who has the time. I'm not sure who did them for you last night." He knew, of course, that it had been Ryman who rubbed them to a high gloss after Edwards installed the tiny transmitter in the heel.

"Well, then, would you thank the gentleman for me?"

"I will do that." Their surveillance tapes had revealed nothing more than a man exercising and trying to kill time. Adler didn't talk to himself, which was exactly what Richard expected. When he learned that Adler had planted microphones in his apartment during Richard's successful campaign to bring Adler to justice, Richard had given up that habit himself. He heard a door open and saw Dak Ho leave the restroom.

Finished with the Danish, Adler set down his coffee cup. "Nature calls."

Richard watched him, followed closely by the two Marines, walk toward the room. Adler nodded politely to Dak Ho as they passed each other. Dak Ho nodded as well. Richard started toward the room. By the time Dak Ho made two steps from Adler, Richard was directly in front of him. A momentary surprise flashed in his eyes, but then he smiled at Richard. "A very popular place this morning," he said. Richard caught a tone in the words, sarcasm, maybe, or hatred. Adler closed the door behind him, and Richard stood staring at the door, logic arguing with instinct. He shook his head.

****

Terra and Erik finished the leg of the fence that ran along the driveway, and now worked about a hundred yards away from the corner along the roadside fence. The fence was in better shape than Terra feared but would take constant attention to keep much livestock inside for long. She pulled a water bottle from her sweatshirt pocket as Erik wrapped the wire around the latest break. She heard a vehicle approaching from the north.

"Let's move away from the fence, ma'am," Erik urged. His hand on her elbow propelled her toward an untidy stack of old wooden fence posts about fifty feet inside the fence just above where the land rolled down into a shallow wash.

"Oh, Erik, it's probably just the car that went by a little while ago." She hated to quit on the fence when they were making good progress but decided to humor him. The pile of fence posts would break the wind for a while, and she could use a few minutes of sitting. Although she had only gained a couple of pounds with the baby thus far, her feet seemed to tire more quickly now. She'd also had to give up wearing her favorite pair of jeans because they felt uncomfortably tight. She saw him sweep his jacket back from his gun and glanced again toward the approaching vehicle. It slowed down near the driveway. She stepped out of the wind by the fence posts as the car slammed to a stop almost in front of them.

****

Richard stood before the restroom door another two seconds, but the insistent whispering of his instinct would not stop. He raised his foot and kicked the door just below the handle. The door flew open as every eye in the room watched. Shock registered on Adler's face as he staggered back from the bin of used towels he was bent over. Richard leaped into the tiny room, slamming Adler against the wall.

"What the hell is wrong with you, Matthews?" Adler sputtered, his face red, eyes wide. One Marine moved in behind Richard. The rest of the people crowded around. He saw Edwards near the door, Harris not far behind him.

"What are you up to?" Richard growled, his left forearm holding Adler against the wall. "Hold out your hands."

Adler raised his arms, empty palms up. "I'm simply trying to take care of private personal needs, Matthews, and you burst in here like a madman."

"Mr. Matthews," Dak Ho's voice came to him. "This is most inappropriate."

"Check the towel bin," Richard ordered the Marine, his gaze still locked with Adler's. "He was going through it when the door came open."

"Have you lost your mind, Matthews?" He felt Adler relax beneath his arm. "Pressure of the negotiations getting to you?" A smile began on Adler's lips. "Maybe you're scared you'll lose another baby." His smile grew. "Or another wife."

Richard increased the pressure of his arm on Adler's chest. "Shut up, you—"

"I found a note, sir," the Marine stood up from the towel bin.

"What does it say?" Richard watched as the color paled in Adler's cheeks.

"It just says, 'hit confirmed,' sir."

Chapter 73

Erik turned toward the car, gun hidden behind his leg from view of the car's occupants. "Get down behind the fence posts, into the wash if you can, ma'am," he said in a low tone. She moved around the pile, hidden from the road, but now exposed to the north wind. Erik stood at the edge of the posts, at such an angle that very little of his body below his shoulders was exposed to the road. He keyed the microphone on his collar, but what he said was so low that the wind blew the words away from Terra's ears.

The rear door on the side of the car away from them flew open, and a man with a rifle appeared over the roof. Erik said something more into the radio and crouched behind the fence posts. "FBI," he yelled. "Throw down the gun and surrender."

A bullet tore through the air over his head, and then a second hit the top fence post. He returned fire, but the car was too far away for a nine-millimeter to be either accurate or effective, beyond punching a hole in the fender. "Get down as far as you can, Terra," he said, firing another three-shot burst.

She heard a car speeding down the driveway. Their backup, she thought, knowing his radio call had brought at least one of the agents from the house. She couldn't believe how quickly life had changed from routine to a fight for survival, of both her and her baby. She wished there was something she could do besides hide. Suddenly, as another rifle shot sounded, Erik spun around and fell against the fence posts, his pistol hitting the ground beside her. She picked it up as he crumpled, blood gushing from his right arm. He blinked hard and reached out his left hand. "Give me the gun."

She shook her head. "You're barely conscious." She peeked toward the road from the opposite side of the post pile that Erik had held. "I'm not planning to go down without a fight."

She heard Erik say, "Officer hit," into the radio as the gunman took aim on the car in the driveway. One shot, and the car spun into the fence they had repaired, stopped halfway through by the deep sand. Both doors flung open, but the rifleman kept up a steady fire that prevented the officers from safely shooting back.

She settled Erik's gun in her hand and steadied herself on the ground with only her hands and head visible to the road. This is no different than Saturday target practice with my dad, she told herself, and stifled her shivering. The first shot she squeezed off shattered the rear window of the car. "That's for my bodyguard," she muttered. The gunman spun toward her as her second shot dug a furrow in the roof. "And that one's for my fence." Before she could get off a third shot, the agents in the car fired on the gunman.

"Okay, you keep the gun," Erik growled, fumbling his backup gun from his ankle holster. Glancing at him, Terra could see that blood had soaked most of the right sleeve of his jacket, and his right arm dangled limp. He gripped the small semi-automatic pistol in his left hand and rolled away from her to cover behind a clump of yucca at the top of the wash. She hoped the sand he rolled through would stanch the blood flow. She saw the dark stain on the ground where he had been sitting and then heard him send two quick shots toward the gunman.

The gunman whirled momentarily from the two agents toward Erik. Terra aimed carefully, caught her breath and squeezed the trigger. This bullet hit the car roof, and she saw the gunman slap his hand over his cheek as if either a fragment of bullet or metal from the car had hit him. Then she heard gunfire from the FBI car. The gunman twirled away from the car and disappeared. The car roared into gear and fishtailed on the sand as the agents shot at it.

Terra crawled below the crest of the wash toward Erik where he lay face down. He was still breathing, she saw as she got closer. Glancing at the road, she saw the other two agents running toward the fallen gunman. She laid Erik's gun down carefully where she could grab it again if needed and pulled off her sweatshirt to use as a bandage.

Erik moaned as the pain of her touch on his arm brought him back to consciousness. "Take it easy, agent," she ordered, wrapping her shirt around his arm. "We got our man."

"Where did you learn to shoot like that?" He winced as she tightened the wrap.

"My dad spent twenty years in the Oklahoma National Guard." She helped him struggle to sit up. "We used to go shooting on weekends he wasn't at drill. He had a nine-millimeter just like his service pistol." She heard sirens, saw the other agents talking into radios. "Just sit still till the cavalry arrives." She grinned at him, trying to cover up the fact that she was shaking inside as she realized the full impact of the danger. "At least that'll teach 'em not to mess with *our* fence!"

Chapter 74

Richard dragged Adler from the restroom and all but threw him against the wall of the anteroom. "Start talking," he ordered. "What does the note mean?"

"I don't know anything about any note, Matthews. I was simply drying my hands—"

Richard grabbed him by the lapels and lifted him six inches off the ground. "You were exchanging messages with someone." He brought his face closer to Adler's. "I want to know who."

"I never saw that note, Matthews."

"Mr. Matthews, is this a personal vendetta?" Dak Ho spoke from a few feet away.

"I'll deal with you in a moment, sir." Richard's voice was low and deadly calm. He did not look away from Adler's face. Adler's gaze flicked to Dak Ho, and then back to Richard.

"Dak Ho, for the time being this is an American situation, and we will allow the Americans to solve it among themselves," Chung Hee said in a quiet voice.

"But the broken door—"

"Dak Ho, let them settle it." Richard heard more authority in Chung Hee's voice than he had ever heard. Dak Ho fell silent.

He gave his full attention to Adler. "All right, Bob," he bit off the name with contempt. "I'll give you one more chance."

"Or else what?" Adler glared at him. "You'll do what? Spank me?" His lips curled in a snarl. "You can't do squat. You can't promise me anything, nor can you even be sure I won't strike a deal that wins me my freedom."

"I can promise you this—" His cell phone vibrated. It had to be Terra; no one else would call him. Anyone else he would have ignored, but Terra knew he should be in negotiations now. Maybe something happened to the baby. He let go of Adler, nodding to the Marine to maintain custody of him. "Terra, now is not a good time—" he began.

"You need to know this." Her voice carried a tone that made him listen. "We were just attacked, a rifleman in a car—"

His heart nearly stopped. "Are you all right?" He could barely choke out the words.

"I'm fine—"

"Mum and Dad? The baby?"

"All fine. Erik was shot, may lose much of the use of his right hand, but the only fatality was the gunman." She paused. "It was almost like they expected us to be at the fence line."

That was too neat a coincidence. "Let me talk to one of the agents." He hated to cut her off, but he had to have more information.

"Agent Driscoll, Mr. Matthews." A crisp, business-like voice came on the line immediately.

"What happened?"

"Just like your wife said, Mr. Matthews. A car with a rifleman attacked them when they were working on the fence along the road. Agent Teague had Mrs. Matthews take cover before the gunman's car stopped and held them off until we arrived." There was a pause. "Although we might not have been able to get him if Mrs. Matthews had not also been shooting at them after Agent Teague was wounded."

"Terra handled a gun?"

"Yes, sir, she's quite an accurate marksman, er, marksperson."

Despite his fear, he felt a tingle of pride, that Terra was good at taking care of herself. But he already knew that from how she had handled Adler. "The gunman was killed?"

"Yes, sir. Dead before we could question him."

"Did you get the driver?"

"Not yet, sir, but we have every law enforcement agency in the country watching for the car. It should be easy to spot, as Mrs. Matthews put several holes in it and shot out the rear window."

"And it was like she said, like they knew she would be at the fence today?"

"Yes, sir, from what we can piece together. We're still investigating, tracing the gun, fingerprinting the body, that sort of thing."

He let out a tense breath. "Keep me posted as you get more information." His voice gentled. "Let me talk to my wife again, please."

"Richard, be very careful." Terra's voice conveyed her fear for him, not herself.

"Me be careful? How about you?" He held the phone away for a second, rested his forehead against the cool wall, as the reality of what could have happened washed over him.

"Richard, you're right, someone there does not want you to bring an equitable peace."

"I know." He took a deep breath, trying to focus his anger and his fear. "We're dealing with it right now." He glanced at the Marine holding Adler against the wall, and then at the rest of the delegates gathered around the show. "I love you, Terra. I'll call you in just a little while."

"I love you, too, Richard. We are all praying for you right now."

"Thanks, love." He closed the phone and stared at the wall for another minute, centering, praying for wisdom and control, getting a grip on his emotions. He spoke to the Marine who found the note.

"Let me see that note, Marine."

"Yes, sir." The Marine handed it to him immediately.

He studied it. Tiny handwriting, a piece of rice paper about twice the size of a postage stamp, edge ragged as if it had been creased carefully to make a neat tear. Not Adler's handwriting, but someone else's. Probably someone who had been able to tap into his phone signals to Terra. No technology his experts were aware of could listen to the conversations he carried on with his staff in his room after it was swept for electronics, but cell phones were another matter. Unless they had encoded scrambling devices imbedded, cell signals could be intercepted. Because they were just using commercial cell phones, he and Terra had been very careful in their conversations. Except for the comment about the fence work. He played a hunch.

"Chung Hee, would you look at this message, please?" He held the note close enough that Chung Hee would have to come very near to examine it.

"Certainly, Mr. Matthews." Chung Hee stood

directly in front of him, studying the message as Richard held it. He made no move to take it from Richard, evidently understanding that the fewer hands on it, the easier it might be to extract fingerprints from it.

"Do you recognize the handwriting?"

Chung Hee looked up from the note to Richard's face. "Not immediately. The script is so small it's difficult to read, much less identify."

Richard hesitated. He was on shaky legal ground, but he knew finding the answer to the note also meant finding the answer to who was sabotaging the negotiations. "Chung Hee, we are on North Korean soil, and because of that, yours is the authority we must defer to." He took a deep breath and plunged ahead. "Would you approve of our experts analyzing the fingerprints on this paper, and then fingerprinting the people present here, until we get a match?"

Chung Hee nodded. "I will approve. If there is someone in our midst who is not what he or she claims to be, that person must be exposed, no matter who it is."

Seong spoke up. "But, Mr. President, what if the Americans manipulate the evidence?"

"We'll do it in cooperation with your personnel, each one confirming what the other finds." He met Seong's gaze. "Fair enough?"

Seong scowled, but agreed. "That is fair."

Chung Hee spoke to Gi Chu. "Get the finest fingerprint technician from Wonson on the way here immediately."

Richard looked at Delmonico, who flipped his cell open and dialed the secure line to the Pacific fleet carrier. Once again, Richard breathed a prayer of relief that his staff was adept at reading a situation. He wasn't sure when he'd have the chance to tell them what had happened with Terra. A minute later, Delmonico snapped the phone shut. "Be here within the hour, boss."

Richard had another request of Chung Hee. "Would you also agree to seal the conference room, holding the people who are here now, with the condition that no one leaves the room except under guard?"

"That is only prudent," he agreed. Seong frowned.

Richard faced the delegates. "Then, ladies and gentlemen, I suggest that we return to the negotiating chamber and wait." He strode to the double doors and paused. "That is, unless someone has a confession to make?" No one spoke. "That's what I thought," he muttered.

He walked toward his chair, as two Marines propelled Adler toward his customary corner to the left of Richard. He slipped into his seat as the delegates began to file back in. His staff and the other two Marines waited in the anteroom, observing.

Chung Hee walked into the room with his shoulders back, no hesitation as he took his seat. Seong followed with a sour expression. Dak Ho was among the last of the delegates to enter the room, and the look he shot Richard spoke resentment. He fidgeted while he waited, glancing more than once at the young woman seated beside him. Her face was pale, tears near to falling from her eyes. Richard stayed silent, watching the delegates, as his staff entered the room and stood near the doors.

Chapter 75

Terra paced the family room, thankful it was devoid of all furniture except the folding stadium chairs she purchased on summer clearance. It gave her more room to walk without stopping. The FBI already sent an agent from Denver to take Erik's place, as well as extra agents to beef up the security presence. Larimer County Sheriff's deputies patrolled the roads around the house. She stopped by the fireplace to pull out her cell phone.

"He'll call as soon as he can." Carrie rose from her chair to put her arms around Terra.

"I know." Terra rested her head on Carrie's shoulder. She took a deep breath and surrendered to the comfort of having family near. Then the restlessness seized her again. She stared out the family room window, south toward the night-cloaked peaks of Rocky Mountain National Park. "It's just that I know something is wrong there."

Paul entered from the kitchen, coffee cup in his hand. "From your description of his conversation, I would say that you are right, Terra." He crossed the room to put one arm around Carrie. "But there nothing we can accomplish by worrying." He set his cup on the fireplace mantel. "Or by wearing a path in the new carpet."

Terra smiled at him. "I know, Paul." She rotated away from the window. "It's just that I feel a terrible sense of danger."

Paul squeezed her shoulder. "I know. I feel it, too." He sighed. "Carrie made dinner all by herself."

Terra caught the twinkle in his eye and laughed despite her fears. "Thanks, Paul, I'm sure Carrie appreciates your humor."

Carrie joined them at the window. "I do, Terra." She elbowed Paul. "I don't always enjoy it, but I do appreciate it."

Shaking her head, knowing she needed a distraction, Terra glanced toward the laptop on the breakfast bar between the kitchen and family room. "Shall we look at more furniture websites?"

"Mrs. Matthews?" The senior agent assigned to them entered the room.

"Yes?"

"We have identified the shooter."

Paul stepped forward. "Who is he?"

The agent consulted the notes in his hand. "Anatoly Temekin, from San Francisco, originally from Russia, St. Petersburg, we think. In the country on a work visa for an importer, but all the info we've turned up says he was a hit man for the Russian mob."

Terra felt a chill. "Is this tied to the situation in Korea?"

The agent gave her a look before he glanced back at his notes. "Not that we've been able to verify yet, ma'am."

Paul spoke up. "Anything on the car?"

The agent shook his head. "Our men only got partial plates. It was a sedan, tan. There are thousands of them on the streets; it may take time to run down."

"Richard may not have much time." Terra pulled out the cell phone. "I'll let him know."

Chapter 76

When the phone vibrated this time, Richard did not chide Terra for the interruption. He was silently watching the delegates and their entourages fret at the waiting. "Go ahead, Terra," he said softly into the phone.

"Richard, are you safe?"

"Yes, Terra, we're on top of the situation." He could hear the fear in her voice.

"And there is a situation right now, isn't there?"

He sighed. She had learned well to read between the lines. "Yes, but I can't discuss it at the moment."

"Well, the FBI has identified the shooter. He's—"

"Hold on a second, Terra." He remembered that Delmonico's phone had the necessary security encoding. "I'll call you right back on another line."

He approached Delmonico seated near the closed doors. The North Korean guards also stationed there eyed him with suspicion. "I need your secure phone, Ray."

Without a word, Delmonico produced the phone.

Richard spoke so only Delmonico could hear him. "We'll need a staff meeting as soon as I finish this call."

Delmonico nodded and rose from his chair to gather Edwards and Harris. While he walked to an empty corner, Richard surveyed the room. Dak Ho looked his direction once, then back at the table when he saw Richard watching. Adler studied Richard, a half-smile on his face. Chung Hee sat relaxed, quiet.

He dialed the number. "Go ahead, Terra." She rapidly outlined what the FBI had told her. It dovetailed with what he had learned from Patmanov and the meeting with Adler on board the aircraft carrier. His blood ran cold as he realized that the hit had to be tied to the succeeding negotiations. It was a trademark of the Red Mafia to not only take out an enemy but his family as well, often brutally. With effort, he kept his voice calm. "Thank you, Terra, that was important for me to know."

"Are you sure you're safe?" Her voice sounded like she was trembling.

"Absolutely, Terra, there are Marines and North Korean security people here."

"The Marines are unarmed, aren't they?"

"Yes, but how did you know—"

"Can you trust the North Koreans?"

"I know I can trust Chung Hee."

"It could be someone North Korean who has been trying to derail things, right?"

"Yes, but it might be someone else, too."

"But whoever it is might have enough influence to control the North Korean security people, couldn't he?"

He had to admit to himself that her fears had brought her to a logical conclusion he had barely considered. "You have a point there, Terra. We'll see what we can do to neutralize it." He glanced at the rest of the room and saw Adler watching him.

"Just be careful, love." Her voice sounded soft, despite her fear. "I want you to come home to us."

"I will come home to you, Terra," he promised. He closed the phone. He saw Adler smiling, which set off warning bells. There must be a plan underway, a plan that Adler was somehow privy to. He scanned the room again. Hyeong conversed quietly with his staff, but they didn't appear to be exceptionally stressed. The Russians sat nearly silent, tense, almost confused by events. Seong looked angry, but Richard had come to realize that this was his normal mood. Chung Hee had his eyes closed, head bowed; Richard assumed he was praying for the outcome. Dak Ho fidgeted and his assistant sat with her head down, hands pressed to her mouth, as if that was the sole means she had of avoiding a total breakdown. He nodded to Delmonico, and within seconds, his staff joined him in the corner.

"What's up, boss?" Delmonico began. "I know you took a call from your wife out there. It sounded like something happened, on top of what is going on here."

He took a deep breath. "Somebody ambushed her."

"Is she okay, sir?" Edwards looked shocked.

"She's fine, FBI killed the shooter, but the driver got away."

"Any leads?" Harris moved closer to him.

"Shooter was Russian mob."

"Sir, that means that the impasse here has to be linked to the heroin." Harris's lips set in a thin line. He exchanged a glance with Delmonico. Both of them knew the reputation of the Russian mafia.

"That's the conclusion I've come to, John." He motioned them closer. "But we have another layer of concern." They gathered close. "The note means that someone who is a party to this is in the room right now. If things get crazy in here at any time, the only ones armed are the North Koreans."

"That's been a concern of mine from day one, sir." Harris spoke softly.

"Mine, too, boss." Delmonico agreed.

"It was the only way we could begin negotiations," Richard maintained. "Still, it may complicate things if it goes bad."

"There's the four of us and four unarmed Marines, sir." Edwards worked through the logistics of the situation. He glanced toward the North Korean security contingent just inside the door. "And four North Korean soldiers, who probably only speak Korean, armed with fully automatic weapons." He sighed. "With another two hundred North Korean troops in the building or close by on the grounds. And a major North Korean military base just a few miles down the road."

Delmonico smiled grimly. "Sound like typical odds to me, boss."

Richard glanced at Delmonico, tension growing within him. "All the more reason to keep this diplomatic and legal." He looked toward the guards at the door. "At least as long as we can."

"How about this, boss?" Delmonico moved closer, as if he were quarterbacking the football huddle he had been a part of through his college years. "John, Ted, and I'll stick close to the door guards, disarm them if the situation warrants. Two Marines can handle Adler, leaving you and the other two Marines to deal immediately with whatever else goes down. We'll assist as soon as the guards are secured." He watched as Harris and Edwards nodded agreement.

Richard took a deep breath. Much now rested on maintaining his cool, on the right tone of voice, the right turn of phrase, or, if that failed, on making the right move quickly enough to save lives. "All right, gentlemen, that's about the best plan we can have, given the situation. I'll brief the Marines, two at a time and station the two not watching Adler to my right to cover that side of the room." He stood straight, ready to handle his responsibility. "And, gentlemen, if you believe in the power of prayer, now would be a good time to offer some up."

"Amen, sir," Edwards responded. Harris and Delmonico nodded.

As they moved back into the room, one of the North Korean guards opened the door to allow a man dressed in the uniform of the North Korean Security Police, complete with covered holster which Richard assumed contained a firearm, to enter the room. He carried a large tool box with him as he reported to Chung Hee. "It looks like the Korean fingerprint technician has arrived." Richard glanced at Delmonico. "Ours should be here soon as well."

Delmonico grunted. "And the fun begins."

Richard stood near Chung Hee, listening as the President briefed the technician on what would be expected of him. Richard understood every word of the instructions, including the order that the technician was to cooperate fully with an American forensic technician. Though his eyes widened for a moment at that news, the man nodded. He requested a table, commandeered from the refreshment area, and set up his equipment.

"May I examine the evidence?" he asked once his equipment was ready. He already wore a pair of sensitive latex gloves. Richard nodded and handed him the saucer with the cup inverted over the scrap of paper, where he had placed it to reduce the handling it received.

"Thank you," the technician said. He seemed surprised that no one had to translate for Richard, and made no move at first to touch the paper, simply studying it from every angle, and taking several photographs of it.

A commotion at the door announced the arrival of the American forensic officer. Harris escorted him to Richard. The man saluted. "Lieutenant Owens at your service, sir."

"You'll be working with Officer Sung, here, double-checking and verifying each other's conclusions." Richard nodded toward the North Korean technician.

The technicians eyed each other with suspicion as they shook hands. The American opened his bag and began to set up his equipment as well. As the tools appeared on the table, the barrier between them began to drop. Sung asked a question about one of the tools.

Owens looked at Sung, then at Richard. "I'm sorry, sir, I don't speak much Korean."

"That's okay, Owens. He just wants to know the technical specs on that tool." He smiled. This exchange was more proof that opening North Korea would integrate them into the rest of the world. "I'll translate between you."

That offer kept him busy for twenty minutes as the two men compared notes and procedures, laying the groundwork for the fingerprinting process. Near the end of the discussion, Richard summoned Chung Hee to assist with translating some of the very technical terms.

Neither Seong nor Dak Ho looked happy to see their leader assisting the Americans.

"Your being helpful to me may not bode well for your Presidency, Chung Hee," he said quietly in English as the other North Koreans watched the process.

Chung Hee did not look at his staff. "Sometimes you have to drive the horses to water, rather than lead them." He met Richard's gaze. "But one can only drive them so far and so fast before the herd scatters."

Finally, the technicians began the process of raising the prints from the paper. Richard watched as distinct print patterns emerged. "Looks like prints from at least four different people, sir," the American technician announced.

"Well, I know at least one of them is mine," Richard said. "Shall we fingerprint me first?" He offered his right hand, the only one he had used to handle the paper. The technicians worked together, assisting each other to make the procedure move smoothly and quickly. When Richard's print was finished, they both pointed out where he had touched the paper. At least they agreed. The Marine who had found the paper should be next. Richard discovered the soldier standing right behind him.

"I'll volunteer to be printed, sir." The Marine offered. "I was next to last to touch it."

"Go ahead." Richard stood aside.

Chung Hee stepped behind the Marine. "I will go next as a gesture of good faith."

Richard glanced toward Adler. Should he force him to go soon, or let him sit and stew? He doubted there was a chance Adler would volunteer to be printed.

Before he could ask for further volunteers, Edwards stepped into place behind Chung Hee. "Harris and Delmonico will get in line one at a time," Edwards explained. That kept most of their emergency reaction plan in place but allowed his staff to eliminate themselves as suspects quickly.

Hyeong stood. "I have no qualms about proving that I am innocent." He took a place in line behind Edwards. His staff followed him.

"Nor do I." Rostopol took the most decisive action he had taken as a delegate as he filed into place behind the South Koreans.

After an hour, Richard asked for a break for the technicians. As they sipped tea and coffee, they pointed out to Richard and the delegates gathered around where Richard and the Marine had touched the paper, their prints clearly evident. None of the other prints gathered thus far matched either of the other designs on the paper.

He sighed. He had known it wouldn't be easy. All of the Marines and his own staff had been fingerprinted. That left only Adler, the North Korean guards, and the rest of the North Korean delegation. Also his most likely suspects. He poured himself a cup of tea and leaned against the wall next to the tea and coffee.

Gi Chu approached him and bowed slightly. "I will go next when the technicians resume their work," he said in English. "If it is not an inconvenience."

Richard studied him. "No inconvenience. I appreciate your volunteering." Gi Chu appeared to be translating the words before he smiled and bowed again. Richard watched him walk to Chung Hee's side. The young man appeared to be humble, intelligent, eager to do the right thing. All of the hallmarks of one who could become a zealot. He hoped that Chung Hee's assessment of the young man proved to be correct. If not, his Presidency would probably be very short-lived.

He finished his tea and made a decision. Setting down the cup, he crossed the room to stand before Adler's chair.

Adler was sipping a cup of coffee, and he eyed Richard over the rim of it. "Not a very productive afternoon of negotiations, Rick."

Richard met the glacial stare. "On the contrary, Bob, I think it's been one of the most productive days we've had."

Adler shrugged and drank again. "Looks can be deceiving."

"Absolutely." He leaned down to put his face at Adler's eye level. "But it's about to get more productive."

"What are you planning to do, dance us a jig on the table?"

"No, you are about to be fingerprinted."

"What if I refuse?"

Richard stood up, smiling. "We're on North Korean soil now, Bob. I hear they have ways of making people comply with orders." He could see both Marines smiling as well.

Adler's face paled slightly, but he shrugged. "I wasn't planning to refuse anyway, just wanted to see what you'd do." He stood and stretched. "I have nothing to hide. You won't find my prints on that note." He started toward the fingerprint technicians.

Richard fell into step beside him. "Maybe not, but I'll bet we'll find your prints all over the plot when we get to the bottom of it."

Adler glanced at him. "I think I'll take that as a compliment, boy."

"Take it any way you want. If you've had anything to do, even far in the past, with what has happened here, you will just be digging yourself a deeper grave."

Adler stopped before the fingerprint table. "A grave is just a grave, no matter how deep." He smiled as he offered his hands for printing. "Just like a prison is still a prison, no matter how nice."

Richard stood and watched as the technicians got clear prints from Adler and compared them to those on the paper. None of them matched. Wiping the ink from his hands, Adler smiled at Richard. "See, my prints are not on there."

"Pardon me for not taking you at your word," Richard said sarcastically. "This would be the first time it's been good with me."

Adler shrugged and moved toward the refreshment table for more coffee. "Whatever, Rick."

Richard watched him. What would he have done with the note, if Richard had not burst into the room? Picked it up with a towel? Flushed it when he finished reading it? How was he communicating with his contact? Richard knew he was getting close to the flash point, when eventually the identity of the remaining prints on the paper would be revealed. How would those identified react? A headache crept up the back of his skull.

He approached Chung Hee, deep in conversation with Gi Chu near the fingerprinting area. He bowed. "Chung Hee, the only parties yet to be fingerprinted are under your authority, and they have not volunteered to be fingerprinted."

Chung Hee nodded his head once. "And you would like me to order them to do so?"

"No," Richard bowed again. "I would like you to ask them." He glanced toward Adler, back in his corner. "Orders should be only for military objectives or prisoners."

Chung Hee, too, looked toward Adler. Richard wondered if Chung Hee had ever heard the story of his feud with Adler. "I will ask them." He lowered his voice and motioned Richard closer. "But if they refuse, they will be ordered to do so."

"And your ordering might be the end of driving the horses to water."

Chung Hee shrugged. "A meteor that burns bright burns up early but spreads much light as it passes." Chung Hee strode toward his staff.

Seong's face went dark. "I suppose you want us to let the Americans print us?" he said in Korean. Though his voice was low, Richard heard his words.

Chung Hee sat in his chair, appearing relaxed. "Yes, it would look better if you volunteered to eliminate yourself as a suspect."

"This is not a criminal matter, Chung Hee." Dak Ho sat forward. "This is about North Korean national security, and the Americans should not be involved."

"Perhaps." Chung Hee shrugged. "But they are involved, and your President believes that it is in the best interest of Chosŏn to cooperate with them."

Seong's eyes narrowed. "You are ordering us to be fingerprinted?"

"I would prefer that you volunteer, but one way or the other, you will be fingerprinted today."

Seong stood. "This will not please the Party, President."

Chung Hee looked at him. "The Peoples Party put me in charge, Seong, and they can remove me if they feel I am no longer representing the people."

Seong compressed his lips in a tight line and marched to the fingerprinting table, followed by the young woman who took notes for him. Dak Ho watched him go and pulled out a cell phone. "Mr. President, if I may make a phone call, we can avoid the unpleasantries—"

Chung Hee took the phone from him. "No calls from here, Dak Ho." He set the phone on the table. "We entered these negotiations in good faith, and we have made much progress that will benefit Chosŏn. To change the rules because we no longer like the outcomes simply makes Chosŏn appear like a spoiled child." He leaned forward. "It is time we grew up and accepted our full role in the world, in a positive way."

Dak Ho glared at Chung Hee, but did not challenge his authority. He spoke to his assistant. "You must be fingerprinted, also." Pale, lips trembling, she rose and walked to the end of the line behind Seong's assistant. Then Dak Ho raised his teacup to his lips to finish his tea before he walked toward the table.

Chung Hee joined Richard where he stood watching the process, as each person was eliminated as someone who had touched the paper. Wiping the ink from his hands, Seong walked toward them as he was exonerated. "Had you been willing to accept my word, I could have sworn to you that I never touched, nor saw that paper."

Chung Hee nodded. "Words are much better if they

are backed by deeds, Seong."

Richard glanced at the line again. Seong's assistant was now being printed. He stepped toward them, to observe. Dak Ho's assistant looked at him. Then her eyelids fluttered, and she toppled toward the table. Richard lunged forward and caught her before she bumped the technicians. Scooping her in his arms, he carried her to a low couch at the north side of the room. Gi Chu hurried ahead of him to sweep pillows out of the way to make a spot for her to lie down. Chung Hee and Dak Ho were close behind.

Richard deposited her gently on the couch, as Edwards brought a dampened napkin that they placed on her forehead. Others in the room gathered around. Richard glanced at the crowd. "Let's give her some room to breathe here, shall we?" Most of them backed a few steps away.

On one knee beside her, Richard rubbed the back of her hand. Her eyes opened, and his was the first face she saw.

She began speaking rapidly in a language Richard did not understand. Gi Chu stepped behind Richard, where she could see him. "Korean please, Bo Bae." She stopped speaking and nodded.

"She grew up near the Manchurian border, and it was the first language she learned," Gi Chu explained in response to Richard's questioning look. "And my mother was from the same region, and I recognized the language she spoke to me as a child."

"What did she say?" Dak Ho edged closer again.

Gi Chu hesitated. "I couldn't catch many of the words. I simply recognized the dialect."

Richard suspected that Gi Chu understood every

word the girl had said. "Thank you, Gi Chu." Richard spoke to Bo Bae. "Are you feeling better now?"

Eyes wide, she nodded at him.

He rocked back on his heels. "Then can you tell us what you just said, in Korean, please?"

She struggled to sit up, and he and Chung Hee reached out to help her. She glanced around the room, until she found Dak Ho, who had moved to the edge of the crowd. She licked her lips. She glanced once more at Gi Chu, and spoke again in the Manchurian dialect.

Gi Chu shook his head. "You must say it in Korean. I can't understand enough to translate."

Richard kept his gaze on her face. He spoke in Korean. "She's afraid of something she wants to tell us, isn't she?"

"Yes, sir," Gi Chu responded.

Chung Hee squatted alongside Richard before her and took her right hand in both of his. "If there is something you need to tell us," he said gently. "Be assured that confession is good for the soul, as well as making punishment lighter. We will not sanction harm to you." He paused. "Or those you care about."

She swallowed hard, then focused on Richard's face. "My fingerprints are on that paper." She gripped Chung Hee's hand hard. "I don't know what it means, I don't speak or write English, but—"

A commotion erupted behind them and instinctively, Richard drew the girl down to shield her with his body. He felt Chung Hee bump against him and realized that Gi Chu had thrown himself across his leader.

He looked toward the door as a half dozen bullets ripped into the ceiling. Most of the delegates gathered around them hit the floor, and he saw Dak Ho wrestling the closest North Korean soldier for his weapon. Delmonico launched a body block at the two of them as Edwards and Harris tried to slip behind the other three soldiers. The two Marines to his right dropped behind the table to crawl toward the group, as one of those with Adler stepped toward them. Both the American and Korean fingerprint technicians stood, toppling their chairs.

Chapter 77

Terra pushed the vegetables around on her plate. Worry sapped her appetite and she couldn't fully appreciate the pork roast Carrie had carefully prepared.

"It seems relatively harmless," Paul commented across the folding table. Carrie snapped her napkin at him.

Terra looked at him then, saw the concern in his eyes and Carrie's. "It's wonderful, Carrie." She propped her chin on her hands, plate forgotten. "I just can't shake the feeling that something awful is happening in Korea right now."

Carrie reached across the table to take her hand. "Terra, no matter what is going on there now, the only thing you can do about it is pray." Terra squeezed her hand, glad of Carrie's understanding. "You also have to take care of yourself both for you and for the sake of the baby." She rose and went to the kitchen. "But I don't think just picking at one meal will hurt you." She carried a tray. "Maybe chocolate caramel chunk ice cream will appeal more to you?"

"Safe haven at last," Paul muttered, pushing his plate aside.

Terra accepted the cup of ice cream gratefully. "Thanks, Carrie." She dipped a spoon into the mixture and licked the ice cream from it. "Whatever is going on, chocolate and caramel make it more manageable."

Paul spoke. "Richard has all the information available to work with, he has a good staff, and I really feel that Chung Hee wants to bring about a peaceful solution."

"I know, Paul." She ate another spoonful of ice cream. "Maybe it's just hormones making me feel this way."

Carrie laughed. "Oh, hormones will give you all kinds of freaky ideas while you're pregnant, Terra, but right now I suspect that you are simply very tuned in to the tension you hear in Richard's voice."

"You may be right," Terra agreed, slurping another bite of ice cream.

The door from Richard's study opened, and one of the agents approached them. Because it was still devoid of furniture, they had adopted it as their command post. "Mrs. Matthews?"

"Yes."

"We found the car." He reached the table.

"Where?" Terra and Paul asked at the same time.

"Denver. Abandoned in a very rough neighborhood."

"Any leads from it?" Paul took up the questioning.

The agent shook his head. "Not much. It was rented at the Denver airport, evidently under a false ID. We're screening passenger lists from flights arriving about that time, following up as much as we can." He stepped closer to Paul. "Car had been pretty well stripped by the time Denver PD found it, and it will take weeks to go through all the fingerprints we could lift from it. We think our best leads will come from the rental agency." He dropped his gaze. "I'm sorry there wasn't more."

Terra finished her ice cream and pulled out her cell phone. "Well, at least it's something." She punched Richard's number. The phone rang and rang before finally rolling over to ask if she wanted to leave a message. She closed it without leaving one. "That's funny."

"No answer?" Paul asked.

"Yeah." She stared at the phone and dialed again. "I kind of expected him to answer right away." Still no answer, so she scanned the log for the call Richard made from the secure phone. She dialed it with the same result. She closed the phone and dropped her chin to her hands again. "Now that really worries me." Carrie stepped behind her to rub her shoulders.

Chapter 78

Richard felt his phone vibrate, as Delmonico, Dak Ho, and the Korean soldier wrestled in a heap by the door. Edwards and Harris stood, hands up, close by them, but not moving. The Marines froze in place, as had both fingerprint technicians. He pulled Bo Bae completely to the floor and could feel her trembling, hear her weeping, beneath his chest. "Do you want to tell me the whole story now?" he said to her in a very quiet voice.

"He made me, showed me what to write, gave me the paper to write it on," she sobbed. "He told me he knew where my family lived, that if I didn't, I would never see them again."

"He who?" His phone vibrated again, and then another burst of gunfire splayed across the ceiling and the upper wall. He heard further commotion in the anteroom, as if more security forces entered that room. Lord, he prayed, if there was ever a time for divine intervention, now would be it.

Chung Hee pulled himself from under Gi Chu's protection. "Soldiers of the Democratic Peoples Republic of Korea," he called in a loud voice. The soldiers at the door and the Korean fingerprint technician faced him. "Hold your fire. Do not shoot except at my command." He struggled to stand in the midst of the huddle of people on the floor.

At that moment, Dak Ho gained control of the gun. On his knees, he took aim at Chung Hee. Seong and Gi Chu stood at the same time, as both Delmonico and the North Korean soldier whose gun Dak Ho had wrested from him threw themselves again at Dak Ho. The gun went off, three shots fired before Dak Ho hit the floor again, unconscious from Delmonico's fist, as the North Korean soldier stomped on his arm and pulled the gun from his hand.

Seong dropped to the floor, Gi Chu trying to catch him as he fell. "How badly are you hurt, Seong?" Chung Hee went down on one knee immediately to examine him.

"Not badly, Mr. President." Seong responded. Gi Chu slipped Seong's coat off to tend the wound.

"Soldier, radio the rest of the security force that the situation is under control," Chung Hee said as he stepped toward the door. One of the soldiers reached for his radio.

Richard pulled himself away from Bo Bae. "Dak Ho?" he asked her. She nodded. "I'll have more questions later." He gripped her shoulder and stood to join Chung Hee. He should have been relieved, that perhaps the culprit behind the impasse had been exposed, but instead, he felt like he had only taken the first step into a hall of mirrors. He feared he would see many false images before he emerged again into reality.

The North Korean soldier whose gun Dak Ho had grabbed laid his weapon near the door, as he and Delmonico together rolled Dak Ho over and pulled his arms behind him. "Your handcuffs, please," Chung Hee requested of the fingerprint technician.

The technician handed them over without

hesitation. Chung Hee then passed them to the soldier, who cuffed Dak Ho. At Chung Hee's direction, two soldiers sat the prisoner in his chair.

Chung Hee faced Richard. "It seems Dak Ho will have a number of questions to answer when he awakens."

"So it seems." Richard caught the sound of Bo Bae's voice again, speaking rapid Manchurian to someone. He saw her talking to Gi Chu with an earnest look on her face. Gi Chu nodded and replied to her in much slower Manchurian, full of pauses and hesitations, as if he did not speak it well at all. Richard walked to her side.

"Is there a problem, Bo Bae?" he said in a quiet voice. Eyes wide, she looked at Richard. She breathed rapidly, as if she was still distraught.

"No, sir, Mr. Matthews," she said slowly in Korean, looking toward his shoes.

He glanced at Gi Chu. "She is upset that her supervisor has been exposed as a traitor to the cause he avowed to support." Richard thought Gi Chu seemed to say with his look that there was much more to what she said than he had revealed, but he was not at liberty to share it.

Richard gave his attention back to Bo Bae. "That is understandable, Bo Bae." He took her elbow to move her toward the opposite side of the table. "A betrayal of trust is a serious thing." He motioned for her to sit and took a chair directly in front of her. "Now, will you tell me exactly what happened with Dak Ho?"

Glancing at Gi Chu, who nodded, she gulped. "It was an honor for me to be selected to serve the people at the seat of government, and to get an advanced education because of it. And then, when the negotiations came up, I was again selected, by Dak Ho personally. But once the negotiations were underway, and you came back from your kidnapping, Dak Ho threatened my family if I didn't cooperate with him." She hesitated, glancing once more at Gi Chu. "In every way." She looked down at her hands, clasped tightly together in her lap.

With sudden insight, Richard realized that Dak Ho must have made physical demands on her, as well as forcing her to participate in his treachery. He touched her hand gently. "Bo Bae, no one will judge you for something you had no choice about."

Behind him, Gi Chu spoke in Korean. "You see, Bo Bae, I told you that you could trust Mr. Matthews."

She nodded. "I am just very—" She did not look up from her hands. "So very dishonored, that I am embarrassed."

"Then help us get to the bottom of this, to redeem your honor and sense of justice." Richard hoped his voice conveyed the sincerity of his words.

She looked at Richard then. Blinking, she swallowed hard. "He asked me late last night to write that note. He never told me what it meant, just what I was to write. Then I folded it in a handkerchief and placed it in his pocket. Then—" She looked down at her hands again. "Never mind about after that."

Richard placed his hand over hers. "Was this the first note he had you write for him?"

She shook her head. "There was one yesterday, and another a couple of days ago."

"What did the one yesterday say?"

"I don't know. I can't read, write, or speak

395

English."

Richard pulled a notepad from the table. "Can you write those notes again for me?"

"I think so." She took the pen he offered her. She wrote slowly, laboriously, basically copying a picture she had seen only once, rather than writing words from memory. When she finished, Bo Bae handed the notepad to Richard.

He stared at the lines on the paper, studying them until they came together to form letters and then words. He looked at Dak Ho, starting to come around. His cell phone pulsated again as he rose from the chair.

Chapter 79

"Richard!" Terra vented all her fears when he answered. "Where have you been? I've called and called—"

"We've had a situation here, Terra." She heard a strain in his voice.

"Are you safe? Is it over?"

"I'm safe. We have it under control, and I think we are getting to the bottom of our problem here."

Hearing his voice made her realize just how frightened she had been. She took a deep, ragged breath. "I was worried."

She heard him sigh. "I know, Terra, but when you called, I couldn't answer the phone."

She had to focus on something concrete, or her fear would consume her completely. "They found the car."

"Where?"

"Denver. Been stripped and handled by a bunch of thugs." She walked around the kitchen bar. "FBI figures it will be useless to find prints from."

"Don't count on it. It could have been made to look that way."

"Yeah, I guess you're right." The fear that dissipated when he answered the phone rose again. "The situation isn't over yet, is it?"

"Not quite." She heard someone talking near him. "I'll call you when things settle down."

She held the phone open after he clicked off. The fear rolled over her like a cold fog. She shivered and closed the phone.

"Still something wrong there?" Carrie asked softly.

"Very wrong." She wrapped her arms around herself. "It's still going on, and he can't tell me what it is."

Paul said nothing, studying the cold fireplace.

Chapter 80

Richard walked toward Dak Ho as he talked to Terra. Still not completely awake, the disgraced foreign minister slumped in the chair. Beside him, Chung Hee bent over Seong.

"I am fine, Mr. President." There seemed to be a new note of respect in Seong's voice.

Gi Chu touched his shoulder. "Mr. Matthews, I need to warn you." His voice was so quiet Richard could barely hear him, even though Gi Chu's mouth nearly touched his ear. "Dak Ho is more dangerous than you realize."

Before Richard could ask a question, Dak Ho awakened. "What is the meaning of me being treated like this?" he sputtered.

Chung Hee stood before him. "You tried to kill your President. Do you expect to be rewarded?"

Dak Ho leaned forward. "I'm simply trying to protect our country from threats you don't understand," he snarled.

Chung Hee remained calm. "It is you who don't understand the world we live in today, Dak Ho." He turned his back to Dak Ho. "We'll see how the Committee chooses to deal with this."

Richard stepped past Chung Hee. "I have a few questions for you, Dak Ho."

Dak Ho glared at him. "I don't have to answer."

Chung Hee responded without facing him. "Your fate would be more positive if you did answer Mr. Matthews."

Dak Ho sat silent, hate distorting his face like one of the mirrors in the hall. Richard glanced around the room, realizing that every hidden motive in the room represented a mirror, reflecting a false image that he had to dig into until he saw the true picture. He stepped forward. "Dak Ho, who were you leaving these messages for?"

Dak Ho looked at the notepad but could not see what was written on it. "I didn't leave any notes." He glared at Richard, his hate for Americans as great as his hate for Chung Hee. "My fingerprints are not on that note."

Richard kept his gaze on Dak Ho's face. "Yes, it's true we haven't found your prints on the note." He moved suddenly close to Dak Ho's face, his hands on the arms of the chair the man sat in. "Because you haven't been fingerprinted yet."

"We will remedy that immediately." Chung Hee motioned to the technician. "Fingerprint him now, please." He moved away. "Without removing the handcuffs."

Dak Ho struggled, but the two technicians together, aided by one of the North Korean guards, were able to get prints of acceptable quality. Dak Ho sat silently defiant when they finished. "Not a match, sir." The American technician held the prints up for Richard to compare.

Richard looked at Bo Bae. "Bo Bae, would you come now and be printed, to prove to us that your words are true?"

She nodded, making her way to the fingerprinting table, careful not to look at Dak Ho. Richard stood behind the technicians, watching as a third print, hers, was matched. Richard looked at Chung Hee. "There is still one print unidentified." He glanced at the North Korean guards. "Will you request their prints?"

Chung Hee nodded. "I will." He faced the guards. "Please, one at a time, go to the fingerprinting table."

As the first of the guards approached the table, Bo Bae stood to leave it. To avoid bumping into the guard, she stepped closer to Dak Ho. He lunged from his chair toward her. She scrambled backwards, crashing into the guard, who tripped into the fingerprinting table. One of the Marines guarding Adler jumped up to catch the table and equipment. Another guard grabbed Dak Ho.

Richard spun toward Bo Bae to help her up, as Chung Hee and the guard pushed Dak Ho toward his chair. Suddenly, in the confusion, Adler appeared behind the Korean technician. Slipping his arm around the man's neck, Adler pulled the technician's sidearm. Moving faster than Richard believed possible for such a large man, Adler backed against the wall, the gun at the technician's head. Once again, the room froze.

Richard pushed Bo Bae behind him as she rose. Where he had stopped to help Bo Bae placed him about ten feet directly in front of Adler. "What do you want, Bob?" he said wearily. After frequent conflicts in college and four years of a campaign to bring Adler to justice, Richard was tired of dealing with him, tired of having a sleeved ace thrown on the table. He remembered the last time Adler had taken a hostage and faced Richard. He knew from experience that dealing with Adler would be pointless, that, no matter the deal,

Adler would not release a hostage unharmed.

Adler raised his chin and glared at Richard. "What do you think I want, rich boy?" Part of Adler's hatred for Richard stemmed from his perception that all of Richard's accomplishments were a result of family name or money.

Richard spread his arms slightly to provide more cover for Bo Bae. "Off hand, I'd guess you want free passage out of this center into North Korea." He met Adler's gaze. "Am I right?"

"That might be part of it." He pressed the gun harder against the technician's temple.

Richard heard Seong's harsh voice. "In North Korea, those who serve the state understand that the state may demand sacrifices of them."

The technician's lips trembled as he responded. "I understand, Minister." One of the North Korean security guards raised his rifle.

"No!" Richard and Chung Hee spoke at the same time. Chung Hee turned to face the guards, standing between the guards and the technician, his back to Adler. "That is the old way. The new way is to recognize the value of each individual."

Seong's mouth set in a tight line, but he did not argue. The guard lowered his rifle from aimed to simply ready.

Richard focused on Adler again. Behind him, Bo Bae slipped into a chair. "What's the other part?"

Adler nodded toward Dak Ho. "Safe passage for him as well, a chopper and pilot on the lawn fueled and ready to go, plus a million *won* in cash before we leave."

"That's about as reasonable as I'd expect." Richard

crossed his arms over his chest, knowing that, even if the helicopter were provided, Adler would be shot while boarding it, or the chopper would be downed. That, however, would mean loss of more innocent lives. "No way you're going to get any of it." He glanced toward Chung Hee. "Even if it was in my power to grant it, which it's not."

Chung Hee stepped to a position beside Richard. "No, you will not receive any of those things." He looked at Dak Ho, staring wide-eyed at Adler. "Why would you want to take Dak Ho with you?" He observed Adler. "He's proved he can't be trusted."

"If you know you can't trust a man, then you are not tempted to do so." Adler responded. "He and I have some unfinished business."

Richard began to scratch the surface of Adler's and Dak Ho's mirrors. He smiled. "I expect he has some unfinished business with you as well." He shrugged. "After all, he was under no suspicion until you blew his cover." He gestured with his right hand. "I know I don't think like you, but if someone was responsible for toppling me from power, I would want him to pay for it." He stepped closer to Adler, chin thrust out, eyes challenging, trying to needle Adler by reminding him it was Richard who dethroned him.

"You would, too, rich boy." Adler accepted the challenge. "You've never been able to see the big picture." He laughed. "Your privileged upbringing makes you think it's always about you."

"You know, Bob, it really is true that one always attributes his own motives to the people he deals with." Because of this, Adler would never suspect what Richard intended to do. If he could find the strength within himself to do it.

"Unless he has a real understanding of what makes people tick." Adler began to smile. "Then he'd know just how to play things to his advantage."

"You've done a good job of that over the years, Bob, I have to give you that." Richard, too, began to smile. Adler had manipulated intelligence and operations for years to maintain tensions in ways he could profit, costing lives in the process. Now, it appeared his plots continued, even from secure U.S. custody. Maybe this situation would bring that to a permanent end.

"Think you've got me outsmarted, don't you, rich boy?" Adler smirked at him.

Richard shook his head. "I don't think it's possible for a normal person to think as deviously as you can."

Adler blinked. "You think you can bait me into doing what you want, eh?" His gun hand relaxed slightly. "You don't understand you don't really matter to me, never have."

"Oh, I don't matter?" Richard stepped closer. "Then why did you order the hit on Terra?"

"What are you talking about, rich boy?" A flicker in Adler's eyes exposed his surprise that Richard made the connection. That flicker told Richard that he made the correct connection.

"Oh, just the sniper that attacked her today, while she was doing something that no one here could have known about without listening to my phone conversation with her."

"And is your dear wife still safe?" Adler's eyes showed no question as to the outcome.

Richard used all his skill to read the glacial gray of

Adler's eyes, the tiniest tremor that crossed the hard face. "That's hard to say."

Something flickered again in Adler's eyes. "Oh, was she injured?"

"Not this time." He maneuvered closer to Adler. "But it's not over yet."

Adler's lips twitched. "What makes you say that?"

Richard waved his hand toward the notepad on the table, still facing Adler. Adler's gaze darted to the table for just an instant. "Just further notes I've intercepted."

"What notes are you talking about?"

"Notes Dak Ho had someone write for him, so his handwriting and fingerprints wouldn't be on them." He moved a half step closer. "Eventually we'll figure out what your half of the communication was." He leaned toward Adler. "I already know you are behind the hit on Terra. And that you had a backup plan in case she got away the first time." He smiled. "You must have learned how resourceful she is when you dealt with her before."

Adler's eyes glittered. "Yes, she's a saucy little bitch, that woman of yours."

Richard kept his voice level, despite the knot of fear in his stomach. He had to push Adler to reveal the rest of what he had orchestrated, but he also needed to use Delmonico's phone to tip the FBI. Lord, please protect my family now, and through what is to come, he prayed.

Behind him, he heard a quiet discussion, Delmonico, Harris, and Edwards speaking in voices low enough he couldn't make out the words. Then he heard Delmonico's phone opened, caught just a few urgent words. He realized his staff had correctly an interpreted Dak Ho's side of the correspondence, even now alerting the FBI that another attack on Richard's family could be imminent. Thank you, Lord, for a very fast answer to prayer, he thought, as he took another step closer to Adler. "Don't expect your Russian goons to just waltz in and take my family hostage."

Adler's lips thinned in a grim smile. "What makes you think they'll be taking any hostages?"

Richard's skin went cold, but he suppressed the shiver that started at the base of his spine. "What makes you think any of your people will survive to get that chance?"

Adler laughed then. "The FBI couldn't protect a rock."

Richard placed himself even closer to Adler. "I don't think they did too bad on building a case against you." He leaned forward. "And capturing you and placing you in custody."

"Custody that I'm about to get out of, rich boy." Adler swung the gun away from the fingerprint technician's temple. "That's close enough, Matthews."

Richard stared into the barrel of the gun, judging the distance from the muzzle to his forehead, calculating how fast he could move, guessing how quickly Adler could squeeze the trigger, how much time he would have before the bullet rocketed from the barrel. He thought about Terra, his child, his parents, and wondered if, when the moment came to act, he truly cared enough about the other people in the room, about the success of the peace mission, to risk his life for their welfare. A verse echoed in his mind. "Greater love hath no man, than he lay down his life for his friends." He stopped, breathing deeply, trying to make

Adler think he was obeying, as he settled his body into a ready stance.

Chapter 81

"Mrs. Matthews?" The lead FBI agent approached her from the doorway of Richard's study.

"Yes?" Terra put down the magazine she had leafed through at least a dozen times without seeing any of the pictures. She rose from her chair, hoping it was news that the crisis Richard was in had been resolved, afraid the news might not be good. Carrie and Paul moved to stand beside her.

"Mrs. Matthews, we've received a tip that there might be another attack." He touched the speaker in his ear. "We have additional agents coming in to surround the house, but I'd like to suggest that you folks all move into an interior room without windows for the time being."

"What room would that be, Barry?" She glanced around the family room. She had fallen in love with this house precisely because every room offered a spectacular view through generous windows. Even the basement was a walkout.

"Well, uh—" He looked around the room, studying each doorway. "What about the utility room?"

"I guess that would work." A room tucked between the garage and kitchen, it contained only a long, narrow horizontal window above the washer and dryer. "But it won't be very comfortable for the three of us to spend the night in."

"No, ma'am, but the word we get is that this will be soon—" The family room picture windows burst inward from a hail of bullets. He drew his gun. "Get down and start crawling that way now!"

Terra already dropped to the floor, her arms wrapped around the back of her head. Paul went to his knees between her and the windows, and Carrie crawled behind Terra, her body forming a barrier between Terra and the front door. "Keep behind me," Paul ordered. Terra nodded, crouching so close to the floor that her belly almost dragged. Paul started for the utility room, Terra close behind, Carrie behind her, when the kitchen's patio door shattered before they had covered three feet.

Paul pulled Terra back to the island of safety provided by the breakfast bar. He pushed her toward it until her back pressed against the wall of the bar. Then he nudged Carrie in beside her. He crouched in front of them, peeping around first one side of the bar and then the other. Three FBI agents, using as cover the narrow walls beside the picture windows, kept guard, firing shots at what targets they could see, evidently trying not to waste ammunition. A chill November wind whistled into the house through the empty windows. Between the cold and the fear, Terra began to shake. "What can you see, Paul?" she asked through chattering teeth.

He pulled off his sweater to wrap around her. "Not a damn thing, Terra." He looked again. "Not a bloody damn thing."

Terra heard gunfire away from the house, snatches of shouting stolen by the wind, and then the gunfire stopped. The agents in the room spoke into their radios, staying alert at their posts. Finally, Barry picked his way across the broken glass toward them. He squatted down to be on their level.

"What's happened, Agent Driscoll?" Paul's voice still carried all the authority he had commanded as a statesman.

"We've neutralized or captured all of the attackers, sir. But we have a tip that there will be at least one more assault tonight." He paused to listen to his radio again. "For additional security, we'd like to move you to a safe house in Fort Collins."

"But we need to cover the windows," Terra protested, protective of her nest. "The pipes will freeze—"

"We'll secure the house, ma'am." Barry gripped her shoulder. "But our first priority is your safety."

"You're sure it's safe to move us now?" Paul glanced around both sides of the bar again.

Barry nodded. "This group is shut down, so we have some time." He met Paul's gaze. "But if there is another attack, we would prefer that you not be here when it comes."

Paul nodded. "We'll go." He took hold of Terra's arms, and she faced him, still shivering. She understood that "neutralized" was an FBI euphemism for "killed." She lost count of how many law enforcement officers she had seen around the house since the attack at the fence line. And Barry said they brought in more. And then there was the gunman dead and Erik injured today. Not even during the feud with Adler had she felt this much danger around her.

Paul's voice reached her through her fear. "Terra, we have to go. They'll take care of the house, and we can come back in the morning."

She fought to shake off the terror that nearly paralyzed her. "Okay, Paul." She moved, to get her balance to stand or crawl, whatever they needed of her. She wanted Richard beside her, wanted to at least be assured he was safe, but she could have neither. She bit her lip. She would focus, she would do what had to be done to protect her baby, and she would survive. "Let's go."

"Good." Barry stood and surveyed both rooms. "Move quickly through the kitchen into the utility room. You'll get into the car in the garage and stay down below the windows until we arrive at the safe house."

Terra stood. "There's plywood in the garage that you can use on the windows."

Paul took her hand and started her moving across the kitchen. "They'll find it, Terra."

Barry followed close behind Carrie, his eyes constantly scanning around them, ready to draw his weapon. "Yes, ma'am, we'll take care of your house."

Chapter 82

Richard stared into Adler's eyes down the muzzle of the gun. Adler smiled and a light that could be madness danced in his eyes. "You've wanted for years to join your beloved Elaine, Matthews." Adler laughed. "Why don't I make that possible for you?" His finger tightened on the trigger. "Now that it's not your goal anymore."

Richard imagined Terra fighting alongside the FBI earlier, remembered how she never gave up against Adler. He thought of the child they would bring into the world. He wanted desperately to share a long life with her and nurture their family. Yet his convictions demanded he take a chance. "Did you really think we were that stupid, Adler? That we didn't know there was a connection between the heroin and the negotiations here?"

Adler's head bobbed up from his aim on Richard's forehead. "What do you mean connection?"

"Between the heroin coming out of here and a distribution network." Richard laughed. "You proved the link when you advised Dak Ho to order the Russian mafia hit on Terra."

Adler's gaze flicked toward Dak Ho, protesting across the room, and in that moment, Richard had only a fraction of a second to act. He leaped forward, grasping Adler's hand and the gun between his palms.

His momentum shoved Adler off balance. He fell, and Richard went down with him, still holding both gun and hand.

Adler lost his grip on the gun as he hit the floor, and suddenly Richard found himself holding it. He shoved the muzzle against Adler's sternum. His finger went to the trigger. He thought of the attack on Terra, his treatment in the hut. A tremor of his finger, a tensing of his muscles, and Adler would be out of his life forever in seconds. The bullet would explode through Adler's heart and no emergency team in the world could save him. He remembered the look on Elaine's face as she died in his arms, and the pain—mental, physical, and emotional—he endured from the attack that killed her. All Adler's doing. No one would condemn Richard for squeezing the trigger; it was self-defense, and the world would be a better place for it. He took a deep breath. Only he knew that he had a choice: he could play God or submit to Him.

"Go ahead, rich boy," Adler rasped. "Go ahead, kill me and end your problems." He laughed as Richard hesitated. "You can't do it now, any more than you could do it months ago in Colorado. And that's the difference between you and me." He reached for the gun.

Richard sprang to his feet, taking the gun with him. Shock on his face, Adler raised his hands. The North Korean guards surrounded him, rifles aimed. Richard handed the gun to the startled fingerprint technician. "I believe this is yours." He faced Chung Hee.

"Chung Hee, this man has committed crimes against your country. Would you like to take him into custody?"

"That would please me very much," Chung Hee responded, smiling.

"I'm an American citizen!" Adler shouted, as the North Korean guards grabbed his arms to jerk him to his feet.

"But, sir," one of the Marines protested. "He's in custody for crimes against the United States as well."

Richard stood with his back to Adler, facing Chung Hee. He understood full well that Adler knew far too many secrets to be allowed to remain alive long in the hands of an enemy. Someone would eventually have to negotiate for his release from North Korean custody. Or neutralize the liability, just as Adler had ordered such hits for years. But for now, Richard really didn't care. "He escaped from our custody while on North Korean soil, Marine. That means he's the prisoner of whoever captures him first, and right now, that is the North Koreans."

"You can't do this, Matthews." Adler's face went dark red. "The President will never sanction it."

"You miss the point, Adler." Richard began to smile. "I'm not doing anything. It's out of my hands." His smile grew. "You took it out of my hands when you made the choice to assault a North Korean police officer."

"You could order me back to American custody." Adler struggled to free himself from the guards.

"I can't order anyone to do anything here. I have no authority."

"But you're in charge! Chung Hee will do whatever you ask."

Richard shrugged. "Maybe. Maybe not." He glanced at Chung Hee. "He's the President of a country, and I'm just a retired diplomat on a temporary job."

"But—" Adler struggled wildly, looking at the grim faces of the guards who held him. "They don't follow Geneva convention rules here. They might kill me."

"Sue me. I really don't care. You don't matter to me anymore." Richard nodded to his staff. "Delegates, recess for the rest of the day and reconvene tomorrow at nine to wrap this up."

"Matthews! You can't leave me here!" Adler shouted.

Richard walked out of the room.

Chapter 83

The "safe house" was the basement of a solitary show home in a new housing development southwest of Fort Collins. Though it was well past midnight, Terra ignored the beds made up in the bedrooms and instead paced the main room of the basement. Carrie sat wearily on the couch, hands clasped together as she watched Terra walk.

"Terra, you really should lie down and get some rest, even if you can't sleep." Carrie covered a yawn with her hand.

"I know, Carrie." Terra stopped pacing to stand in front of Carrie. "Why don't you go rest a while?"

Carrie stood to put her arms around Terra. "I can't sleep any more than you can." She glanced toward Paul coming down the stairs for probably the tenth time since they had arrived at the house three hours ago. "Anything new to report, dear?"

Paul shook his head. "Nothing yet." He dropped into the recliner that faced the couch. "But they behave like they expect something." He pushed the chair back, raising his feet. "The agent upstairs acts like he's the star quarterback, and he's stuck at a dance recital instead of on the football field."

Carrie went to the chair and curled up on the arm of it, leaning her cheek against Paul's head. He grasped her hand and held it without saying a word. A lump

416

rose in Terra's throat as she realized how attuned they were to each other. She blinked back tears as she wondered if she and Richard would ever have the chance to develop such harmony. She faced the couch and felt Carrie's hands on her arms.

She dropped her head to Carrie's shoulder and let the tears come. She not only had a bad feeling about what was going on with Richard, she feared that the safe house was no safer than her own home proved to be.

Upstairs, a radio crackled, and they heard the agent speaking quickly. Terra lifted her head and she and Carrie looked toward the stairway at the same time. Paul dropped the footrest on the recliner, as the agent clattered down the stairs. The agent stopped at the foot of the stairs, a broad smile creasing his face. "Folks, I think it's all over but the paperwork."

Paul stood. "Are you sure?"

The agent nodded. "We captured ten suspects, wounded three, killed four, and we have teams with dogs searching around the property now, in case we did miss some."

"Were any agents hurt?" Terra asked. With the number of assailants involved, she suspected the agents were vastly outnumbered.

The agent faced her, surprise registering on his face. Evidently, he expected more curiosity about the battle. "Couple of minor wounds." He glanced at Paul. "We had eight agents, plus Larimer County officers, Colorado Highway Patrol, a couple of guys from Homeland, and one from Drug Enforcement." He laughed. "The ones we captured will deal with the whole alphabet of federal agencies before we're done with them."

"Do you think this was the last attack?" Paul's eyes were serious.

"The agent in charge seemed to think so. He had some info from CIA. Seemed to think it was tied to a Russian mafia drug operation." He glanced at Terra. "Your husband must have pissed off some really mean big dogs there in Korea."

"When will we be safe again?" Terra just wanted to settle into her home, plan a life with Richard, and concentrate on them becoming a family. Yet, somewhere deep inside, she understood that, with Richard, family life would never be as simple as most people found it.

"We recommend that you spend the night here and then wait until we have scoured the area one more time tomorrow in the daylight before you go home." He smiled for Terra. "You may not get breakfast or lunch at home, but you should be able to have dinner there."

"Thank you." Exhaustion from the constant tension of the past twenty-four hours hit her then, now that at least this crisis appeared to be over. If she only knew that Richard was safe, she thought she could probably sleep ten or twelve hours straight. "Lord, please keep him safe," she prayed. "And bring him home safely. Soon." She looked at Carrie, and Carrie reached out to brush her hair back from her face.

"Why don't you try to get some sleep now, Terra?" She studied Terra's face. "You look tired."

She sighed. "I am tired, Carrie, and I do think I'll lie down for a little while now." She took a step toward one of the basement bedrooms. "Will you and Paul sleep, too?"

Carrie nodded, and Paul spoke up. "I only hope my snoring won't keep you awake." Carrie smiled and wrapped her arm around his.

Terra smiled, as the weariness settled into her bones. "The only thing that could wake me tonight would be a call from Richard." As if in response to her wish, the cell phone at her waist rang. She grabbed it before the first tone ended. "Richard?"

"Terra, I love you." His voice sounded weary, but also carried a note of excitement. "Are you okay?"

"We're fine. We had some excitement here, but FBI says it's over now."

"I'm sorry about that." He paused, regret in his voice. "I learned that something was planned, but I couldn't let anyone know for a while. Delmonico finally got a chance to tip our people off."

"That's how they knew there was going to be a second and third attack."

"Where are you now?"

"FBI brought us to a safe house." She glanced at the agent. "I think our home will need some more work before we can live in it again."

"I don't care about the house, as long as you and the baby and Mum and Dad are safe."

"We're safe, Richard." She hesitated. "Is your situation over?"

"That's the good news." That explained the excitement in his voice. "We got to the bottom of what was going wrong here, and we should wrap up tomorrow." Her heart leaped with hope. "I'll be home in a day or so." He paused. "Home for good."

Chapter 84

Ryman knocked on Richard's suite door. "Chung Hee is here for you, sir."

Richard paused in his packing. "Let him in, Ryman."

"Congratulations, Richard," Chung Hee began, offering his hand. "On a fine job of bringing a winning solution for everyone involved."

Richard took his hand in a firm handshake. "Everyone except Adler and Dak Ho."

Chung Hee nodded. "Perhaps I should rephrase my congratulations." He smiled. "On a fine job of bringing a fair solution to everyone." He tapped Richard's shoulder. "I would say they will be getting exactly what they deserve."

"Still, I know that there are those in your country who are not happy about the way we resolved things, and got Adler back in U.S. custody within an hour."

"There were those who wanted us to hold Mr. Adler until he revealed some of the security secrets he keeps." Chung Hee smiled. "But, perhaps, with the assistance of your DEA, we will be able to break the drug organization within Chosŏn, and that will take some of the pressure off my government."

"And there were others, who know some of what he knows, who wanted him silenced." There were moments when Richard wondered if he had done the right thing by letting mercy stay his hand in Adler's case. Like the siren in Greek mythology, Adler could tempt others to ruin by twisting the truth. Information he revealed could lead to more death and deception. Even back in U.S. custody in a secure Federal prison, he would be a dangerous viper. "There is a long road ahead." He knew that what they had accomplished in the weeks of negotiation was only the beginning, that there would need to be a strong and steady hand at the helm to keep the process moving ahead. "Will you be able to get the cooperation you need to keep the agreements on course? Will they allow you to let the nuclear inspectors in?"

"The treaty is to be signed next week, and the inspectors will arrive the next day. The food is ready to begin distribution tomorrow, with Gi Chu in charge. I will personally hand out the first few boxes." Chung Hee shrugged. "I think I have proved to the Party that I truly have the best interests of Chosŏn at heart, but who knows how they will feel in a month, six months, a year?" He met Richard's gaze. "You know as well as I do that when you agree to serve your country, your life ceases to be your own."

Richard stared into his eyes for a moment. The elation he felt at being finished here began to evaporate. "I know." He studied the clothes he was folding for his bag.

"But there also comes a time when you have to let someone else carry the ball." Chung Hee reached out to grip Richard's shoulder. "Now it's my time to carry the ball, my friend, and I sincerely hope that your days of ball carrying are over." He paused. "I was happy to hear that your dear wife and parents escaped any injury when they were attacked."

"Thanks. The authorities are still trying to run down all the leads, and I think some of them will bring them back here." When Terra told him the extent of the damage to the house, the number of agencies that responded, and the nature of the men involved in the hit, Richard shuddered to think what could have happened.

"And that means that they may provide more information that can assist us with the changes we've begun."

"Yet—" He dropped the clothes into the bag, unfolded. "I feel like we've only scratched the surface of what needs to be done." He glanced down at his hands. "And there's at least one player unidentified."

Chung Hee nodded. "We are continuing to work on that last print. We've printed the guards and are starting on the maintenance and food staff now." He smiled. "I won't just let that go." He reached into his pocket. "But your purpose here has been accomplished. You opened the dialogue, you placed the focus on what is best for the people, not just the rulers of Chosŏn, you exposed the ones behind the unrest—"

"Did you know someone would try to sabotage the negotiations?" Richard wondered if his friend had used him as bait, just as he had used Adler, as Adler had once used him.

Chung Hee shook his head. "I knew that many of the reforms I wanted to initiate met with resistance, but I wasn't sure it was related to sabotage. I thought there was an equal chance it was just fear of change in general." He pulled a package from his pocket. "I want you to have something to remind you of what happened here." He glanced at Richard's bearded face, then dropped his gaze to Richard's hands. "Besides the physical reminders you will carry the rest of your life."

"There's no need." Reluctantly, Richard took the package Chung Hee placed his hands. He fingered the silken wrapping.

Chung Hee smiled. "I know I didn't have to, but I wanted to let you know how deeply I am in your debt. And to bring a line into a circle."

Richard pulled the package open slowly to reveal a worn leather-bound Bible. He looked at Chung Hee in surprise. "Is the country so open already that you can buy these anywhere?" He knew that in the not-so-distant past, Christians had been persecuted for their faith by being run over by steam rollers—while alive.

Chung Hee shook his head. "This one is one of my personal Bibles, the one the priest gave me that afternoon in Cambridge. I was able to have it shipped in as I gained the trust of the ruling members of the party." He looked down. "But it is my hope that the time is not far off when my people can live out their faith—any faith—without fear."

Richard tried to hand it back to him. "I don't want to take your only Bible, especially one this special," he protested.

Chung Hee stopped him. "It's not my only Bible. But it is one that I have read often, my favorite translation, and it means something to me. Something that you were a part of. That is why I want you to have it." He smiled. "Besides, like I told you, the Lord has written His words in my heart, as He will in yours, but you have to first let them engage your mind." He closed his hands over Richard's around the Bible. "Read it with your heart as well as your mind, and may you find the comfort in it that I have found." He turned to leave. "We will need its wisdom, as well as courage and strength, to continue the work you have begun." He paused at the door. "You will find the encouragement you will need to raise your son or daughter there as well." He opened the door. "I wish you peace and long life, my friend. May God keep you in His grace and mercy."

Richard stood staring after Chung Hee long after the door closed behind him. He wondered what the future held for the enigmatic man. He wondered, too, what the future held for him, and if their paths would ever cross again. Once again, he fingered the worn leather. Quietly, he placed the Bible in the bag he would keep with him on the plane for home. Home. Terra. A child of his own. A life where he would be responsible for nothing more than providing for his family and raising his children to be good citizens. He closed the last of his bags, looked around the room one more time, and walked toward the door. He flipped open the cell phone. "Terra, I'm on my way home to stay."

Epilogue

She wielded the scissors with great care, ensuring even margins on the article she cut from the newspaper. She smiled as she skimmed over it before placing it between a coffee table book on Washington, DC, and another on the Colorado Rocky Mountains, to press out the fold marks. Then she picked up the latest *Time* magazine. There on the front cover, waving to the press as he exited a helicopter in Seoul, posed her hero, Richard Matthews. Fresh from his successful negotiation of the near-crisis with North Korea, he was touted in the magazine's lead article as a candidate for *Time*'s man of the year, perhaps even the Nobel Peace Prize. She settled back on her bed to re-read the article, touching the photos of him with reverence.

At the final photo, though, she frowned. That photo showed him embracing his wife at Dulles International Airport, just before a limousine whisked them away for a state dinner at the White House. She was a part of the crowd that greeted them, but the pushy press people had kept her from being able to see much, as they shoved their way to the front of the huddle. His arm protectively around his clinging little wife, he declined interviews at the time.

She got up from her bed to perch on the chair before her desk. Placing the magazine in her multi-function printer, she scanned in the final photo. It took her nearly two hours to be satisfied with the result, but when she printed out her work, her image had replaced Terra Matthews beside Richard. She smiled and slipped her print into a frame beside her bed. Shutting down her computer, she put her scissors away, tossed the rest of the newspaper and laid the *Time* magazine on her nightstand.

One more week, she thought. Just one more week, and I'll be moving. Careful research had convinced her that the best place to settle would be Fort Collins, Colorado. Home of Colorado State University, where she could blend in with students, and where she heard rumors that Richard had tentatively agreed to teach a writing class the next semester.

She laid her head on the pillow and gazed at the photo she had created. She had been close to him once, but she moved too fast, and he rejected her. Her cheeks burned as she remembered pressing her room key into his hand at a writer's conference. He had given it to the hotel desk as one he found on the floor. Then when she bribed the maid to let her into his room, he shoved her out.

But she had done her homework in the interim, working two jobs and saving every penny to afford the plastic surgery that changed her nose to that of his first wife. Monthly visits to a stylist made her dark hair the shining gold of Elaine Matthews.

Now all she had to do was bide her time until she could enroll in his class and make him notice her. She imagined the difference had it been her and not that gold-digger who greeted him at his return. She would have made sure there was some private time before the state dinner, maybe even made him want to decline the

White House invitation. She reached out to gather the photo and hug it against her as she drifted to sleep.

A word about the author...

I vividly remember when I first considered writing. I was less than five years old, galloping about our yard at the farm, probably pretending to lead a cavalry charge or round up a stampede. On one of the few smooth limestone slabs that made up our sidewalk, I paused and turned to face the east, where the yard sloped down into a grove of evergreens that led to our garden and the highway. I focused on something far beyond the highway, even past the hay meadow and the locust-forested pasture. "Maybe I should write books," I thought. "Someone has to." I pondered this momentous choice for a while. Then I decided that it would be more logical for people who could read to write books, and galloped off again.

Like many people, I began writing in my teens. Unlike others, though, the stories within would not allow me to stop. Ideas clamor "Pick me, pick me!" to be let out of the files and into a completed story. A thirty-year career in government has afforded me insight into the layers of motivation that keep the world turning—and authors writing about it.

http://katherinepritchett.com/

Thank you for purchasing
this publication of The Wild Rose Press, Inc.

For questions or more information
contact us at
info@thewildrosepress.com.

The Wild Rose Press, Inc.
www.thewildrosepress.com